DARK IS THE NIGHT

DARK IS THE NIGHT

A DEATH & TEXAS WESTERN

WILLIAM W. JOHNSTONE

and J.A. JOHNSTONE

PINNACLE BOOKS
Kensington Publishing Corp.
www.kensingtonbooks.com

CHAPTER 1

Leon Armstrong turned when he heard the door open to discover the now-familiar image of Cullen McCabe in the doorway. Armstrong hurried to the telegraph window to fetch a telegram from the drawer. "Mornin', Mr. McCabe," he greeted him.

"Mornin'," Cullen returned. "Mr. Thornton, over at the store, said you have a telegram for me."

"That's right, I do," Armstrong said. "It came in day before yesterday. I told Ronald to let you know if you came into the store, in case I didn't see you." He handed an envelope to Cullen and stood waiting, hoping Cullen might comment on the message. When he failed to do so, Armstrong commented, "We like to deliver telegrams as soon as we can, but with you not living in town, nothing we can do but hold it till we see you."

"No problem," Cullen said as he folded the telegram and stuck it in his pocket.

Armstrong was itching inside with curiosity about the quiet man whom no one in the little town of Two Forks knew anything about, except him. And the only thing he knew was that, from time to time,

Cullen McCabe received a wire asking him to report to Michael O'Brien in Austin. The telegrams never said what the meetings were about, and the reason Armstrong was so curious was the fact that O'Brien was the governor's aide. Of course, Ronald Thornton had dealings with McCabe, but according to Thornton, they always consisted of a minimum of words to place an order for supplies. The only noticeable difference in the size of his orders was whenever they came after he had received one of these telegrams from the governor's office. And as Thornton had predicted, when Cullen returned to his store, after picking up his telegram, he placed a larger order for supplies than he normally did. Being the speculator that Thornton was, he guessed that the quiet man of few words had gotten another notice to travel.

When Cullen had completed his order, Thornton thanked him for the business, then commented, "From the size of that order, I'd figure you were fixin' to take a little trip."

"Is that so?" Cullen replied, and gathered up his purchases without further comment.

"I can give you a hand with those," Thornton offered.

"Thanks just the same," McCabe said, "but it's no bother. I'll just make a couple of trips. That way, you won't have to stand out there holdin' 'em while I pack 'em in the sacks on my packhorse." As he said, he left half of the supplies on the counter while he rearranged his packs, then returned to get the rest as Clara Thornton came into the store. "Ma'am," he said politely as he passed her on his way out.

When McCabe was out the door and in no danger

of hearing him, Thornton greeted his wife. "He's on the road again," he said.

"Did he tell you that?" Clara asked, every bit as curious about the man as was her husband.

"He didn't have to," Thornton insisted. "I could tell by the order he placed. I knew when Leon said he had another one of those telegrams from the governor that McCabe would be gettin' ready to travel."

"Huh," Clara snorted. "Maybe he just ain't plannin' to come into town for a while," she offered sarcastically. "I declare, you and Leon Armstrong will have everybody in town thinkin' Cullen McCabe is some kinda mystery man, just because he doesn't talk much."

"Is that so?" Thornton replied, standing at the front window now. "Then how come he's headin' straight to the blacksmith?"

"Maybe he needs something from Graham Price," Clara suggested, again sarcastically. "Why does anybody go to the blacksmith?" She walked back to the front window to stand beside her husband to watch Cullen approach Graham Price's forge. "You and Leon oughta take a lesson from him, so you wouldn't gossip so much."

"You're just as curious as I am," Thornton replied. "Don't try to make out like you ain't."

The object of Thornton's curiosity led his horses up the street and tied them at the rail in front of the blacksmith shop. Graham Price looked up from a wagon rim he was hammering out on his anvil. When he saw Cullen, he paused for a moment to say, "Howdy. Give me a minute and I'll be right with you." Cullen nodded, and Price continued to hammer out a section in the rim before dunking it in a barrel of water beside his anvil. "Yes, sir," he said then. "Your name's McCabe, ain't it? What can I do for you?"

"I'm thinkin' Jake here needs some new shoes," Cullen said. "Can you take care of him this mornin'? I'm gonna have to take a little trip sooner than I expected. If you can't, I'll . . ."

That was as far as he got before Price interrupted. "No problem a-tall," he said. "I can get right on it, if you wanna wait. It'll take me a little while. Have you got someplace else you've gotta go while you're in town?"

"I have," Cullen answered. He didn't expound on it, but he had planned to have himself a big breakfast at the dining room next to the hotel on this trip to town. It was something he had never treated himself to in Two Forks and he figured he'd see if they had a decent cook. "I'll leave both horses here, but I think I'll take most of that load off my packhorse. No sense in makin' him stand around with all that on his back."

"You can just put it over in the shade of that tree," Price said, nodding toward a large oak at the back of his shop. "I'll get started on your horse right away."

"Much obliged," Cullen said, and led the horse to the back, where he relieved it of most of the heavier sacks. That done, he walked up the street to the hotel and the Two Forks Kitchen beside it.

"Mornin'," Porter Johnson greeted him when he walked in the door.

"Am I too late to get some breakfast?" Cullen asked.

"Almost," Johnson replied, "but Gracie ain't throwed out everything yet. She's still got a little pancake batter left and we've got plenty of eggs and bacon. Set yourself down and I'll go tell her to rustle you up something." He started for the kitchen, then paused.

"Pancakes, bacon, and eggs all right with you?" When Cullen said that would suit him fine if the eggs were scrambled, Johnson continued to the kitchen. When he returned, he was carrying two cups of coffee. "Mind if I sit down with you?"

"Don't mind at all," Cullen said. "I was afraid I'd gotten here too late to catch breakfast." He had a feeling that the owner of the Kitchen was curious to find out more about him.

Johnson placed one of the cups before Cullen and sat down at the table. He didn't take long to confirm Cullen's suspicions. "Your name's McCabe, ain't it?" Cullen nodded. "I've seen you come into town a time or two," Johnson said, "but I believe this is the first time you've come in here to eat."

"That's a fact," Cullen answered simply, and tried a sip of the hot coffee.

"Ronald Thornton says you've got a place somewhere down the river," Johnson went on, determined to get some information on the solemn man. "You got a family? We're always glad to welcome new families to Two Forks."

"Nope, no family," was Cullen's short reply. He could sense Johnson's impatience, but he was not inclined to make small talk as a rule, and specifically not in Two Forks. The less people knew about him here, the better. His rough little cabin downriver from the town was not in an easy spot to find, and it served his purposes when he needed some peace and quiet between jobs. After a while in the solitude he preferred, however, he was usually ready to take on the governor's next assignment for him. So he was gratified to discover there was a telegram waiting for him when he came into town today.

"You don't strike me as a farmer," Johnson commented. "You in the cattle business?"

"Nope," Cullen answered, then sat back to give Gracie room to set a plate on the table before him.

"You're lucky you came in when you did," the stocky gray-haired woman said. "Porter came in the kitchen just when I was fixin' to empty that batter into the hog's bucket. So them's the last of the pancakes. Big feller like you might want more. If you do, you'll have to settle for cold biscuits."

"I'm sure that stack is plenty," Cullen said. "I 'preciate you goin' to the trouble. They look mighty good."

Johnson waited for Gracie to back away before continuing his questioning. "You ain't farmin' and you ain't raisin' cattle. What is your line of business?"

"Just one thing and another, I reckon," Cullen replied.

"You don't talk much, do you?"

"I reckon I've already talked a lot more since I sat down here than I figure I need to," Cullen said. He was saved from further interrogation by Gracie O'Hara.

"Porter, why in the world don't you let the poor man eat his breakfast?" She stood, hands on hips, shaking her head. "How's that coffee, honey?" she asked Cullen. "You need some more?"

"No, ma'am, not just yet."

In spite of Gracie's reproach, Johnson was about to continue, but was interrupted when the door opened and another customer walked in. Glancing up at Porter's face, Cullen detected an obvious expression of irritation as he pushed his chair back and got to his feet. "Sonny, what are you doin' back in here? Sheriff

Woods told you not to come back here anymore. You still ain't ever paid me the money to fix that table you busted up, and you was supposed to do that as soon as you got outta jail."

"I'll pay you the money when I get it," Sonny said. "Right now, I've only got enough to eat some breakfast. And that stack of flapjacks that feller's eatin' suits my taste this mornin'."

"You're too late for breakfast," Johnson said. "This feller here just made it before Gracie cleaned up the kitchen and started workin' on dinner."

"If you can feed him, you can feed me," Sonny replied. "You owe me more than the trouble it takes to cook some flapjacks. After you went cryin' to the sheriff about that little ruckus with them two cowboys, he locked me up for two nights." He aimed a sassy smile in Gracie's direction, standing near the kitchen door. "Get your sloppy old ass in there and cook me some flapjacks."

"I ain't got no more batter," Gracie replied calmly. "Them's the last of it."

"You lyin' old . . ." Sonny started, then stopped and eyed Cullen for a few moments, who seemed to be making an obvious attempt to ignore him. He grinned, thinking Cullen's attention to his breakfast was really an attempt not to cause him any reason to come after him. "Never mind, old woman," Sonny said, "I'll just have them that feller's fixin' to eat. Bring me a clean plate."

Cullen had hoped it wouldn't come to this, but evidently, he was getting an unwelcome introduction to the town bully. He put his knife and fork down and turned his attention to the smirking young man. "What's your name, friend?"

"None of your damn business," Sonny replied, still sneering defiantly, "and I sure as hell ain't your friend."

"His name's Sonny Tice," Gracie volunteered, "but it oughta be Sonny Trouble."

Cullen nodded in response, then turned back to him. "All right, Sonny, it appears to me that you ain't ever been taught how to talk to ladies. So, you owe this lady an apology for your rough language to her. And you also don't know it ain't polite to interfere with folks eatin' their breakfast. Just lookin' at you, I'd guess you went to the saloon before you decided to come here lookin' for breakfast. So the best thing for you is to go back to the saloon and tell them you're hungry. Most saloons can fix you up with something to eat, even at this time of day. It won't be as good as these pancakes I'm fixin' to eat, but maybe it'll do till you get sobered up some."

Sonny was struck dumb for a few moments, astonished to hear the calm scolding coming from the stranger. Finally, he found his voice again. "Why, you dumb prairie rat," he blurted. "You're fixin' to get your ass whupped."

Still calm, Cullen shook his head impatiently. "There you go again. You haven't heard a word I've been tryin' to tell you. You're gonna have to get outta here now." He paused. "After you apologize to the lady."

"Like hell I will!" Sonny responded, and reached for the .44 on his hip. Anticipating his move, Cullen grabbed Porter Johnson's coffee cup and threw the contents into Sonny's face, coming up out of his chair at the same time. When Sonny reeled, Cullen drove his shoulder into him, driving him backward to land on the floor. Still trying to draw his pistol, even though flat on his back, Sonny looked up at the formidable man standing above him, his weapon in his hand.

"Is it worth dyin' over?" Cullen asked calmly when Sonny started to pull his .44. Sonny realized at once that he had no chance. Scowling at Cullen, he raised his hands in defeat.

"All right," Sonny said. "You got the jump on me this time. I'm goin'." He started to roll over and get up from the floor.

"Hold it!" Cullen ordered, and cocked his Colt .44. "Apologize to the lady first."

Straining to contain his anger and embarrassment, Sonny nevertheless said, "I'm sorry, Gracie." He glared back at Cullen. "Now can I get outta this dump?"

"Yep, and when you think about it some, maybe you'll change the way you treat people," Cullen said, and turned to go back to his chair.

"McCabe!" Gracie screamed. Cullen looked back to see Sonny standing in the doorway, his pistol aimed at him. There was no time to think. He fired at almost the same time Sonny pulled the trigger and felt the sting of the bullet that grazed his upper arm. About to fire a second shot, he hesitated when Sonny's gun fell from his hand and he dropped to his knees, already dead from the shot in his chest. With his eyes seeming to be staring into the next life, Sonny remained on his knees for a few moments before he collapsed onto his side. Cullen returned his .44 to his holster and remarked calmly, "Sorry about that. There wasn't much else I could do."

Stunned, Porter Johnson could do nothing but stare until Gracie broke his trance. "You're shot!" she exclaimed to Cullen.

He looked down at his arm. "I reckon I am," he said, "but it ain't much, just a graze."

"You might need to see Doc Taylor. Better let me take a look at it," she said. When Cullen said it was nothing, she insisted. "Slip outta your jacket and take your shirt off." He could see there was no use in arguing with her, so he let her take a look at the wound. As he had said, it was a minor creasing of his skin, doing more damage to his shirt and jacket than it did to his arm. She led him into the kitchen and cleaned the wound with a wet cloth before tying a clean cloth around his arm.

He was still in the process of buttoning the shirt when Clyde Allen, the owner of the hotel, walked in with the sheriff. Seeing Johnson still standing there looking at the body of Sonny Tice in the doorway, the sheriff exclaimed, "What the hell, Porter? What happened here?"

"That ain't my doin'," Johnson replied. "He drew down on McCabe and McCabe done for him."

"McCabe?" Sheriff Woods asked, "Who's McCabe?"

"That would be me," Cullen said, coming from the kitchen when he heard them talking.

Not waiting for Cullen to offer any explanation, Gracie spoke up. "That foulmouthed bully finally ran up against somebody who wasn't afraid of him. He waited till McCabe turned his back and then he drew down on him. He got what he deserved."

Calvin Woods turned back to Johnson. "Is that what happened, Porter?" Johnson replied that it was, but he went into more detail, describing the incident as it actually happened with emphasis on the quick reactions demonstrated by Cullen. After listening to his accounting, the sheriff said, "I reckon it was bound to happen. Sooner or later, he was gonna pick on the wrong man." He looked at Cullen. "Well, looks like there ain't no doubt it was self-defense, McCabe. What's your first name?" When Cullen replied, Woods asked, "When I go back to my office, I don't reckon I'll find any paper on Cullen McCabe, will I?"

Cullen smiled. "Reckon not."

"I'll tell Walter Creech to pick up the body," Woods said. "Then I suppose I'll have to ride out to tell old man Jesse Tice his youngest son is dead. That ain't something I look forward to. He ain't gonna take it too well, so if I was you, I'd make myself scarce, and I mean like right now. Sonny's got two brothers and his death ain't likely to set too well with 'em. And I don't want another shoot-out in my town, so the best thing for you to do is to get outta town."

"I'll be glad to," Cullen said. "Just as soon as Graham Price shoes my horse, I'll be on my way. He ain't likely finished yet, and I've got some pancakes that are pretty cold by now, but I might as well eat 'em, since I've gotta wait, anyway."

Woods reacted with a look of disbelief. "Mister, I don't think you're catchin' my drift. I'm tryin' to save your life. Those Tice boys are gonna come lookin' for the man that killed their brother. That ain't a guess, and I ain't sure I'll be able to protect you. It'll make my job a helluva lot easier if you ain't here."

"I 'preciate what you're tellin' me, Sheriff, and like I said, soon as Price finishes with my horse, I'll be on my way. I don't want trouble any more than you do."

Woods shook his head, exasperated with Cullen's apparent lack of urgency. "I'll take my time ridin' out to Tice's place, but I damn sure have to tell the old man about it pretty soon. I'd rather not have him find out on his own and wanna shoot up the town over it. Gimme a hand, Porter, and we'll drag Sonny out the door, then I'll go get Walter to pick him up." Cullen sat back down at the table to finish his breakfast. Clyde Allen, mute to that point, said he would help. Cullen heard Woods mumbling to them as they carried the heavy carcass outside. "It's bad enough havin' gunfights in the saloon without us startin' to have 'em in the dinin' room."

Gracie came to stand beside Cullen. "Sorry 'bout your pancakes. I'm warmin' up some syrup on the stove. Maybe that'll help 'em a little bit."

"Much obliged," he said. "How far is Tice's place from here?"

"'Bout four miles or so," she said. "Calvin was tellin' you the truth about the Tice boys."

"I believed him," Cullen assured her, "but I can't go till the blacksmith's through with my horse. Maybe it'll take the sheriff a little while to go out to tell Tice. And it'll take Tice a little while to come back here lookin' for me. And I ain't had my breakfast yet, so I might as well eat."

She had to chuckle. Shaking her head, she said, "McCabe, you're one helluva strange man. I wonder if you care whether you live or die."

"I don't," he said softly. She chuckled again, with no way of knowing the truthfulness of his short reply, or that it was the primary reason he was the one man so qualified to do the job the governor hired him to do.

CHAPTER 2

It was a little before noon when Cullen picked up his horses at the blacksmith's shop. As he had promised Sheriff Woods, he rode straight out of town, taking the road north to Austin. It was a full day's ride to that city, so he planned to arrive there before noon the following day. Gracie had said it was four miles out to Jesse Tice's farm. That should give him enough time to put a good bit of distance between him and the Tice boys by the time they rode into town. Had he been a little more thorough when looking into the situation, he might have asked her in which direction the Tice farm lay. As he was to find, Jesse Tice's farm was north of Two Forks about four miles, just off the road to Austin. He got his first clue when he met Sheriff Woods on his way back to town.

"McCabe!" Woods blurted when he pulled up before him. "Where the hell are you goin'?"

"Austin," Cullen answered matter-of-factly.

"I thought you had a place south of town somewhere," Woods exclaimed. "Are you just lookin' for trouble?"

It took only a moment for Cullen to figure out why

the sheriff was upset with him. "You're fixin' to tell me the Tice place is north of town, right?" Woods didn't answer, but his expression of disbelief was sufficient to tell Cullen he had guessed correctly. "Right off this road, I expect," Cullen continued, and received a nod of confirmation. "Are they right behind you?"

"No," Woods said, "but they won't be long in comin'. They're about as riled up as you would expect. I told 'em there were two witnesses to the fight, and Sonny pulled his weapon first. But it didn't do much to settle the old man down. I warned 'em that I didn't want any trouble in Two Forks over this, and Jesse said he was comin' in to get his son. I told him there ain't no law against that." He paused to look behind him before continuing. "But, mister, you'd best get movin' now. You ain't even a mile from the trail that leads to the Tice farm. If you don't wanna meet Jesse and his two boys, you'd best let that bay feel your heels."

"Pleasure talkin' to ya, Sheriff," Cullen responded, then promptly took the sheriff's advice and nudged Jake into a brisk lope. He had no desire to thin the Tice family out any more than he had already, so he held Jake to that pace until he was past a trail leading off toward the river. He guessed that to be the trail to the Tice farm and he continued on for another couple of miles before he reined Jake back to a walk. He counted himself fortunate to have avoided a meeting with Jesse Tice and his two sons. He hoped that he hadn't caused trouble for Sheriff Woods and the folks in Two Forks. He had no regrets for the killing of Sonny Tice beyond the trouble it might cause them. Sonny had made his choice and he paid for it with his life. What Cullen did regret, however, was the sudden notoriety cast upon him in a town where he didn't exist, as far as most of the population had been concerned. Prior to this day, he had only an occasional business relationship with Ronald Thornton and Leon Armstrong, and that was the way he preferred to keep it. Now he was known by half a dozen people. *I wonder if I should have let Sonny have the damn pancakes*, he thought, but decided it would have only emboldened the young bully to challenge him further. *What's done is done*, he told himself. *The only thing for me to do is report to Michael O'Brien at the governor's office and get on with whatever he's called me in for.*

Sheriff Woods saw them ride into town, their horses laboring as they pulled them to a hard stop in front of Walter Creech's shop. He left his office and hurried over to intercept them. Seeing the sheriff, Jesse Tice demanded, "Where's my son?"

"Just like I told you, Mr. Tice," Woods replied. "I had Walter Creech take care of the body, so it wouldn't come to no harm. He'll turn him over to you. There ain't no charge or nothin'."

"Damn right there ain't," Jesse said. "Now, where's the man that shot him?" he asked as Creech walked out of his shop, having heard the commotion.

"You're welcome to take your son, Mr. Tice," Creech said. "I took the liberty to clean away some of the blood. It was about all I could do for him."

"Go in there and see," Tice told one of his sons, and Samson, the eldest, immediately obeyed. Tice turned back to the sheriff and demanded again, "Where's the jasper that shot him?"

"I can't say," Woods answered. "He left town right after the gunfight, so I don't know which way he went."

"He went out by the stable, Sheriff." Surprised, Woods turned to see Walter Creech's six-year-old son pointing toward the north road to Austin, the road that Tice had just ridden into town. All attention turned immediately to the boy, who stood there grinning, still pointing north, thinking he had been helpful.

Creech quickly turned him around and sent him back inside the shop. "Go back to the kitchen with your mama," he told him. "Go on, now," he prodded when the boy was reluctant to leave. A glance in Woods's direction told him the sheriff was not pleased with the boy's efforts to help.

"I just rode in on that road!" Jesse Tice bellowed. "How long has he been gone?"

"I don't know," Woods answered. "He lit out right after the gunfight," he lied.

Samson came back out the door at that moment, so Jesse waited to hear what he had to say. "Sonny's in there," Samson reported. "He's laid out on a table with a sheet over him."

"Where was he shot?" Jesse asked.

His son responded with a blank expression, then answered, "In the Two Forks Kitchen is what they said."

"No, you jackass," Jesse retorted. "Where was the bullet hole?"

"Oh." Samson paused. "Right square in the middle of his chest."

"Like the witnesses said," the sheriff was quick to point out, "Sonny was facin' the man who shot him. It was a gunfight, fair and simple." He declined to mention the part when Sonny had attempted to shoot Cullen in the back, thinking that might not set too well with the grieving father. To give the old man a little bit of satisfaction, he said, "Sonny got off a shot, grazed the other fellow's arm."

Jesse considered that for a moment, then said, "You ain't never told me that feller's name. What does he call hisself, this hotshot gunslinger?"

"I don't know that that's important," Woods stammered. "The main thing is he's gone from here to who knows where."

"I got a right to know who killed my boy!" Jesse stated forcefully.

"Cullen McCabe," Woods blurted, when all three Tice men dropped their hands to rest on the handles of their guns. "But he's long gone now," he said, in an attempt to derail the old man's thoughts of vengeance. "Here comes Jim Tilly," he said, nodding toward the owner of the stable, walking toward them. "I had him keep Sonny's horse for you. I reckon you wanna put Sonny's body on his horse and take him home now."

"I reckon that can wait," Jesse replied. "I'll get Sonny and his horse as soon as we get back. A man shoots my son has to answer to me. Get mounted, boys." Samson and Joe were quick to climb into their saddles. Without another word, Jesse wheeled his horse and led his two sons out the north road to Austin.

Left to puzzle over their departure, the three men involved looked at one another helplessly. Walter Creech was the first to speak. "Well, I never . . . What am I supposed to do with the body? There ain't no tellin' when he'll be back for it."

Jim Tilly shook his head in wonder. "Well, I reckon I'll have to feed his horse." He smiled at Walter. "I

don't reckon you'll have to do that with the body."
He laughed at his joke, but the other two didn't
join him.

"I hope McCabe ain't wastin' no time," Woods said.
"I tried to hold Tice back as much as I could, but my
jurisdiction ends at the city limits. Ain't nothin' I can
do to help him outside of town."

Unaware that he had a three-man posse on his tail,
Cullen was intent upon creating some distance between him and Two Forks, nonetheless. It always
paid to be cautious, but he figured if Jesse Tice was
looking for him, he would likely go downriver,
hoping to find his cabin. If he was lucky, maybe Tice
wouldn't find his cabin. He had left nothing in it
that he couldn't afford to lose. He never did when
he was going to be gone even for as long as a day.
That was the reason he could decide to ride on to
Austin when he got O'Brien's telegram, instead of
having to return to his cabin.

It was only a full day's ride to Austin from Two
Forks, but he had gotten a late start, so he would ride
until dark and camp overnight, then arrive at the governor's office before noon tomorrow. He already had
a spot in mind, a creek about twenty miles from
Austin, where he had camped before. As he had estimated, the sun was settling down behind the trees
guarding the creek when he approached it. A whinny
from Jake told him that the bay was ready to take a
rest. "I reckon we could both use a little rest," he told
the horse as he turned him off the road and walked
him upstream about forty yards to a small grassy
opening. After relieving his horses of their burdens,

he let them go to the water before he went about the business of a fire and supper.

He settled for beef jerky and coffee on this night. He had treated himself to a big breakfast late that morning, although his pancakes had been allowed to get cold. And he would most likely buy a meal in Austin tomorrow, so jerky and coffee should do for tonight. When he had finished his supper, he let his fire die down to no more than a warm glow. It was not a cold night and there was no use to build up a fire that would announce his presence to anyone passing in the night. Normally, if he knew someone was trying to track him, he would take precautions to keep from being jumped in his bedroll, maybe roll up a dummy blanket near the fire while he found a place to hide. He gave it some thought, still of the opinion that, if Tice and his sons went after him, they would more than likely head south of Two Forks, looking for his cabin, instead of heading north. In view of that, he figured the odds were against their catching up with him before he got to Austin in the morning. That would be the time to be extra careful. With that thought in mind, he poked the fire up a little, so it would be easier to start up again in the morning, then he turned in, planning to start early the next day.

Although they pushed their horses hard, Jesse and his sons were making a slow process of their pursuit of Cullen. It was too dark to follow any tracks on the well-traveled road to Austin. Determined to catch up with him, however, Jesse continued on into the night, stopping at every creek and stream to send his two sons to look for a camp, Joe upstream and Samson downstream. It was the only way he could be sure they didn't pass by McCabe's camp in the darkness, and he naturally assumed his son's killer would have to stop for the night. It was the third such search that produced results. Joe came back to the road to announce, "I found him, Papa! 'Bout thirty-five or forty yards up the creek. I woulda shot him, but he's kinda curled up against a tree, and I was afraid if I missed, he'da found some cover."

"You done right," Jesse said, having already decided that he should have the first shot at his son's killer. "Tie these horses here, and we'll all three slip up on him. Samson, you cross over to the other side. Me and Joe will come at him on this side. Don't nobody get too trigger-happy and shoot before we all get close enough. I wanna make sure there ain't no chance we'll miss, so watch for my signal. If I wave my hand at you, just stay where you are until you hear me shoot. Then you can cut loose." All three experienced hunters, they took to the banks of the creek and moved quietly upstream toward the sleeping man.

When they were within about fifteen yards of the camp, Jesse signaled a halt. He was now able to understand why Joe had not chanced a shot. Their target had spread his blanket up close around the base of a sizable tree, in effect giving himself protection against anyone sneaking in to take a shot at his back. *Pretty slick*, Jesse thought, *but it don't protect him from the front.* "We need to cross over to the other side with Samson," he said to Joe. He waved his arm back and forth several times before Samson saw his signal and waved back to signal he was waiting.

Samson looked back when he heard them coming up behind him. "What's the matter?" he whispered.

"There ain't no clear shot comin' up on him on that side," his father answered. "But he's wide open from this side."

"Where's his horses?" Samson asked. "I don't see no horses."

"Most likely in that grass on the other side of the trees. Make sure you don't shoot that way," Jesse cautioned. "We can always use a couple of good horses. We'll wade across the creek before we start shootin'. Be careful and don't go splashin' across and wake him up before we're ready." Eager to begin the execution, they carefully entered the thigh-deep water and pushed silently across, their rifles ready. After advancing undetected to within ten yards of their sleeping victim, Jesse pulled the trigger of his Henry and set off a barrage of .44 slugs that ripped the unprotected target as well as the tree trunk to splinters. "That's enough!" Jesse shouted when the sudden silence signaled that all three magazines were empty. With a hoot and holler from Joe and Samson, the three Tice men hurried up the bank to witness the damage. Only seconds later, they were stopped cold to stare at the bundle of tree branches wrapped in an old blanket, now shot to pieces. "Watch out!" Jesse blurted, trying to look in every direction at once. "He's tricked us! Get back to the creek!"

Looking wildly from side to side, expecting bullets to start flying, both sons ran back to the creek and the cover of the bank. Two steps ahead of them, their father hunkered down under the creek bank, desperately searching the darkness enveloping the creek. "Where the hell is he?" Joe asked frantically while hurrying to reload the magazine on his rifle, dropping several cartridges in his haste.

"This don't make no sense," Jesse mumbled, then ordered, "Get back to the horses! He's up to somethin'." He didn't have to repeat it. They ran back down the creek bank, recklessly crashing through berry bushes and laurel branches, not at all in the stealthy manner used in their advance upon the camp minutes before. "Keep your eyes peeled!" Jesse called out unnecessarily. When he arrived mere seconds behind his two sons, it was to find them standing dumbfounded in the little gap where they had left the horses. But there were no horses. "What the . . ." Jesse started, then looked around him frantically, thinking it wasn't the right place.

"He stole the horses!" Samson whined. He and his brother started searching the bushes in a wide circle. "This is where we left 'em." He turned to his father. "What are we gonna do?"

Already working on that, Jesse said, "We're gonna find us a good spot to protect ourselves 'cause he'll be comin' after us, sure as hell." They started combing the bank at once, looking for a spot they could defend from all directions, and hopefully, one that would not permit McCabe to get too close without being seen. Thinking they had very little time to find that place, they quickly settled for a deep gully close to the edge of the water. With little room to spare, they hunkered down in the gully to await the attack they were sure was coming. Their rifles reloaded, they sat facing in three different directions, their eyes searching the dark shadows under the trees. Still, there was no sign of attack. Hours passed with not a sound from the trees beyond that of a whisper of a breeze that tickled the leaves of the trees along the creek bank.

The first rays of the new day caused Samson, who

was facing the east, to blink as the trees and bushes began to take shape and separate from the veil of darkness of the night just past. As he stared, bleary-eyed from the night of constant vigilance, he suddenly detected movement in a stand of berry bushes. Quick to react, he raised his rifle and fired, startling his father and his brother into action as well. "I got him! I got him!" Samson bellowed. "I saw him drop!"

"Be careful, damn it!" Jesse warned when both sons started to scramble out of the gully. "You mighta hit him and you mighta missed. He might be playin' possum."

"I can see him where he fell!" Samson exclaimed. "He's still layin' in the bushes. He ain't moved."

"You be careful," his father repeated. "He might be tryin' to pull a trick on us. Spread out," he ordered when they left the protection of the gully. "You see the first little wiggle, cut down on him."

They continued to advance, slowly and cautiously, halfway expecting McCabe to suddenly spring up and start blazing away. When within several yards of the bushes, it became apparent that Samson had been right when he claimed he'd shot him. Although still dark in the shadows of the trees, they could make out the motionless body, and it showed no signs of moving. On a signal from Jesse, they suddenly parted the bushes to thrust their rifles through, ready to fire a volley into the carcass of a young deer. "Damn!" Jesse cursed, and paused to look around him as if expecting to see someone laughing at their foolishness. He dropped to one knee in an effort not to present such an obvious target. Joe and Samson did the same, taking the cue from their father. "What are we gonna do, Papa?" Samson asked.

Jesse didn't have an answer for him, so he took a long moment to try to come up with one. He feared that he and his sons were caught in an ambush, but he couldn't understand why McCabe didn't spring it. He had killed Sonny—what was he waiting for now? "We need to find our horses," he finally decided. "We find them and we'll most likely find him. He musta got in behind us and took our horses back where his are tied." Looking into the faces of his two sons, he could see they were still uncertain, so he reminded them, "He still ain't but one man against three of us. We've just gotta find where he's hidin', and I'm bettin' that's back there on the other side of his camp where he had his horses."

Once again, they followed the creek back to the campsite. Approaching it cautiously, they found no one there, so they continued on past the line of trees to the prairie beyond where they had figured his horses were. There was no sign of him or the horses. It was now to the point where all three Tice men were not only confused, they were uncertain about what was happening to them. McCabe had to be playing games with them, but for what purpose? "That gopher has found him a hole to hide in," Jesse finally announced.

"It must be a big hole," Joe commented, "if he's got all the horses in it with him."

"He couldn'ta got very far from here," Jesse said. "We've just got to find him." They started a search then, up one side of the creek and down the other, checking out every likely place to hide all the horses. The sun was high in the sky when it finally registered with them. "He stole our horses and took off." The reality of it struck with the force of a sledgehammer:

while they were sneaking up on his camp to kill him, he had simply circled behind them, taken their horses, and ridden away in the darkness. Left on foot, twenty miles from the town of Austin, and more than that from home, they were helpless to do anything about it. Their only option was to walk back to their farm, which was about a twenty-five-mile hike. In any case, it made no sense to start out for Austin, even presuming that was where McCabe was heading. They would need money and horses for that, two items they were now short of.

Both sons stood gaping at their father while he was obviously trying to think until Samson asked, "What are we gonna do, Papa?"

Jesse cocked an eye in his direction, as if irritated by the question. "What the hell do you think? We're gonna start walkin'. He skunked us good and proper and there ain't nothin' else we can do."

"I'm hungry," Joe complained, "and that's a long walk without somethin' in my belly."

When Samson said he was hungry, too, Jesse said, "I reckon we'd best go back and butcher that deer you shot. We might as well have us a good breakfast before we start for home." Three dejected-looking avengers turned and walked back along the creek to the spot where the deer was killed. To a man of Jesse Tice's violent nature, it was just as painful to have been so obviously outfoxed as it would have been to have gotten shot by the man who killed his son. He vowed to store the name Cullen McCabe in his memory and hope for the opportunity to cross his path again one day.

CHAPTER 3

Satisfied that he had avoided unnecessary killing, Cullen found himself about ten miles from the town of Austin when the sun rose high over the treetops in the distance, indicating a stream or creek. He had uncertain thoughts about the possibility of pursuit by Jesse Tice and his sons, so he changed his mind about sleeping next to his fire. His instincts had been right on, because he had watched one of the Tice boys as he sneaked along the creek toward his camp. With his rifle aimed at the unsuspecting man, he hesitated when the man stopped to join two others who crossed over from the other side of the creek. He decided then what he would do. He quietly saddled Jake and loaded his packhorse again, then led them back down the creek, where he found three horses tied in the trees.

He could not be sure how much time he had before they discovered he was not in the camp, so he took the reins of all three horses and rode back toward the road, leading them along with his pack-horse. He was on a wide circle around the creek when he heard the barrage of gunfire back at his camp. Figuring they had been fooled by his dummy, he rode back to the road and headed north.

Now, as he approached a wide stream, he knew he would have to rest the horses. Jake and his packhorse were not so much in need of rest, but the three horses he stole were fairly worn out. He imagined they had been ridden pretty hard in Tice's efforts to catch up with him during the night. To lighten their burdens a little, he had stopped after riding about five miles from his camp and dumped their saddles. Then, to make it a little easier on himself, he had rigged a lead rope, so he didn't have to hold on to their reins. When he reached the stream, he rode back from the road a good distance, as he usually did, and tied the lead rope to a wild cherry tree, leaving the rope with enough slack so the horses could reach the water. Since he had not slept during the night just past, he made himself comfortable with his back against a tree to take a little nap, confident that Jake would warn him if he had visitors.

He rode into Austin around noon and rode straight to the stable where he had kept Jake and his packhorse before. The man who owned it was a friendly fellow by the name of Burnett and he had mentioned to Cullen that he was active in the business of buying and selling horses. When Cullen pulled up in front of the stable, he met Burnett coming out. Burnett stopped and waited until Cullen dismounted before offering a greeting. "McCabe, right?"

"That's right," Cullen responded. "I'm surprised you remembered my name."

Burnett smiled. "A man like you ain't hard to remember. What brings you back to town?"

"Just back to do a little business. I don't reckon I'll be in town longer'n just today, but knowin' you're in the business of buyin' horses, I thought I'd bring these three by to let you take a look at 'em."

"Is that so?" Burnett asked. "I didn't know you were in the horse-tradin' business." He took the reins of one of the horses and took a look in his mouth.

"I'm not," Cullen replied, "but from time to time I pick up an extra horse or two. This just happens to be one of those times. I've got some business to take care of and I don't wanna bother with takin' these horses back to my place."

Burnett walked around the other two horses, taking a closer look. "They ain't what you'd call pick of the herd, but I don't see anything wrong with 'em. Where'd you get 'em?"

"I picked 'em up on my way from south of here. Don't worry, nobody's gonna come lookin' for 'em. I ain't a horse thief."

"I never thought you were," Burnett was quick to respond, "not for a minute." He broke out a friendly smile for him. "What kinda price you lookin' for? I might not be able to meet it."

"You just give me what you think they're worth to you," Cullen said. "If it's a fair price, I'll take it."

Burnett hesitated while he pretended to study the three horses. Finally, he said, "I'll tell you what I'll do. I'll give you eighty dollars for the three of 'em. How's that?"

"Done," Cullen replied, to Burnett's surprise. He had expected to do some bargaining.

The extra horses off his hands, Cullen's next stop was the governor's office. He tied his two horses at the hitching rail near the back stairs and walked up to the second floor. Just as he was going to walk into Michael O'Brien's outer office, the door opened, and he collided with Benny Thacker on his way to dinner. The short, elf-like man who was O'Brien's secretary, recoiled upon impact with the solidly built larger man, and would have fallen if Cullen hadn't reached out to catch him. "Sorry," Cullen said.

"Mr. McCabe!" Benny blurted, embarrassed. "I apologize. I should look where I'm going."

"No, it's my fault, I reckon," Cullen offered. "I shoulda knocked on the door." He released Benny's arm and asked, "Is Mr. O'Brien in? He sent me a telegram."

"Yes, sir, Mr. McCabe," Benny replied, still flustered. "Please come in. I'll tell Mr. O'Brien you're here." He turned at once and went to O'Brien's office, tapped on the door, and stuck his head in.

Within a few seconds, O'Brien opened his door wide. "Cullen McCabe," he greeted him. "Come on in, man. I'm glad to see you got my wire. I hope you're ready to go again, after your little vacation." It had been two weeks since Cullen had returned from his last job in the little town of Bonnie Creek.

"Tell you the truth," Cullen said, "I wasn't sure I'd hear from you again."

O'Brien looked genuinely surprised. "Why would you think that? You did a helluva job in Bonnie Creek.

The governor was highly pleased with the results, and from what we've been able to learn, it was almost entirely because of your work there. Now he wants to see if you can have the same kind of results in another situation. You ever hear of a town called New Hope?"

"Can't say as I have," Cullen replied.

"You've heard of Fort Griffin, I expect," O'Brien said.

"I reckon everybody's heard of Fort Griffin," Cullen said. The town had earned a reputation as one of the wildest towns in the state of Texas, earning it the nickname of *Babylon on the Brazos*. The army built Fort Griffin on the rolling hills between the Trinity River and the Clear Fork of the Brazos to control the Indians after the Civil War. The town of Fort Griffin sprang up below the bluff and soon attracted every form of outlaw as well as honest settlers and businessmen. While he had never been to Fort Griffin, Cullen was well aware of its reputation. "You thinkin' about sendin' me to Fort Griffin?" He asked the question, thinking if that was the case, it would take a hell of a lot more than one man to tame that town.

"No," O'Brien said with a chuckle. "The Texas Rangers have been keeping quite frequent company with that town"—he paused—"and with very little success in taming it, I might add. The honest people of Fort Griffin decided to leave the town to the outlaws and form their own town, even petitioned successfully to form a new county. They named it Shackelford County and their new town, Albany." He smiled at Cullen and shook his head. "Long story short, Albany soon attracted half the miscreants from Fort Griffin."

"You're sendin' me to Albany?" Cullen asked.

"No, again," O'Brien said. "Still looking for a town

to serve honest ranchers and farmers, a group of merchants abandoned Albany a year ago to set up another new town. About sixteen miles northwest, on the Brazos River, still in Shackelford County, they formed the town of New Hope." He paused for emphasis before continuing. "McCabe, Governor Hubbard would very much like to see these folks make a success of their venture. He's hoping you might be effective in helping them avoid the lawless element that embedded itself in Fort Griffin and Albany. But, not surprising, New Hope is already attracting the criminal element that flocked to Fort Griffin. There's been a good bit of trouble involving saloon shootings and property destruction, but also some cattle rustling. There are several small ranchers near that town and they've generally been overwhelmed by one gang in particular. They call it the Viper Gang." He shrugged when his last comment caused Cullen to raise his eyebrows. "Don't ask me how they came up with that name." His presentation finished, he sat back in his chair and waited for Cullen's response.

"I'll see what I can do," Cullen said, never understanding what the governor thought one man could possibly do if the situation was already out of hand.

"Good," O'Brien replied enthusiastically. "You want us to notify the mayor of New Hope that you're coming to help them? Or do you prefer to go up there unannounced, like the last job?"

"All the same to you, I'd rather ride up there without them knowin' the governor sent me," Cullen said. "It's easier to get a better idea of what's goin' on."

"We've got no problem with that, any way you want to do it. We can't argue with the results you achieved last time. And I can assure you the governor will be happy to hear you've agreed to go up there." He got up out of his chair and extended his hand. "Now, I was just about to go get something to eat when you came in. Whaddaya say we go down the street to the Capitol Diner? Steak or pork, they're both good there, and every once in a while, they'll bake a first-rate chicken potpie. You interested?"

"Reckon so," Cullen replied, and favored O'Brien with one of his rare grins.

"Good. And I'll fill you in on what's going on in New Hope while we eat." He picked up a folder with some papers in it. "You can leave your firearms here in my office, like you did last time. I'll lock my door, since Benny's gone to dinner." He knew Cullen was not comfortable leaving his weapons unguarded, even there in the capital, and he knew without asking that Cullen's horses were tied at the rail by the back door of the building instead of in front.

After the short walk to the restaurant, Cullen was aware of the looks of curiosity that came his way when they walked into the dining room. He remembered the same stares that greeted him the last time he had visited there with O'Brien. They were led to a table in the very back corner of the room and Cullen had to wonder if that was because of his sturdy workingman's outfit and wide-brim hat. It didn't seem to bother O'Brien, however, as he exchanged pleasantries with several people sitting at the tables they passed. One of his acquaintances, upon seeing the diminutive O'Brien dwarfed by the towering man behind him, was inspired to jape him. "Hey, Michael, when did you hire a bodyguard?"

"Ever since I knew I had to eat in here with all you crooks," O'Brien joked back.

When they were seated, a waiter came with menus, which Cullen was not accustomed to. It always seemed amazing that the place offered so many choices of meals, and if that wasn't enough, the waiter informed them that they had the chicken potpie that O'Brien had mentioned. Cullen went for that with no hesitation. He couldn't remember if he'd ever had one or not. He didn't think his late wife, Mary Kate, had ever baked one for him. But then, there were a lot of things he couldn't remember since Mary Kate and the children were taken from him. So much of his life before that time had somehow been blacked out of his mind.

The potpie proved to be as good as O'Brien said, and the coffee was hot and plentiful, even considering the many trips the waiter had to take to fill his cup. Cullen could have suggested that a full-sized cup would have cut down on the trips, instead of serving the coffee in such dainty little china, with handles you could use only a thumb and forefinger to hold. He was afraid he was going to drop it. After they finished the meal, O'Brien opened his folder and started introducing Cullen to the principal citizens of New Hope, starting with the mayor, Ernest Robertson, who was the owner of the hotel. "I don't know much about him, or any of the others, for that matter," O'Brien said, "but I do know of a few names we've been able to learn." He proceeded to list them. "Franklin Bass, the preacher of the First Baptist Church; Jack Myers, owner of New Hope General Merchandise; Burt Whitley, owns the stable; and the sheriff's name is Alton Ford. There's at least one saloon, too, but I don't know the owner's name."

"Reckon the first thing I'll have to do when I get to town is go in the saloon, so I'll know his name," Cullen japed. "I doubt I'll remember the other names by the time I get there. If I remember right, Fort Griffin's a good ride from here. Hell, I might not remember my own name by the time I find New Hope."

"I'm giving you this list of names to take with you," O'Brien said, "and when we get back to the office, I'll show you where New Hope is on the map."

They finished up the last of the coffee and walked back to the office. Cullen went straight to the giant map of Texas on the wall behind O'Brien's desk. O'Brien pointed to a small *X*, printed with a pencil. Beside it, also printed with a pencil, was the name *New Hope.* Cullen held his finger on it, then looked down to find Austin. "Like I said, it's a good ride from here." He took the ruler O'Brien handed him and started measuring the distance in miles. He came up with a total of over two hundred miles, as the crow flies. "Allowin' for all the problems the map doesn't show, I expect it'll take four and a half to five days to get there, without killin' my horses."

"Whatever," O'Brien said with a shrug. "I'm sure you'll get there as quickly as you can. I imagine you're planning to start first thing in the morning."

"I'll start this afternoon," Cullen said. "I've got no reason to hang around Austin."

"In that case, you'll probably want to get to the bank as soon as you leave here." He handed him an envelope. "Here's a check for one hundred dollars. That should take care of your expenses for a while. We don't know how long you'll be in New Hope, but if you have to have more, there's a telegraph office at Fort Griffin." He paused, waiting to see if there was anything more from Cullen. When there was nothing, he wound up the meeting. "Well, I guess we've covered all we know about the problem. Nothing to add to it but wishing you good luck. I know Governor Hubbard would have wanted to wish you good luck, too, but he's out of town this week."

"Maybe next time," Cullen said, not particularly interested in seeing the governor. He strapped his Colt .44 back on, picked up his Winchester 73, and with a quick nod of his head, said good-bye to O'Brien. Passing through the outer office, he gave Benny Thacker a quick nod as well. Benny returned it, doing his best to appear stern. As O'Brien had suggested, Cullen led his horses down the street to the bank, where he had an account. He cashed the expense check, and with the money he got for the Tice horses, he felt he was flush for a good while. If he was not wasteful, and he never was, he could stretch the supplies he had bought in Two Forks to last him until he reached New Hope. If he was lucky, he might run up on a deer between here and there. It was close to four o'clock when he climbed aboard Jake and set out for Shackelford County and the town of New Hope.

As it turned out, it took him six days to reach the little settlement. It would have taken him less time than that, had he not taken one day to do some hunting. He struck the river south of the town as the sun was sinking beyond the hills on the fifth night. Since he had never been to New Hope, he wasn't sure how close he was, so he decided to make camp there by the river, then follow it north in the morning until he found the town. He pulled his saddle off Jake and unloaded his packhorse to let them get a drink of water before he gathered enough wood to build a fire and get some supper started. He was enjoying his second cup of coffee when he spotted the two riders approaching his camp. In the fading twilight of early evening, it was hard to determine who his visitors might be until they were about forty yards away. But it was obvious that they were aiming for his campfire. Friend or foe, there was no way to tell, so he prepared for the latter and picked up his rifle and backed slowly away from the fire.

When still about twenty yards away, one of the riders called out, "You there in the camp! We're comin' in. All right?"

"Come on in, if you're peaceful," Cullen answered, and knelt on one knee, his rifle ready.

They rode right up to the fire before pulling up to look his camp over, both riders with rifles out and lying across their thighs. "Where's the rest of your friends?"

The man who asked was obviously the one who had called out before. Cullen quickly decided the two were father and son because the other rider looked to be no more than fourteen or fifteen. "You're lookin' at all the friends I've got," Cullen said, and nodded toward his horses at the river's edge.

This seemed to puzzle the man for a few moments. "Looks like you're cookin' a little supper there. Enjoyin' some good beef, are ya?"

Cullen realized then what the visit was about, and he could see that the man was not totally confident in what he was trying to do. "Is this your range I'm campin' on?"

"That's a fact," he said, "and I've been missin' a few head of cattle."

"That's what I figured," Cullen said. "Well, if you holster those weapons and step down, I'll invite you to try a strip of that meat on the fire. Then you can tell me if it's beef or deer meat. You can tell the difference, can't you?"

"That's deer meat you're cookin'?" the man stammered.

"Why don't you tell me? Is that your son?"

"Yeah, that's my boy. How'd you know that?"

"I just figured," Cullen said. "You and your boy step down and help me eat up some of this venison. I shot a little buck yesterday and the meat ain't gonna be good much longer, so I need some help. I'll make another pot of coffee to wash it down."

"Well, I'll be . . ." the man started, obviously greatly relieved. Cullen guessed that he was not comfortable in the image he was trying to take on for his son's benefit. He returned his rifle to his saddle sling and told his son to do the same. Then he stepped down and immediately apologized for his impolite reception. "My name's Fred Thomas. I own this little piece of land next to the river, and that's my son, Sammy."

"Cullen McCabe," he said, and shook the hand extended to him. "Hope you don't mind me stoppin' tonight on your land. I'll be on my way in the mornin'—headed to New Hope. Maybe you can tell me how far it is from here."

"Five miles," Sammy spoke up. "We thought you was one of them Viper Gang rustlers."

"Viper Gang?" Cullen repeated. "Who's that?" It was the name Michael O'Brien had mentioned, but he was interested to hear their comments on the gang.

"Nobody knows for sure," Fred answered. "They just showed up around here in the last six months or so. They'll cut out part of a herd and drive 'em off to market, Fort Worth or somewhere else. And when they ain't rustlin' a bunch to sell, they'll still butcher a cow every time they want some beef. We thought that was what you were doin'. Sorry," he apologized again. "You say you're headin' to New Hope? You fixin' to look for some land to buy?"

"Ain't decided," Cullen replied, "but I heard it was a new town just startin' up, so I thought I oughta go take a look at it."

"Well, we could sure use some more honest folks. Most of us came out here from Fort Griffin and Albany to get away from the outlaws, and damned if they ain't startin' to find New Hope now." He helped himself to a strip of venison. "That sure is deer meat, all right. You got family?"

"Nope, just me," Cullen answered as he took the coffeepot Sammy brought back filled with water.

"This is mighty neighborly of you," Fred remarked. "But there ain't no need to waste your coffee on us. We oughta be invitin' you back to the house for supper. If you're goin' to New Hope, you'll be passin' right by the house on your way." He turned to point north. "It ain't but about a quarter of a mile up the river."

"Thanks just the same," Cullen said, "but I'll be fine right here, and I'm supposed to meet somebody for breakfast tomorrow in New Hope." It was not the truth, but he didn't feel inclined to spend more time with Fred Thomas and his family. For one thing, he asked too many questions."

"Oh well, that's too bad," Fred replied. "Who are you supposed to meet?"

Cullen had to pause a moment to think. "The mayor," he said. "Mayor Roberts." He hoped he had the right name. He didn't.

"Robertson," Fred said. "You mean Ernest Robertson. He owns the hotel."

"Right, that's who I meant. Like I said, I've never been to New Hope." He was beginning to regret ever having been discovered by Fred Thomas and his son. Thankfully, Fred finally said he and Sammy had to get back to the house because his wife would think something had happened. He invited Cullen to come with them, but Cullen begged off, saying he had traveled a long way that day and needed to get some sleep.

"Maybe we'll see you in the mornin'," Fred said in parting.

"Maybe so," Cullen said while thinking, *Don't count on it.* Fred Thomas seemed to be a friendly enough fellow, but Cullen was reluctant to cause his wife the trouble of cooking extra food for a visitor she wasn't expecting. In addition to that, he was eager to get to New Hope to get a feel for the situation there and try to figure out if he could be of any help.

CHAPTER 4

Cullen took a wide circle around Fred Thomas's ranch house early the next morning before coming back to follow the wagon road along the river that led to town. Approaching it from the south, the first structure he came to in New Hope was the First Baptist Church. It was a small building, the wood siding still new enough not to have the weathered look of the rest of the structures he could see up ahead. Right beside the steps to the door, there was a roughly lettered sign that announced that Reverend Franklin Bass welcomed all residents and their guests to attend services on Sunday. There was a wide empty lot between the church and the next building, which was the stable with a barn and corral behind it. He planned to leave his horses there but decided to ride up the street and back before he did. He thought it would be a good idea to take a room in the hotel, so he decided that would be his first stop. A little gnawing in his stomach reminded him that he had skipped breakfast. He hoped the hotel had a dining room.

As he proceeded up the street, he saw only a few people about. Each one paused to give him a looking-

over as he slow-walked Jake up toward the hotel. He
passed the saloon, a wide building with glass windows
across much of the front facade. The only sign of life
was in the form of an obvious drunk, seeming to be
passed out while sitting in a chair propped on two
legs, leaning against the wall. Cullen glanced up at the
sign on the porch roof that proclaimed the saloon to
be THE TEXAS HOUSE. While he walked Jake slowly by, a
young man wearing a badge stepped up on the porch
and approached the drunk. He appeared to be having
a conversation with him that resulted in the drunk
getting to his feet and attempting to walk away. When
it became obvious that he was in no shape to make it
on his own, the law officer helped him make his way
to the jail, which was just beyond the post office.
Cullen pulled Jake to a stop and watched until they
went inside the jail. *No doubt to let him sleep it off,* he
thought. He couldn't help thinking about that part of
his life that he had spent as sheriff in the little town of
Sundown. It now seemed a hundred years ago. He
nudged Jake again and continued up toward the end
of the street and the hotel, thinking New Hope appeared to be a peaceful little town, not at all as wild as
Michael O'Brien had thought. He wondered if he had
ridden all the way from Austin for nothing. *Of course,
there was that trouble Fred Thomas complained about,*
he thought, *with the cattle rustlers.* "We'll give it a
couple of days," he announced to Jake.

He pulled Jake up at the hitching rail at the New
Hope Hotel, stepped down, and looped the reins
loosely over the rail. When he stepped up on the
porch, he paused and sniffed a couple of times. He
was certain he detected the aroma of coffee and
bacon in the air. *Good,* he thought, *they've got a dining*

room. Inside the front door, he found James Levitt searching for something under the check-in desk. Cullen stood, waiting for a couple of minutes for the hotel clerk to discover him. When it became obvious that he was too intent upon finding whatever it was he was looking for under the counter to realize he had a customer, Cullen tapped on a bell sitting on the counter. Startled when the bell sounded right over his head, Levitt bolted upright and banged his head on the bottom of the counter. He made no sound in response to the pain, but backed away from the desk and straightened up. Startled for the second time when he rose to encounter the formidable figure of Cullen McCabe standing before the desk, he attempted to speak, but Cullen spoke first. "That had to hurt like hell," he said. "Didn't mean to surprise you."

"Not at all," Levitt replied, his head still ringing from his encounter with the front desk. "Can I help you?"

"I'd like a room," Cullen answered, "on the front, with a window."

Levitt took a look at the rugged face before him, unshaven since leaving Austin six days before, and decided he was not looking at a proper gentleman, maybe even a holdup about to take place. Cautious now, he nevertheless started to explain. "Sir, the front rooms upstairs cost three dollars a night. We have cheaper rooms with no windows for a dollar a night."

"I'll take one of the three-dollar rooms," Cullen said, much to the clerk's surprise.

"We ask that you pay in advance," Levitt said. "How long will you be staying with us?"

He was further surprised when Cullen pulled a roll of bills out of his pocket and peeled off six dollars. "Couple of days," Cullen said, "maybe more. We'll see." He had no intention of staying in the hotel longer than two days. He didn't care much for hotels, preferring to sleep in his own camp, or with his horse in the stable. But he thought he might like to sleep in a bed for a night or two, after six straight days in the saddle. "I'd like to clean up before I eat breakfast. You do have a dinin' room, right?" Levitt assured him that they did, indeed.

After the clerk showed him to his room and presented him with the key, Cullen went back downstairs to get his saddlebags, as well as a sack he carried clean clothes in, which was on his packhorse. He took the bags up to his room, then came back down to take his horses to the stable.

Burt Whitley stood in the door of the stable, watching the stranger on the bay horse as he came back down the street. *Big fellow,* he thought, *wonder if he's another gunman come to town, looking to make trouble.* He had happened to see him pass by when he went up to the hotel and he wondered then if it meant more trouble for New Hope. When Cullen rode up and dismounted, Burt walked out to meet him. "What can I do for you?"

"I'd like to leave my horses with you," Cullen said. "I'm stayin' at the hotel, and I'd like to leave my packs with 'em, if you don't mind."

"I'll be glad to take care of 'em for you," Burt said. "Ain't seen you in town before. You gonna be stayin' awhile, or just passin' through?"

"Don't know for sure," Cullen said. "I don't know much about New Hope, so I reckon I'll just look the town over, then decide if I wanna stay awhile."

"Reckon it depends on what you're lookin' for," Burt said, not at all sure the stranger would be good for the town. "There's some honest, hardworkin' folks in New Hope—not much money, just folks tryin' to make a livin'. We've got a post office now, and an honest sheriff, but we ain't even got a bank."

"Is that a fact?" Cullen replied, almost tempted to laugh. He got the impression that Burt might be suspicious that he was looking the town over to see if there was anything worth taking. James Levitt, back at the hotel, was cautious as well. Maybe the governor was right, maybe the townsfolk were concerned about losing their town to the criminal element. "Well, I'm just interested in the town to see if maybe I wanna recommend it to some friends of mine who wanna find a place to start a ranch."

That seemed to relax Burt's caution a little. "Well, that's just what the town has in mind, and we've got a pretty good start on makin' this a jim-dandy place to settle. My name's Burt Whitley. I moved my business over here from Fort Griffin."

"Cullen McCabe," he responded, "from down in Two Forks in Hays County."

"Well, I hope you find what you're lookin' for in New Hope. I'll take good care of your horses."

"I 'preciate it," Cullen said. "I'm gonna go back up to the hotel and get some breakfast." He left Burt still wondering what he really was looking for in New Hope.

The next stop was the washroom off the back porch of the hotel. When he was cleaned up, he proceeded to the dining room. He was met at the door by a slightly built, balding man who introduced himself as Raymond Monroe. "Come in, Mr. McCabe," he said.

"James said you needed some breakfast, and this is the best in town, right here in the hotel." He led him over to a side table. "You can leave your firearms right here on this table. We have a policy of no firearms in the hotel dining room. I promise you, no harm will come to them, and you can pick 'em up after you eat." Cullen didn't resist—he expected as much. "Set yourself down anywhere you like, at the big table or one of the small ones, whatever suits you. Lottie will be with you in a minute. You want coffee, I reckon."

"Right," Cullen replied as Monroe walked toward the kitchen.

In a couple of minutes, a tall, lanky woman of no discernable age came from the kitchen, carrying a cup and saucer in one hand and a large coffeepot in the other. She came to stand before Cullen, who had not decided where to sit. "I brought your coffee," she said. "You gonna drink it standin' up, or are you gonna set yourself down somewhere?"

"I'll sit," Cullen answered, and sat down at one of the small tables opposite the long table in the center of the room, where a party of three men were in the middle of breakfast.

A lively conversation between them had come to a halt when Cullen had entered but was resumed when he sat down. "Hey, Lottie, how 'bout bringin' that coffeepot down here?" one of the men called out.

"Keep your shirt on, Hiram," she said. "I'll be there in a minute." She turned back to Cullen and asked, "You want the breakfast special, honey, or you want something else?"

"What's the special?"

"Eggs, grits, bacon, and biscuits," Lottie answered. "Eggs any way you want 'em."

"That sounds good to me," Cullen said. "Scramble the eggs." She gave him a confirming nod, then walked over to the long table to refill their coffee cups. There was some exchange of playful bantering between the men and the lanky waitress that Cullen had no interest in hearing. The only comment that registered with him at all was when Lottie answered a question, saying she didn't know who he was. A short time later, she came from the kitchen with his food. At almost the same time, the little breakfast party broke up, with a couple of the men declaring that they had better go to work. One of them remained, however. He stood up, picked up his cup and saucer, and walked back to Cullen's table.

"Looks like I ran those boys off," he said to Cullen. "Mind if I sit down and join you?" He paused, then added, "If I won't be disturbing your breakfast."

Cullen glanced up at him, then looked around at the empty dining room. "I reckon not," he said. "Have a seat."

He pulled a chair back and sat down. "My name's Ernest Robertson. I own the hotel and I just wanted to welcome you as a guest. I'm also the mayor of New Hope." He offered his hand.

Cullen shook it and said, "Cullen McCabe. Pleased to meet you." Robertson was one of the first people in town he wanted to meet, so he was pleased to have the mayor approach him. Maybe that way, he could find out more about the town than he would have if he was asking questions. So, he poured some honey on his plate from a jar on the table, dabbed a biscuit in it, and asked, "You welcome every stranger who comes to town, or just the ones who check in the hotel?"

Robertson laughed. "No, but I saw Burt Whitley a

little while ago, and he said you were looking the town over to see if you might recommend it to some friends of yours."

"Is that a fact?" Cullen replied. "Yeah, Burt seems like a nice fellow. Course, I just rode into town this mornin', and it appears to be a quiet little town. But I met a fellow on my way in yesterday. Fred Thomas, he said his name was, and he was worried about some trouble with cattle rustlers—said somethin' about a Viper Gang. Is there anything to that story, or is it just a story? 'Cause that could make a big difference for somebody lookin' to settle here."

Robertson could not hide his immediate alarm to Cullen's remark, but he quickly recovered with a wide smile. "Fred Thomas is a fine man. He's got a wonderful wife and son, but Fred tends to exaggerate sometimes. I don't deny the fact that there have been some incidents of cattle rustling in Shackelford County. What part of Texas are you coming from?" When Cullen said he was from Hays County, Robertson said, "I expect there has been some cattle rustled down there, too. Right?" When Cullen allowed that to be true, Robertson continued, "This is Texas, man, cow country. You're gonna have some people who rustle cattle all over the state. But we've created New Hope with the idea of good, churchgoing people making sure our town won't be taken over by outlaws. We've got an honest sheriff, who isn't afraid to face any outlaws who think they can take over this town, like they did in Fort Griffin and Albany." He paused then, when he saw the patient reaction to his passionate defense. "You'll have to excuse me," he said, "I get a little heated up when I'm talking about our town."

"I can see that," Cullen said as he took another bite of biscuit.

"How long are you going to be in town, Mr. McCabe?"

"Oh, I don't know." Cullen shrugged. "Couple of days, I reckon, till I decide it's time to move on."

"Are you in the cattle business?" Robertson was aware that Cullen had never volunteered anything regarding his line of work. When Cullen answered his question with a single answer of "Nope," Robertson asked, "What is your line of work?"

"One thing and then another, I reckon," Cullen answered, and signaled Lottie to bring more coffee. Back to Robertson, he changed the subject. "I swear, that was one fine breakfast. I expect I'll be back to try supper."

Robertson realized he was not likely to get any information on Cullen's personal occupation, for whatever reason, but his natural reaction would cause him to be suspicious. So, he gave up on the effort to find out more about him. "Glad you enjoyed it," he said. "I'll have to tell Monroe you said so." He got up from the table when Lottie arrived with the coffeepot. "Hope you enjoy your stay in New Hope," he said, and walked out of the dining room, still not sure about the caliber of the stranger.

"His Honor, the mayor, was really givin' you the business," Lottie said as she filled his cup. "He's tryin' to find out if you're a peaceful settler or another damn gunslinger. Which are you?"

He had to laugh at her brazen lack of diplomacy. "Neither one," he answered. "Good food," he added.

"I'll tell Bea you said so," Lottie said. "She's the one who cooked it." She remained beside the table for a few moments, watching him as he walked out.

"Come back to see us," Raymond Monroe invited as Cullen buckled his gun belt at the weapons table by the door.

"I'll do that," Cullen replied, then he picked up his rifle and went out the door.

Monroe went immediately to intercept Lottie on her way back to the kitchen. "Whaddaya think?" he asked. "Did he give you any idea he was really lookin' the town over for some settlers lookin' for a place to build? Or you think maybe he's one of those outlaws just sizin' the town up—maybe those Vipers?"

"Hell, I don't know," Lottie answered. "It's hard to get much of anything out of him. I reckon we'll find out, if he hangs around town for a while." As far as the so-called Viper Gang was concerned, no one had ever claimed to be a member of that gang. She wondered if it actually existed.

Most of the afternoon was spent looking the rest of the town over, in order to get a better feel for New Hope. Cullen was interested to find out if the other merchants shared the same dedication to the future of the town as did their mayor. Or were their thoughts more like those of Fred Thomas? He stopped in the general store to buy a new shaving brush and met the owner, Jack Myers, and his wife, Mildred. When he walked by the blacksmith shop, Hiram Polson called out a hello, so he stopped for a while to talk. Hiram reminded him that he had seen him that morning in the hotel dining room. He was back at the dining room at suppertime and welcomed back by Raymond Monroe and Lottie Bridges. After another excellent meal, he made it a point to stick his head in the kitchen door to compliment Bea Rivenbark on the cooking.

He had checked out almost every establishment with one exception, The Texas House. He was saving that for evening, figuring that if there was a trouble-some element in the town, they would be showing up in the saloon, coming out of their holes like cock-roaches at night. There were already a few horses tied at the rail in front of the saloon, and a definite hum of business coming from inside when Cullen walked in. As was his custom, he carried his rifle in one hand as he looked the room over. It was noisy, as drinkers usually were, but all seemed peaceful enough. He walked up to the bar, where he was met by a bald little man with a thick mustache that twitched from side to side when he spoke. "Howdy stranger," the bartender greeted him. "You must be the mysterious stranger who's been all over town today. I was beginnin' to wonder if you were gonna come to see me."

"That so?" Cullen replied. "Mysterious, huh, what makes you think it was me?"

"Big feller, don't talk much, and you ain't ever been in here before. I figure it was you. What you gonna have?" Cullen asked for a shot of whiskey. The bartender poured it, then introduced himself. "I'm Deke Campbell."

"Cullen McCabe," he said. "You the owner?"

"No, sir, that would be Johnny Bledsoe, settin' at that table against the wall." He pointed to a man sit-ting with a woman that Cullen figured was a working girl. "You need to talk to Johnny?"

"Nope," Cullen answered. "I just came in to have a couple drinks of whiskey before I turn in for the night."

He tossed the whiskey back and slammed the glass back down on the bar. "That stuff's got a bite," he exclaimed, and signaled Deke to pour another.

Deke started to pour, but stopped, the bottle hovering over Cullen's glass. Cullen turned to look toward the door to see what had captured Deke's attention. He saw three men standing just inside the door, obviously looking the room over. "Uh-oh," Deke muttered. "That ain't good." Still holding the bottle over Cullen's glass, he turned his head to exchange glances with Johnny Bledsoe. Johnny nodded slowly, causing Deke to call a young woman standing near the end of the bar talking to a customer. She broke off her conversation and came at once. "Darlene," Deke said, "go get Alton. Tell him that feller's back and he brung two more with him." She paused only long enough to look toward the three at the door before hurrying toward the kitchen door.

"Trouble?" Cullen asked when Darlene disappeared through the kitchen door.

"What?" Deke mumbled, still distracted by what he had seen at the door. "Oh yeah, sorry . . . I forgot what I was doin'." Then another thought occurred to him. "Them fellers, standin' at the door, are they friends of yours?"

"Nope," Cullen answered. "Can't say as they are, but it looks to me like you know 'em."

Deke continued to study Cullen's face for a long moment, trying to decide if he could believe him. Finally, he said, "That big one in the middle with the fancy vest was in here three days ago. He pushed a young ranch hand named Davey Douglas, from downriver, into a fight and shot him dead. I just sent

Darlene to get Alton Ford, he's the sheriff. Alton had to let that feller go because Davey didn't have no better sense than to stand up to him when he called him out. But Alton told him we didn't want his kind in New Hope and told him not to come back."

Cullen tossed his second drink back after Deke finally remembered to pour it. He shook his head when Deke started to fill the glass again, then took a long look at the three men surveying the barroom. It didn't take an experienced lawman to recognize trouble like the kind he was looking at now. He remembered the young lawman he had seen that morning, taking a drunk to sleep it off, and he hoped the young man was a deputy. The three he was watching at the moment appeared to be as rough as a cob and too much for that young lawman to handle. Maybe there was an older, more experienced sheriff.

After only a few moments, the three men picked their victims. They swaggered past the table where Johnny Bledsoe was sitting, heading for a table near the back, where a three-handed poker game was in progress. As they walked past, the man in the fancy vest reached down and grabbed the arm of the woman sitting with Johnny and pulled her up out of her chair. "Hey!" she cried out. "Take it easy. I ain't no horse!"

"Is that right?" he replied. "But I bet you've been rode as much as my horse. Ain't that right?" His comment received a loud chuckle from his two friends as he proceeded to pull her along with him. Bledsoe got to his feet but made no attempt to stop them. Instead, he looked to Deke to see if he had sent for the sheriff. A nod from Deke told him that he had. The noisy hum that had filled the saloon suddenly stopped as the other customers became aware of the three men.

Approaching the three-handed card game, one of the strangers announced to the men playing cards, "Clear outta there! This here's our table. Ain't that right, Slade?"

"That's right," the man in the fancy vest answered. "That's our table, all right."

One of the card players started to protest. "You can't just walk in here and take any table you want. There's other tables. You can use one of them." He got to his feet to look for Johnny Bledsoe to complain, only to be met with the fist of the grinning brute, flush on his nose. The blow was hard enough to knock him backward over his chair, and before he hit the floor, all three guns of the unwelcome guests were out, daring anyone else to protest. The other two men who had been playing cards helped their friend up from the floor and wisely headed out the door.

There was a definite standoff in the saloon, with no one willing to draw the troublemakers' attention to focus on them. Cullen knew he was going to have to step in, but he was not ready yet. So far, the only real damage was a punch in the face, and it was obvious that no one was going to challenge the three. So, like Bledsoe and Deke, he decided to wait for the sheriff. With no sign of any other protests, the man called Slade and his friends had a good laugh before holstering their weapons. "Bartender!" Slade yelled. "Bring a bottle and some glasses back here!" At that moment, the sheriff walked in and Cullen was disappointed to see that it was the same young man he had seen that morning. He realized that his first job in New Hope would be to keep the sheriff from getting killed.

"Well, lookee here, boys," Slade taunted. "It's the fearless sheriff come to welcome us to town. Last time I was here, he held a gun on me and ran me outta town."

"That's right," Sheriff Alton Ford said as he walked back to the table. "And I told you then not to come back to New Hope, or you'd be arrested."

"That you did, Sheriff." He turned to his two companions. "That's a fact, boys, he told me he was gonna arrest me if I came back." He returned his sneer back to the sheriff. "But whaddaya know? Here I am again and I ain't got no intention of goin' to your stinkin' jail, so what are you gonna do about that?" Seeing her chance to escape, the young woman quickly backed away when he released her arm to face the sheriff.

"I'm placing you under arrest," Alton said, and drew his pistol. The other customers who had been watching, suddenly backed away when the gun came out.

Slade and his companions continued to smirk at the sheriff's attempt. "I ain't wantin' to be arrested," Slade said. "Whaddaya gonna do about that, shoot me?"

"If I have to," Alton said.

"You pull that trigger and my two friends will gun you down before you can get off another shot. Or maybe you think you're fast enough to get all three of us. I think the best thing you can do is put that pistol back in your holster and get your ass outta here."

There was no doubt in Cullen's mind that the three outlaws had come to town with the explicit intention to kill the sheriff. And he couldn't risk delaying action any longer because he could see that young Alton Ford was just as intent upon standing up to them. With all eyes riveted on the sheriff, Cullen was able to slowly move through the spectators crowded against the wall until he sidled quietly up beside the outlaw who had punched the card player. "Hey," he whispered. Surprised, the man turned in time to get the full force of Cullen's rifle butt in his face. He dropped heavily to the floor, causing both of the other outlaws to reach for their guns. "Pull it and you're dead!" Cullen warned. Fully as surprised as the two outlaws, Alton nevertheless realized the odds were suddenly reversed and he held his .44 on Slade, ready to shoot if he tried to pull his pistol. Cullen reached down and pulled the fallen man's weapon from his holster, while he was still struggling to get to his hands and knees. Cullen tossed the pistol over to Bledsoe, who was standing gaping with the other spectators. Then, with the barrel of his rifle pressed against the back of Slade's partner, Cullen lifted his and Slade's pistols, tossing them to Bledsoe as well. He looked at the sheriff then. "You bring any handcuffs with you?"

"One pair," Alton replied, still dumbfounded by what had just taken place.

"I expect you might wanna clamp 'em on Mr. Slade there. Maybe Deke's got some rope somewhere."

"I sure have," Deke responded eagerly, and ran into the kitchen. He was back in a minute with a coil of rope.

Cullen quickly tied the hands of Slade's partners behind their backs, then helped the fallen man to his feet. "Looks like you're all set to take your prisoners to jail," he said. "If you want, I'll go with you and help you guard 'em while you're lockin' 'em up."

"I'd appreciate it," Alton said.

Cullen gave Slade a shove to get him started and the angry man responded with a threat. "I don't know who you are, but if I ever get free, I'm comin' for you."

"I wouldn't be surprised," Cullen replied, then asked Alton, "All right if I shoot him, if he starts to run?"

"I think that would be allowed under the law," the sheriff replied. They escorted the prisoners out the door and marched them up the street to the jail, where Alton had to evict the drunk still sleeping in one of the two cells to make room for his prisoners. Cullen stood by while Alton put them in and locked the cells, then had them back up to the bars to free their hands.

"Just what the hell are you arrestin' us for?" Slade demanded. "We didn't do nothin'."

"Disturbing the peace, resisting arrest, threatening an officer of the law, and ignoring an order to stay outta town," Alton answered, doing his best to sound professional. "Now, what are your names?"

"Go to hell," Slade answered.

"Well, I heard him call you Slade," Alton said. "Is that your first or last name?"

"None of your damn business," Slade replied.

Alton looked at the other two. "Names?" He got a similar response from both. "All right, if that's the way you wanna play it." He pointed to the prisoner with a nose that was now swollen to twice its normal size. "You'll be Jackass Number One." Then he pointed to the other one and said, "Jackass Number Two."

"How long are you figurin' on keepin' us here?" Jackass Number Two asked.

"That depends on how long it takes to find out your real names," Alton said. "Most likely it'll be a good while. I'll get you some water and a slop bucket. Tomorrow, I'll see about getting you fed." With that, he walked out of the cell room and closed the door.

Out in his office, he spoke directly to Cullen for the first time. "You're McCabe, right?"

"That's right, Sheriff, Cullen McCabe."

"I heard you were in town today. Ernest Robertson said you were thinking about bringing some folks here to settle. Some of the folks were concerned that you might be here, looking the town over for some other reason that might not be good for New Hope." When Cullen just shrugged, Alton continued, "I expect you might have saved my bacon tonight. Why did you decide to step in when you did?"

"'Cause you needed the help," Cullen said. "You were lookin' at some pretty slim odds."

"I guess I was, at that," Alton said, "but I couldn't let 'em chase me outta the saloon. We've got to teach men like that that they can't come here and do as they like."

"Don't you even have a deputy?" Cullen asked.

"No," Alton replied. "Up to about six months ago, we didn't really need a deputy. Then we started seeing these drifters starting to show up in town. Maybe after what you did tonight, some more of the men in town will be willing to step forward."

"Maybe so," Cullen said with a shrug, not very confident about it, especially if these three tonight might be members of a large gang of rustlers and gunfighters. "I reckon you'll soon find out if these three belong to a gang or not."

"Are you just passing through town? Or are you gonna be here awhile?" Alton asked.

"Tell you the truth, I hadn't decided, but I reckon I'll stay for a couple of days or more, long enough to get to know the place a little better, anyway. Like I told the mayor, I told some friends of mine that I'd look the town over to see if it's a good place for them." That was the story he had tossed out on the spur of the moment, so he figured he'd better stick with it.

"Well, I'm mighty glad you showed up," Alton said, and extended his hand. "And I wanna thank you again for helping me out."

CHAPTER 5

After leaving the jail, Cullen returned to The Texas House, where the hum of business had resumed, with even more of a buzz now, following the event that had just happened. "Here he is," Deke Campbell announced to no one in particular.

Johnny Bledsoe, standing at the end of the bar, came over when he saw Cullen come in. "McCabe," he greeted him, "did you and the sheriff get our guests checked in all right?"

"Yep," Cullen answered. "The sheriff locked 'em up."

"You need another drink?" Deke asked, and held a bottle ready to pour.

"Nope," Cullen said. "I just came back to pay for the two I've already had. After that little fracas here, I forgot I hadn't paid you for my whiskey."

"I swear! An honest man!" Bledsoe exclaimed. "Those two drinks are sure as hell on the house. You sure you don't want another one? Hell, if it wasn't for you, we mighta had to go lookin' for a new sheriff tomorrow. Pour him another drink, Deke."

Cullen held up his hand to stop Deke. "Thanks just

the same, but two's my limit tonight. I'm fixin' to turn in pretty quick. But I 'preciate the offer."

Bledsoe was not willing to let him walk out of the saloon until he found out a little more about him. After witnessing the way Cullen had so effectively disarmed three dangerous gunmen almost in the blink of an eye, he was not ready to believe the story he was telling around town. He had a reason to come to New Hope, and Bledsoe wasn't ready to believe he was there to see if the town welcomed settlers. "What's your hurry, McCabe?" Bledsoe asked. "You oughta stick around awhile, have a drink with me. Maybe you could use a little time with Nancy, or Darlene. They both know how to make a man relax." As if to confirm it, both women favored Cullen with a smile.

"Well, now, Bledsoe, as temptin' as you make that sound, I reckon I'll have to pass that up. They're both fine-lookin' ladies, but I'm payin' for a hotel room and I wanna see if that bed is as comfortable as the mayor says it is. I've been in the saddle for six days in a row and I'm ready to get some sleep." He had a feeling Bledsoe was itching to find out why he was really in New Hope, and his "ladies" would most likely have a lot of questions for him.

"You don't know what you're missin'," Bledsoe said.

"Probably more'n I could handle," Cullen said, and headed for the door. Outside, he hesitated, thinking about whether or not he should check on his horses. He decided he trusted Burt Whitley when he said he would take good care of them. *He's most likely locked up for the night, anyway,* he thought, and started for the hotel. The business with Bledsoe was still on his mind and he was a little concerned that he was getting too much attention. He preferred not to draw too much attention to himself, but he was in town only one day and people were talking about the takedown in The Texas House. He might as well have pulled out his official papers and worn his shiny badge, he told himself, knowing that would be the last thing he would do.

He got another dose of the hero treatment when he walked into the hotel and found Ernest Robertson waiting for him. Robertson's word of appreciation seemed genuine to him, a simple thank-you for helping the sheriff make the arrest, but he made no attempt to interrogate him. He did find it strange that the mayor said he and his wife, Eunice, appreciated it, and was further surprised when Robertson told him he was giving him a special rate on his room. "Half the rate, for as long as you're here," Robertson said.

After a good night's sleep, he woke up with a strong appetite for breakfast. Remembering the one he had the day before, he planned to find out if that was one of Bea Rivenbark's rare days, or if the cooking was that good every day. After he strapped on his gun belt and picked up his rifle, he stood at the window and watched the street below for a few minutes. A more peaceful little scene could not be imagined. With that image in his mind, he went downstairs to the dining room, where he was met at the door by Monroe. "Good mornin', McCabe. Find yourself a chair and I'll send Lottie out with a cup of coffee." Cullen returned the greeting and took a chair not too far from the table he had deposited his firearms upon. He was beginning to wonder if the dining room was open because there was no one else there. But in a few moments Lottie appeared, carrying two cups.

"Mornin'," she said. "You're an early riser."

"I reckon," he replied. "I thought for a minute you weren't even open yet."

"We're open. In about fifteen or twenty minutes, they'll start to come in for breakfast. I'll get yours started. You want the same thing you had yesterday, or you wanna try some of Bea's pancakes?" That sounded pretty good to him, remembering the last time he had ordered pancakes and had to eat them after they had turned cold. Maybe he would get a chance to eat these while they were still hot, so he told her to back them up with some sausage and grits. She left the extra cup of coffee on his table and went to the kitchen to give Bea his order. She was back right away and proceeded to sit down at the table with him. "Before it gets busy in here, I'm gonna have some coffee, myself. You mind if I join you?"

He broke out one of his rare smiles. "I·reckon not," he replied, since she had already seated herself.

Detecting the subtle hint of sarcasm in his reply, she shrugged and said, "If I waited for you to invite me to sit down, you might not have." She shoveled two heaping spoonfuls of sugar into her coffee, enough to cause him to wince. "What?" she asked, seeing his expression. "My disposition is so sour, I have to take a lot of sugar to keep me from killin' somebody some days in here."

"I hope this ain't one of those days," he said.

She laughed in response and concentrated on stirring her coffee for a few moments. "You don't talk a helluva lot, do ya?" He shrugged in response. "Monroe told me what you did in The Texas House last night—

said you didn't do a lot of talkin' then, either, but you sure as hell got the message across."

"Things just happened the way they did," he said. "Coulda turned out either way. I just happened to be close enough to give the sheriff a hand. If I hadn't been there, most likely one of the other men would have stepped in to help." He was not happy with the way Lottie was trying to inflate his actions.

"Hogwash," she said. "Most of the men in this town woulda stood right there and watched those three gunslingers shoot Alton Ford down." She looked at him as if daring him to refute it. "I'll bet the mayor thanked you for steppin' in."

"He did," Cullen admitted, thinking it useless to try to change her perception of the incident in the saloon. "He thanked me, even said his wife thanked me."

"Well, she oughta thank you," Lottie insisted. When the expression on Cullen's face told her that he didn't understand, she went on to explain. "Course, you wouldn't know, would you? Alton Ford is Eunice Robertson's younger brother. That's the only reason he got the job as sheriff, not that anybody's complained about it. So far, he seems to be tryin' to do a good job." She was interrupted then by a loud yell from Bea in the kitchen. "I reckon your pancakes are done," Lottie said with a chuckle. "Monroe got her a little bell to ring when an order's ready, but she don't ever remember to ring it." She got to her feet but paused a moment to motion with her head toward Monroe, who was hurrying into the kitchen. "She's still got her back up about havin' to cook breakfast for those three in the jail. Monroe didn't tell her till this mornin'." She chuckled and followed Monroe into the kitchen to pick up

Cullen's breakfast. She left him to consider what he had just learned about the town's sheriff and how difficult an inexperienced lawman could make New Hope's chances of avoiding the same fate Fort Griffin had suffered. He reminded himself then that he couldn't have been much older than Alton when he took the job as sheriff of Sundown, Texas. His thoughts were distracted then when a couple of the hotel guests came into the dining room, their timing coinciding with Lottie's arrival at the table with his breakfast. "Reckon I've gotta go back to work now," she said, took a quick gulp of coffee, then left to wait on the two customers. He was just as glad. She was a source of information, but he allowed that a good percentage of it might come from her personal opinion.

On the positive side, the pancakes were as good as he had ever had anywhere else. Feeling his hunger satisfied, he paid Monroe for his breakfast and walked down the street to the stable. At least, he now knew why Ernest Robertson had been so grateful for his preventing the sheriff's death at the hands of Slade and his two friends. And there was no doubt in Cullen's mind that that would have certainly been the result. He wanted to know more about Alton Ford and he thought Burt Whitley might be a good source of information. He wanted to check on his horses, anyway.

"Good mornin', McCabe," Burt called out when Cullen walked into the alley between the stalls. "I was just fixin' to feed your horses."

Cullen returned the greeting and went into the

stall where Jake was. The placid bay gelding greeted him with a nudge of his muzzle against Cullen's chest. "How you doin', boy?" he said as he stroked the horse's neck. "Is Burt treatin' you all right?"

Burt stood there and watched him for a few moments before opening the conversation Cullen knew he wanted to talk about. "Heard you got a chance to meet some of our new friends in the saloon last night." When Cullen failed to reply, he continued, "I saw Johnny Bledsoe a little while ago. He said if you hadn'ta jumped in to help him, Alton Ford mighta got gunned down."

"That was a possibility, I expect," Cullen said. "And if Alton hadn't been covering that Slade fellow, I mighta got gunned down. Your sheriff's young, but he wasn't afraid to stand up to three pretty rough-lookin' fellows. I heard he's the younger brother of Ernest Robertson's wife. How'd it happen that Robertson's brother-in-law got the job as sheriff?"

"Oh, there wasn't no under-the-table deal on that," Burt was quick to reply. "We've got a town council. I'm on it, and we had a problem findin' a sheriff. Nobody wanted the job, even though we weren't havin' any real trouble with outlaws at the time. Eunice Robertson said her brother was workin' as a deputy in some little town east of Fort Worth. She got in touch with him and he was willin' to try it for a while. Nobody on the town council objected, so we gave him the job. Well, like I said, we didn't have any trouble to amount to much, so he just stayed on as the sheriff. And you gotta give him credit, he ran that Slade character outta town last week." He paused to shake his head slowly. "Trouble is, it looks like he's set himself up for more of what we had last night. Three of 'em showed up last night. What if they're all part of that Viper Gang? If they are, there may be more comin' after those three in jail."

"You're the second one to say something about the Viper Gang," Cullen said. "What do you know about them? Is there really a Viper Gang? Or is that just some horseshit somebody made up?"

"I believe it," Burt was quick to admit. "I mean, course there ain't nobody come ridin' into town claimin' they was the Viper Gang. That's just the name somebody here in town started callin' them. I reckon because they're nothin' but a bunch of low-life snakes. There's been cattle rustlin' on several of the small ranches in the county, and every time it was done by a dozen or so rustlers, too many for the average small rancher around here to fight. They usually cut out fifty to two or three hundred head, a number they can move pretty fast. And they have enough men to drop some back to stop anybody trying to catch up with 'em."

"Anybody say they know where these Vipers come from?" Cullen asked. "They got a camp somewhere?" He couldn't believe a gang the size Burt was describing could have a camp that no one had ever found.

"If they have, ain't nobody in New Hope ever seen it," Burt claimed. "Ernest got in touch with the Texas Rangers and complained about it. They've been to Fort Griffin more'n once lookin' for the same type of rustlers. They didn't find a trace of 'em and that town turned into the wildest outlaw hangout in the state. It's the reason I came to New Hope, and now the son of the devil have followed me over here." He looked at Cullen and shook his head. "Trouble is, it ain't just cattle rustlin'. There's also robberies of all kinds, and there's been some people killed when they tried to resist. I'm sorry to have to tell you about all this 'cause I know you were hopin' to find a peaceful place for your friends to settle. But that's the way things are goin' in New Hope right now."

"I 'preciate your honesty, Burt. It sure makes you wanna look before you leap," Cullen said. "I think I'll hang around a day or two longer, though. I ain't in any particular hurry to move to somewhere else to look. As a matter of fact, I was thinkin' about taking Jake out today to look at some of the land around New Hope. I'm afraid if I don't work him a little bit, he might get to likin' it too much."

"You takin' your packhorse, too?" Burt asked.

"Nope, I'll just take Jake. I'll be back in town tonight, in time to put him back in the stable." He waited a few minutes, since Burt was about to feed his horses when he came in. Jake might as well have a portion of oats, he decided.

After Jake was fed, Cullen climbed up into the saddle and turned toward the north end of the street. Past the saloon and the post office, he slow-walked his horse through the quiet little town. Approaching the jail, he saw Alton Ford sitting on the wide stoop in front, his chair balanced on two legs as he leaned against the wall. "Mornin', Sheriff," Cullen called out as he rode past.

"McCabe," Alton returned. Cullen was not inclined to stop and talk. He assumed the sheriff was not having any problems with his prisoners, judging by his calm appearance. Cullen nudged Jake into a casual lope and followed the north road out of town.

"Hey!" Slade Powell yelled. "Where the hell's our supper?"

Sitting at his desk, Alton Ford ignored him, but when he continued to shout and Red Grimsley joined in the protest, Alton went into the cell room to quiet them down. "You might as well knock it off," he said. "It ain't quite time for your supper. It'll be here directly. Yellin' like that ain't gonna bring it any sooner, and if you don't quiet down, I'm not gonna give it to you when it does get here."

"I'm glad to hear that, Sheriff," Slade responded. "We thought maybe you were asleep in the other room, and you mighta forgot all about your poor prisoners in here."

"You got some whiskey somewhere?" Luther Hill asked. "I need some medicine, I got a lot of pain and I can't breathe through my nose. That sidewinder busted it. You're supposed to take care of your prisoners, ain't you? How 'bout that doctor? There's a doctor in town now, ain't there? I need to have him take a look at my nose."

Alton wasn't sure if he should ask Doc Worley to come to the jail to look at a prisoner or not. "It doesn't look that bad, Jackass Number One. We'll just give it a chance to let the swelling go down. Doc ain't likely to give you any whiskey for it, anyway." Doc Worley had a drinking problem and Alton doubted he would waste a single drop on an outlaw. He was saved momentarily from further harassment from his prisoners when he heard someone come in the office. He looked out the cell room door and saw Lottie Bridges carrying a large basket and a coffeepot. "You can quit your complainin' now," he said to his prisoners. "Your supper's here." He went out into the office to help her.

"I brought another coffeepot from the dinin' room," Lottie said. "At least this one's big enough to give your guests a couple of cups apiece and I won't have to carry it back and forth." She placed it on the little stove in his office. "Hell, you ain't even got a fire in the stove," she complained. "You want me to build one for you?"

"I'll do it," he said. "It wasn't cold in here, but I'll build a little fire, enough to warm that coffeepot."

"Tell her to come on in here with that supper," Slade yelled, recognizing a woman's voice. "After we eat, we might have us a little party."

His comments might have been meant to embarrass the woman, but they were wasted on Lottie. "I'd rather party with a hog," she yelled back at him.

She heard the chuckling from the cell room, then Slade called back again. "Well, we've got Luther in here. He's pretty damn close to a hog. Ain't that right, Luther?"

"Oink, oink, oink," Luther sang out to Red and Slade's loud guffaws of laughter.

"I'm sorry, Lottie," Alton apologized. "I'll take the basket and coffeepot, and you'd best let me take care of the supper. I didn't think they'd act up like that."

"Don't worry yourself about it," Lottie tried to assure him. "I don't pay any attention to brayin' donkeys." Sensing his embarrassment, however, she didn't linger after giving him the basket.

"I ought not give you your supper, seein' as how rude you were to Miss Bridges," Alton said when he brought the basket of food into the cell room. "You oughta be glad you're gettin' some decent food."

"Yeah, well, we're real sorry about that," Red said. "Ain't we, Slade?"

"Yeah, we sure are," Slade replied. "Open the cell door and you can just hand them plates to me."

"I don't think so, Slade," Alton said, wary of an attempt to escape. "We'll keep usin' the slot here." He pointed to a horizontal slot built into the cell door, just big enough to accommodate a plate of food. One by one, he passed the plates through. "I've got your coffee warmin' up on the stove. I'll be back with it in a minute or two."

As he said he would, Alton returned, carrying three cups and the coffeepot. He set the pot on a small table by the door, then proceeded to fill the cups. "One at a time," he said again, "and I'll hand you a cup through the bars." He drew his pistol with one hand and picked up a cup with the other. "Just so you don't get any ideas," he said when Slade pretended to be surprised by his caution.

"I'm startin' to think you don't trust us," Slade said as he stepped up to take the hot coffee through the bars. Red and Luther quickly stepped up to the bars behind him.

"I don't," Alton said, and held his gun trained on Slade as he passed the cup through to him.

Slade reached for the cup of steaming hot coffee, but appeared to bump it in the process, causing hot coffee to spill on his hand. "Yow!" Slade roared, and jumped back. Startled, Alton reacted by trying to keep the coffee from spilling on his hand, forgetting the gun in his other hand for an instant. That instant was enough for Luther to reach through the bars and trap

Alton's gun hand. Before Alton could react to prevent it, the simpleminded outlaw crushed his hand with brutelike strength, preventing him from cocking the gun. Luther yanked the surprised lawman's arm, slamming him up against the bars. Then he easily wrenched the pistol from his hand while Slade and Red held Alton firmly against the bars. Grinning like a pet retriever that just fetched a quail to his master, Luther handed the pistol to Slade.

"Well, now, Sheriff," Slade taunted him, "things have turned around, ain't they?" His face right up against the shocked young man's, he said, "There's only two things that can happen here right now, and only one that can keep you alive, so you listen real good. If we turn you loose and you walk over and get me that key to this cell door, we'll walk outta here and leave you in this cell. That's all we want, to get outta here. Now, if we turn you loose and you decide to run for it, I'll shoot you down before you reach the door. Me and my friends here won't be any worse off than we already are, but you'll be deader'n hell. So, what's it gonna be? You feel like dyin' just to keep us in here?"

Too shocked to think clearly, Alton was not even aware of the blood running down the side of his face, the result of his impact with the bars when Luther slammed him against the cell wall. He did not want to lose the first prisoners he had locked in jail, but he didn't see that he had any option other than to let them escape. He was aware more than ever that he did not want to die. He made one feeble attempt to discourage them. "Give me back my gun and I'll forget you tried this escape." All three laughed in response. "If I get the key and let you out, and you shoot me, everybody will hear the shots, and you won't get away."

"That's right," Slade said. "That's why you know we won't shoot you. All we want is to get outta here. You can tell everybody that somebody passed us a gun through the window, so they won't know we took it away from you. We're wastin' time, so if you don't fetch that key hanging on that hook over there, I'm gonna end up shootin' you, anyway. Let him go, boys."

They released him, and he quickly stepped back away from the bars, to stand there, hesitating. He looked at the smirking face of Slade, the pistol cocked and aimed at him. He took a quick glance at the cell room door, now seeming to be ten yards away. He suddenly exhaled, not realizing he had been holding his breath. It was not worth dying for, he decided. No one would know how it really happened. He would do as Slade suggested and tell everybody that a gun had been slipped in through the window. He turned then and got the key from the hook on the opposite wall.

As soon as Alton turned the key in the lock, Slade pushed the cell door open. Still holding the gun on him, he told Alton to step inside the cell. Alton did as he was told. "I kept my side of the deal," he said when he walked in. "You said you won't shoot me if I unlocked the cell."

"That's right, I did," Slade replied. "And I aim to keep my word. I said I wouldn't shoot you. I never said I wouldn't kill you." He winked at Luther. The grinning brute suddenly grabbed Alton, wrapped him up with a choke hold around his neck, then gradually choked the life out of the unfortunate young sheriff.

Slade stood watching until the last breath of life was gone. "Now, that's what I came back here to do."

Wasting no more time, the three outlaws went into the sheriff's office to recover their weapons, helping themselves to additional ammunition in the process. Once they were armed again, they felt in control of the whole town with not even the young, ineffective sheriff to worry about. "I'd like to see that big baboon that jumped us," Red Grimsley said. They left the jail and walked brazenly down the middle of the street past the saloon, looking right and left, hoping somebody would challenge them. No one dared, not even when they went into the stable to get their horses. "Where the hell is that jasper that owns this place?" Red asked, thinking that there should be somebody around that early in the evening.

"Maybe he saw us walkin' down the street and got the hell outta here," Slade said. "I swear, I was hopin' to get to shoot at least one hero before we left town." Everyone laughed at his remark, with the exception of Burt Whitley, who was lying behind a hay bale in the loft overhead, trying not to inhale deep breaths, in case they might be heard. As Slade had suggested, he had seen the three outlaws when they approached his stable. Unfortunately, he had no time to get down, and no way to defend himself, since he wasn't wearing his gun. He just hoped they would saddle their horses and leave without doing any damage to his place, or stealing any horses. They showed no indication of being in a hurry, considering they had evidently just broken out of jail, a fact that caused Burt to wonder if Alton was aware of the escape. This time of day, Alton might be up at the hotel, eating supper.

Finally, he heard the men below preparing to

leave. When he heard them ride out of the stable, he got to his feet and went to the hayloft door, where he got a glimpse of them as they rode out the north road. Relieved, he went down the ladder and hurried straight to the tack room to get his gun belt out of one of the bins. Even though the threat was over, he felt the need to be armed. Everything seemed to be in order, which came as a relief also. It appeared that the three had taken nothing more than their horses and saddles. Then he thought he'd best run up to the jail to see if Alton was there.

CHAPTER 6

"In jail?" John Prophet responded loudly, scarcely able to believe it.

"That's what I said," Stumpy Spratte replied, then repeated what he had just reported. "All three of 'em was locked up last night after a little trouble in the saloon. Feller I talked to said Slade called the sheriff out and the sheriff put all three of 'em in jail."

"How the hell did he do that?" Prophet demanded, thinking of the image of the young tenderfoot lawman he had formed from descriptions told to him by his men. He had big plans for the town of New Hope, so he had purposefully not visited it with any of his men. "Were they drunk?"

"That ain't what this feller told me," Stumpy continued. "He said he had some help, said it was a stranger that stepped in and broke Luther's nose, then got the jump on Red and Slade."

Prophet tried to picture that but still found it difficult to believe. Slade Powell was not an easy man to get the jump on. He knew Slade was still hot under the collar for getting run out of town a week ago by a sheriff who didn't look old enough to shave. There was no talking him out of going back to draw the sheriff into a gunfight. Prophet was not against it. He planned to gun down any lawman they persuaded to take the job, anyway. But he told Slade to take Red Grimsley and Luther Hill with him, just in case the sheriff had some help. And now to find out all three of them were in jail, it didn't just irritate him, it infuriated him. He was planning to go after a sizable herd of cattle in the next day or two and he wanted all of his men to move them. But more important than that, he didn't want Slade to become well known by the people of New Hope, because he would be useless to him if he did.

Stumpy watched Prophet as he obviously thought over what he had just been told. It was easy to see he was mad as hell. "I thought about helpin' 'em, but I knew what you said about raisin' too much hell in that town till we was ready to take it over."

Prophet cocked an eye at the sawed-off gunman. "Good thing you didn't," he finally said. If those people in that town find out how many of us are fixin' to own it, they'll have the Rangers over here, or the damn soldiers, like they did at Fort Griffin."

"What are we gonna do, Boss?" Stumpy asked. "Just leave 'em in jail? Ain't no tellin' how long they're gonna keep 'em locked up."

Prophet didn't answer right away. He was still trying to decide what would be best in the long run. Everything he had done up to this point was to follow a plan he devised to take over a town. And when the people split off from Fort Griffin and Albany to make New Hope, he knew it was ripe for his picking. He had assembled eleven of the roughest outlaws he could persuade to follow him. And he had delivered on his promises to keep them well paid by rustling cattle and robbing the stage lines. After every job, they returned to hole up in this hideout far up a little stream in the rolling hills west of the Brazos. He had not objected to his men's needs to go into town and raise a little hell as long as they didn't all go into town at the same time. The idea was never to let the townsfolk know they were a gang, instead of two or three drifters looking for a drink of whiskey and a game of cards.

The decision he was going to have to make now was whether or not to ride into town and break the three men out of jail. It would be easy enough to do, but in doing so, he might destroy his plan to run the town for his benefit. Taking over the sheriff's office was in the plan, but not at this stage. He had to establish himself in New Hope first before bringing some of his men in as deputies. He wanted the merchants in New Hope to feel they were protected and he had planned to use Slade as one of his deputies after he was installed as the new sheriff. But that was not going to happen if he rode in and broke him out of jail.

"You want me to tell the boys to saddle up?" Stumpy asked, thinking they would surely be going in to free their three comrades.

"No, damn it," Prophet replied. "I need to think about the best thing to do right now. Let 'em sit in that jail for a while, till I'm ready. I told Slade he could kill that sheriff, but to make sure it was a duel, face-to-face. And then he ends up in jail, all three of 'em. I want to know how that happened." His thoughts were interrupted then when Slim Bradshaw opened the cabin door.

"Three riders comin' up the trail from the river,"

Slim said. "Riker said it looks like Slade and them, but it's gettin' too dark to be sure. I'll go take a look."

Prophet walked out on the front stoop of the cabin to wait. He wasn't worried about three men, even if it wasn't Slade, Red, and Luther, not with eight hardened gunmen in his camp, plus himself. In about five minutes, the riders appeared, climbing the winding trail that snaked its way through thick growths of stunted oak trees before coming out in the clearing and the camp. He could hear Riker calling out to them and knew it was Slade. Prophet stepped off the stoop and went to meet them at the corral.

"You don't have to worry 'bout that prissy sheriff in New Hope no more," Slade announced. "Luther wrung his neck like a chicken."

"Anybody on your tail?" Prophet asked.

"Nope," Slade said. "You know we ain't gonna lead nobody up here. Wasn't any need to worry, anyway. Those folks are too scared to come after us, right, Red?"

"That's right, Boss," Grimsley replied. "We walked right down the middle of the street and there wouldn't nobody show their face. We took our time gettin' on our horses and there still weren't nobody in sight when we rode out."

"Is that so?" Prophet responded. "How the hell did you get outta jail?"

"How'd you know we was in jail?" Slade asked, surprised. He hadn't planned to admit that they had been arrested, and he had advised Red and Luther to keep it to themselves as well.

"Stumpy was in town and some fellow told him the three of you got yourselves thrown in the jail by the sheriff," Prophet said. "I'd be mighty interested to know how that happened."

"He had some help," Slade quickly responded. "I called him out, just like I told you I would, and he had this other jasper, big feller, almost as big as Luther. He jumped us from behind, flattened Luther's nose, and had us at gunpoint before we had a chance to do anything. Ain't that right, Luther?"

"That's right, Boss," Luther said. "Look at my nose. I didn't see him comin'. But we got even. I wrung his neck, like Slade said."

"The big fellow?" Prophet asked, thinking they might have someone else to deal with who would be tougher to deal with than the sheriff.

"No, I wrung the sheriff's neck," Luther answered. "That feller weren't there when we broke out. Else, I'da wrung his, too."

Stumpy spoke up then. "That feller that told me they was in jail said some drifter stepped in to help the sheriff, somebody just passin' through town. I expect he mighta left town already."

"If he helped the sheriff arrest three big badmen," Prophet suggested sarcastically, "he most likely stayed around so the folks could buy him drinks."

"He had a chance to show his face when we were walkin' down the middle of the street," Slade countered. "I'da loved it if he had."

Prophet was undecided what he should do at this point. He wondered if this "big fellow" who had stepped in, might be someone being considered to replace Sheriff Ford. It had come sooner than he had anticipated, but maybe he should move in and make his pitch to take the job. They should be anxious to fill the job as soon as they could, what with the recent troubles they had had, thanks to visits from his men. *A man's a fool not to take the opportunity when it's laid at his feet*, he thought. He made up his mind. "We're not goin' after those cattle tomorrow. It's important that I go to New Hope to see if I can salvage something outta the mess you three made there today."

It was a town in distress that Cullen returned to that evening. He was met at the stable by Burt Whitley when he brought his horse back to his stall. "Evenin', Burt," Cullen greeted him when he walked out of the tack room. "Glad I got back before you locked up. I rode Jake pretty hard today. I think he's earned a portion of oats." He could tell by Burt's anxious expression that he was waiting to tell him something. "Something goin' on in town tonight?"

"My Lordy, yes," Burt replied. "There's a whole lotta somethin' goin' on. For starters, Alton Ford is dead." That captured Cullen's attention at once. "And the three prisoners have escaped," Burt continued.

"They shot Alton?" Cullen blurted.

"Well, no, they didn't shoot him, but he's dead. Doc Worley said they choked him to death. Then they walked down the street, darin' anybody to stop 'em, came down here, and got their horses. I woulda tried to stop 'em, but they caught me up in the hayloft without my gun."

Cullen didn't say anything for a long moment while his brain processed this unexpected occurrence. He had counted on young Alton Ford to quickly grow into his job, just as he had in the little town of Sundown. Aware then that Burt was awaiting some comment following his confession, Cullen said, "It's a good thing you didn't try. One of 'em might have gotten a shot at you."

"Well, at the time, I didn't know they had killed Alton," Burt said, still intent upon justifying his lack of action. "I saw 'em comin' and figured they'd escaped, but like I said, I was up in the loft and my gun was in the tack room."

"You'da been a fool to try to stop those three gun-slingers," Cullen assured him. "It's never a good idea to bring a pitchfork to a gunfight, even if the odds ain't three-to-one against you."

"I reckon you're right," Burt said, nodding thoughtfully. "I kinda wish I'da had my gun, though."

"I reckon the mayor and his wife are pretty upset," Cullen said. They not only lost Eunice's brother, the mayor lost his sheriff as well.

"I reckon," Burt replied. "They're havin' a funeral for Alton tomorrow at the church. I expect half the town will be there. After we get Alton in the ground, we're gonna have to start all over again to find us a sheriff." He cocked a serious eye at Cullen. "Don't suppose you'd be interested in takin' that job, would you?"

"Not at all," Cullen said. "I've got business elsewhere. I'm just passin' through your town."

"What kinda business are you in?" Burt asked.

"Like I told you yesterday, just one thing and then another. Now, I'm in New Hope to look over the lay of the land as a favor for a friend." To discourage Burt from asking more questions, Cullen quickly changed the subject. "I'm too late to get supper at the hotel and I'm about to starve. So, I reckon I'll go get some of that chuck over at the saloon."

"You goin' to the funeral tomorrow?" Burt asked. "Everybody I've talked to said they'd be there."

"I don't think so," Cullen answered. "I don't think they'd care if I was there or not, since I'm just passin' through town." He didn't say so, but he thought it might be a good idea to keep an eye on the town while most of the people were at the funeral. Slade and his two friends might think that a convenient time to pay New Hope another visit.

Burt Whitley had been correct in saying most of the town would gather at the First Baptist Church the next day. The few rows of pews were filled in the modest church when Reverend Franklin Bass said the opening prayer beside the open casket of Alton Ford. It was one of many prayers from the inspired preacher, alternating with inspirational hymns forced out of a small organ by the reverend's wife, Ruby. When six strong men carried the coffin out, Ernest Robertson and his grieving wife followed it to the cemetery. After the graveside burial service was completed and condolences were offered by their friends and neighbors, the group of mourners began to disperse. The mayor helped his wife up into the buckboard, then walked around to the other side to find a stranger standing there waiting for him. Puzzled, Robertson hesitated, trying to remember if he had seen him before. Tall, black hair, and a neatly trimmed mustache, he carried himself with an air of authority. When he spoke, his voice was deep and distinctive.

"Mayor Robertson," he said, then nodded at Eunice, who was staring at him, as puzzled as her husband. "Ma'am." He removed his hat. "I hope you won't think I'm intrudin' on this sad occasion, but I just wanted to express my sympathies in your time of strife."

"That's mighty thoughtful of you, sir," Eunice

replied. "Forgive me if I can't recall your name. It must be the sorrowful occasion that's impaired my memory."

"No, ma'am, not at all. You don't know me. I was just passin' through New Hope on my way to Kansas, and I heard about the murder of your brother. The fact that he was an officer of the law, made me want to come to honor him at his funeral. You see, I'm a lawman, myself, and I'm on my way to Dodge City. The city council has been tryin' to persuade me to come up there and take the job as chief marshal. I don't really wanna leave Texas, but I told 'em I'd talk to them about it. I reckon they're impressed by my record down in San Antonio, but Dodge is just another big, wild town. I cotton to the smaller towns, like your town." He stepped back then. "Anyway, thank you for your time. I hope I haven't delayed you." He put his hat back on as if about to walk away.

"What's your name, mister?" Robertson stopped him.

"My name's John Prophet," he said, "spelled like the holy man, and not the money you get when you sell a horse for more money than you paid for it."

"Well, Mr. Prophet, I think it was a mighty unusual occurrence that caused you to stop in New Hope at this particular time." Robertson extended his hand. "You say you're on your way up to Kansas to talk about the marshal's job? If you haven't already agreed to anything up there, maybe you should think about taking a job right here in New Hope." He motioned for Prophet to take a few steps away from the buckboard. Eunice might find talking business to be disrespectful of her departed brother, but this seemed an unbelievable opportunity.

"Well, sir, to be honest with you, I haven't agreed

to anything with the folks up there," Prophet said. "It didn't occur to me when I rode into town that there might be a job openin' right here. That's mighty interestin'."

"I'd say it's more than a coincidence that a lawman named Prophet happens to show up in New Hope right at the time when the town needs one," Robertson went on, his enthusiasm growing by the minute. "I hope the fact that we're burying our sheriff wouldn't discourage you from considering our town." He shook his head slowly. "Sheriff Ford was a fine young man, but I'm afraid he was just too young for the responsibility of the sheriff's job." He felt empathy for his wife's mourning of her younger brother, but he, possibly like everybody else in town, had never had much confidence in Alton's ability to handle the job. His death, if anything, was the obvious proof of that. "I believe you should consider taking the job as our sheriff. You said you didn't want to leave Texas. Looks to me like that might be the answer to that problem. Whaddaya say we talk about it this afternoon?"

Prophet made a show of acting surprised. "Well, I never . . ." he started, then said, "I certainly agree that you need a man with experience, which I have a great deal of when it comes to keeping the peace. Maybe there was a reason I happened by here today. Where do you wanna meet?"

"I own the hotel," Robertson said. "Why don't you meet me in the dining room about five o'clock?" He stole another quick look toward his wife. "I'd say sooner, but there's bound to be lots of visitin' and such after the funeral," he said, almost whispering.

"I'll be there," Prophet said, and they shook hands once again. Robertson stood by the buckboard a few moments longer, watching his prospect for sheriff walk away. He couldn't help thinking that the man's physical bearing seemed to suggest authority. *Sorry, Alton,* he said to himself, *but this might be a lucky day for New Hope.*

"Well, look who's back," Lottie Bridges sang out when she saw Cullen walk in the door of the dining room and pause at the table by the door to remove his pistol. She waited for him at the table he always picked. "I figured you'd headed outta town, on your way to wherever. I reckon you heard about Alton."

"Yeah," Cullen replied, "Burt told me about it when I got back last night."

"You didn't come in for supper last night," she said.

"I got back too late to catch supper here, so I ate some stew Rena cooked up at The Texas House."

"You didn't come to breakfast this mornin'," Lottie reminded him. About to scold him, she stopped when she remembered. "Oh, I forgot we were closed on account of the funeral. You want coffee?"

While he waited for Lottie to return with his coffee, Ernest Robertson walked in. He paused beside Cullen's table long enough to speak. "McCabe," he acknowledged.

"Mr. Mayor," Cullen returned. "Sorry to hear about Alton's death."

"Yes," Robertson replied. "Terrible thing, terrible waste of a fine young man. It's a damn shame we live in a state where men like those three outlaws congregate." With that, he walked away and seated himself at a table in the back corner of the room. Cullen was just as glad he did. He preferred to concentrate on his supper, especially after his experience with Rena's stew the night before. He had sat, drinking his coffee, no more than five or six minutes when another man walked into the dining room. A stranger, he had to be informed by Monroe to surrender his weapon. He did so without argument, then promptly proceeded to the table in the corner as Robertson signaled to catch his attention.

Lottie returned to Cullen's table with a plate of food but stood staring at Robertson and his guest at the back table before putting the plate down. "You waitin' for me to beg for it?" Cullen asked finally.

"Sorry," she said, and placed it before him. "There's been talk about a stranger that hit town today, and I reckon that's gotta be him. James Levitt says he overheard Ernest sayin' something about a new sheriff, and Alton Ford just stuck in the ground this mornin'." Her comment served to perk Cullen's interest in the stranger as well. She went back to their table to see if they were going to eat supper. In a couple of minutes, she returned to the kitchen. On her way past Cullen's table, she whispered, "That's the new sheriff."

He had to admit, this latest development could serve to make things interesting, depending upon whether or not this new sheriff had what it takes to keep the peace. If he could do the job that was required, then it appeared that the governor might have sent him all the way from Austin needlessly. The sooner he found out, the better, so when he had finished eating, he got up and walked back to the table. "I didn't go to the funeral," Cullen said, "so I ain't had a chance to tell your wife how disappointed I was to hear about Alton's death. I wish you'd tell her I'm sorry for her pain."

"Appreciate you saying so, I'll tell her," Robertson said. He looked at Prophet and said, "McCabe here is one of the guests in the hotel. He's the fellow I told you about who helped Alton Ford capture those three outlaws." Turning back to Cullen, he said, "McCabe, meet John Prophet. He's going to take Alton's place as sheriff of New Hope." He grinned and said, "Looks like you're one of the first in town to know."

"Well, I reckon I'll wish you better luck than Alton had," Cullen said.

"I think you can count on it," Prophet answered. "I don't intend to have any need for the citizens of New Hope to help control crime in this town."

"John here has quite a bit of experience as an officer of the law," Robertson said. "I expect things will be a lot different around here when some of these trouble-making drifters find out there's an experienced sheriff on the job."

"Might at that," Cullen commented. "Where were you workin' before, Sheriff?"

"I've served the law in several places," Prophet replied, "most recently in San Antonio."

"Sounds like you've got the right kind of experience, all right," Cullen said. "I hope everything works out just fine for you and the town."

"'Preciate it," Prophet said. "The mayor says you're just passin' through town."

"Yep, just like I told the mayor, I'm tryin' to get a good look at the land around here. I'm thinkin' about ridin' up toward Fort Griffin today, but I'll be back here tonight. I'll most likely be around for a couple of days or more before I head somewhere else." He left them to talk about their plans for New Hope, stopping to pay Monroe for his supper on his way out. It would appear that New Hope's problems were over, and maybe they weren't. Cullen had a worrisome feeling about John Prophet. He was almost too perfect for the job. *I think I'll hang around for a few days to see how things work out,* he thought, *but there's one little trip I'd like to make tomorrow.*

CHAPTER 7

It was only about sixteen miles to Fort Griffin, so Cullen decided to eat breakfast in the hotel before taking the ride. In addition to a fine breakfast, cooked by Bea Rivenbark, he got a full report on the meeting between the mayor and John Prophet. According to Lottie, they remained at the table long after they finished supper. She, as was her nature, managed to stay within earshot for a good part of the discussion between the two. And from what she could hear from her eavesdropping, Prophet was going to be allowed to hire a couple of deputies. "I know the rest of the merchants are gonna be tickled to hear that," Lottie said with a giggle. "Hell, it was hard enough to get 'em to agree to pay Alton by himself."

"Sounds like this fellow, Prophet, is figurin' on settin' up a regular police force," Cullen said, and took one last gulp of coffee. It seemed to be at least one more deputy than a town of its size called for. "I hope it all works out for you folks here in New Hope." He got to his feet. "I've got a little ride to take. Maybe I'll be back in time for supper."

"We won't be holdin' our breath," Lottie replied, falling back to her usual sarcastic state of mind.

Burt Whitley was in the process of cleaning out stalls when Cullen arrived to pick up his horse. Whitley offered to get Jake from the corral for him, but Cullen said he could do it himself. "You comin' back?" Burt asked.

"Yeah, I'll be back," Cullen answered. "You've still got my packhorse." He went to the tack room and picked up his saddle. "You heard about the new sheriff?"

"I heard a rumor last night," Burt answered. "Then I saw a feller loadin' some packs in the sheriff's office this mornin', so I figured it must be true. Course, I ain't seen him up close, but from a distance, he don't look like the youngster that Alton was. I'm waitin' to see if he brings his horse down here to the stable." He walked out with Cullen when he led Jake out of the corral. "How 'bout you? Have you met him?"

"Yeah, I met him last night," Cullen replied, and climbed up into the saddle. "He's talkin' a pretty strong game—might be a lot different around here, if he's as tough as he talks."

"Good, we need it," Burt said, sighed once for the job awaiting him, and went back to work on the stalls.

"Yonder he comes," Luther Hill blurted, "the piece of dirt that broke my nose! Just like Prophet said, he's headin' to Fort Griffin. Wonder what he's goin' there for."

"Who gives a damn?" Slade replied. "Prophet said to stop him. He thinks he could be trouble if he decides to stay in New Hope, and Prophet's got a pretty good nose for troublemakers. All I know is I'm gonna enjoy puttin' a bullet between his shoulder blades."

"The hell you say," Luther came back. "I'm the one got my nose broke. I oughta be the one that shoots him."

"We're both gonna shoot him," Slade replied impatiently. "Fill him so full of lead till his horse can't tote him."

"Oh, I thought you meant you was gonna be the only one to take the shot."

"The reason I picked this spot near the creek was because the road crosses it where there's a wide-open space on both sides." Slade tried to appease his slow-witted partner. "He's ridin' the road, so he'll be right out in the open till he gets to the trees on the other side. So, as soon as he clears the trees on that side, we'll fire away."

"Oh, I got it," Luther said, and grinned.

"Just don't shoot till he rides out of the trees," Slade reminded him. "'Cause once he's in the clear, he ain't got no place to take cover." He shook his head, exasperated with the slow-thinking child in a brute's body. He had rather Prophet hadn't sent Luther with him. He didn't need help waiting in ambush for one man, but Luther wanted to go. He was still a little disgruntled that Prophet talked his way into the sheriff's job, and Slim and Riker were going to be hired as his deputies, a job that Slade wanted. Prophet explained that neither he, Red, nor Luther could be appointed as deputies because they were known by the whole town as the three prisoners who had escaped. Worse yet, they had killed the sheriff. Slade understood, but it still stuck in his craw that Riker and Slim would be enjoying the benefits of being deputies while he would have to lie low. His thoughts were interrupted then when he saw McCabe entering the clump of trees south of the creek. "Get ready, he'll be comin' outta those trees in about two minutes." Rifles already cocked, both men positioned themselves to cut their target down.

On the road, Cullen rode easy in rhythm with Jake's comfortable gait. Following a wagon road that wound across open prairie, he was approaching what appeared to be a fairly large creek, its course outlined by trees. At the point where the road crossed the creek, there was an especially thick clump of trees, and a random thought floated through his mind. *That's a perfect spot for an ambush.* As if thinking the same thing, Jake's ears, which were seldom still, suddenly pricked up and he snorted. That was usually his way of saying things didn't seem exactly right ahead. "Are you tryin' to tell me something, boy?" Cullen muttered. He thought back on the conversation he had with the mayor and Prophet the night before. At the time, he had sensed a suspicious attitude on the part of the new sheriff, almost as if he was competing with him for the mayor's favor. Now he remembered saying that he was thinking about riding up to Fort Griffin. *That wasn't too smart,* he told himself. Jake had suddenly become cautious, and Cullen had become uneasy, himself. *I might be playing head games with myself,* he thought, *but I think I'd rather be overcautious than blissfully dead.*

He did not vary from his approach to the creek, continuing on the road until he reached the first large clump of trees. At that point, he turned Jake off the road and rode through the trees, paralleling the creek for a distance of about forty yards before crossing over to the other bank. He figured that if there was anyone in ambush, they would be watching for him to come from the south side of the creek, and not this side, and he might possibly get behind them. Halfway thinking he was letting his imagination run away with him, he made his way back toward the road, leading his horse through the thick growth of trees. He stopped suddenly when Jake nickered. Looking ahead of him, he spotted movement in the leaves of the low limbs. Thinking he had almost stumbled into the ambush, he took a few cautious steps backward until he could reach his rifle and pull it from its sling. He looped his reins around a low branch and left Jake behind as he cautiously moved toward the spot where he had seen movement. A few feet at a time, he moved from bush to bush, approaching the trees hard by the bank of the creek. He raised his rifle, knowing he would have to be quick to crank a cartridge into the chamber and fire, not wanting to alert his ambusher before he could actually see him. One last branch obstructed his view, and when he carefully pulled it aside, he discovered two horses tied in the trees by the creek, but no riders. Down on one knee, his rifle ready, he scanned the creek beyond, looking along the bank until he could see a wide space in the trees right where the road crossed the water. Then he spotted them, two men, kneeling behind a low bluff, their focus riveted to the open space.

"What the hell's he doin'?" Luther whispered, his eyes glued to the road. "Where is he?"

Slade didn't answer. It had been five minutes or more since they had lost sight of him. But on their last sighting, he had followed the road into the trees. He should have gotten to the creek by now. "I don't like the look of this," he said, moments before he heard the sound of a rifle cocking. "Get down!" he yelled just before he heard Luther yelp when he caught the round in his shoulder. Slade dived over the bluff to take cover on the other side of it, leaving Luther to fend for himself. In a rage, the angry brute turned to face his attacker, firing blindly into the brush. Cullen recognized him then as Jackass Number One, so named by Alton Ford, and probably the one who strangled the young sheriff. He didn't hesitate. His next round hit Luther square in the chest.

Seeing Luther fall backward and roll down the bank, dead, Slade scrambled on all fours along the bluff until he felt it safe to get to his feet and run. When he did, Cullen caught a glimpse of him and threw one shot after him before he disappeared into the trees. It had been only a glimpse, but he thought he'd seen the outlaw called Slade. It made sense, considering the other one was also one of the three escaped prisoners. Now it was a question for Cullen as to what best to do. Rather than chase after Slade and run the risk again of blundering into an ambush there in the trees, he decided to withdraw and see if Slade would come after him. To give him incentive, Cullen backtracked and picked up the two horses he had stumbled upon in the trees. He quickly led them back to his own horse, then he rode in a wide circle to come back to the road a quarter of a mile north of the creek. In the process of leaving the creek, he made no effort to disguise his trail. In fact, he made sure enough branches and limbs were broken to leave a clear trail. He had no idea where their camp might be, or if Slade would start hoofing it for home, once he was sure he was not being hunted. But remembering the man Slade was, and he felt sure it was Slade, he was willing to bet against it. He fully expected him to come after him to recover his horse, so he continued to follow the road to Fort Griffin, looking for the first suitable spot to set up his own ambush.

He had ridden no more than a couple of miles when he came to a place he thought would do just fine for his purposes. It was a kink in the otherwise straight trail where the road looped around a low mesa before continuing north again. The mesa was just high enough to hide the horses and afforded him the individual cover of a narrow gully that ran to the road. It was barren of trees or high brush, which made it seem an unlikely place for ambush. *Now we'll see if Mr. Slade has the motivation to come after me on foot,* he thought. He climbed up to the top of the mesa to take a look back the way he had come. There was no sign of anyone on the road for as far as he could see. He sat down inside the top of the gully and waited. While he waited, he thought about the ambush he had just avoided, and whether or not it could possibly be connected to the hiring of the new sheriff of New Hope. There was certainly reason enough for Slade and his partner to seek revenge against Cullen for causing their capture. But could it also be connected to John Prophet? If not, it was one hell of a coincidence the two of them would be waiting in ambush for him on the road to Fort Griffin. Cullen was finding it difficult to get that notion out of his head. So much so, that he decided it would be worthwhile to try to capture Slade and take him back to New Hope and see how Prophet responded. He was still turning that over in his mind when a form appeared on the road in the distance. *I figured,* Cullen thought.

He sat where he was for a while, watching the form as it gradually became closer, walking doggedly, carrying a rifle in one hand, his head down as if his eyes were focused on the road at his feet. When a little closer, Cullen confirmed his original assumption. It was the one called Slade, all right, and it would be a simple shot to just cut him down and be done with it. But he was still of a mind to take him back to New Hope to face Prophet. He made his way back down the gully next to the road, where he took a knee and remained hidden. In a few minutes, Slade appeared, looking neither right nor left, intent only upon putting one foot in front of the other, in a desperate attempt to somehow catch up. Cullen let him walk past the gully before he stepped out behind him. With his rifle cocked and raised, he issued an order. "Stop right there, or I'll cut you down." When Slade abruptly stopped, Cullen ordered, "Don't turn around. Drop the rifle on the ground." Slade hesitated for only a moment, obviously making a decision, then dropped the rifle. "All right," Cullen continued, "with your left hand, reach over and pull that handgun out and drop it. Be careful. I've got no reason not to shoot you." When Slade did as he was instructed, Cullen asked, "Did John Prophet put you two up to this ambush?"

Slade didn't answer for a few moments, then asked, "Who the hell's John Prophet?"

"Maybe you know him by another name," Cullen said. "He's the man you work for, the man who sent you to kill me."

"I don't work for any man. What are you fixin' to do now, shoot me?"

"I'm thinkin' that over," Cullen said. "It depends on how much trouble you give me when I take you back to jail."

"Can I turn around now? I'd like to face the devil that's fixin' to shoot me."

"If you don't give me any trouble, you'll live to see another day. We'll ride back to town and you can deal with the new sheriff, the one you say you ain't ever heard of. So, turn around, and do it real slow."

"All right, I'm turnin'," Slade said, making a show of deliberate motions as he turned. Halfway around, he suddenly whirled, at the same time pulling a belly gun from his belt. The .44 slug from Cullen's Winchester slammed into his chest, and he stumbled backward several steps before collapsing, the dark scowl of anger stamped forever on his face.

"Have it your way," Cullen remarked casually, even though he would have liked to see what Prophet would have done had he been able to take Slade back to New Hope. Slade had denied knowing Prophet, but Cullen was not totally convinced of that. And now that this little distraction was over, he decided to continue on his way to Fort Griffin. First, he thought it the considerate thing to move Slade's body from the middle of the road. Being a practical man, he removed Slade's gun belt and searched his pockets for anything of value. He found a small amount of money, but he was in possession of two extra horses and saddles. Those he would sell, maybe in Fort Griffin, he thought. He dragged Slade's body over to the gully and rolled it over to fall inside. Then he set out again for Fort Griffin.

* * *

It was still early in the afternoon when Cullen arrived in the town at the foot of the hill below Fort Griffin. Riding down the main street, he went directly to the stable at the far end, where he was greeted by the owner, Homer Wilcox. "Howdy," Wilcox said. "You lookin' to board them horses?" He openly eyed the two bearing empty saddles.

"Howdy," Cullen returned. "Nope, I ain't sure I'll be in town that long. I just thought I'd ask you if you're interested in buyin' a couple of good horses, saddles included, for a reasonable price—save me the trouble of leadin' 'em back to New Hope with me."

"I ain't really buyin' no horses right now," Wilcox said, reciting a standard response by every buyer of horses Cullen had ever dealt with. "How'd you come by them?"

"It doesn't really matter, does it?" Cullen answered. "They ain't stolen, and there won't be anybody comin' to look for 'em. I guess you could say they were left to me when the previous owners didn't have any use for 'em anymore. The point is, I'm willin' to sell 'em, both horses and both saddles, for one hundred dollars." He felt pretty sure it would not be the first time Wilcox had bought horses with uncertain backgrounds.

Wilcox did not respond at once but proceeded to more closely inspect the two horses. When he finished, he took a close look at the saddles. Then he looked at Cullen and said, "Eighty dollars."

"You got yourself some horses," Cullen said at once, surprising Wilcox. "Now, you can tell me where the telegraph office is."

"That's up on the hill at the fort," Wilcox said. He took the reins of the two horses and led them over to the corral and tied them while he went inside to get the eighty dollars. While he waited, some idle thoughts entered Cullen's mind. It occurred to him that he seemed to be in the horse-trading business of late. He was making more money selling horses than working for the governor, and the price always seemed to be eighty dollars. He sold Burnett three horses for eighty dollars in Austin. Wilcox was only getting two horses for the same amount, but he got two saddles thrown in.

With his extra horses converted to cash, Cullen rode up on the hill to the fort overlooking the Clear Fork of the Brazos River, where a soldier pointed out the telegraph office for him. Inside, he was surprised to find a civilian operating the telegraph. The operator, identifying himself simply as Henry, told Cullen the wire was used for military purposes only. "I'll be back in a minute," Cullen said, and went back to his horse. When he returned, he was carrying his special agent badge and the official papers stating his name and position, bearing the official seal of the governor. Henry was sufficiently impressed and eager to accommodate him. "I need to telegraph John Prophet in the sheriff's department in San Antonio and request that he wire me back here as soon as possible." Henry wrote the message down, then sent it. "How long before we get a response?" Cullen asked.

"Not long usually," Henry said, "at least when it's a military wire, but this is going to the sheriff's office, so it may come back right away, and it might be a while." He shrugged helplessly.

"I'll wait around a little while in case they come right back," Cullen said, then changed his mind. "I'm kinda hungry. I think I'll go back downtown and get something to eat. Is there a decent place to eat down there?"

Henry glanced at the clock on the wall. "Well, the hotel's got a decent dining room, but you're kinda in between dinner and supper right now. You'll be better off going to Mullin's Saloon. He's got a woman in his kitchen that'll fix you up with something, as long as you're not looking for anything fancy."

"Much obliged," Cullen said. "I'll be back in a little while." Outside, he climbed back into the saddle and descended the hill to leave Jake at the hitching post in front of a weathered building with a sign that proclaimed it to be Mullin's.

"How do?" Mullin asked when Cullen walked in. "Ain't seen you in here before. What's it gonna be?"

Cullen looked around at the almost empty room. There were only four customers sitting at the tables, two working on a bottle of whiskey, and two sitting at another table playing blackjack. The blackjack players appeared to be having an argument over a turn of the cards. Cullen turned his attention elsewhere. Spotting a large coffeepot sitting on the edge of a large iron stove, he decided to take a chance. "How old is that coffee on the stove over there?"

Mullin turned to look, as if only now aware there was a coffeepot over there. "That coffee was made fresh this mornin'," he said. "I just got through drinkin' a cup of it, myself, a few minutes before you walked in."

"Lemme have a cup of it," Cullen decided. "Got something to eat with it?"

Without answering him, Mullin yelled, "Sue, you got anythin' left to eat in the kitchen?"

"Nothin' but some salt-cured ham and cold biscuits," Sue yelled back. "Who's wantin' it?"

"I don't know," Mullin yelled again. "Some feller just walked in wantin' somethin' to eat." He looked back at Cullen then. "Are you anybody?" When he saw Cullen's puzzled expression, he said, "I mean somebody I've ever heard of. John Wesley Hardin was in the saloon at the other end of the street about a week ago. Big feller like you, I thought you might be somebody, too."

"I'm not anybody, just somebody who's hungry," Cullen replied. "Tell Sue to fix me up a couple of those ham biscuits."

Mullin promptly yelled the order back to the kitchen. Then he reached under the counter and pulled out a coffee cup, took a look inside, then blew some dust out of it. The gesture gave Cullen pause, but he decided the coffee in that pot was likely strong enough to kill anything living in the cup. Mullin handed the cup to Cullen and said, "Help yourself."

After filling his cup with coffee that appeared as black as sin, Cullen walked over to sit down at a table to await his food. It came shortly, carried by a tiny gray-haired woman. Two biscuits on a plate, and they didn't look as bad as he had expected. The coffee, however, turned out to be a test of his manhood, but he decided its purpose was to kill anything harmful on the ham. The argument at the card game across from him began to increase in heated exchange and soon turned into a shouting match of accusations. By the time Cullen finished the first biscuit, the shouting match was followed by the first punch and progressed into a full-fledged fistfight. Cullen glanced up at Mullin, who was still seated on a stool behind the bar, showing no interest in the fight now shifting back and forth in the middle of the floor. Soon they knocked over their table, with each combatant giving as good as he got. The two men quietly drinking whiskey at the other table, like Mullin, paid little attention to the two brawling card players. Cullen figured it was no concern of his, so when the two, still swinging wildly, lurched into his table, he merely picked up his coffee and his plate just as the table went upside down, and walked over to finish eating at the bar. Both fighters showed signs of exhaustion as they lay on the floor until one of them got up and walked out the door. The other one soon got up and followed him.

His food finished, Cullen paid Mullin, who was still sitting on his stool while Sue came out of the kitchen and started righting the tables and chairs the fight had scattered. "That happen very often?" Cullen asked.

"Every now and then," Mullin answered. "That's just the Willis brothers, they ain't never handled their whiskey worth a damn, and they both cheat like hell at cards."

Cullen rode back up the hill to the telegraph office. When he walked in the door, Henry greeted him with the news that he already received a reply from the San Antonio sheriff's office. It informed him that there was no one by that name employed in that office, nor had there ever been. It confirmed what Cullen had suspected since first meeting John Prophet. Prophet wasn't who he said he was. Cullen realized that it didn't mean Prophet wouldn't be a good sheriff, and it didn't tie him to Slade and the other two outlaws who broke out of jail with him. But it branded him a liar and a man to keep an eye on. He would not be the first town marshal who had ridden on both sides of the law. Some of them turned out to be successful lawmen. "Was there a name sayin' who sent the message?" Cullen asked.

"Yep," Henry replied. "It was sent by Sheriff Prentice Porter."

"Much obliged," Cullen said.

Since there was a good bit of daylight left, and Jake had had plenty of time to rest, he decided to start back to New Hope right away. It wasn't that much of a journey and he should even have enough light to look for Jackass Number One's body when he got back to the creek where the ambush was staged. There was no use in leaving the man's weapons to rust in the woods, and like Slade, he might be carrying some cash money. So, it was worth the time to go back and find that spot where the big man tumbled over the bluff and rolled down near the water. It would probably be a good idea to make sure the body wasn't in the water, too, in case he wanted to take a drink downstream from the spot.

He found it was no trouble to find Jackass Number One's body. It was sprawled on the sand below the bluff, a good twenty feet from the water's edge. After he relieved it of weapons and cash, he decided not to move it. It would be convenient for the coyotes and buzzards to feast on it close by the water, so they could drink while eating.

CHAPTER 8

He got back to the hotel late that night, too late to catch supper at the dining room, but he was hungry, so he decided to get something at The Texas House. Before going there, he decided he'd best try to catch Burt before he locked the stable for the night. Burt was in the process when Cullen pulled Jake up at the door. "Good thing you showed up," Burt said. "'Cause I was fixin' to go to the house right now."

"Sorry to hold you up," Cullen said as he stepped down. "Go ahead, if you're in a hurry. I'll take care of Jake and put the padlock on the door when I leave."

"Nah," Burt said, "I ain't in no hurry. You wanna feed him some grain?"

"I expect he'd appreciate it," Cullen replied. Curious then, he asked, "Has the word got around about the new sheriff?"

"Oh yeah," Burt said while he waited for Cullen to remove his saddlebags before loosening Jake's cinch. "The word's got around, all right. That feller's a fast mover. He's already moved himself into the jailhouse and today he was walking around town introducin' everybody to his deputies, two of 'em. They was in here. He told me their names but blamed if I can remember 'em now. I reckon I was still thinkin' about the sheriff tellin' me that I'll be takin' care of their horses at no charge." He took Jake's bridle and saddle and parked them on a rail in the tack room, still talking. "I told him that I never took care of Alton's horse at no charge, and he said that was part of his deal with the mayor. He said things were gonna change around here." He turned to give Cullen a helpless shrug. "I talked to Ernest about it, and he said we were all gonna have to do our part to keep law and order in town. He said he's givin' Prophet a free room in his hotel." He smirked. "Said he wouldn't ask the rest of us merchants to make any sacrifice that he wouldn't make."

It sounded to Cullen like Prophet was setting himself up to run the town. "What about his two deputies? Are they gettin' free rooms, too?"

"Nah, I think they're gonna bunk in the back of the sheriff's office, like Alton did." His remark called to mind something else. "Like I said, I don't remember their names, but they've got a look about 'em that makes you wanna keep your hand on your money pouch. I talked to Deke today. He said the sheriff brought 'em in the saloon today to give him the same story he gave me. Deke said one of 'em was in the saloon not long ago with a couple of drifters, and they picked a fight with a couple of ranch hands from the other side of the river. Maybe it'll be different now that he's wearin' a badge, but I don't know." He paused to scratch his head while he thought about it. "I reckon maybe it's a smart thing to have deputies that ain't afraid to mix it up with an outlaw if they have to. I don't know," he repeated. "Seems kinda odd to me, though, that this fellow, Prophet, was just passin' though town just in time for Ernest to offer him the job as sheriff. Now, the next day, he's already found him two deputies. Where the hell did they come from?"

It seemed odd to Cullen as well and served to fit right in with his suspicions about the new sheriff's motives. It was obvious to Cullen that Burt was not sure the new sheriff was a wise move on Ernest Robertson's part. The fact that the mayor had seen fit to offer Prophet the job without talking it over with the rest of the town council was bound to make some of the merchants unhappy. He suspected Robertson acted out of fear that the town had been left without any semblance of law and order and vulnerable to the same fate that Fort Griffin and Albany had suffered. As far as Cullen's mission was concerned, after this turn of events, he was not sure what he might do to help New Hope protect itself. That is, if they needed his help. He was convinced that John Prophet lied about his experience as a San Antonio lawman, but he might be just the man New Hope needed to insure their future.

It was highly unlikely to be a coincidence that a man Prophet just hired as a deputy had been seen in town with a bunch of drifters, however. Cullen had to suspect that Prophet might be in cahoots with a lot of the troublemakers the town had tolerated. There was still the issue of increased cattle rustling, and that ordinarily didn't come under a town sheriff's responsibility. So, Cullen decided his primary mission was to try to find any trace of the so-called Viper Gang in some effort to find those responsible for the rustling.

He was not willing to rule Prophet out as a part of that gang. "Well, I reckon you'll just have to see how things go after your sheriff has had a chance to run his office," Cullen said. "I'll see you tomorrow. Right now, I'm goin' to The Texas House to see if I can get something to eat."

When he went into the saloon, he was to find the subject of his conversation with Burt, standing at the bar, talking to Deke. Both men turned toward the door when he walked in. Cullen was certain he detected a look of total disbelief on Prophet's face. But it was only for a second, before his usual countenance of authority returned. It could be easy to assume that the sheriff had never expected him to return. "Howdy, McCabe," Deke greeted him. "I thought you'd left town."

"Just for the day," Cullen said. He nodded to Prophet. "Sheriff."

"McCabe," Prophet returned. "Like Deke here, I thought you'd moved on."

"Nope," Cullen replied. "I'm still lookin' around at the land available in the county, so I think I'll be operatin' outta New Hope. It's a lot more peaceful town than Fort Griffin or Albany. Besides, there's a lot of changes goin' on in New Hope right now. Ain't that right, Sheriff? I think it'd be right interestin' to see how it all turns out."

Prophet studied him carefully while he spoke, giving Cullen the feeling that he was being judged. Confirming it, Prophet commented, "You know, McCabe, I don't recollect you ever sayin' what business you're in. As sheriff, I like to know what everybody's business is, especially people who are just driftin' through town."

"You mean like you and me, right? I was just driftin' through town and decided to stay awhile when I thought it a good place to settle. You were just driftin' through and decided to take the sheriff's job."

Prophet gave him a patient smile. "I don't think it's the same situation at all," he said. "I was on my way to talk about a job. Where were you headin'?"

"Why, I thought I told you yesterday when I was talkin' to you and the mayor. I'm up here scoutin' out land for some friends of mine who are thinkin' about leavin' San Antonio and startin' a cattle business up this way. You've been workin' in the sheriff's office down that way. Ain't that what you said?" He paused to receive a nod from Prophet. "Well, like I said, this friend of mine, his name's Prentice Porter, is the one who told me to look around this part of the country. Seein' as how you came here from San Antonio, you mighta run into Prentice."

"Don't know if I have, or not," Prophet replied. "I don't recollect the name."

"You'd remember if you had," Cullen said, "big fellow, rides a big Palouse stallion."

"I may have seen him," Prophet allowed. "He sounds familiar, but I ain't the best at rememberin' names."

I reckon not, Cullen thought, *seeing as how you don't even remember the name of the sheriff of San Antonio.* To Prophet, he said, "I reckon that's the way it is with a lot of us." The conversation hadn't told him anything that he hadn't already surmised, it had simply told him that his suspicion was correct. At this point, however, he decided not to call Prophet on the lie he was selling the town, preferring to wait awhile yet, to see what he was up to. The best possible situation would be a case where Prophet sincerely wanted to do a respectable job as sheriff for the town. If that was the case, and Cullen was not convinced that it was, then what harm could the man's shady background be? He decided that his job now was to make sure the sheriff ran an honest and diligent office. In the meantime, he could look into the business of cattle rustling. Turning to Deke then, he asked, "Reckon Rena has anything left in the kitchen? I could use some supper." He couldn't help saying to himself that he hoped whatever she had would be better than the stew she served him the last time he ate there.

"I've gotta take a turn around town," Prophet said abruptly, finished a drink Deke had poured for him, and headed for the door.

"What's eatin' him?" Deke wondered. "When he came in, just a few minutes before you did, I thought he was gonna set down at a table and stay awhile." He shrugged and said, "I'll go see if Rena can fix you up with somethin' to eat."

"That devil just came strollin' in the saloon!" Prophet roared when he stormed in the door of the sheriff's office, startling both of his deputies.

"Who?" Slim Bradshaw responded as he jerked his feet off the desk and sat up straight in the chair.

"That darned McCabe!" Prophet exclaimed, and pointed a finger at Pete Riker, who, until that moment, had been stretched out on a cot against the wall. "Did you do what I sent you to do last night?"

"I sure as hell did," Riker answered. "And Slade and

Luther said they would head out early this mornin' to do the job."

"Did you tell them the road to Fort Griffin?" Prophet demanded.

"Road to Fort Griffin, that's what I told 'em, and Slade said they'd get up that way early, so they could pick 'em a good spot to ambush him. I told 'em word for word what you told me to." He shrugged and added, "Maybe he didn't ride up that way."

"Maybe," Prophet fumed. "Get on your horse and get up to the hideout and find out why McCabe is still walkin' around. You can tell Slade he'd better have one helluva good reason why he messed up that one simple job."

"Now?" Riker responded. "Damn, Boss, it's almost dark. That trail up that stream is hard enough in the daylight. Can't it wait till mornin'?"

Prophet, steaming over seeing Cullen alive after he had ordered him killed, took a few moments to calm down. "I wanna know tonight why the job didn't get done. Damn it, when I tell somebody to do somethin' . . ." He trailed off, still heated up over seeing McCabe alive.

After Prophet settled down, Slim asked him, "What's got you worried about that jasper, Boss? I don't see how he can cause us no trouble. He's just one man, and nothin' but a drifter. I expect he'll be movin' on in a day or two, anyway."

"I don't trust him," Prophet said. "I got a feelin' he was thinkin' about takin' over this town, himself."

"If he was, he sure as hell oughta know better by now," Slim insisted. "But hell, if you want him dead, we can arrange that right here in town. We don't have to ambush him nowhere." He paused to chuckle.

"We'll arrest him for disorderly conduct, then shoot him when he tries to escape."

"That sounds like a helluvan idea to me," Riker said.

"Maybe so," Prophet allowed, "but I still want you to ride up to the hideout. No, wait." He paused. "I think I'll ride up there myself, and I'll do it tonight. I want the boys to get ready to go after that herd south of town. We've already waited longer'n I planned to."

"Whatever you say, Boss," Riker said, happy to be relieved of having to make the ride himself. "The Viper Gang is gonna strike again. Just wait till the boys hear the name the town gave us," he cackled. "You best be careful goin' up that snaky climb. Me and Slim will keep the peace in New Hope, won't we, Slim?"

Johnny Bledsoe popped in the saloon soon after Rena brought Cullen a plate of beans and corn bread. She had apologized to him for not having any meat left. "I threw the last few pieces of it in the hog bucket not thirty minutes before you came in," she had told him. "And the beans were about to go next, but this'll stick to your bones till breakfast, I reckon." He had assured her that it would be fine, and that he hadn't had corn bread in a long time, so he was looking forward to it. Thinking again about the stew she had made, he had approached the plate of food cautiously, determined to eat it, no matter what. He found to his surprise that it was really very good, and he cleaned his plate. These were his thoughts when Bledsoe walked over to talk after he visited a couple of other tables to say hello.

"Mind if I join you?" Bledsoe said, and pulled a chair back but waited for Cullen's nod. Like everyone else

Cullen had seen since he got back from Fort Griffin, Johnny wanted to discuss the new occupants of the sheriff's office. As soon as he sat down, he asked, "Whaddaya think about our new sheriff and his deputies?"

Cullen was frankly surprised that he asked, so he said as much. "I reckon it's more important what you and the other merchants think about 'em, since I don't live here. What do *you* think about 'em?"

"I think I'd rather have Alton back, if you want an honest opinion," Johnny said at once. "That was hard luck that brought him down. And this new jasper strikes me as somebody lookin' to get rich in the job, and maybe run the town from the sheriff's office."

Cullen was surprised. Burt Whitley had been concerned, but was still hoping for the best, while Bledsoe held the same suspicions that Cullen held. He was further surprised that Johnny confessed his feelings to him, a stranger as much so as John Prophet. He was about to continue but stopped when two men Cullen had never seen before walked in the saloon. Judging by Bledsoe's sudden pause, he was prompted to ask, "Are those two the sheriff's deputies?"

"Yep," Bledsoe answered softly as they walked over to the bar. "There's our two noble protectors of the citizens of New Hope, come in to get a free drink of whiskey, courtesy of me, damn it. The one with the fast-draw holster is Riker. I think they call the other one Slim. I don't remember his name."

"Everythin' all right in here tonight?" Riker asked Deke, over at the bar. "We're just makin' our rounds to make sure there ain't no trouble in town."

"Yeah," Deke answered curtly, "everything's all right in here."

"Well, that's good," Riker said. "You might as well pour us a drink, long as we're in here." Deke set a couple of glasses on the bar and poured. While he did, Slim looked over the room. When his gaze fell on the table where Cullen and Johnny were seated, he asked, "Ain't that your boss settin' there?" When Deke said that it was, Riker asked, "Who's that feller he's settin' with?"

"His name's Cullen McCabe," Deke answered.

Riker looked at Slim, nodded and winked. "I figured that must be Mr. Cullen McCabe. He's the feller that got the jump on Slade and broke Luther's nose."

"That's right," Slim replied. "Maybe we oughta go over and have a little talk with him, let him know we don't stand for no troublemakers in our town."

"Looks like you're gonna get a chance to meet 'em," Johnny said to Cullen when the two deputies started toward their table. He turned in his chair to face them. "Somethin' I can do for you boys?"

"Yeah," Riker answered him, but directed his conversation toward Cullen. "Your name's McCabe, ain't it?" Cullen said that it was. "Well, McCabe, I'm gonna have to order you to leave this saloon."

"Oh?" Cullen responded. "Why is that?"

"On account of your reputation as a troublemaker. We got reports of you startin' a fight in here and bustin' a feller's nose," Riker replied, "and disturbin' the peace. Sounds to me like you and saloons don't mix. You can't handle your liquor. So, get up from there and get outta here."

"I'm not drinkin' anything but coffee," Cullen patiently replied. "I'm just eatin' a little supper, so I reckon you don't have anything to worry about." He remained seated, calmly watching the belligerent deputy's reactions.

"Riker, ain't it?" Johnny Bledsoe interrupted.

"That's right," Riker answered, "and you're the owner of this saloon, right?"

"I am," Johnny answered. "Well, Riker, somebody has told you the wrong story on how that criminal got his nose broken. He and two of his friends were gettin' ready to kill our sheriff, but McCabe stepped in and helped the sheriff arrest the three of them. So, he's welcome in my saloon anytime."

His comments caused Riker to pause, unsure. He had already decided to force Cullen's hand, knowing Prophet wanted him dead, but also knowing that Prophet didn't want it to appear to be outright murder. So, he continued to goad Cullen in an effort to make him angry enough to defy him. Then it would be a plain-and-simple question of who was fastest with his six-gun, and Riker was sure he already knew the answer to that one. His eyes locked on Cullen's, he said, "Get on your feet. I ain't gonna tell you again."

Completely aware of what Riker had in mind, Cullen did not budge. "What are you gonna do if I don't, shoot me for eatin' beans and corn bread?"

"You're wastin' my time," Riker responded. "I think a little time in jail will teach you a little more respect for the law. Get up from there, or I'll shoot you right where you're settin'."

"I'm not goin' to jail and that's for sure," Cullen said. "I haven't broken any laws and I haven't given you any reason to arrest me, so I'm gonna warn you. If I get up, I'll cut you down at the first hint of a move on your part. So, why don't you and your grinnin' partner

over there just forget about this little party you're tryin'
to start and leave peaceful people alone?"

A slow smile began to work its way across Riker's
face. He recognized what he thought was an attempt
by Cullen to bluff his way out of facing him in a gunfight. He glanced at Slim and winked. Slim answered
with a grin, well aware of Riker's speed with the Colt
.44 he wore. *Prophet's gonna be tickled*, he thought.

"You had your chance," Riker stated, and took a
step backward to give himself room, his right hand
hovering over the handle of his gun.

"I warned you," Cullen said. He slowly pushed his
chair back and started to get on his feet. Not taking
any chances, Riker didn't wait for him to stand up.
He reached for his pistol, only to stare in shock at
the pistol in Cullen's hand when it came from under the
table as he was rising. Riker's knees sagged at once
when Cullen's bullet smacked him in the chest, his
dying effort sending a shot into the floor. Before
Riker's body hit the floor, Cullen shifted his aim
toward Slim, but Slim made no move to retaliate,
instead gaping openmouthed in disbelief. When he
looked from Riker's body to Cullen's .44 waiting for
his response, he held his hands up in front of him.
"I warned him," Cullen reminded Slim.

"Yes, sir, you sure did," Slim replied, "and I ain't
thinkin' 'bout nothin' but draggin' him outta here.
This will be up to the sheriff to say what happens
next. This ain't the end of it."

Shocked as much as Slim and everybody else in
the saloon, Johnny was frozen speechless for a few
moments. When Slim asked Deke to help him carry
Riker out, Johnny quickly spoke up then. "You tell
the sheriff what happened here. McCabe didn't do

anything to get arrested. Riker called him out. It was self-defense." Slim didn't answer. He wasn't sure how he was going to explain it to Prophet.

Johnny Bledsoe turned to look Cullen in the eye. "I don't know what the hell that sheriff will do about this! Maybe you'd best get on your horse and ride!"

Cullen was already trying to decide what to do himself. He hadn't anticipated having one of Prophet's deputies come after him in such a blatant attempt to kill him. He didn't have the opportunity to find out how fast Riker really was because he had taken the precaution to put his pistol in his lap when he saw them come in. There was no doubt now that Prophet somehow thought he was a threat to his plans. Whatever they were, Cullen was sure now that they did not bode well for the town of New Hope. And that was going to be hard to sell to Ernest Robertson, since he had jumped at the chance to hire Prophet. Cullen glanced at Bledsoe, staring expectantly at him, so he said, "I don't intend to run when I haven't done a damn thing to have that deputy come after me. Besides, I just put my horse up for the night. He needs a rest. I reckon I'll just wait till mornin' and see what happens."

"Well, you'd better watch yourself tonight," Bledsoe said. "I'm surprised the sheriff ain't come back here yet." He shook his head in indication of the complicated event. "You can count on me and Deke to tell Prophet exactly how that shootin' went down, and you better make yourself scarce."

"They ain't the only ones that saw what happened," Darlene spoke up then. "Me and Nancy saw the whole thing." The two women had not uttered a peep until Bledsoe said something about witnessing the shooting.

"I seen it, too," Rena spoke up from the kitchen door. "He was aimin' to kill you."

"Maybe you're right," Cullen said, "I 'preciate it." He pulled out some change to pay for his beans and corn bread.

"Never mind that." Bledsoe stopped him. "It was worth your supper to have one of those bastards shot. Now get outta here and go out the back door, so you don't run into the sheriff," he directed, unaware that Sheriff Prophet was on his way to the Viper camp at that moment.

Back in the sheriff's office, Slim Bradshaw had worked himself into a nervous state. He and Riker had messed up when they got the notion to go after McCabe. Prophet was going to raise hell when he came back in the morning and found out that Riker was laid out on the undertaker's table. They had planned to have McCabe's body on that table, as a nice little surprise for Prophet. He was going to be mad as hell.

Slim had thoughts of going back in the saloon to attempt to arrest McCabe, but soon decided there was too much possibility that it would end in the same way as their first encounter with him. He wished Prophet hadn't ridden off in the dark to go back to the hideout. Then another thought entered his mind. What if there was some other kind of trouble happening in town tonight? Prophet would expect him to take care of it. At first, when Prophet picked him to be one of his deputies, he thought he would enjoy it. Now he was not so sure.

CHAPTER 9

"Now, who the hell is that?" Elmo Dalton blurted when he heard a sound like that a horse might make on the rocky stream leading up to the hideout. He picked up his rifle and moved out of the light of the small fire he had been nursing. Any time someone approached the cabin from the creek below was cause to be cautious, late at night, even more so.

"Maybe it's Slade and Luther comin' back," Tiny Watkins whispered as he positioned himself to receive any unwelcome guests. Slade and Luther were long overdue. A few long seconds passed before they heard the call.

"Hey, up there! It's me, John Prophet, don't nobody shoot!"

"Well, I'll be . . ." Elmo muttered in surprise before calling back, "Well, come on up, Boss." He and Tiny stood at the head of the trail and waited until Prophet climbed up the narrow path, leading his horse. "What in the world are you doin', ridin' around in the middle of the night? Is everything all right?"

"It's the first time I ain't ever run when the sheriff came callin'," Tiny saw fit to joke. As soon as Prophet stepped down from the saddle, however, he realized that his boss was not in a joking mood. "What's the matter, Boss?"

"Where's Slade?" Prophet demanded.

"Don't know," Elmo answered. "Him and Luther left at sunup and ain't ever come back. We thought that mighta been them when we heard you comin' up the trail, thought maybe they went into town after they done for that jasper you sent 'em after."

This was not news Prophet wanted to hear—McCabe came back, but Slade and Luther didn't. He had a feeling he knew what had happened to them now, and the thought of it served to increase the rage already gripping his insides. "That smug so-and-so," he muttered, causing Elmo and Tiny to exchange puzzled glances. It infuriated Prophet to think that McCabe had come back to New Hope, just as casual as you please, never mentioning an ambush or the fact that he had killed two men. And Prophet knew without doubt that was exactly what had happened. He knew from the beginning that McCabe was going to get in his way. This song and dance he was hoodwinking everybody in town with, that he was looking for land for some friend, might fool them, but he knew a crook when he saw one. *And the difference is, he's got to build a gang to take control, and I've already got one.* The thought gave him some confidence, even though it appeared McCabe was concentrating on taking his men out. It was reasonable to assume that he had lost two of his men this very day. He suddenly felt an urgency to get back to New Hope, but he reminded himself of the need to rustle another herd of cattle to sell. "Where's Clute?" he asked.

"In the cabin with the rest of the boys," Elmo said,

and stepped aside to keep from getting run over when Prophet strode toward the door. When he was out of earshot, Elmo looked at Merle Blake and commented softly, "He's got his back up over that McCabe feller, ain't he?" They followed him into the cabin to see the same surprised reactions they had just experienced.

"Damn, Boss," Red Grimsley exclaimed, "what are you doin' up here?" He was playing cards with the three other men.

"I came up here to get you boys off your lazy behinds," Prophet replied. "I'm runnin' low on cash, so I know damn well you boys are. It's time to get to work before these small ranches get ready to move their cattle to market. So, that's the first thing we're gonna get done. We'll start with that Thomas fellow, south of New Hope. He ain't got no crew, just him and his son. He can't drive 'em to market with just the two of 'em, so he'll be gettin' ready to combine with a couple of the other small ranchers to drive their cattle up to Dodge. I need to have you boys get in there and take them cows while he ain't got no help to stop you. You've been keepin' an eye on 'em, Clute. How many you think he's got now?"

"I figure he's got close to three hundred head," Clute Bishop said. "Ain't you goin' with us, Boss?"

"Not this time," Prophet said. "I've got too much I gotta take care of in town. I'm puttin' you in charge of it, Clute. You can handle it."

"Sure I can," Clute said at once. He was a little surprised, since it was usually Slade who took charge when Prophet wasn't on the drive. "Same as always, I reckon, drive 'em to that buyer in Fort Worth." Curious then, he asked, "What about Slade? Ain't he goin'?"

"No, Luther, neither," Prophet said. "I gave the two

of them a simple job to do, and it looks like they couldn't handle it."

"McCabe?" Clute asked. He was well aware of the job Slade had been charged with.

"He's still alive and lookin' pretty damn healthy," Prophet replied. "And that's the reason I've got business in town. Sooner or later, he's gonna make a mistake and that's when I'll shoot him."

"I reckon we could go after Thomas's cattle tonight, if you want us to," Clute said.

"No, wait till tomorrow night," Prophet said. "You boys ain't ready to go tonight. Take tomorrow to get everything ready. You need to ride across the river to see where he's grazin' 'em, so you don't spend a lot of time lookin' for 'em. Then clean out his whole damn herd tomorrow night, and you'll be halfway to Fort Worth before he can round up enough help to come after you." Clute assured him that he could be counted on to do the job.

Cullen stayed in his room in the hotel until it was time for the dining room to open for breakfast. He was somewhat surprised that he had not had a visit during the night from Sheriff Prophet, unaware as he was that Prophet had left town. Another look out his window at the street below told him there was nothing out of the ordinary going on, as the town woke up to another day. There was something more to be determined, and that was the mayor's reaction to his having shot one of his new deputies. He figured he might possibly find that out this morning in the dining room. So he put on his gun belt and picked up his rifle, then he went to the door and stood there for a minute or two, listening, before he turned the key in the lock and opened the door. There was no one in the hall. He stood staring down the hallway toward the last room, the room that Robertson had provided for the sheriff, and considered knocking on the door. After thinking about it for a few seconds, he decided if there was to be any investigation of the shooting, the sheriff could come to him. *Meanwhile*, he thought, *I need some coffee.*

He was met by Monroe at the door of the dining room, and he greeted Cullen with a simple, "Mornin'," and nothing more. He silently watched Cullen as he propped his rifle against the table reserved for weapons, waited for a few moments before reminding him. "And the pistol," he said.

"I don't know about that," Cullen said, hesitating. "I shot a deputy sheriff last night."

"I heard," Monroe replied.

"Well, I don't think it would be too wise for me to surrender my weapon under the circumstances. If the sheriff and his deputy come in here, they're gonna be wearin' their weapons. Right?"

"The rule is, if you wanna eat in here, you have to leave your weapons by the door," Monroe insisted.

"But that doesn't apply to an officer of the law, does it?" Cullen asked. Monroe shrugged, but didn't answer, so Cullen persisted. "So, if the sheriff comes in here after me, whether I'm guilty of something or not, I'm supposed to defend myself with a knife and fork. Is that right?" Monroe shrugged again. They were obviously at a standoff, until Lottie settled it.

"Oh, come on, Monroe," she said impatiently. "Don't be a damn fool. He ain't gonna start any trouble." She turned to face Cullen. "Set yourself down at that little table in the back corner. I'll give you another napkin to spread over your pistol, so you won't upset any of the guests if they come in for breakfast this early." Turning back to Monroe, she said, "McCabe shot that damn Riker when he drew on him. It was self-defense."

"How do you know that?" Monroe replied.

"'Cause I saw Deke Campbell this mornin' on his way to work. He said everybody at The Texas House last night will tell you Riker tried to shoot McCabe. McCabe had no choice, he had to defend himself."

"I didn't hear all that," Monroe said. "All I heard was you shot another man in the saloon, and this time it was a deputy sheriff." He hesitated for a moment, then asked, "If that's what happened, why do you need to wear that gun in here?"

"'Cause the sheriff mighta heard the same version you did," Cullen said.

While Monroe paused to consider that, Lottie grabbed Cullen's sleeve and pulled him away. "Come on, McCabe, set yourself down and I'll get you some coffee." Monroe shrugged once again and went into the kitchen, hoping there wouldn't be a shoot-out in his dining room.

As Lottie had directed, Cullen sat down at the table in the corner and draped a red-and-white-checkered napkin over the handle of the Colt .44 at his side. The spunky waitress brought him a cup of fresh hot coffee and lingered to watch him test it. "You ain't off to a very good start with our new sheriff and his deputies, are you?"

"Don't seem that way, does it?" Cullen replied.

Hands on hips, she stood, studying him for a few moments. "What I don't understand, is what in the world you're still hangin' around New Hope for. Most people that ran into the kind of luck you've had, couldn't wait to get outta this town. But you're still here, not that you ain't welcome, at least in here, anyway."

"I don't know," Cullen said. "It's just a nice town and I think my friends would like to find a place around here."

"Your friends," she scoffed. "I don't know what you're up to, but you ain't lookin' for no land for anybody. What are you up to?"

He simply stared at her for a few seconds, wondering if his ruse was that transparent to anyone else. Finally, he shook his head slowly, and locking his gaze on hers, asked, "Can I trust you to keep a secret?" When she nodded solemnly, he said, "It's Bea Rivenbark's cookin'. You can't get cookin' like hers anywhere else in Texas."

"Kiss my foot," she bellowed. "I've a mind not to bring you any breakfast." She spun around and proceeded to the kitchen to see if his breakfast was ready.

In spite of her threat, his breakfast was not slow in coming and he was not quite finished with it when he had a visitor. He saw Ernest Robertson when he came in the side door from the hotel and stop to talk briefly to Monroe. Then he walked back to Cullen's table. "McCabe," the mayor greeted him.

"Mr. Mayor," Cullen returned.

"Mind if I join you?" Robertson asked, and Cullen invited him to sit down. Lottie was right behind the mayor and asked if he was going to eat. "No, just coffee," he replied. Cullen got a feeling he was not there just to pass the time of day. "A problem has come up that I'm hoping you can help me solve," he started. "I find myself kind of caught in the middle of an uncomfortable situation."

"Got something to do with your new sheriff?" Cullen asked.

"Well, yes, as a matter of fact," Robertson said.

"I figured that," Cullen said, "and I'm kinda surprised the sheriff hasn't come by to see me this mornin', since that business with his deputy last night."

"I expect he'll be looking for you as soon as he finds out about Deputy Riker." When Cullen seemed puzzled, Robertson went on to explain. "Sheriff Prophet was out of town last night on some sort of investigation, according to Deputy Bradshaw. Bradshaw said he expected him back fairly early today."

"Well, that explains it," Cullen said, "but you still have a situation and you want my help?" The mayor suddenly looked extremely uncomfortable. Cullen had a pretty good idea about what was coming. "You're kickin' me outta your hotel, right?" Just from the brief exposure he had experienced with Prophet, he was not surprised.

"No, no," Robertson quickly responded. "I'm not kicking you out. It's just that you had told me you wanted that room for only a couple of days, and now I have a reservation problem. And you recall that I gave you a reduced rate for that room. It's just that I find now that I need the room back."

"Wouldn't have anything to do with the fact that it's a better room than the one at the end of the hall, would it?" Cullen asked, referring to Prophet's room.

It was obvious that McCabe saw right through his attempt to mask his dilemma, so he quit trying to disguise it. "Damn it, McCabe, I agreed to give Sheriff Prophet the best room in the house, and like I said, you told me you were going to be gone in two days." He paused, then quickly repeated, "And I let you have that room at half price. I would never have done that if I had any idea you were staying longer."

"Well, don't worry about it, Mr. Mayor. I kinda expected it. I'll move outta the hotel after I finish my breakfast. Fair enough?"

"I'm not saying you have to leave the hotel," Robertson quickly reacted. "We have smaller rooms downstairs behind the kitchen for a dollar a night. For you, maybe even seventy-five cents, if you think that would be satisfactory."

"No, thanks just the same," Cullen said. "I'll go ahead and move out, soon as I finish my coffee." He nodded to Lottie when she held the pot up for him to see. "You want some more coffee?"

Robertson shook his head and got to his feet, having never taken a swallow of his coffee. "I sincerely hope there are no hard feelings because of this," he said.

"Not at all," Cullen said. "I don't waste time on hard feelin's. I understand you're caught between a rock and a hard place. Like I told you when I got here, I didn't plan to stay in your hotel but a couple of days."

The mayor looked relieved at once. "Thank you, McCabe," he said. "I appreciate your understanding." He turned and hurried off.

"What's eatin' at him?" Lottie asked when she filled Cullen's cup.

"He was just tellin' me it was time for me to get outta his hotel," Cullen answered. "He didn't say anything about the dinin' room, though. I reckon that'll be up to Monroe."

"You think it was because you shot that deputy?"

"I expect that had something to do with it, but I think it goes deeper than that. He might be upset about the shooting, but probably more concerned about what your sheriff will do when he finds out about his deputy. I ain't surprised, he's got to stand behind the man he hired."

While Cullen finished his coffee, then went upstairs to vacate his room, there was another meeting going on. Sheriff Prophet had returned to his office and was receiving news that he had lost a deputy. "Don't tell me that!" Prophet shouted. "Don't tell me that!" Slim Bradshaw literally trembled as he dutifully reported the death of Pete Riker. Seething with anger that threatened to consume him, Prophet demanded, "Is he dead? Is McCabe dead? 'Cause I don't see him in that cell!"

"I couldn't arrest him, Boss," Slim pleaded. "There was too many witnesses that saw Riker pick a fight with McCabe, and they saw Riker reach for his gun. I thought you'd want me to act like a lawman would, you know, not arrest a man for self-defense." When Prophet merely scowled in disgust for his excuse, Slim said. "I set up outside the saloon after that with my rifle. I was fixin' to shoot him when he came outta there, but he musta gone out the back door 'cause he never showed up." It was a lie. He had actually retreated to the safety of the jail, but he hoped it would temper Prophet's disgust for him.

That was only one of the things on the sheriff's mind. He had lost another member of his gang, bringing the total to three, just since he had become sheriff. And every one of them was killed by McCabe. His first inclination was to shoot him on sight, but he had planned to convince the people of New Hope that he was a fair-dealing professional sheriff. It would shock a lot of people if he simply eliminated McCabe as he preferred, but McCabe had to go. He decided he would order him out of town, then if he resisted, he would shoot him. "Come on," he said to Slim. "We're gonna go call on Mr. McCabe."

With Slim at his elbow, Prophet walked briskly up the street to the hotel. They walked in the front door to find Ernest Robertson talking to his desk clerk at the front counter. Robertson looked as if stunned at first but managed to quickly recover. "Good morning, Sheriff. James and I were just discussing plans to move you into a better room, now that one's available."

Forcing himself to play his part, in spite of his impatience, Prophet said, "Why, thank you, Mr. Mayor but what I'm here for now is to talk to Cullen McCabe. Is he in the hotel?"

"No," Robertson said, "Mr. McCabe moved out of his room this morning. He left right after he had breakfast. I told him I had to have that room for you. I offered to move him into a smaller room downstairs, but he preferred to leave." He grinned at the sheriff expectantly, thinking he would be pleased, but Prophet seemed annoyed.

The sheriff turned around and headed for the door with only a quick, "Thank you," for Robertson. "Come on," he said to Slim, "we need to get down to the stable."

The sheriff and his deputy found Burt Whitley in the back of the stable, replacing a broken board in an empty stall. "Which one of these horses belongs to Cullen McCabe?" Prophet asked.

"None of 'em," Burt replied. "His packhorse used to stay in this stall I'm workin' on. McCabe packed up his horses and left, not thirty minutes ago."

That gave Prophet pause. He took a second to think about it. "Gone, huh?" he finally spoke. "Did he say where he was goin' or when he was comin' back?"

"Nope, for a fact, he didn't," Burt answered. "I don't know if he's comin' back. He didn't say, but he packed up everything he owned and took the north road outta town."

Both Burt and Slim stood watching Prophet's reaction as he considered what he should do about it. Finally, he decided. "Well," he said, "makes no difference now, does it? I was comin' to tell him it was time for him to leave town, so I reckon that takes care of that."

Openly surprised, Burt couldn't resist asking, "You were comin' to run McCabe outta town? What for?"

"Maybe you've been too busy repairin' your stalls," Prophet answered, his tone thick with sarcasm. "McCabe shot one of my deputies last night, and I ain't about to let something like that go unpunished."

"I heard from some of them that saw it that your deputy called him out, then pulled on McCabe and tried to kill him before he even got up from the table," Burt said.

"Maybe that's one version," Prophet said, "but it ain't the right one. The right one is, you don't ever pull a gun on any officer of the law, and that's the one we're goin' by in this town."

"Right," Burt responded, not willing to jeopardize

his own standing with the sheriff. At the same time, however, he didn't like the sound of a policy that gave a lawman absolute power over all the people. He wondered if the mayor knew he had hired a tyrant who planned to take total control of the town. He had a feeling McCabe had already come to that conclusion and knew that Prophet would be coming for him. Why else would he suddenly leave town when he had said he was going to hang around for a few more days? The more Burt thought about it, the more he was convinced McCabe had done the smart thing.

Outside the stable, Prophet headed back to the jail. "Jump on your horse and ride out to the hideout before the men go after those cows tonight. Bring Red Grimsley back to town with you. I need to have two of you in town in case there's somebody else that's gonna cause problems."

"Whatever you say, Boss, but that sheriff had Red in jail with Slade and Luther. Ain't that gonna be hard to explain to folks here?"

"Damn," Prophet swore. "I forgot about that." He fumed over that for a few minutes. The reason he told Slim to bring Red, was because Red was more dependable to keep his wits about him as well as being a good gunhand. "Hell, bring him anyway. I doubt if anybody in town got a good look at him, and even if they did, I'll tell 'em he didn't know Slade and Luther. He was just havin' a drink with 'em and he tried to tell 'em to back down."

"I don't know, Boss," Slim said, scratching his head thoughtfully. Even as naive as he was, Slim didn't think that a good idea. He couldn't help wondering if

Prophet was so intent upon owning the town that he was ignoring common sense.

After a moment, Prophet seemed to return to rational thinking. "Bring Merle, instead. They don't know him."

"Right," Slim responded. "If I know Clute, he'll wanna know exactly where that herd is sleepin' tonight. So, he'll most likely be comin' down from the hideout early enough to set up camp a little closer to that herd before dark. He'll do the scoutin' while he's still got a little daylight. I'll head up there right now and me and Merle will be back here before dark."

CHAPTER 10

When Cullen had left the hotel that morning, he had taken the precaution of walking behind the buildings on the one main street. When he started to cross the open space between the hotel and the general store, he paused when he spotted the sheriff and his deputy on their way to the hotel. Thinking about that now, Robertson had told him that the sheriff was out of town the night before. So, Cullen thought it a good bet that, if Prophet was connected to the Viper Gang, he could permit himself to assume that was where the sheriff was last night. And if that was the case, the hideout was close enough to allow Prophet to ride in and arrive early. It was still only suspicion, but he was finding it hard not to believe Prophet was connected to the gang rustling cattle in the county. It was common thought in town that the notorious Viper camp was impossible to find. Cullen was of the opinion that the fact of the matter was, nobody wanted to find the camp where a large gang of robbers and killers waited. Now it was time somebody tried to find it, he decided.

It was his gut feeling that the mysterious camp must

lie north of New Hope, so he followed the river back
toward a ridge made up of roughly wooded hills,
scarred with multiple ravines and cuts and no land to
attract settlers. The farther he rode, the more the
country looked suitable for little more than raising
rattlesnakes and maybe lizards. It seemed ideal for use
as an outlaw hideout, however. As he continued along
the river, he encountered just one rugged ravine after
another leading up to hills covered with occasional
stands of scrubby oaks. After a ride he estimated to be
about ten miles from town, he was beginning to
believe the camp didn't exist. Thinking about his
speculation that it was not that far from New Hope, he
thought maybe he had just missed any evidence of a
hidden trail and decided to turn back to search more
closely. Looking up ahead, he decided he would continue to a thicker growth of trees on the bank about
fifty yards farther and turn around there.

When he reached the clump of trees, he paused
there to let his horses drink before turning around
and starting back the way he had come. When he
came to a spot, after a couple of dozen yards, that was
even with a wide ravine on the other side of the river,
he thought it a good idea to ride up it to take a better
look at that section of the river. So, he turned Jake off
the bank and crossed over. The ravine was wide
enough to permit him to ride his horses halfway up
the hill, then he dismounted and climbed the rest of
the way on foot. When he reached the top, he found
that it afforded him a good view of a long section of
the river. He started a visual search of the river and
looked for evidence of a trail. It didn't take long
before he was convinced that, if there really was a
hideout, it was nowhere near this place. Ready to

move on, he turned to descend the ravine, then
stopped suddenly when a movement far down the
river caught his eye. He stared at the spot until it eventually took shape as it moved toward him—a rider,
following the same trail he had just left!

He looked at once at his horses, halfway down the
ravine, thinking they might be seen from the trail. He
decided it highly unlikely, since the trail was on the
other side of the river and the sides of the ravine were
deep enough to hide the horses. The only way they
might be seen would be when the rider was exactly
even with the mouth of the ravine and happened to
look across the river at that point, the same way he
had discovered it. He decided it not likely, unless this
was just his unlucky day. With his rifle ready, just in
case, he knelt so as not to provide a silhouette on top
of the hill, and waited to watch the rider approach. As
the man got closer, Cullen thought he looked familiar, and when he passed directly in front of the ravine,
Cullen identified him. *Deputy sheriff*, he thought, *the
one called Slim. Wonder where he's heading.*

If his suspicions were right, Slim might be on his
way to the Viper camp. Hopefully he would lead him
there. Not wanting to risk falling in behind Slim too
close, he waited to let him put a little more distance
between them, so he remained where he was and continued to watch him. When Slim reached the thick
clump of trees where he had turned around, Cullen
figured it safe to get in behind him. He rose up from
his knee but froze when Slim suddenly stopped. Had
he seen him? *Impossible*, Cullen thought, besides, Slim
was not looking back toward him. Instead, he looked
ahead and behind, as if making sure no one was
watching. Then he turned his horse toward a bank of

large laurel bushes and drove his mount forward, disappearing between the bushes. "Well, I'll be . . ." Cullen started, then hurried down the ravine to his horses.

With his Winchester across his thighs, he rode slowly up to the point in the trail where Slim had disappeared between the bushes and drove Jake through them. Beyond the bushes, he found himself in a small stream. It wandered snake-like down from the hill above and a low mountain behind the hill. A narrow path had been beaten out beside it, bearing numerous hoofprints. The path up was steep and he could see marks in the earth where Slim's horse had evidently slipped on the difficult footing. Cullen saw at once that it was out of the question to try to follow Slim while he was leading a packhorse, so he decided the best thing for him was to go up it on foot. Turning his horses around was the next problem he faced, for the path up the hill was little more than a gully. When he finally accomplished that, he rode up the river a little way and tied the horses in a stand of pines.

Hurrying back to the stream, he pushed through the bushes again and started up the steep trail, keeping a sharp eye ahead of him, in case he might suddenly pop up in a clearing with a gang of outlaws waiting to welcome him. Figuring he was probably about halfway up the hill, he stopped when he heard sounds above him from someone coming down. Without hesitating, he dived over the edge of the gully and rolled several yards down against a tree trunk. In a matter of seconds, a string of riders appeared, making their way carefully down the steep path. With no thoughts that there could be anyone within miles of them, they alternately laughed and cursed as their horses fought to keep from stumbling.

Lying there against the tree, Cullen could hear them, but he couldn't see them, so he crawled up away from the tree until he could see the heads of the riders above the sides of the gully. He spotted Slim at once and assumed he must have come to get the others. None of the others looked familiar until the last rider passed and he recognized Red Grimsley, one of the men who had escaped from the jail, when Alton Ford was killed. He had no doubt that he had found the Viper Gang. Slim and Red were definitely connected to the gang and Slim was working for Prophet. So, it was easy to assume that Prophet was connected to the gang as well. Cullen counted eight men descending the trail. What he needed to know now was, where were they going?

When he was sure there were no more, he climbed back over the side of the gully and followed them down to the river. Standing in the thick bushes that hid the trail, he watched as the gang of men rode back toward New Hope. Concerned now that the town of New Hope was not going to know what hit them, he hurried back to his horses. There was no hope of getting around the outlaws to warn the town. The only thing he could do was follow them and maybe help from behind, if they were intent upon overrunning the town.

When within a couple of miles of the north end of town, the riders stopped, evidently talking over their plan of attack. After a few minutes, however, two of the riders—he couldn't be sure, but he thought it might be Slim and one other man—continued on toward town. The other six turned on a wide angle as if to go around the town. He could assume only that they intended to come into the town from a different direction. "Damn," he murmured, "they're gonna attack like a party of soldiers." He decided to stick with the six riders.

For whatever reason, the outlaws were evidently planning to ride in on the wagon road that led into town from the east and ended between the stable and the saloon. When the gang struck that road, they crossed it and continued on to the south. He realized then that he had guessed wrong, they weren't going to New Hope at all. They had something else in mind and the first thing he thought of was the reports of cattle rustling, the problem that had caused him to be sent there.

When they were well past the town, the outlaws cut back to intercept the trail by the river again. Cullen figured they must be close to the range where he had met Fred Thomas and his son, Sammy, the day before he first rode into New Hope. When the outlaws came to a sharp bend in the river where the trees had grown close on the banks, they pulled up and rode into them. Cullen hung back, waiting to see if they came out again farther down the river, but he saw no sign of them. He wanted to get closer, but he thought it too risky unless he crossed over to the other side of the river, hid his horses, and worked his way up closer on foot. So that's what he did, thinking all the time that things would be a lot easier, had he not brought his packhorse with him. But when he had left New Hope that morning, he had planned to camp outside of town.

With Jake and the packhorse tied in the trees, he was able to work his way up to a point almost directly across the river from the outlaws. They appeared to be

making camp, which puzzled him, until he watched
them a little while. They were doing a lot of talking,
most of it from one who looked to be the boss. After
he was done, two of the men climbed on their horses
and rode out of the trees. When they reached the trail
by the river, they continued on across it, then split,
one going almost dead east, the other on a more
southerly course. Cullen realized then what the gang
had in mind. They were getting ready to rustle Fred
Thomas's cattle. The two men who just rode out were
scouts, sent to find the main herd. More than likely,
they would not move on the cattle until nightfall. He
thought about the man, Thomas, and his young son.
There was no way the two of them could protect their
cattle from the six men he was following, even if they
were keeping watch. This was why the governor sent
him to New Hope, to find out if the threat of rustling
was real, so now it was up to him to see if he could
spoil this little party. Like the rustlers he was watching,
he needed to find out where that herd was grazing.
And he figured the best way to do that was to go to
Fred's house and ask him. And while he was at it,
maybe he could help them hold on to their cattle. He
went back to get his horses, then continued riding
south on that side of the river. When he was past the
rustlers' camp, he crossed back over and followed
the trail to Thomas's ranch house.

Fred Thomas looked out the open end of his barn
and saw the lone rider approaching his house. It
wasn't one of the neighboring ranchers, but he
looked familiar. Then he remembered the big man
with the fresh venison. He propped his pitchfork

against the side of the stall and walked out into the barnyard to meet him. "How do?" Thomas greeted him. "Didn't expect to see you again. Did you find what you were lookin' for?"

"More or less, I reckon," Cullen answered him.

"I'm sorry, but I can't remember your name," Thomas said.

"Cullen McCabe," he said

"Right," Thomas responded. "Then you're the fellow that had a little run-in with some of those drifters in town. I heard you helped the sheriff out of a jam in the saloon. Step down and we'll go up to the house and see if my wife's got any coffee that ain't too stout. Maybe she can find something to eat with it, too."

"Thanks just the same," Cullen said. "It ain't been that long since breakfast. I just came back to see if I could help you hang on to your cattle." Fred naturally looked confused by his statement, so he went on to explain. "I think you're gettin' set up for a raid on your cattle tonight."

"Say what?" Fred replied. "What makes you say that?"

Cullen detected an expression of immediate distrust on Fred's face, as if he was being hoodwinked. "I know you were complainin' to me about the so-called Viper Gang and how they felt free to help themselves to your beef whenever they felt like it. Well, I think now they've decided to help themselves to your whole herd." He paused to let that sink in, but he could see that Fred was only growing more suspicious of the messenger. "I followed a gang of six riders to your range. Four of 'em are camped on the river about two miles north of here and two of 'em rode out across your range. My guess is those two are the scouts, tryin' to find your main herd, and when it gets dark, the six of 'em figure on moving your entire herd right outta here."

"My Lord in heaven!" Thomas reacted, obviously devastated. He said nothing for a long minute while the thought of the loss resonated in his brain. "How do I know you ain't trickin' me? Maybe you're ridin' with that gang of rustlers."

"I reckon you don't," Cullen replied. "But if I was fixin' to steal your cattle, I most likely wouldn't come to tell you I was."

Trembling now with the thought of losing his entire investment, Fred admitted, "I guess you're right. I can't lose my cattle now. I've just built a herd big enough to drive to market. This spring was gonna be our first year. We were gonna drive our herd with Snyder's and Williams's. They're both bigger'n I am, and they've got the cowhands to do it." He shook his head from side to side. "Me and my boy have worked our asses off keepin' those cows alive."

"In that case, I reckon we'd best do what we can to keep the Vipers from runnin' off with 'em," Cullen said. "Where are the cattle?"

Thinking there was no use not to trust Cullen at this point, Thomas said, "They're grazin' on the lower part of my range, in a little valley that runs down to the river."

"How far from here?"

"A little over a mile and a half," Thomas replied. "You think we oughta go drive 'em back close to the house? Maybe those rustlers won't bother 'em if they're close to the house."

"I don't think these men will care if they're close to

the house or not, and I don't wanna alarm you, but I don't think they would plan on leavin' any witnesses. You, your boy, and I are gonna be pretty busy tonight, so it's probably a good idea to keep the cows where they are. And that'll keep the rustlers away from the house. That would be better for your wife, wouldn't it?"

"Of course," Fred said at once. "I wasn't thinkin', was I?"

"Let's go take a look at that valley, all right?" Cullen suggested. "How 'bout if I leave my packhorse here till all this is over? Then you'd best tell your wife and son what's goin' on."

"Right," Thomas said. "I'll go tell Naomi where we're goin'. Sammy's with the cattle." He hurried away to the house while Cullen took the packs off his packhorse.

Cullen paused briefly to watch Thomas as he hustled off to the back door of his house. He hoped he could count on Fred and his son when the time came to face six hardened outlaws. When he had removed the packs from his horse, he let it out in the corral with Fred's horses and waited. In a few minutes, the kitchen door opened, and Fred stepped out. He paused on the steps, the screen door still open, while he was obviously talking to his wife. He could well imagine the woman's concern after hearing what was about to take place. She stepped outside the door then and peered in Cullen's direction. Probably to see what kind of man her husband was going to ride off with, he thought. Cullen didn't like the idea of leaving the woman alone and unprotected any more than Fred did. But he believed there was little danger of any trouble for her. The Viper Gang was after the cattle, and if they were a mile and a half or so away, there should be no contact with her.

Fred left the kitchen steps and started back to the barn while Naomi remained there to watch until he went in the barn to saddle his horse. *She's sure as hell going to make sure she recognizes me,* Cullen thought, not really blaming her for thinking this whole story might be a double-cross of some kind.

Sammy Thomas reined his horse to a stop when he spotted the two riders approaching. He recognized his father but wondered about the man riding with him. Then when they were a little closer, he remembered the big man on the bay horse, the man they had shared some deer meat with the week before. He nudged his horse again and continued driving the small bunch of strays back to the herd. "What's goin' on, Pa?" Sammy asked when Fred and Cullen pulled up beside him.

"You remember this fellow, don't you?" Thomas asked. Sammy said that he did, that he was the man they had once accused of killing one of their cows. "That's right," Thomas said. "His name's Cullen McCabe and he's come with some bad news."

"Has it got anything to do with that other fellow?" Sammy asked. When his father asked what fellow he was talking about, Sammy explained. "A little while ago, I looked over toward the west ridge." He pointed to a low ridge where one lone oak tree stood like a silent sentinel at the mouth of the valley. "There was somebody settin' on a horse under that tree, sat there awhile, watchin' me round up some strays. Then he turned around and rode off."

"Well, they've found the herd," Cullen said to Fred, "and I don't expect they'll do anything until tonight. But I ain't always right, they might come after 'em this afternoon, thinkin' there ain't nobody to stop 'em. It's best to be ready just in case, but I still think it'll be tonight. It'll be a lot easier for 'em after dark, especially if they think you don't know anything about it. It'll be easier for us to stop 'em in the dark, too."

"Whaddaya talkin' about?" Sammy wanted to know.

"McCabe says we're about to get our cattle rustled," Fred answered. "That rider you saw by the oak tree was lookin' for the herd. He's already on his way back to tell the rest of the gang."

"Dang," Sammy exclaimed. "If I'da knowed that, I'da took a shot at him."

"Whaddaya think we oughta do, McCabe?" Fred asked.

"I expect we'd best keep a sharp eye for the rest of the afternoon and try to keep most of the cattle back down close to the river," Cullen suggested. "When they come, there'll be six of 'em. With a herd the size of yours, I'd guess they'll get a couple of men behind 'em to stampede 'em. The other men will ride the flanks and the head and try to guide the herd out the north end of this valley. So I think we need to set ourselves up tonight at the north end and sit tight till they get their men in position. Then, when the men in the rear start the stampede and the cattle start runnin', they'll be drivin' them toward us. If we start shootin', we can take out the lead men and most likely cause the cattle to scatter all over this valley." He paused to give both father and son a serious look. "Right about now, I need to ask how committed you are to savin' your cattle. Because there's gonna be some lead flyin' hot and heavy, and there's a good chance you might catch some of it." He was especially concerned about young Sammy.

"Like I already told you," Fred replied, "this herd represents all I've invested to build a real cattle ranch. I lose it, I lose everything." He looked at his son. "I don't know about Sammy, though. I'm thinkin' it would be best if you go back to the house and take care of your mother. It anything happens to me, it's up to you to look after her."

"I was thinkin' the same thing," Cullen said. "And I think the two of us can still cause that herd to scatter and save most of the cows."

"No, sir, Pa!" Sammy demanded. "I'm stayin' right here with you. You need another gun and I'm a damn good shot. You know that. This ranch is my whole life, too, and I'm willin' to fight for it. As far away from the house as the cows are gonna be, Ma oughta be safe where she is. Besides, I don't plan on either one of us gettin' shot."

Cullen didn't say anything, preferring to let Fred handle it. Fred just stood there for a long moment, gazing at his son, without replying. Cullen thought he could detect a twinkle of pride in Fred's eye as he looked at Cullen and said, "I reckon there'll be three of us."

"All right," Cullen said. "I expect we'd best pick out three good spots to hide in when it's time for our guests to show up. We can rest our horses up good because they're gonna be workin' hard tonight, if everything happens the way we think it will."

"It's gonna be a while before dark," Fred said. "I don't know about you, but I'm liable to get pretty hungry by the time we're through this night."

"I think you've got plenty of time to go back to the house and get yourself something," Cullen said. "Ain't no use fightin' on an empty stomach. I'll keep an eye out here while you're gone."

"I've got a better idea," Fred suggested. "We'll send Sammy back to get some food for all of us." That plan was endorsed by all three, so Sammy got on his horse and headed for the house.

CHAPTER 11

The afternoon went fast enough, helped along by a sack of ham biscuits, courtesy of Naomi Thomas. As Cullen had predicted, there was no sign of cattle rustlers even as the sun began to sink lower behind the distant hills to the west. As darkness began to settle upon the valley, they decided it was time to retreat to the hiding places they had selected that afternoon. When Fred started to put out the fire they had built to make coffee, Cullen suggested it was a better idea to leave it burning, even throw a few more limbs on it. "They're most likely expectin' to see one person watching the herd at night, knowin' there ain't but two of you to do all the work," he explained. "Most of the year, the cattle are scattered all over the range, but now it's roundup time when you've got all your cows ready to drive to market. They come ridin' in here tonight and there ain't no sign of a single soul to watch 'em, it ain't gonna look right. One little fire burnin' and everything will look peaceful and right." Fred saw the sense of that reasoning, so he left the fire to burn, and the three of them went to their chosen places to wait. "Remember," Cullen said as they left, "make enough noise, so they'll think there's more than three of us when the shooting starts."

Young Sammy Thomas knelt in the narrow ravine he had selected for his hiding spot. With his horse tied to a slender bush farther up the ravine, he waited with nervous apprehension for what would be the first dangerous confrontation in his fifteen years. He was not afraid. In fact, he was eager to show both his father and the stranger, Cullen McCabe, that he was equal to a man's responsibility. After what seemed hours, he began to wonder if McCabe had been wrong about the rustlers and he started to get fidgety. For the third time, he checked his Winchester 66 rifle to make sure it was fully loaded when he heard their horses. He quickly whipped the rifle toward the sound, ready to fire. He had to caution himself to remember that Cullen had said to hold his fire until the rustlers started the stampede. In a few seconds, he saw two horses walking slowly past the ravine as the outlaws took their positions on his side of the herd. It wouldn't be long now! He felt his hands trembling, so he moved his hand away from the trigger guard, afraid he might accidentally pull the trigger.

Some fifty yards east of the boy, Cullen waited as well. From his position, he had not seen any riders, but Jake had alerted him of their presence, so he knew it would not be long before the party started. Suddenly, the still night air was shattered by the sounds of gunfire near the river and there was an immediate vibration as if the herd of cattle were one gigantic organ. All at once the herd started moving as the shooting increased and soon the cattle were running wildly toward the mouth of the valley. Cullen held his rifle up and cranked out three quick shots as he galloped straight toward the charging cattle. On cue, Fred and Sammy began firing as well. As a result, the stampeding cattle became confused and the lead cows turned to the side. In a frantic effort to turn them back, Clute Bishop tried to head them off. It was then he saw the rider charging toward the front of the herd. He immediately shot at him. Seeing Clute at almost the same time, Cullen heard the snap of Clute's shot as it passed close by his head. He leveled his rifle and knocked Clute out of the saddle.

Seeing Clute go down, Stumpy Spratte swung over from the other side of the frantic cattle, his six-gun blazing at Cullen, until a shot from Sammy's Winchester slammed into his back. He was dead when he galloped past Cullen to slide out of the saddle some twenty yards farther. With all semblance of order lost now, the cattle turned back on themselves and scattered as the shooting continued, the main part of the herd now heading toward the river. Realizing that all was lost, with no possibility of capturing the herd of cattle now, Elmo Dalton's objective switched to survival. Seeing Tiny Watkins coming up behind him, he yelled, "Let's get the hell outta here! It's a damn trap!"

"Where's Clute?" Tiny yelled back at him.

"Dead! I saw him go down!" Elmo shouted. "Where's Pick and Red?" They were the two men at the rear of the herd who started the stampede.

"Done for, and I ain't seen Stumpy. Let's get outta here." He didn't wait any longer, gave his horse his heels, and didn't look to see if Elmo followed or not.

Seeing two men riding full out in retreat, Cullen and Fred threw several more shots after them to hurry them along their way. The job now was to calm the cattle down and keep them from scattering any further. But first, Cullen wanted to account for two missing men. "There were six in the gang, and I didn't see but two that got away. Those two near the lead cattle are both dead. I saw them go down and they ain't moved since. How 'bout the other two, anybody see 'em?" Nobody had, but there was a lot of lead flying and Fred couldn't tell for sure if he had hit everybody he aimed at. While they were trying to settle the cattle down, two horses with empty saddles showed up. "That's a good sign," Cullen said, "but it doesn't mean they're dead. It just might mean they're walkin'. We need to account for all six of 'em."

When the cattle were calm again, the three of them started searching through the middle of the herd, looking for the two missing men. Their search finally turned up another body before they gave up. Cullen recognized him as the other man who had been jailed with Slade and Luther. So, they could only account for five of the six raiders. "Well, whatever happened to the other one, we know he's on foot," Fred said. "I expect we'd best watch out he ain't hidin' somewhere fixin' to take a shot at us."

"Dependin' on how bad he was hit," Cullen said, "he mighta just crawled off somewhere to die. If he was gonna take a shot at one of us, I expect he would have done it while all three of us were standin' here talkin'. I reckon we'd best keep a sharp eye till we do find him. Chances are, if he's not wounded too bad, he's walkin' back the way he came, hopin' he'll find a horse somewhere." After he said it, he paused to think about the possibilities, then decided to make another suggestion. "Fred, just to make sure, why don't you ride on back to your house to make sure your wife is all right?"

"You think that maybe . . ." Fred started. "Right, maybe that would be a good idea," he said when the picture of his wife confronting a wounded outlaw came to his mind. His house was only a little over a mile and a half away, not a long walk, if you were not wounded too badly. He didn't hesitate further, ran to his horse, and, looking back at Sammy, said, "You stay here and help McCabe, son." In a matter of seconds, he was in the saddle and on his way home.

When at last it looked as though the cattle were settled down for the night, Sammy rode back to the ravine where he had taken cover. A short distance from the place he had knelt to shoot from, he found what he was looking for. Leading his horse slowly up to the body of a man known to his companions as Stumpy Spratte, Sammy stood staring down at the dark, still corpse. He felt a shiver run the length of his spine. When he had seen him firing as fast as he could at Cullen, he had simply taken aim and fired. It was the same as he would have done if the target had been a deer, or a coyote, or wolf. But this had been a man, a human being, although one with evil intent. It seemed he could not make himself look away from the face, frozen in agony, the result of Sammy's shot. So entranced was he, that he didn't hear Cullen behind him until he spoke. "I reckon you ain't a boy no more," Cullen said softly, causing Sammy to recoil as if firing a gun. He took a step backward and looked as if he wanted to explain, but Cullen spoke again. "I reckon I wanna thank you for savin' my life. I never saw this fellow behind me. It was a good shot and you killed an evil man that no doubt has caused a lot of pain for a lot of folks. But it wasn't any fun, was it?"

"No, sir, it wasn't no fun at all," Sammy answered meekly.

"Good," Cullen said. "As long as you feel that way, you don't have to think you did anything wrong. You just stepped up and did a man's job, and if you're lucky, maybe you won't ever have to shoot a man again. Now, how 'bout jumpin' on your horse and go after that little bunch of cows wanderin' off to the north there?" He pointed to a small group that had broken away from the main herd. Sammy climbed up into the saddle and went after them. As soon as he left, Cullen tied a rope around Stumpy Spratte's boots and let Jake drag the body up into the ravine Sammy had hidden in.

Naomi Thomas heard the shooting when it started and immediately bowed her head and asked the Lord to protect her men. Seated by the fireplace in the parlor, she had waited to hear it ever since she had sent the biscuits and ham back with Sammy, after telling him to be particular about the way he handled them. "I don't want your Mr. McCabe to think I sent biscuits with dirty fingerprints all over them," she had told him. Her husband had said she should be in no danger, since the men they thought were coming had no objective other than running off with their cattle. Even so, she could not relax enough to go to bed, choosing to sit in the rocking chair by the fireplace and await the morning. Feeling her eyelids getting heavy, she decided to go to the kitchen to see if there was any coffee left in the pot. She did not want to fall asleep.

Even though she had let the fire in her stove die

out, the iron stove was still warm enough to keep the little bit of coffee left in it warm. Had she not had her mind on the long time it had been since the shooting stopped, she might have noticed that the back door to the kitchen was slightly ajar. But her concentration was fixed upon the coffeepot she held over her cup. In the next instant, she dropped both cup and pot on the stove when a beefy arm suddenly trapped her from behind, pinning her arms to her sides, and she felt the cold, hard muzzle of a pistol pressed against her head. Terrified, she screamed, causing the arm to jerk even tighter. "You make another sound and I'll blow your brains out," he warned her.

Too frightened to move, she began to feel dizzy, but dared not faint for fear she might never wake again. Finally, she found her voice. "Please, don't hurt me," she pleaded.

"I'm gonna hurt you plenty if you don't do what I tell you," Pick Pickens promised her. "I've got a hole in my side and I need to stop the bleedin', and you're gonna do that for me, so get me somethin' to tie it up with."

Realizing then that he was not going to hurt her, at least until she had bandaged his wound, she forced herself to think calmly. "I've got some old sheets we use for bandages in the bedroom. I'll go get one," she said, thinking about the shotgun in the corner of the bedroom. "I'll be right back."

"I'm shot in the side, not in my head," Pick said with a sneer. "We'll go get the sheet together, and you'd best know that I ain't in the mood to play games. So, if you get any ideas about tryin' to pull a fast one, just take my word for it, I'll kill you deader'n hell. Now get movin'."

He released her, so she could go get the sheet,
waiting for her to pick up the lamp from the kitchen
table. Then he followed right behind her with his
pistol aimed at her. In the bedroom, she went to the
closet and pulled an old sheet down from the shelf.
He watched her every move closely, lest she try any
tricks, and when he spotted the shotgun leaning in
the corner by the bed, he gave her a wry smile. Under
his constant gaze, she ripped several strips from the
sheet that already showed signs of having been used
for that purpose before. "Hurry up," he scolded. "I
ain't plannin' on hangin' around here all night."

"I'm hurryin' as fast as I can," she replied as she
took one piece of sheet and folded it into a square to
press against the wound. "I'll tie this with these long
strips."

"You got any whiskey?" Pick demanded. When she
hesitated, he warned her. "Don't you lie to me. Get
the damn bottle!" She went at once to a cupboard and
got a bottle half filled with whiskey. When she handed
it to him, he uncorked it and splashed some of it on
the wound in his side, grimacing with the pain. Then
he turned the bottle up and took a couple of long
pulls from it. "You want a drink?" She quickly shook
her head, causing him to laugh. "If I wasn't in such a
hurry, I'd stay here, and we'd have us a party. You
ain't that bad-lookin' for a lady old enough to be my
mama. Hell, your hair ain't even all the way gray yet.
It's more like possum-gray. Hell, I wouldn't kick you
outta the bed," he said, enjoying the look of disgust
his lewd remarks brought to her face. Then he took
the bandage from her and slapped it over his wound
and ordered, "Tie it up. It's gonna be daylight soon

and we don't wanna be here when your menfolk come home for breakfast. Right, darlin'?"

She tied the bandage around his body, tight enough to slow the bleeding, and he had just struggled into his shirt again when they heard the footsteps and the voice from the kitchen. "Naomi! Where are you?" Fred called out. "You know you left the door open?"

Before she could yell to warn him, Pick grabbed her by the throat, pressed the gun against her temple, and whispered in her ear, "If you wanna live, you tell him you're in the bedroom."

"I'm in the bedroom," she called back, her voice quaking with fear.

"What's the matter, hon?" Fred called out as he walked down the short hall toward the light coming from the bedroom door. "You sound like you're ailin', or some . . ." The last word trailed off as he stepped in the bedroom to discover his wife with a gun held to her head.

"Now, you be real careful what you do right now," Pick warned him. "You've done put one bullet in me, so I feel like I already owe you for that one. We'll call it even if you do like I tell you. First thing is you need to take your left hand and unbuckle that gun belt, and let it drop on the floor." Fred did as he was instructed. "Who else is outside?" Pick asked.

"Nobody. There's just me."

"That better be the truth 'cause, if I find out you're lyin', I'll blow her brains out."

"I ain't lyin'," Fred said.

"We'll see, won't we?" Pick allowed. "All right, we're fixin' to leave now. What's your name, anyway?"

"Fred Thomas."

"All right, Fred, you're gonna lead us outta here. You can tote the lamp. Walk back through the kitchen and go out the back door, real slow. We'll be right behind you and remember, I'm holdin' a .44 with a hair trigger right up against your wife's head. So don't do nothin' dumb." Fred took the lamp and led them out to the back door, then went outside where they found his horse still standing by the back steps. When Pick saw the horse, he felt compelled to express his appreciation. "Nice work, Fred, you left me a horse, saddled and ready to go. I was wonderin' if I was gonna have to go saddle one of those in the corral yonder. You've been doin' real good so far, so don't mess up now and get yourself shot. You can climb back up the steps now. Me and the missus are fixin' to take a little ride. If everything goes the way I want it to, I'll let her go after I see there ain't nobody chasin' me. I'm gonna have to keep the horse, though. You got a pretty good trade. My horse is back yonder in the middle of your cattle herd somewhere and he's totin' a helluva lot better saddle than this one." He smiled at Naomi. "Let's go, sweetie. Stick your foot in that stirrup. Come on," he pressed when she seemed to have trouble lifting her foot high enough to reach it. Impatient, he grabbed her behind with his free hand and boosted her up, causing her to release a little squeal in response. Fred started to react, but Pick's reflexes were quicker, shifting his gun hand to cover him before he could make a move. "Try it, if you're tired of livin'," Pick invited. "Back up against that door." When he did, Pick quickly stepped up in the stirrup and settled behind the saddle.

Once he was behind her, Pick put one arm around her and pulled her up close against his chest while holding the .44 against her side with his other hand. "Now, we're gonna ride outta here close together, like we was one person," he said, giving her a little squeeze to emphasize his point. "So, if there's anyone else sneakin' around here gettin' a notion to take a shot at me, they're gonna most likely hit your wife, too."

"There ain't nobody else to take a shot," Fred pleaded. "You've got no call to treat her rough like that. Let her go."

"I will, when I'm ready," Pick said. "You just stand quiet, like I told you and I won't shoot unless I have to. The only reason I ain't already shot you is because I don't want that crew of yours to hear the shot." He gave Naomi another squeeze. "All right, sweetie, you're gonna do the drivin' 'cause my hands are full. Pick up the reins and let's go."

Afraid not to do what he ordered, Naomi leaned forward to pick up the reins resting on the horse's neck. All three were startled by the sudden sound of the impact of a .44 slug against Pick's chest. It was followed a second later by the distant report of a Winchester 73 rifle. Too stunned to react at once, Fred stared in horror as Pick and Naomi, still locked together, keeled over sideways and fell to the ground. Shocked into action then, he jumped from the steps and rushed to take the pistol from Pick's hand. "Naomi!" he cried out, horrified, as he pulled Pick's arm from around her waist.

"I'm all right," she said, finally coming to her senses after her fall from the horse. "I thought I was shot, but I don't think I am now." Fred pulled her away from Pick's body and helped her to her feet. She immediately threw her arms around him, hugging him with all her might. "I thought I was dead for sure," she whispered. They remained standing beside the body of her abductor, the couple still shaking from their close encounter when she suddenly said, "There." He turned to see what had caught her eye, to discover Sammy running toward them. Behind him, walked the imposing stranger called Cullen McCabe.

"Everybody all right?" Cullen asked as he approached the joyous reunion of the small family.

"Thanks to you, I reckon," Fred replied. "But I swear, McCabe, that was a damn risky shot to take. I reckon the good Lord was watchin' over us today. He sent us a miracle."

"Maybe so," Cullen allowed, "but I had a clean shot when your wife bent over, or I wouldn't have taken it."

Sammy took over then, eager to tell his parents about it. "McCabe said the cattle were settled down enough to leave 'em, and we still hadn't found hide nor hair of this feller here. So he said we'd best get back to make sure you and Mama were all right. When we spotted Pa's horse standin' by the kitchen steps, McCabe said he didn't like the look of that, so we rode up behind the barn. By the time we got off our horses and moved around where we could see the house, we saw Mama and this feller get up on Papa's horse." He looked over at Cullen then and grinned. "I was 'bout to go crazy. I wanted to run to help you, but McCabe told me I was liable to get you both shot. And all the time he just kneeled down at the corner of the corral with his rifle aimed at that feller, waitin', and all of a sudden, bam! He pulled the trigger. Scared me to death." He looked at Cullen again and grinned.

"I guess I need to thank you for savin' my life," Naomi said to Cullen.

"Not at all, ma'am," Cullen responded. "I expect

you most likely saved your own life. If you hadn't bent over when you did, I couldn't have risked takin' the shot."

Fred Thomas could only shake his head after Cullen's response. The image of Naomi sitting on his horse, so tightly held by the despicable outlaw, was one he would never forget. So vivid was his memory of it, that he was able to recall the distance between Naomi's back and Pick's chest to be no more than a handspan when she leaned forward to pick up the reins. *The man is a hell of a lot more confident in his shooting than I am*, he thought.

Rising once again to her position as the ruler of her house, Naomi decided it time to put the incident behind them and get on with the day. "Sammy," she ordered, "go in the house and get my stove a-goin'. We're gonna need some hot coffee and some breakfast." She turned to her husband and Cullen. "If you two would please do something with that body, I'd appreciate it."

"Yes, ma'am," Cullen replied. She promptly spun on her heel and went up the kitchen steps. "That's a right spunky woman you're married to, Fred. You got any particular spot where you wanna bury this rustler?"

Fred said he knew just the place. "On the other side of the hill behind the barn, same place I buried a little mule I had. The two of 'em oughta enjoy each other's company. I'll go get a couple of shovels." He went to the barn and Cullen took a coil of rope from Fred's saddle, tied one end around Pick's boots, then led the horse as it dragged the body over toward the barn. After they dragged the body around to the far side of the little hill behind the barn, they put it in the ground and returned to eat the hearty breakfast awaiting them.

The question that came naturally to be discussed was, if the raid they had successfully defended against was by none other than the notorious Viper Gang. If it was, then the gang had suffered severe casualties on this unsuccessful raid. Of the six men that attempted to steal the cattle, only two managed to escape with their lives. Cullen joined in the speculation, although he refrained from expressing all his suspicions. He was convinced that the gang was tied around New Hope's new sheriff. In prior reports regarding the Viper Gang, other ranchers claimed the raids were carried out by eleven or twelve riders, too many for the smaller ranchers to fight. There were only six riders in this attempt to steal Fred's cattle, but if you added the other men Cullen was convinced had ties to the sheriff, you would come closer to the number originally reported. These included the onetime deputy, Riker, plus Slade and Luther. Add another deputy, presently in town, and if you included Prophet, you had the right number for the Viper Gang. There was evidence enough that they were all connected, with Prophet calling the shots.

Sitting at the table, listening to the happenings of the night just past, Naomi rejoiced in the defeat of the Vipers, but she was naturally concerned about the future. "What if they come back to try it again?"

"We cut those six rustlers down to two men," Fred said. "I don't reckon those two are gonna think about comin' back to try it again." He reminded her that they were scheduled to combine the herd with those cattle belonging to John Snyder and Tim Williams two days hence. And once that happened, there would be plenty of men to protect the herds. "Don't you think so, McCabe?"

"I'd have to agree with you, Fred," Cullen answered. "I think we mighta cut the heart out of the Viper Gang last night." He didn't share his other suspicions with them, but he was convinced he knew where the brain of the gang was located. And that was his next priority, but he was of a mind to hang around on Fred's range until he moved his cattle to join Snyder's and Williams's.

"I think it's high time somebody said thank you for what you've done for us," Naomi said.

"Oh hell, yes," Fred blurted, just realizing that he hadn't done so. "If you hadn't come to help us, I reckon our cattle would be on their way to market without us. We owe you a helluva lot."

"I figure that fine meal I just had oughta take care of it," Cullen said.

Cullen's casual dismissal of his contribution to him, his wife, and son suddenly caused Fred to wonder why the man, a stranger, risked his life to come to their aid. "McCabe," he started, then began again. "As good a friend as you've been to me and my family, I figure I can call you by your first name. So, it puzzles me, Cullen, why did you risk your neck to jump in this fight on our side? I swear, I can't see a thing you had to gain besides our friendship."

Cullen wasn't prepared for the question and wasn't sure how to answer it. He didn't want to be honest about it and tell him that he was sent there by the governor to try to stem the cattle rustling. When he decided on his answer, it seemed to be the right one. "I'd say your friendship is as good a reason as I can think of." All three of them beamed at him.

"What are your plans now that you've helped save the Thomas family?" Fred asked. "You still lookin' for good land for your friends?"

"Yeah, I reckon so," Cullen answered. "You say you're supposed to join your herd with your neighbors' in two days?"

"Day after tomorrow," Fred repeated. "Some of Snyder's crew are gonna come help me drive 'em. I'll take the wagon into town tomorrow to pick up some supplies for Naomi and Sammy." He glanced at his son and smiled. "Maybe Sammy will be goin' on the drive next year, but this year we need him to stay here to look after his mother."

"That sounds like a good idea," Cullen said. "I was thinkin', if you don't mind, I'd like to camp on your range till your cattle are gone. I'll stay outta your way—just thought I'd like to see that the drive starts all right."

"Course you can," Fred said at once. "I'd appreciate it! You can stay here at the house with us, if you want."

"'Preciate it, Fred, but I'd just as soon move around on my own. I've got my packhorse here with everything I need to camp, and maybe we'll bump into each other. Just don't take a shot at me, if you see me hangin' around." He winked at Sammy.

After breakfast, he loaded his packhorse and wished Fred a good sale for his cattle, then said goodbye. Fred stood beside his wife while they watched Cullen ride away. "I swear, I still don't know why he done what he done," he said. "How many men do you know woulda bothered to save our bacon?"

CHAPTER 12

Sheriff John Prophet was standing by the front window of The Texas House, drinking a glass of beer when he saw the two riders lope by the saloon, riding in the direction of the jail. Shocked, he almost spilled his beer as he stepped closer to the window panes. "What the hell . . . ?" he muttered, not realizing he had blurted it aloud.

"What's the matter, Sheriff?" Deke Campbell asked.

Prophet turned at the sound of his voice and stared at him as if he hadn't known he was there. "Nothin'," he finally answered. "I got some business at the jail." He placed the half-finished glass of beer on the nearest table and headed straight for the door.

"What lit a fire under his tail?" Darlene asked Deke, and walked to the window to see. "He's headin' to the jail, all right." She turned back and laughed. "He didn't even finish his beer."

"Reckon not," Deke said. "It ain't no money outta his pocket."

When Prophet stormed into his office, he found Elmo and Tiny talking to his two deputies. All four turned to face him when they heard the door open.

"Are you crazy?" Prophet raged. "What the hell are you two doin' here? You're supposed to be halfway outta the county by now. You left four men to drive that herd to Fort Worth?"

With no choice other than wait for his rage to simmer down, neither man offered an explanation. Their very presence had already told him that something had gone wrong. It was just a matter of how bad it had been, so they stood speechless until he finally allowed them to explain. "There ain't nobody left but me and Tiny," Elmo said. Not sure what he meant, Prophet made no response other than to gape wide-eyed at him, waiting for some clarification. "It was a trap," Elmo continued. "They was waitin' for us. They knew we was comin' after the cattle last night."

"How did they know that?" Prophet demanded. "How the hell could they know?"

"I don't know, Boss, but they knew. Didn't they, Tiny?"

"They knew, all right," Tiny answered, "and waited for us to start the stampede before they came down on us hard."

"One man and his young son?" Prophet replied in disbelief.

"They had more'n just the two of 'em," Elmo insisted. "There was shootin' comin' from all around us. I saw Clute go down right after the stampede started, but it was so dark it was hard to tell who was a friend and who wasn't."

Tiny spoke up again. "Red and Pick was both knocked off their horses. I saw that. I don't know what happened to Stumpy. I thought I was the only one left till I run up on Elmo. By that time, the herd was scattered all over hell and back. There wasn't nothin' else we could do against that many men, so we decided it weren't gonna be any good for two more of us to get killed."

Prophet had remained quiet during the few minutes of their explanation, but the sting of the utter defeat of his plans burned like a live coal in his gut. The magnitude of the disaster was almost impossible to believe. After a string of half a dozen successful raids on Texas cattle ranches, without the loss of one single man, to now lose four in a raid on one man and his son was inconceivable. What to do at this point? At the moment, Prophet was at a loss. In a period of a few days, he had been reduced from a gang of twelve men to one of five men. He let himself dwell on that setback for only a few moments longer before his confidence and determination returned. He was the sheriff of New Hope, and with his four men, he could still own it. As for the Viper Gang, he liked the name and he would rebuild it. "All right," he said, "we got our asses kicked this time. But we ain't whipped, not by a long shot. I aim to own this town before we're through, then when the time's right, we'll clean it out and move on to another territory. You two go on back to the hideout and keep outta sight for a while. I'm gonna find out where Fred Thomas found the men he had last night. I'm thinkin' they musta come from one of the ranches he's drivin' cattle with. We just might start thinnin' that crop out some."

"We're runnin' kinda short on supplies up at the camp," Elmo said. "How 'bout if me and Tiny pick up some coffee and flour and some beans from the store here, maybe a little bacon, too?"

"You got any money?" Prophet asked.

"Hell, I figured we'd just take it," Tiny said.

"Use what little bit of sense you've got, damn it," Prophet scolded. "I'm the sheriff. I can't let these people think I can't protect them from thieves. I'll give you enough to buy what you need." Then, considering the simple man's lack of common sense, he added, "And don't tell 'em you got the money from me."

"Right," Tiny said. Elmo looked at Prophet and shook his head, as he followed the simple man out the door.

It was midafternoon when Fred Thomas drove his wagon up beside the general store owned by Jack Myers. Jack and his wife, Mildred, greeted him warmly. "Haven't seen you in town in a while," Mildred said. "How's Naomi? She didn't come in with you?"

"No, ma'am," Fred replied. "She's doin' just fine. She didn't come in with me because our old sow just had pigs and I reckon Naomi don't think the mama can take care of 'em without her help." He went on to tell Jack about the attempt to steal his cattle the night before and the dangerous situation Naomi had landed in.

"Well, thank the good Lord that Naomi wasn't hurt too bad. They musta been some of that Viper Gang," Jack said. "But there wasn't but six of 'em?" Fred said that was the number. "I reckon they figured that was as many as they needed with you without any help but Sammy. Even with McCabe, they still outnumbered you two to one. You lose any cows?"

"Nary a one," Fred answered proudly.

"Well, good for you, Fred," Jack said. "I expect you're the first one those Vipers have got skunked on."

With his supplies loaded on his wagon, Fred left

the store and drove his wagon down to the saloon. He wanted to buy a bottle of whiskey to replace that used by the wounded outlaw, Pick Pickens. "How do, Fred," Deke Campbell greeted him when he walked in. "What's your pleasure?"

"I need a bottle of corn whiskey," Fred answered. "And I'll take a little shot of whatever you're pourin' at the bar to celebrate."

"What are you celebratin'?" Deke asked.

"My little visit from the Viper cattle rustlers last night," Fred said proudly, eager to repeat the same story he had just told Jack Myers. When he had finished, he tossed his shot of whiskey back and smacked his lips, satisfied.

"Nobody but you, your boy, and McCabe," Deke commented. "That's worth celebratin', all right. I didn't know McCabe was back in town. Lucky for you he is, ain't it?"

Two men enjoying a drink of whiskey at a table close by the bar listened with interest to Fred's accounting of the night just past. When he had finished, the two deputies got up and walked out. "Put them drinks on the sheriff's bill," Slim said to Deke as they passed the bar.

"Right," Deke answered, and waited for them to walk out the door before he commented lowly, "and I'll hold my breath till he pays the damn bill."

"You ain't gonna like what we just heard over at the saloon," Deputy Sheriff Merle Blake announced as soon as they walked in the door of the sheriff's office. His comment was met with a scowl from Sheriff

Prophet, who had heard nothing but bad news of late. "Your old friend McCabe is back in town," Merle continued. "At least, he's back close to town. He was in that little ruckus last night at the Thomas place." As he had expected, Prophet's face twisted up immediately.

"And that ain't all," Slim chimed in. "There weren't but three of 'em, Thomas, his son, and McCabe. They routed Clute and the boys right proper. We just heard Thomas braggin' about it, how they done for four of 'em and the other two run off with their tails between their legs."

"I want him dead," was Prophet's initial response. His face remained strained, as if twisted by sheer frustration. How could one man destroy his whole gang, one by one? "I want him dead," he repeated, and slammed his fist on the desk hard enough to spill coffee from his half-filled cup.

There seemed to be no question that his proclamation was a direct order. His two deputies seemed uncertain, however. It was Merle who asked the question. "You mean that, Boss? You want him shot on sight, or arrest him first, or what?"

Although furious enough to have him shot on sight, Prophet wisely checked his desire for revenge. McCabe had established himself as a weapon against crime in the little town, and it would almost certainly derail his efforts to build the sheriff's department as the ruling force in town if he blatantly shot him down. "No, don't shoot him if there are any witnesses around," he ordered. "But if there's no one to see you do it, then, by God, shoot the man. I don't want it tied to this office."

"What if he breaks the law and resists arrest?" Merle asked.

"That's different," Prophet said. "Then you can shoot him, but make it look like you ain't got no choice."

Slim didn't have to think about that very long to see that they had a free license to provoke McCabe into a confrontation. And if not that, to simply keep an eye on his movements in the event one of them might find him in a situation with no witnesses. He and Merle agreed that the second one was the preferred method of elimination.

"Where is McCabe?" Prophet asked then. "Did he come to town with Thomas?" Slim said that he wasn't with him in the saloon. This caused Prophet to speculate. "He's up to something. I don't know what it is, but he's hangin' around this town for some reason. It don't make any sense, unless he's figurin' on cuttin' us out and cashin' in, himself." The more he thought about it, the more he became convinced that McCabe was his competition for control of the town. "Merle, I want you to take a little ride out to the Thomas ranch and see if McCabe is hangin' around there." He paused to make sure. "And if you can catch him out away from the house, shoot him. Slim, you go on back to The Texas House, in case he shows up in town. If he does, I wanna know."

Merle took the short ride out to Fred Thomas's ranch, leaving the river road when he spotted the wagon in the distance ahead of him, realizing he was about to catch up with him. There was a low ridge that ran parallel to the road about seventy-five yards to the east, so he decided to put that between him and the road. The first thing he wanted to find out was whether or not McCabe was at Fred's house. Riding at a lope, he easily rode past the wagon, hidden by the gently rolling ridge, and was able to find himself a small patch of trees at the foot of it where he could see the house and barn. With his horse tied to some scrubby laurel bushes, he walked up to the trees and sat down to watch the house. In a short time, the wagon appeared and headed straight for the barn. Merle figured that, if McCabe was at the ranch, he'd most likely come out to help Fred unload the wagon. It didn't take long to determine there was no one at the barn to help, not even his son. *If he ain't at the house, he must be with the cattle,* Merle thought. He waited awhile longer to be certain before getting back on his horse and going in search of the herd.

He thought there was a pretty good chance that the herd was still grazing in the same shallow valley Clute and the boys had found them in before. Recalling Elmo Dalton's account of how they had found the cattle, Merle found the valley with little effort. Although there were few trees on the rolling prairie, the lay of the land afforded him adequate cover to get within one hundred yards of the outer edge of the herd. He set himself up behind one of the few trees standing. A small tree, it grew with double trunks that formed a vee, allowing him to crouch behind them while steadying his rifle in the fork. It was a comfortable distance for his rifle. All he needed, he told himself, was something to shoot at. To his disappointment, there was no sign of McCabe, no one at all, in fact, which he found to be strange.

After a short period, during which he decided he

was wasting his time, he was about to move back to the ranch house again, when a rider suddenly appeared. Coming up from behind the rearmost cows, the rider circled around beside the herd. When he got close enough to tell, Merle saw that it wasn't McCabe. It was the boy, Fred's son. He continued to watch, waiting to see if McCabe might join the boy. When it appeared that he would not, Merle laid his front sight on Sammy and rested his finger on the trigger. It would be no trouble at all to knock him out of the saddle from that distance, and the more he thought about it, the more inclined he was to do it. It would be a fitting payback for the Viper men who were shot on that ill-fated raid. He cocked the hammer back and held the rifle steady. "It'd be an easy shot, wouldn't it?" The voice cut through him like a knife and he froze, unable to move. "Now, ease that hammer back down."

"I weren't gonna shoot nobody!" Merle finally found his voice. "I was just seein' what kinda shot it woulda been!"

"It woulda been the last shot you ever made," Cullen said. "Now, leave the rifle where it is and crawl back outta that tree trunk." Fearing he was about to die and knowing he couldn't even attempt to lift the rifle up and turn to shoot without being blocked by the trunk, he did as Cullen said. "Who the hell are you? Let's have a look at you," Cullen ordered. Like a dog caught eating chicken eggs, Merle crawled backward and turned over to face Cullen. Seeing the badge Merle wore, Cullen said, "One of Sheriff Prophet's deputies and it looked to me like you were fixin' to murder Fred Thomas's son."

"No, no, I weren't!" Merle pleaded. "I swear, I was

just sightin' on him. I wouldn'ta never pulled the trigger."

"Is that a fact?" Cullen replied. "But you pulled the hammer back on that rifle. What are you doin' out here, hidin' behind a tree, anyway, if you weren't fixin' to shoot?"

Thinking as fast as he could force himself to, Merle declared, "I was lookin' for rustlers. That's what I was doin'. After we heard about them rustlers that hit this herd last night, I just came out here to make sure they didn't come back."

"Is that a fact?" Cullen replied. "Did Sheriff Prophet send you out here? I thought he was the town sheriff. I didn't know he was a county sheriff." Holding his rifle on the trembling man, he cocked his chin as if thinking hard. "I don't know if you're a real deputy or not. You mighta stole that badge."

"I'm a deputy!" Merle insisted. "Anybody in town knows I'm a deputy."

"Anybody?" Cullen asked. "I'll tell you what, we'll go to town and ask Sheriff Prophet if you're his deputy."

"You don't wanna do that!" Merle blurted, picturing the scene if McCabe paraded him back before Prophet. "Sheriff Prophet might not like you doin' that."

"I'd think he'd appreciate it," Cullen said, "havin' me wantin' to make sure nobody goes around impersonatin' a law officer. You've got a badge. How 'bout handcuffs? You got handcuffs, too? No? Well, lucky I brought some rope, ain't it? Roll over on your belly and stick your hands behind you." He pulled Merle's six-gun from his holster and stuck it in his belt.

Somewhat confident now that he wasn't going to shoot him, Merle said, "You're makin' a big mistake, mister. You can't treat a law officer this way. Sheriff Prophet's liable to put you in jail for messin' with his deputy."

"I reckon that's a chance I'll have to take," Cullen said as he grabbed Merle's wrists and tied them together. Then he took hold of his arm and picked him up on his feet. "I brought your horse up here, so you wouldn't have to walk." After he helped him up into the saddle, he led the horse back down the slope where Jake was waiting. With his devastated prisoner behind him, inwardly moaning about the reaction he was going to cause Prophet, Cullen started toward town.

CHAPTER 13

"Well, I'll be . . ." Burt Whitley mumbled to himself when he looked out the door as two riders rode past the stable. Not sure he could believe his first glance, he hurried to stand outside the door. "What in the world?" he mumbled again when a second look confirmed it. Cullen McCabe, astride his big bay gelding, was leading one of Sheriff Prophet's deputies, his hands tied behind his back, up the middle of the street. Curious to see where McCabe was taking the deputy, Burt walked up the street behind them. The riders on the two horses caught Hiram Polson's eye as well, and he laid his hammer aside and fell in step with Burt as Cullen led Merle past the blacksmith's shop. Rapidly becoming a parade, they picked up a couple more intrigued spectators, including Johnny Bledsoe, when they passed the saloon.

On the other side of the saloon, Slim Bradshaw sat on the tiny front porch of the sheriff's office. When he looked down toward the stable and saw the small crowd coming his way, he got up from his chair and took a longer look. It was enough to make him swear, then he stepped just inside the office door. "Boss, there's a damn parade marchin' up the street this way, and you ain't gonna believe who's leadin' it."

"Now, what the hell?" Prophet mumbled, and came to the door immediately. His patience already spent, what with the recent failures he had suffered, he was not in a mood to suffer another setback. "McCabe," was the one word he uttered when he stepped out to look.

"That's Merle behind him," Slim said. "It looks like he's got his hands tied behind his back. What the hell is he doin'?"

Prophet didn't answer him but walked to the edge of the porch to await the confrontation, a dark scowl prominent upon his face. By the time the parade reached the jail, it had attracted an audience of a dozen or more of the town's citizens, sprinkled here and there with a drifter or a drunk. All of them, too curious to pass up the opportunity to spectate, followed close behind the deputy's horse. Fighting hard to control his anger, Prophet remained standing there, saying nothing, until Cullen reined Jake to a stop in front of the steps. Then, with just one word again, he said, "McCabe," more a curse than a greeting.

Cullen answered with one word only as well. "Sheriff," he responded, sounding almost like a cheerful greeting in contrast. They remained in a silent confrontation for a long moment, one standing defiantly, the other in the saddle, equally defiant, each taking full measure of his adversary. After what seemed a long empty space, with no sound other than that from an out-of-tune piano in the saloon down the street, Cullen spoke. "I thought I'd bring your deputy back to ya. I reckon he musta got lost. I found him south of here on Fred Thomas's range."

"Is that so?" Prophet asked. "And you had to tie his hands behind his back?"

"Well, it seemed like the safe thing to do. When I found him, he was lyin' up between the forks of a tree, fixin' to shoot Fred's boy, Sammy. So I didn't wanna take a chance on him tryin' to shoot me." His comment generated a low murmuring among the spectators that had gathered around the two horses.

Now fighting an impulse to simply shoot the man he had come to despise, Prophet struggled inside to control his emotions, knowing the damage his raw emotions might cause in his quest to own the town. "Well, I reckon that's one version of what really happened, but you did the right thing, bringin' him to me. I'll deal with him appropriately." He cringed then when Merle opened his mouth.

"I swear, Boss, I told him I weren't really gonna shoot that boy. I was just takin' aim like I woulda done if he had been one of them rustlers."

"Shut up, Merle!" Prophet spat. He turned to Slim, who was visibly fidgeting, not sure if there was going to be a gunfight or not. "Slim, go untie his hands and get him inside." Turning back to Cullen, he said, "I'll take it from here. You folks go on about your business. The show's over." His eyes never left Cullen's, seeming to promise that this was not the end of it between them.

The gathering dispersed to discuss the incident just witnessed in smaller conversations among themselves. It was difficult to decide what to make of it, but the animosity between the sheriff and the rugged stranger was blatantly apparent. Cullen watched as Slim untied Merle's wrists and stepped back to let Merle dismount. Then he pulled Merle's pistol from his belt, broke the cylinder and emptied the cartridges. "Here," he called to Merle, and tossed the empty weapon to him. Looking back at Prophet again, he said, "I wouldn't wanna get arrested for stealin' it." Then he backed Jake up six or seven yards, keeping his eye on Prophet until wheeling and riding off toward the stable.

He was taking his saddle off his horse by the time Burt walked back to the stable, and he walked in asking questions. "Was what you said the truth? Did you catch that deputy fixin' to shoot Fred Thomas's boy?"

"That's what it looked like to me," Cullen answered. He pulled Jake's bridle off and let him out in the corral. "He was lyin' behind that tree with his rifle aimed at Sammy Thomas, and while I watched him, he cocked the hammer back with his finger on the trigger. To me, that says he was gettin' ready to shoot."

"Lord have mercy," Burt replied. "A deputy sheriff. Whaddaya reckon the sheriff will do to him?"

"That's what I'm waitin' to see," Cullen answered. "I expect it'll come down to his word against mine, and I'm thinkin' Prophet will stand by his deputy."

"I expect you're right," Burt said, and shook his head when he thought about it. "Damn, McCabe, you've made yourself one hell of an enemy. You shoulda shot that deputy when you caught up with him and let somebody else find him."

"I thought about it," Cullen said. Then, changing the subject, he said, "I wanna leave Jake here to rest up a little while. I'll be goin' back outta town later this afternoon."

"Sure," Burt said. "You'd better keep a low profile around town, though. You ain't too popular with the sheriff's department."

"Yeah, I'll do that," Cullen said, although he had

no intention of doing so. To the contrary, he figured the best thing for his own safety was to be very prominent and make sure there were always witnesses wherever he was. The more witnesses, the better, for he was convinced Prophet was still planning to convince the people of New Hope that they had hired not only a tough sheriff, but an honest one. He had seen enough at this point to suspect Prophet was without a doubt connected to the Viper gang, and it was his strong feeling that he was the leader of it. He saw his responsibility to the governor to be the elimination of Prophet and his followers. In a world without morals, the simplest course of action would be to kill them out like you would a nest of rattlesnakes. He had already cut their numbers down. But rather than take on the role of assassin, he strongly felt that the people had to come to discover the evil of the man for themselves. That might not be easy, for some of the people, the mayor prominent among them, believed Prophet to be the ideal man for sheriff.

Counting on Mayor Ernest Robertson's belief in his qualifications as well, Prophet was prone to worry now that he might be swayed to change his mind if McCabe continued to get in the way. The man was like a plague that kept rising up unexpectedly. Prophet decided he could wait no longer. His initial instincts about Cullen now seemed correct and it was apparent to him that the only solution was to eliminate the man—the sooner, the better. He turned to Merle. "I'm firin' you," he announced. When Merle immediately started to protest, Prophet snapped, "Shut up and listen. When the people in town hear that I fired you, they ain't gonna be surprised at all that you'll blame it on Cullen McCabe for that little show he put on today. Matter of fact, they'll expect you to wanna call McCabe out for costin' you your job as deputy. So you call him out, only you make sure he ain't holdin' a gun in his lap this time." He glanced over at Slim then back at Merle, who still looked uncertain. "You two have been runnin' off at the mouth about wantin' to just shoot the scoundrel. Well, Merle, now you've got good reason, unless you don't think you're man enough for the job." He paused then, waiting for Merle's reaction.

Merle didn't reply at once. He wasn't sure he wanted to stand up to the formidable stranger, but he didn't want to trash his stock with the gang by refusing to. "Hell," he finally offered. "I sure as hell ain't scared of callin' him out, or nobody else. I'm as fast as the next man with a six-gun."

Eager to see such a face-off, Slim spoke up. "A man as big as he is ain't usually all that fast with a six-gun," he encouraged. "Ain't nobody seen him in a real contest. You can't go by that thing in the saloon with Riker. McCabe already had his gun in his hand. That sounds to me like somebody who knows he ain't fast enough to stand and draw fair and square."

"That's what I was thinkin'," Prophet said. Like his two deputies, he had no idea how fast McCabe might be with his sidearm, but he appeared to favor a rifle. It was a gamble that Prophet figured he couldn't lose on. If Merle beat him and shot him down, the problem was solved, and the sheriff would get credit for firing his deputy, even though there would be no charges against Merle. He would simply send him back to the camp and replace him with Tiny or Elmo.

That was the result Prophet preferred. However, if McCabe proved to be faster than Merle, it might still be possible to arrest McCabe, and eventually kill him in a jailbreak attempt.

Prophet and Slim both stood looking at Merle, waiting to see how he was going to respond to Prophet's challenge. Merle knew his reputation with the gang of outlaws was at stake, so in spite of a decided reluctance, he accepted the challenge. "Hell," he bragged loudly, "I ain't a-scared to face that jasper. There ain't no yeller streak runnin' down my back."

"I knowed you'd say that," Slim responded at once. "He's as good as dead. Let's go find him. Anybody know where he went?"

"After he left here, he was headin' down toward the stable," Prophet said. "You can start there."

"Ain't you goin' with us?" Slim asked.

"No," Prophet answered him. "I can't go out and try to set up a gunfight. How would that look for the sheriff to be doin' that? I'll wait here till I hear gunshots, then I'll come runnin'."

"I reckon that would look bad to the good people of New Hope at that," Slim said. "Come on, Merle, let's go down to the stable."

When they got to the stable, Burt told them that Cullen had left his horse there, but he was gone, and he didn't say where he was going. "Mighta gone to the saloon," Slim said. "Come on, Merle." Merle looked as if he might need a drink, anyway, and willingly followed Slim back up the street, even though he hoped Cullen wasn't at the saloon. When they got to The Texas House, Slim told Merle to wait while he took a look inside to see if McCabe was there. "It would look like a setup if I was to go walkin' in there with you," he said. So, while Merle stood nervously waiting, Slim walked up beside the door and peered inside. He was back in a few seconds. "He's in there, down at the other end of the bar, talkin' to the bartender. You go on in and I'll come in after, so folks won't think the sheriff had anything to do with callin' out McCabe."

Becoming more reluctant by the minute, Merle eased the .44 he wore up and down in his holster several times to make sure it was free and easy. He tried to swallow, but his throat was so dry he couldn't. "I'm gonna need a drink first," he said to Slim when he passed him and entered the saloon.

In the midst of telling Cullen how he had happened to come to work for Johnny Bledsoe, Deke paused when he saw Merle come in the door. He remained silent as he watched Merle step up to the other end of the long bar, then went down to wait on him. "What can I get for you? Deputy Blake, ain't it?" Seated at a table, talking to a farmhand, both Darlene and Nancy turned when they heard Merle come in. When they saw who it was, they returned their attention to the young farmhand.

"Gimme a shot of whiskey," Merle replied in as husky a voice as he could affect.

"Right," Deke said, reached under the bar for a glass, then poured the drink. Then he waited while Merle downed it and slammed the empty glass down for another.

After Merle downed the second one, he waved off a third. Knowing Slim was standing right outside, peering at him through the window, he summoned the little bit of nerve the whiskey had inspired.

"McCabe!" he blurted. "Because of you, I lost my job. Sheriff Prophet fired me."

"Is that a fact?" Cullen replied. "I'm sorry to hear that. I reckon a lot of folks would say you just took a step up in your life."

Merle paused, not sure how to respond, since he didn't know if he had been insulted or not. So he started all over. "You cost me my job."

"I understand that," Cullen said.

"You owe me for two shots of whiskey," Deke inserted, "since you ain't a deputy no more."

Already confused, Merle glanced at Deke, then turned back to Cullen at the other end of the bar. "I'm callin' you out, McCabe. Right here. We're gonna settle up."

It was very apparent to Cullen that Merle's heart was not in the challenge he was issuing. He suspected that he had been put up to the job by Prophet. "I've already had a gun on you today, and I didn't shoot you. I caught you aimin' to shoot a young boy. I shoulda shot you then, but I didn't. Now, why are you comin' in here wantin' to get shot again?"

"You cost me my job," was all Merle could think to reply.

"It wasn't a job you were any good at, anyway," Cullen said. "Who told you to come in here and call me out? Was it the sheriff?"

"What? No!" Merle reacted. "Nobody told me to. This is my idea."

"Well, it's a bad idea. It's liable to get you killed. If Prophet really has fired you, the best thing for you to do is get on your horse and put this town behind you. Maybe you can find some honest work somewhere."

Rapidly becoming unraveled, Merle was getting

more and more confused by Cullen's refusal to take his challenge seriously. The response he was getting from McCabe was not one he expected. To make matters worse, he glanced at the door and discovered that Slim had stepped inside to watch, evidently wondering what was taking so long. Realizing at last that he had succeeded only in making himself seem to be a fool, he acted in anger. "Draw, damn it!" He reached for his six-gun as he said it, and in his haste, pulled the trigger before his gun was leveled at Cullen. His bullet glanced off the top of the bar between Deke and Cullen, causing Deke to dive under the bar, and scattering Darlene and Nancy and their young man. Cullen was left with no choice but to put Merle down. Looking almost relieved, Merle dropped his pistol and held on to the bar for a few moments before sinking to the floor.

When he heard Merle drop to the floor, Deke crawled out from under the bar to find a somewhat astonished McCabe, his six-gun in hand. "I swear," Cullen uttered, "I didn't think he would do it."

"It sure didn't look like he wanted to do it," Deke said, having been of the same opinion as Cullen. "Else, I sure as hell wouldn'ta been standin' right beside you." He took his bar rag and rubbed a six-inch scar on the top of his bar. "He left a pretty good burn mark on my counter."

Their discussion was interrupted then by a voice from the door. "What's goin' on in here?" Slim called out. "What was them shots?"

"You watched it," Cullen answered. "Maybe you know more about what's goin' on than we do. Looks to me like you and your boss were finally able to get this poor fool killed."

"Is that so?" Slim came back. "From where I'm standin', it looks like there ain't no doubt about who shot who." He walked over to the end of the bar and looked down at the body. "That's Merle Blake," he announced, as if he didn't know before. About to carry on his charade further, he was interrupted then when Sheriff Prophet came in the door, followed by a couple of spectators who had heard the shots.

"What's the trouble here, Slim?" Prophet asked. "I heard shots." Cullen was sure he detected the disappointment in the sheriff's face when he discovered him still standing.

"We got a shootin' here," Slim answered. "Looks like McCabe put a bullet in Merle Blake's chest. "It mighta been outright murder. I was right outside, and I never heard but one shot."

"Bullshit!" Deke exclaimed. "Blake there came in here and did the best he could to get McCabe to draw. When McCabe wouldn't do it, Blake pulled on him and shot at him. McCabe didn't have no choice, he had to shoot then."

"That's the truth, Sheriff," Darlene spoke up. "Everybody in here saw it."

"Right here's where his shot tore a scar on the top of my bar," Deke said, pointing to the six-inch mark on the counter, "and damn near hit me."

Their immediate defense of Cullen brought a scowl to Prophet's face. He glanced briefly down at Merle's body as if blaming him for his stupidity. Back at Cullen then, he said, "Trouble just seems to hang around you, don't it? You've already killed Deputy Pete Riker. Now, you've even killed a deputy I just fired. It makes me think you got some particular dislike for law officers."

"Just some law officers," Cullen said, "the kind that

ain't sure which side of the law to stand on." He could feel the tension building in the barroom while everyone waited for the sheriff's remarks.

"I'm plannin' on runnin' a peaceful town here," Prophet began, "so, I think it's about time you moved on. If you're the cause of any more trouble for New Hope, I'm gonna have to lock you up."

"Thanks for the warnin', Sheriff, but I ain't so sure you have the authority to tell me to move on, since I ain't broke any laws. And I'm not a vagrant, I pay for every service I get. I don't know of any complaints from any of the merchants I've done business with here in town. Do you? If you do, maybe we oughta go talk to 'em together and straighten any problems out."

"You're a smart-ass, ain't you?" Prophet uttered between clinched teeth. Things had clearly failed to work out as he had hoped after he had literally coerced Merle Blake into seeking a gunfight with McCabe. *One by one,* he thought as he continued to glare at the troublesome stranger. His gang of twelve had been chopped down to himself and three men, and all because of Cullen McCabe. Prophet still saw it as a contest between the two of them for complete control of the town, and he feared that McCabe was rapidly winning the favor of the town's citizens. *A shot in the back would take care of it, and the time has come for that.* The thought caused a thin smile to trace a line across his face. "You think about what I said, McCabe. Maybe the healthiest thing for you would be to get on that bay horse of yours and ride on outta New Hope."

"That sounds like a threat," Cullen said.

"It's good advice, that's what it is," Prophet replied. "I just don't believe you've got much of a future in New Hope."

"I'll take it under consideration. You may be right. Maybe I'll ride on back to San Antonio, talk to my old friend Prentice Porter. You remember him, he's the sheriff in San Antonio. I'll tell him you said hello." He watched for Prophet's reaction, but it was no more than a return of the thin smile.

Prophet turned to Deke. "You can drag that corpse outta here." Back to his deputy, he said, "Slim, pull his cartridge belt out from under him and see what he's got in his pockets." He waited until Slim had finished, then walked close to Cullen on his way to the door. "You'd best think about what I said. This town ain't big enough for both of us."

CHAPTER 14

Sheriff John Prophet was not in a good mood, and aware of that, Slim Bradshaw sat in the corner of the office nursing a cup of coffee and keeping as quiet as he possibly could. On the other side of the room, he could hear Prophet muttering to himself, until finally he announced, sarcastically, "I'm goin' to talk to His Honor, the mayor. I need more money to run this town." He was especially angry over the loss of Fred Thomas's herd of cattle, cattle that he had planned to steal and sell at a nice price. He had sent Tiny Watkins and Elmo Dalton out to the Thomas range that morning and they said the cattle had already been moved to John Snyder's range, and combined with Snyder's and Williams's cows. Prophet was furious when he got that news, even though he no longer had enough men to make another try, had Thomas's cattle still been there. The reason his men had failed was Cullen McCabe. And the more he thought about his loss, the madder he became, until he could hold it no longer. "Slim," he blurted, startling his deputy. "Ride out to the hideout again. Tell Tiny and Elmo to go back to that ranch before dark. McCabe ain't stayin' in town no more. I figure he's been campin' on Thomas's place somewhere, most likely close to the house. Tell them to find his camp and put him under the damn ground. I've had enough of his trouble."

Slim got up immediately. "I'm on my way, Boss." He was just as happy to ride out to the camp, rather than continue to hang around while Prophet was drowning in his fit of anger. Prophet followed him out the door but turned to storm up the street to the hotel.

Ernest Robertson was in his office behind the clerk's desk of the hotel. He looked up, surprised, when the sheriff walked past his startled desk clerk without a word of explanation. "Sheriff, is something wrong?" Robertson asked.

"There sure as hell is," Prophet replied. "It's time me and you had a little discussion about the way this town is bein' run." Robertson was too astonished to respond, even had he thought to, since Prophet didn't pause. "For one thing, the salaries you're payin' me and my deputy ain't nearly enough to cover all my expenses to keep this town safe. I need a raise. And the next problem is the interference in my job from Cullen McCabe and the fact that everybody in town seems to have a blind eye on what he's up to."

When there was finally a pause in Prophet's discourse, Robertson, still baffled by the sheriff's outburst, managed to ask a question. "What is it that you think McCabe is up to?"

"What anybody with a grain of sense oughta be able to see," Prophet replied. "He's tryin' to make as much trouble for me as he can, so he can convince you that he oughta be sheriff. I'm tellin' you, he's lookin' to run this town, never mind you and the town council."

Robertson continued to be amazed by the sheriff's outburst. "I think maybe you have read McCabe's intentions wrong," he said. "He's said all along that he doesn't intend to stay in New Hope, and he'll be leaving any day now."

"There!" Prophet exclaimed. "You see what I mean? He's even got you fooled. What reason has a drifter like him got for hangin' around a town where he's already shot and killed two deputy sheriffs? And that ain't all. He's shot two more men outside of town." This was news to Robertson and when he asked what two men the sheriff was referring to, Prophet said, "Nobody you know, I reckon, but he shot 'em. There were witnesses seen him when he done it."

Totally unprepared for the sudden charges brought by his new sheriff, Robertson was at a loss as to how to respond. From the short time Cullen McCabe had been in town, it seemed that all those in contact with him thought him no danger to the town, In fact, he had been more closely thought of as a friend to the town. As far as the shootings of the two deputies, everyone who witnessed the incidents said that McCabe had acted in self-defense. Robertson found it hard to believe Prophet's charges, but what if they were accurate? "I'll tell you the truth," he finally decided. "I'll call a special meeting of the town council and we'll discuss the charges you've brought to my attention. As for your request for more money, I'm sure I told you that we hadn't planned on salaries for two deputies to begin with, but we came up with them. You understand that it's not me that pays your salary, don't you? It's the town council, so we have to talk about it. I'll call for a meeting and, of course, I'll notify you, so you can attend."

Prophet was not totally satisfied with the mayor's response to his appeal. He had wrongly expected an immediate answer. He hesitated, thinking to threaten if his demands weren't addressed at once. But in a moment of coolness, he decided he'd better not push the issue before the council met. "'Preciate your attention to this thing," he said, as calmly as he could affect. "My interests are just what's best for the town. Let me know when you have the meetin'." With that, he walked out of the office, ignoring the polite greeting tossed his way from the desk clerk when he passed by.

When he had gone, Robertson walked out to the front desk and shook his head in concern. "Is everything all right, Boss?" James Levitt asked.

"I don't know," Robertson answered honestly. "Sometimes I can make some really dumb mistakes." That was all he offered his clerk, not anxious to admit that he had been premature in hiring a sheriff without conferring with the other members of the council. "Maybe it'll all work out."

As the sun began to settle down below the long line of hills on the western side of the Brazos, the two riders pulled up on the top of a low ridge to take a look up the wide valley leading to the river. "Hell," Elmo Dalton complained, "it'll be plum dark by the time we scout that long valley, and we might not see his camp if we was to ride right by it. He oughta be campin' here by the river."

"You're right," Tiny Watkins said. "It'd be a waste of time. Besides, I'm gettin' hungry."

"We mighta been wastin' our time already," Elmo suggested. "While we've been ridin' around out here, he might be settin' at the table in the ranch house, havin' supper with Thomas's wife, since her old man rode off on the cattle trail."

Tiny chuckled at the thought. "You might be right. Wouldn't that be somethin' if ol' McCabe was comfortin' Thomas's wife while him and his son are driving cattle north? If he is, maybe they might invite us to supper, so why don't we go take a look at the house?"

"Suits me," Elmo said, thinking more of the woman than the possibility of finding Cullen there. He gave his horse a nudge and headed for what looked to be a ravine that led down to the valley floor. Tiny turned his horse to follow him. Halfway down the narrow ravine, Elmo's horse suddenly stopped and reared backward, almost falling against Tiny's horse. "Whoa!" Elmo blurted, holding on to keep from coming out of the saddle.

"What the hell?" Tiny exclaimed as he tried to back his horse up the ravine. "Snakes?" he asked, thinking Elmo's horse might have stepped into a rattler's nest.

"No!" Elmo answered after he backed his horse and dismounted. "It's somebody a-layin' there. I can't see too good in this damn gully, but I reckon he's dead 'cause he didn't move when my horse damn near stepped on him." He reached in his vest pocket and pulled out a match, then walked back down to the neck of the ravine. Kneeling down close to the body, he struck the match on his belt buckle, then held it close to the face of the corpse. When the flame flared up, it revealed the twisted features of Stumpy Spratte. Elmo recoiled at the sight, dropping the match in the dirt.

"What is it?" Tiny exclaimed.

"It's Stumpy and he looked like he was starin' straight into hell."

"Lemme see," Tiny said, and stepped down from his saddle.

"Help yourself," Elmo allowed, and led his horse past the body. "I've done seen all I wanna see." He went on to the mouth of the ravine to wait for Tiny to satisfy his curiosity.

When Tiny led his horse down beside Elmo's, he was shaking his head slowly. "Ol' Stumpy," he finally commented, "and he looked like he was just fixin' to say somethin', didn't he? He was sayin', *It don't look too good where I'm headin', boys.*" Then he chuckled at the thought.

"You know, you're kinda sick in the head," Elmo told him. "Let's go take a look around that ranch house."

"I wonder where the rest of the boys are," Tiny said as he stepped up into the saddle again.

"I don't know and I'd just as soon let 'em lay right where McCabe left 'em," Elmo said, and gave his horse a nudge.

They followed the same trail that Pick Pickens had walked that night, figuring correctly that it probably led to the ranch headquarters. A short ride brought them within sight of the house and barn. In the darkness, they pulled up to within a hundred and fifty yards to look it over before deciding what to do. While they watched, the back door of the house opened, and a woman stepped out on the steps. They could hear her calling out something but were unable to understand what she said. In a few seconds, a man carrying a lantern walked from the barn and went to the house. "There he is!" Tiny exclaimed. "And she's callin' him in to supper, I bet."

"I hope she made plenty," Elmo commented. "Killin' makes me hungry."

"Looks like ol' Prophet is gonna get his wish," Tiny speculated. "If we can slip up there real quiet-like, we might catch him settin' at the table with his back turned, and get the job done before the beans get cold." He gave his horse his heels and loped off toward the back of the barn. Elmo was close behind, and once they reached it, they quickly dismounted and tied their horses at the corner of the corral. Then they eased around to the front corner of the barn, guns drawn, and paused there to see if anyone came out the door. "Looks like they're in there to eat supper, all right."

"You know, soon as we shoot him down," Elmo said, "there ain't no reason to shoot the woman right away. I mean, if she's halfway decent-lookin'."

Tiny snickered. "Hell, even if she ain't." Both of the same mind then, they made a dash across the barnyard to the back of the house, where they stopped to listen before attempting to enter. With his .44 cocked and ready, he eased up the back steps and pressed his ear against the door. "I can hear 'em talkin'," he whispered. Elmo took a quick look right and left, then stepped up behind Tiny, who slowly opened the screen door for Elmo to hold while he cautiously turned the kitchen doorknob and eased the door open just far enough to peek inside. What he saw was what he had hoped to see, the man they came to kill, seated at the table, his back to the kitchen door.

The woman was standing beside the table, a large bowl in one hand. She was filling his plate with a large serving spoon. A sly grin slowly crept across Tiny's unshaven face as he whispered to Elmo, "He's settin' there, helpless as a lamb. He ain't even wearin' a gun."

This was enough to excite Elmo. It meant that he was at their mercy. They could even take the opportunity to let him see who it was who was going to kill him. It would make up some for the members of the gang he had cut down. When Tiny asked if he was ready, he nodded, and they burst through the door, their guns leveled at the unsuspecting two.

Naomi screamed, dropping the large serving bowl on the table as she backed away, terrified. Startled by his mother's actions, Sammy tried to get to his feet but stumbled over his chair and landed on his side on the floor. "What the . . ." Elmo started, then said, "You ain't McCabe!" He looked at Tiny and said, "Prophet said McCabe was here." The two outlaws stood with their guns aimed at the two helpless victims for what seemed like a long time before Elmo demanded, "Where's McCabe?" When Sammy started to get to his feet, Elmo pointed his gun directly at his head. "Don't you move."

When Naomi saw the direct threat to her son, she found her voice. "He doesn't know where McCabe is. Now, get out of my house!"

"We just might stay for supper," Tiny sneered, "and maybe a little later, if you behave yourself. Now, we're gonna ask you again, and this time I better hear a better answer. Where is McCabe?"

"I'm right here." The voice came from the kitchen door behind them. Elmo spun around but was not quick enough to avoid a bullet in his chest. Seeing his partner's fate, Tiny did not make the same attempt. Instead, he grabbed Naomi, who was cringing in fear for her life, and aimed his pistol at her.

"All right," Tiny said, "you got the jump on us, but I'm fixin' to blow a hole in this woman's head if you don't drop that gun on the floor."

"If you drop yours, I won't shoot you," Cullen said. "I'll take you into town to jail."

"Ha!" Tiny scoffed. "You ain't in no place to give anybody orders. I said drop it, or this pretty lady gets it in the head." He had no sooner uttered the last word of his threat when Cullen's .44 slug impacted with the side of his head and he crumpled to the floor, his pistol still cocked.

Naomi collapsed to the floor as well, her nervous system shutting down as a result of the brief moments of terror, the second such incident in as many days. Sammy cried out, "Mama!" Thinking she had been shot, he scrambled across the floor to reach her.

"She's all right," Cullen said to him as he carefully took the cocked pistol from Tiny's hand and released the hammer. "She just fainted. Get a cloth and soak it in cool water and put that on her forehead. She'll most likely come around pretty soon." While Sammy hurried to find a cloth, Cullen grabbed Elmo by his boots and dragged him out the back door. Unfortunately, it was not soon enough to prevent Elmo from leaving some blood on Naomi's kitchen floor. Cullen shook his head apologetically and returned to get Tiny. When he had dragged both bodies out of the house, he returned to the kitchen to find Naomi recovering from her faint. "Are you all right, ma'am?"

"I guess I am now," she replied rather weakly. "Who were those men? Why did they want you?"

"I'm sorry they came here but I reckon they had killin' me in mind. I don't know why they thought I'd be here," Cullen said.

"One of 'em said Prophet said you'd be here," Sammy said.

It was by a stroke of good luck that he had been there when he was needed. He had thought it a good idea to keep an eye on Naomi and Sammy for a few days, so he had camped by the river not far from the house. He counted it pure luck that he had decided to take a ride by the house just after dark. And when he saw the two horses tied at the corner of the corral, he had hoped he wasn't too late.

She thought for a second, then looked at her son, who was still holding the wet cloth to her head, and smiled. "Well, all I can say is thank the good Lord you were here." She paused and added, "again."

"Amen to that," Sammy said. "Were they part of that gang that tried to rustle our cattle?"

"I'm pretty sure they are," Cullen answered. "I woulda liked to have taken that one into town to the jail, but he wouldn't listen to reason." He would have liked to see what Sheriff Prophet would have done with Tiny as a prisoner.

"He had that gun to Mama's head," Sammy said, unable to hide some concern for the risky shot Cullen took. "How'd you know you could kill him before he pulled the trigger?"

Cullen understood both their concerns. "Well, I knew if I shot him in the head, his brain would shut down right away. And I noticed his pistol wasn't cocked, so I had time to take the shot." It was not entirely true. He knew Tiny's brain would most likely shut down if his aim was on the mark. Tiny's gun was cocked, but Cullen was sure enough of the shot to take it. He figured there was no point in letting them think he was reckless. Sammy didn't reply but nodded his head slowly, satisfied that Cullen knew what he was doing. "How 'bout givin' me a hand with those two bodies," Cullen said. "I'm gonna load them on their horses and take 'em back to their boss. You can help me heft 'em up, especially that big one."

"Who's their boss?" Sammy asked.

"Don't know for sure," Cullen replied, "but I'm thinkin' it's the sheriff of New Hope."

His comment brought a look of surprise to both their faces. "Sheriff Prophet?" Naomi responded. "Do you mean that?"

"I'm afraid I do," Cullen answered, "and you're the first people I've admitted that to. But I figure you're not gonna be in town in the next couple of days, so I might as well tell you. Everybody's gonna know whether I'm right or wrong in the next few days, if I don't miss my guess."

"He said the sheriff told him you would be here," Sammy reminded them.

"Well, I do declare," Naomi exhaled, finding it hard to believe. She looked at Sammy and shook her head. Then, suddenly recovering from the perilous incident she had just survived, she announced, "Go load those bodies while I get this food ready. It's just getting cold while we stand around here gabbing."

"Thank you just the same, ma'am," Cullen replied. "But I reckon you didn't figure on havin' another mouth to feed for supper. I can find something in town."

"In the first place," she replied, "my name's not ma'am. You can call me Naomi, since Fred and I have decided we can call you Cullen. In the second place,

I fixed enough food for four people, so you might as well help us get rid of some of it. All right?"

"Yes, ma'am," Cullen said, failing to interpret her look of impatience as she rolled her eyes up. "I mean Naomi," he said then, bringing a chuckle from Sammy.

At approximately the same time Cullen sat down to supper with Naomi and Sammy, a meeting of the town council of New Hope was in session at The Texas House. Attending the meeting, and the cause of it, was Sheriff John Prophet. The first and only matter on the agenda was a complaint from the sheriff regarding what he charged was underpayment for his services. Right from the start, there was scant sympathy for the sheriff's insistence on employing two deputies. "Hell," Hiram Polson, the blacksmith, interrupted, "Alton Ford did the job without no deputies and he didn't get as much as we're already payin' you."

"And look what happened to him," Prophet replied. "If you want someone to do the job, you have to pay for a professional like me and the men I need to do the job."

"I don't know about anybody else," Jack Myers spoke up then, "but I'm paying thirty dollars a month for the sheriff's office, and danged if I can see anything I'm getting for it. Most months, that accounts for all the profit I make."

"You ain't been robbed, have you?" Prophet snapped.

"I wasn't robbed when Alton was sheriff," Myers fired back.

"Hell, Jack," Johnny Bledsoe said, "it costs me more'n that for the whiskey the sheriff and his deputies drink up. I don't know about the rest of you, but if we're gonna vote on this, I'm votin' *hell no*."

His statement was followed by a general rumbling of like statements, causing Mayor Robertson to call for order, banging on his table with a claw hammer he was using as a gavel. "Let's try to keep it orderly, gentlemen," Robertson said. "Sheriff, I think we've heard your argument for increased funds and two deputies. You can be excused now and the council will consider your request."

"Consider my request?" Prophet echoed in anger. "How'd you like to see your town without me and my deputy to keep you safe in your beds at night? You might be thinkin' you'd be safer with McCabe in my office, but you'd soon find out you were wrong."

His outburst was met with stony silence. No one but the mayor knew what he was ranting about, and Robertson had hoped that Prophet would not bring his suspicions up before the council. Confused, those in attendance looked around at one another to see if anyone knew what Prophet was talking about. Finally, Burt Whitley asked, "What's he talkin' about, Ernest? Is Cullen McCabe interested in the sheriff's job? He ain't never said anything to me about it."

"No, no," Robertson was quick to reply. "McCabe hasn't ever talked to me about the sheriff's job. I doubt he'll be around much longer, anyway."

His answer to Burt's question brought a thin smile to Prophet's face. "You're probably right about that, Mayor. A man like McCabe might disappear any day now." He stood before the small gathering for a few moments, glancing from face to face, as if memorizing each one. Then he announced that he had work to do to protect all of them while they sat around in the saloon. With that, he stormed out of the room.

Behind him, he left a barroom of astonished citizens and the buzz of quiet discussion. When he was sure the sheriff was out of earshot, Johnny Bledsoe asked, "Is it just me? Or does anybody else suspect we might have us a sheriff that's plum loco?" There were more than a few of the others who agreed with his assessment. The question was soon dumped at Ernest Robertson's feet, also voiced by Bledsoe. "You ain't tellin' us everything, Ernest. What the hell is he talkin' about with McCabe?" Robertson finally told them that Prophet had come to him with a story that McCabe may have said he was just passing through town, but in fact, he was scheming to wrest the sheriff's job from him with plans to run the town. He said that the sheriff was also ranting about McCabe killing two of his deputies.

The meeting turned into a noisy discussion with Burt Whitley, who reminded them that both deputies had forced the fight with McCabe. It continued to go back and forth until Raymond Monroe asked, "What if Prophet ain't really loco? Maybe we mighta all been sucked in by McCabe and his story about lookin' for land for some friends of his."

"Maybe you oughta ask him," Deke Campbell said, standing by one of the front windows. "If you want to, now's your chance. He's ridin' by the saloon right now and he's leadin' two horses with a body lyin' across the saddle on each one of 'em."

There was a rush to the window by several of the men. "Danged if he ain't," Hiram Polson confirmed. "Two bodies, deader'n hell."

"Where's he goin'?" Bledsoe asked.

"Looks to me like he's headed for the sheriff's office," Hiram answered. Then a moment later, "Yep, that's where he's goin'."

The saloon emptied and all, except for Deke, Darlene, Nancy, and Rena, the cook, filed out into the street and headed toward the jail. By the time they got there, Cullen had tied the two horses with bodies on them to the hitching rail in front of the sheriff's office. He reached down and knocked loudly on the floor of the porch, aware seconds later of the mob in the street behind him. The door to the office opened halfway and Slim looked at Cullen standing there, then the gathering of people. He quickly stepped back inside and told Prophet he had a problem. Reading the concern in Slim's message, Prophet stepped out on the porch. "What the hell is this all about?" Prophet demanded, looking at the bodies on the two horses, then at the gathering of spectators.

He was as much surprised by the sudden gathering of spectators as Prophet was, but Cullen nevertheless proceeded with the message he had planned to take to the sheriff. "I'm just returnin' your property to you. I reckon by lookin' at 'em you've probably already figured out they weren't able to do the job you sent 'em to do. I gave 'em the choice of comin' back to town sittin' up in the saddle, but they decided they'd rather come back this way."

"What the hell are you talkin' about?" Prophet demanded. "I never saw those two men in my life."

"How can you be so sure of that before you take a look at 'em?" Cullen countered. "Layin' across the saddle like that, in the dark to boot, it's kinda hard to tell, ain't it?"

"You've got a helluva lot of nerve showin' up here

with two men you murdered and makin' out that I know who they are," Prophet charged, having assumed that Cullen was somehow responsible for the crowd of people that had followed him, a crowd made up mostly of the council members Prophet had just left in the saloon. Turning to the spectators, he said, "You see now what's goin' on? It's like I told the mayor, he's tryin' to take my job, and he don't care who he kills to do it. Ain't no tellin' who these two poor souls are he's killed this time."

"Let me help you there, Prophet," Cullen said. "They're the two men you sent out to Fred Thomas's range to find me, only I found them first. I found 'em in the kitchen with Fred's wife and son at gunpoint. If that doesn't jiggle your memory, maybe you'll remember 'em as the last two saddle tramps in that gang you've been hidin' out." He paused a moment to see how Prophet would respond to a reference to the gang. From the sheriff's twisted face, Cullen guessed he was burning inside with anger, so he gave him another nudge. "By my count, that cuts the number of your gang down to two, you and your deputy. Ain't that about right?"

Close to choking on the hatred he felt for this man who now openly accused him in front of the members of the town council, Prophet could not immediately reply. One glance at his deputy told him he would find little backup there. His natural impulse was to draw his six-gun and shoot McCabe point-blank, but he struggled with his urge to act, desperately trying to maintain his composure. "I see what you're tryin' to imply here," he said after a moment, his voice calm and commanding now. "You've got these folks all up in the air about the recent killin's in town—all of 'em by you, I might add. Then you bring in a couple more bodies with a wild story that they're my men." He paused to shake his head slowly. "Lord knows who these poor devils were and where you found them. But this circus has gone on long enough." He turned to Ernest Robertson. "Mr. Mayor, I suggest you might set up a court and try to find out what McCabe is up to. In the meantime, all you folks get outta the street and get back to your own business, so I can take care of mine."

"That ain't a bad idea, Sheriff," Cullen responded. "I think it's time for a trial. Matter of fact, we could bring Mrs. Thomas and her son in and see if they know where I found these two poor devils."

After the sheriff's apparent sense of confidence, it was difficult for some of the people to determine who was right, McCabe or Prophet. The spectators began to disperse, as the sheriff had ordered, but certain members of the town council gathered around the mayor as they walked back toward the saloon. "We're gonna have to decide something about this mess," Johnny Bledsoe insisted. "We ain't got a judge, but we can set up a court to try to find out which one of those two men are tryin' to take over our town, and my money's on Prophet. I don't know why McCabe is still hangin' around New Hope, but I do know that every man he shot got what he deserved." His comment was quickly seconded by several others.

"I think Johnny's right," Jack Myers said. "We need to do something about it, but what have we got to work with? We don't have any evidence or anything like that. So, how are we supposed to have a trial of any kind?"

"We could bring Mrs. Thomas and her son in, like McCabe said," Burt Whitley suggested. "That would tell us if McCabe was tellin' the truth about shootin' those two men." His suggestion was met with general agreement and the discussion continued. By the time they had returned to The Texas House, it was decided that they would have their trial and Prophet and McCabe would be notified to attend it, two days hence.

When Burt returned to the stable, he found that Cullen had put his horse in an empty stall. "I wasn't sure you'd be back here tonight or not," Burt said.

"I wasn't sure, myself," Cullen said. "But I ran into those two jaspers, so I brought 'em back to town. So, if it's all right with you, I'll sleep here tonight."

"Sure, it's all right with me. You oughta be in town, anyway. We've decided to have that trial somebody suggested and you'll likely wanna be here for that, right?"

"You say that like you think I might decide it's a better idea to leave town," Cullen said.

"I wouldn'ta been surprised." Burt shrugged. "I mean, with all the talk about the gunfights you've gotten into, wouldn't have surprised me a-tall if you decided it weren't worth foolin' with."

"No, I'll stick around. I think New Hope's worth foolin' with."

"Well, then," Burt announced, "consider yourself notified that the council requires your presence at a public meeting in The Texas House day after tomorrow at ten o'clock in the mornin'." He punctuated it with a firm nod of his head. "I wasn't supposed to tell you until tomorrow. Hiram Polson's supposed to officially notify the sheriff. And like you said, Ernest is sendin' somebody out to notify Mrs. Thomas and her son."

"That's a good idea," Cullen said. "Naomi Thomas said those two men held a gun on her and asked her where I was. There ain't no doubt they were lookin' for me." As soon as he said it, he realized the danger involved. "You're not supposed to notify me till to-morrow?"

"Well, that's what Ernest said to do."

"In that case, I'll be leavin' here early in the mornin'." When Burt asked if he was skipping town after all, Cullen said, "No, I'll be at the Thomas ranch when she's notified."

CHAPTER 15

He was already up and had Jake saddled when Burt opened up in the morning. He sensed that Burt was a little bit skeptical about his urgency to leave town before breakfast, so he tried to assure him that he would be at the Thomas ranch, as he had told him the night before. "And I'll sure be at the hearing tomorrow mornin'. I'll leave my packhorse here. I'll just take my bedroll and some coffee and bacon in my war bag. That'll take care of me for one night."

"I'll see you tomorrow," Burt said as Cullen stepped up in the saddle and rode off toward the south end of town. He stood there watching him until he disappeared around a patch of trees in a curve of the road. He hoped like hell he wasn't wrong about the big man who had seemed to turn up every troublemaker in town during the short time he had been there. Cullen McCabe had impressed him as the kind of friend a man could count on. He hoped he hadn't read him wrong. "I reckon we'll find the answer to that tomorrow if he don't show up for the meetin'," he muttered. Then he remembered the packhorse in the corral. "He'll be back."

* * *

Sammy Thomas stood at the corner of the pigpen down below the barn, holding a bucket that he had just emptied into the trough. He was watching the litter of baby pigs attacking their mother when he glanced up to see a rider approaching from the river road. The rider didn't have to get very close before he was recognized, so Sammy walked toward the house to meet him. "Mornin', Cullen," he greeted him. "I didn't know you were gonna be comin' out here this mornin'."

"Mornin', Sammy," Cullen returned the greeting. "I didn't know I was, myself, till last night. I just thought I'd ride out and let you and your ma know you'll be gettin' some company from town sometime today."

"Who's comin'?" Sammy asked, and Cullen told him that it would be someone to tell them about a meeting of the town council. "You just missed breakfast," Sammy informed him. "Ma's gonna be mad at you for not gettin' here in time for breakfast."

"No matter," Cullen said. "I brought a little something to eat with me. I didn't wanna surprise her again right at mealtime." He stepped down and put Jake in the corral. "I'll leave his saddle on him. I'll be doin' a little ridin' after I talk to your mama. Let's go see her."

Cullen hung back a little to let Sammy go in first, in case Naomi was not dressed to receive guests. He waited on the kitchen steps while Sammy sang out, "Ma, Cullen's here."

"Where?" he heard Naomi respond. And when Sammy told her he was on the back steps, she asked, "Well, why doesn't he come on in?"

Hearing that, Cullen tapped on the door and walked in. "Mornin', Naomi," he said, this time removing his hat when he entered. "Sorry to drop in on you so early, but I wanted to talk to you about something."

Pretending to be irritated, Naomi stood with hands on hips and scolded, "Why are you showing up here this late? You should have been here when breakfast was ready."

"I told you," Sammy said with a wide grin on his face.

"I wasn't figurin' on breakfast," Cullen said. "I didn't wanna put you out any. I just wanted to tell you about somebody comin' out here today."

"Well, sit yourself down at the table and you can tell me while I rustle you up something to eat." She hesitated and asked, "You haven't eaten, have you?" When he shrugged his shoulders, but didn't answer, she said, "I didn't think so." She laid several strips of bacon in the pan, turned to take a look at him, then laid a couple more strips in the pan. She picked up a basket of eggs and asked, "How do you want 'em?"

"I'll eat 'em any way you fix 'em, but I'm partial to scrambled."

"Then I'll scramble 'em," she said. "Now, what is it you came to tell me?"

He told them about the confrontation with Sheriff Prophet the night before, when he returned with the two bodies, and the hearing scheduled for ten o'clock the next morning. She and Sammy sat with him at the table, drinking coffee, while he told them why the mayor and the town council wanted to know whom they could believe. "So, I wanted to let you know somebody will be out here today, to inform you that they want you to be at that meetin'. And if you don't mind, I'll hang around to make sure everything's all right."

"Well, I'll gladly tell them about those two killers who broke into my kitchen last night," she said at once, "threatening me and my son." She looked Cullen straight in the eye. "And after what you've told me about Sheriff Prophet, I know why you're really out here—and I appreciate it. You're a good man, Cullen McCabe."

"Most likely nothin' to worry about," Cullen said, "but there's no use to take a chance." When the coffee was finished, he got up from the table. "Thank you for the breakfast. I'll be around and I'll try to keep outta your way." He walked to the door and waited for Sammy to follow. When he did, they walked to the barn, talking. "I wanted to talk to you alone, Sammy. I want you to keep your eyes open today and make sure you know where your ma is all the time. All right?"

Sammy nodded vigorously. "You think that sheriff might send somebody to shut us up?"

"I don't know," Cullen answered frankly, "but I don't see any reason not to be ready just in case he does. You keep your rifle handy. I'm gonna be scoutin' in a close circle around the place, but I'll be checkin' on you folks right regular. All right? I've seen you in action, so I know you can hold up your end of it, and I'll see you in a little bit."

"You can count on me," Sammy said confidently.

"I know I can," Cullen said as he wheeled Jake away from the corral and started out of the barnyard at a lope. Sammy went straight to the house to get his rifle and make sure it was loaded.

Cullen did not know for sure just what resources Prophet had left to use. He felt certain, however, that he had accounted for all the gang that had been hiding out up at the outlaw camp. And if he had figured right, the death of the two men he had killed the night before left Prophet with only one man to do his dirty work. And that was his deputy. Prophet was unlikely to do the job himself, so if he was planning to silence Naomi and Sammy, Cullen expected he was on the lookout for one man, Deputy Slim Bradshaw. He even considered the possibility that Slim might be the messenger sent to deliver the summons to Naomi and Sammy. If that was the case, he would have to be damn sure he accompanied them back to town. These were the thoughts that occupied his mind as he guided Jake across the separate approaches to Fred's ranch, never straying far from the wagon road that led to New Hope.

It was midmorning when he spotted a rider on the road from town. He pulled Jake to a stop on top of a low rise a few yards off the road and waited. As the rider approached, Cullen was glad to recognize James Levitt, the hotel desk clerk. He waited until Levitt was within thirty yards of him before riding out of the trees to meet him on the road. His sudden appearance was enough to make Levitt rein his horse to a sliding stop. "Mr. McCabe!" he blurted, looking somewhat uncertain.

It occurred to Cullen then of the possibility that

Levitt wasn't sure which side of the law he stood on, so he made a quick effort to set him at ease. "Mr. Levitt," he called out in a friendly tone, he hoped. "I reckon you're on your way to the Thomas ranch. I'll ride along with you."

"Mayor Robertson sent me to deliver a message to Mrs. Thomas," James quickly informed Cullen. "The whole council knows I'm taking the summons to her."

It was obvious that Levitt wanted him to consider that, in case he had interfering in mind. So, Cullen said, "Couldn'ta picked a better man for the job. It's good they sent somebody who could explain to Mrs. Thomas the importance of havin' her show up tomorrow."

"Well, I suppose that's right," Levitt allowed, relieved that Cullen showed no aggressive tendencies.

"I'll go with you to make sure nobody stops you from doin' your appointed duty," Cullen assured him, wheeling Jake in beside him, and they proceeded along the road to the ranch. When they came within sight of the house and barn, Cullen was pleased to see Sammy walk out of the barn, his rifle in hand. As soon as he recognized Cullen, he waved, and Cullen returned the signal. Sammy went to the house then to inform his mother that the messenger Cullen had told them about had arrived.

When Cullen and Levitt rode up to the front of the house, Naomi stepped out onto the porch and waited for Cullen to speak. "This is James Levitt, Naomi, he's come to give you a message from the mayor of New Hope."

Levitt hesitated, in case Cullen would say more. When he didn't, Levitt stated, "Yes, ma'am, Mrs.

Thomas, Mayor Ernest Robertson and the members
of the town council respectfully ask for your attendance at a town meeting tomorrow morning at The
Texas House at ten o'clock a.m."

"The Texas House?" Naomi responded. "You're
holding this important meeting in the saloon?"

"Yes, ma'am," Levitt replied, then quickly added,
"There won't be any alcoholic beverages sold until
after the hearing is finished. Mayor Robertson wanted
to hold it in the church, but some of the council said
there was more room in the saloon." Cullen could
well imagine Johnny Bledsoe active in that decision.

It was obvious that young Mr. Levitt was fearful that
the choice of meeting places had somehow offended
the lady, so Naomi set him at ease. "You tell the mayor
that I'll be there at ten o'clock tomorrow."

"Yes, ma'am, I surely will," Levitt replied. "I'll get
back to tell him right away."

"And in case anybody wants to know," Cullen said,
"I'll escort Mrs. Thomas into town." When Levitt got
on his horse and headed back toward the road,
Cullen said to Naomi, "Won't take us an hour to ride
to town unless you wanna take the wagon." She told
him that she had rather ride her horse, so he said he
would have it saddled and waiting for her at about
nine. That settled, he climbed back on his horse and
rode toward the low ridge to the east of the ranch
house. "You be back here at noon," she called after
him. He acknowledged with a wave of his hand,
knowing that meant he was going to get a good
dinner. The rest of that day was spent in a rather
casual surveillance of the ranch in close to the house.
If there was to be any attempt to silence Naomi, he

didn't expect it to occur in broad daylight. Prophet would wait till after dark, not wanting to risk having his deputy seen by anyone.

Slim Bradshaw opened the door of the sheriff's office and announced, "The blacksmith wants to see you, Boss."

"What about?" Prophet asked, and when Slim replied that he didn't say, Prophet said, "Well, tell him to come on in."

Hiram Polson stuck his head in the door, not really wanting to go inside to talk to the sheriff. "I'm supposed to officially tell you the town council is havin' a meetin' tomorrow mornin' at ten o'clock at the saloon and we think it's important for you to be there."

"Is that right?" Prophet responded sarcastically. "You're officially tellin' me, huh? Is McCabe gonna be there, too?"

"I don't know if he is or not," Hiram answered. "All I'm supposed to do is tell you about it. Are you gonna be there?"

"Oh yeah, I'll be there, all right," Prophet said.

"Good, I'll tell 'em," Hiram said, and closed the door.

Listening to the exchange on the porch, Slim couldn't help thinking it a bad idea. From what he had heard after the first meeting with the council, he was concerned that Prophet might lose control of his temper altogether if this meeting was anything like the first one. When Hiram walked off the porch, Slim went inside the office. "Whaddaya think, Boss? You gonna go to their meetin'?"

"You heard me say I was, didn't you?" Prophet

replied. "And if it don't go the way I want it to, I just might decide to put the fear of God into those big-shot storekeepers. I've been holdin' back, but I reckon it's time I let 'em know who's gonna run this town."

This was not what Slim wanted to hear at this particular time, when their strength had been reduced to just the two of them. In his opinion, it would be best to appear as cooperative with the town council as possible, because Prophet might be right about McCabe. He might be out to replace him as sheriff. And if Prophet raised too much hell about him, the council might decide he was too much of a hothead to run the sheriff's office. Slim was reluctant to broach the subject when Prophet was as wound up as he was about it, but he thought to give it a try. "You think this might be a good time to draw back a little bit and let the mayor think we're ready to do what the council thinks best?"

"Draw back?" Prophet erupted, his dark eyebrows almost touching as he screwed his face in response. "What the hell kinda talk is that? Don't tell me you've gone petticoat on me, too. Hell, no! Now's the time to clamp down on 'em hard. Let 'em know who's boss."

"You know there ain't but the two of us, don'tcha?"

Prophet didn't answer right away. Instead, he glared at Slim for a long moment. "You ain't goin' soft on me, are you? 'Cause if you are, I need to know right now."

"No, sir, Boss," Slim immediately responded. "You know better'n that. I was just wonderin' if we oughta try to shine up to these folks a little, so they don't start gettin' ideas that we're gonna ride 'em till they're dry, then leave after it's too late to stop us. Least, that's what I thought your plan was when we hit this town."

"Plans change," Prophet said. "We hadn't counted on McCabe when we first hit town."

Thinking it no use to try to talk him out of whatever he was planning to do, Slim caved in. "You're the boss," he said. "Whaddaya figure on doin'?"

"I'm thinkin' it ain't gonna do us any good for that Thomas woman to shoot her mouth off about Elmo and Tiny coming to her house, lookin' for McCabe." He paused to shake his head and grumble, "Those two morons. If they hadda shot the woman, we wouldn't have to worry about her tellin' the council about it."

"Yeah, but don't nobody know Tiny and Elmo was members of our gang. All she can say is they come lookin' for McCabe." He was still hoping to get Prophet's mind off his determination to silence everyone. "How can anybody prove we knew them at all?"

"We don't know what those two fools mighta said to that woman and her son," Prophet insisted. "The only way we can be sure they didn't tie us in to it is to shut her and her son up." Slim knew then what was coming next, and he was reluctant to go along with it. "After dark," Prophet said, "you need to ride out to that ranch and pay a little visit to 'em. 'Cause I know they told her to come to the meetin', too."

"What about McCabe?" Slim asked.

"What about him?" Prophet came back. When Slim just shrugged, reluctant to say what he feared, Prophet said, "If he shows up, shoot him, and that would take care of a lot of things."

"If that's what you want, I reckon I can ride outta town tonight without anybody noticin' and see if I can get a shot at 'em," he said, although he knew he was not sure he was going to try very hard. He didn't feel exactly right about the wanton killing of a woman and a young boy, in spite of all the other bad things he had done in his life. As far as Cullen McCabe was concerned, he had developed a cautious fear about a man who had methodically gunned down every hardened gunman who had come up against him. The man even looked invincible. Slim decided he was not going to find out.

Prophet studied his deputy intensely for a moment, as if evaluating the truthfulness in his agreement to do his bidding. "I'd rather do the job on McCabe, myself," he said, "and the gal and her puppy, too. But folks would notice if I was outta town tonight." He paused again, still watching Slim closely. "I know I can count on you. You won't let me down. And if we get McCabe outta the way, things are gonna be a whole lot easier for us."

"That's right, Boss, I ain't never let you down."

Burt Whitley came back from supper to find Deputy Slim Bradshaw in the stable, his horse saddled and a packsaddle on one of the other horses that belonged to the sheriff's department. "Can I help you with somethin', Deputy?" Burt said, accustomed to the sheriff and his deputy leaving saddling for him to do.

"Nope," Slim answered. "I reckon not."

Burt realized Slim was loading the packhorse as if preparing to be gone for some time. "You fixin' to head out?" Burt asked, thinking it pretty late in the day to start on a long trip.

"Not till in the mornin'. I'm gonna head out before sunup," Slim said. "So, I'm gonna go ahead and take my horses tonight. I'll be startin' out before you open up in the mornin'."

Burt shrugged, not really interested in what the deputy was planning to do. He went into the tack room to work on a harness he had intended to mend that he had promised the postmaster in the morning. It didn't take him very long, but when he came out, Slim was gone. "Glad he didn't hang around here," he mumbled, and started closing up for the night. When he had closed the padlock on the stable door, he decided he'd like a little drink before he went home to bed. There was no little woman waiting for him, Burt being a widower, so he didn't have to answer to anyone. When he walked by the sheriff's office, he glanced over that way. It registered with him that he didn't see Slim's two horses tied out behind the jail, but he didn't care enough to give it more thought.

When he walked into the saloon, there were a few of the regulars sitting around, and fairly conspicuous at a table near the bar, sat Sheriff John Prophet. It was unusual to see the sheriff lingering in The Texas House. He usually sent his deputy to fetch a bottle of Deke's best whiskey to drink in his hotel room. Burt sidled up to the bar at the far end from Prophet's table. When Deke walked over to serve him, Burt softly commented. "I see you've got a real highfalutin guest in your establishment tonight."

"Yeah, ain't that somethin'," Deke replied, just as softly. "I can't say that it's been too good for business. He's been settin' there for the most part of an hour."

Almost as if he had heard the conversation between Deke and Burt, Prophet got up from the table and announced to no one in particular, "I reckon I've set around this saloon long enough." He made it a point to walk by the bar and place his empty glass on it. "I'll be at the hotel if anybody needs me," he said to Deke, then walked out the door.

"What the hell was that all about?" Deke wondered aloud. "He don't ever come in here and just sit around like that. He only had a couple of drinks the whole time he was here."

"Don't ask me," Burt said. "I can't say I'm sorry he left, though."

Prophet walked across the street to the jail to make sure he had locked the door, before heading back up the street to the hotel. Ordinarily, Slim would be in the office all night, but since he had sent Slim on a special mission that night, he locked the door. He had made his unusual visit to the saloon to make sure there were plenty of witnesses to the fact that he was in town this evening. He intended to make sure someone at the hotel saw him when he went up to his room. He trusted Slim to get the job done that Elmo and Tiny had failed to do. He had never thought those two had one brain between them, anyway. Slim had left the jail right after dark to get his horse from the stable before Burt Whitley locked up. He expected him back in town before sunup in the morning. *And plenty of the good citizens will know for sure that I never left town tonight*, he thought, *even if somebody sees Slim.* He had considered the possibility that Slim might not succeed in killing the Thomas woman and her son, and get a shot at McCabe, too. As long as McCabe didn't see him kill the woman and boy, he was in the clear. McCabe could say he sent Slim to kill them, but he couldn't prove it without witnesses. Even if there were witnesses, no one could prove that he had sent Slim to do the killing. He would simply fire him, just as he had supposedly fired Merle Blake. He didn't care for the idea of being cut down to himself alone, but he was confident that Slim could handle the job. As soon as McCabe was eliminated, he would build his gang again, back to the strength it was before his path crossed McCabe's. He pulled his pocket watch out of his vest pocket and took a look at it. *He's had plenty of time to get down there,* he thought. With a little luck, maybe Slim might already have finished the job. The thought brought a wicked smile to his face as he walked into the hotel. "Evenin', Levitt," he said when he found James still at the front desk. Astonished by the almost cheerful greeting, the young man responded with one of his own. He couldn't remember the sheriff ever having offered a polite greeting before.

Prophet announced that he was going upstairs to bed, confident that his plan was most likely in full operation. And morning would bring the news that neither the Thomas woman nor one Cullen McCabe showed up for the town's special meeting. So he went to sleep looking forward to the meeting. This was without the knowledge that his deputy, at that moment, followed the Brazos, as it approached its confluence with Paint Creek, some sixteen miles north of New Hope. He was not a brilliant man, but Slim Bradshaw had seen enough signs of a man losing his mind to decide he was not going to be the final sacrifice. Slim had been satisfied with his lot, riding for Prophet, but they should have stuck to their business of rustling cattle and robbing stagecoaches. When Prophet first got this notion of capturing a whole town was when Slim knew that he should have left. When he had seen time and again Prophet's casual willingness to send his men to do his dirty work, he should have known that sooner or later his turn would come. Still not brave enough to tell Prophet he could not shoot down a woman and her son, nor face up to Cullen McCabe, his only option was to run. So, better late than to end up like the rest of the boys, he was heading toward Indian Territory. He figured to reach Gus Welker's trading post on the Wichita River by late afternoon the following day. Gus was a longtime friend of any number of outlaws and Slim could stay there till he decided what he was going to do.

While Slim was heading north, Cullen was unrolling his bedroll on the front porch of Fred Thomas's house. Both he and Sammy had kept a sharp eye on the Thomas house and barn and all the outbuildings, including the pigpen. There had been no sign of anyone for all that day and well after supper that evening. Still, Cullen did not trust Prophet to miss an opportunity to silence any negative testimony to the foiled attack by the two men at the ranch. So, he decided to sleep on the front porch, expecting Slim to show up sometime during the night, or in the early hours of the morning.

CHAPTER 16

Cullen awoke to the crowing of Fred Thomas's rooster, right at the break of dawn. His first impulse was a mild panic, knowing he had been asleep, and he quickly threw his blanket aside and reached for his rifle. Hearing no sounds other than the rooster, he pulled on his boots and walked around the house, looking for anything out of the ordinary. He rounded the corner of the house by the kitchen just as the back door opened and Sammy walked out, carrying a bucket. "Mornin'," Sammy said when he saw Cullen. "I gotta go milk the cow. I started the fire up again in the stove. Ma will be up in a few minutes and start fixin' breakfast."

"Right," Cullen responded. "I'm lookin' forward to it." He stood there a few moments after Sammy went to the barn, just looking around him. He found it hard to believe they had gotten through the night with no visitor. He had been certain that Prophet would send his deputy to do the job. "Well, I was wrong," he said to himself. "If it's gonna happen, it'll be on the way into town." With that thought in mind, he knew he would be scouting the road to town on both sides all the way into New Hope, looking for any sign of a sniper. Before he did that, however, he saddled his horse and rode a wide circle around the low line of hills east of the house, then tracked along the bank of the river west of the house. He was looking for any sign of a rider who might be inclined to set up with a long-range rifle. He found nothing, and the fact that he didn't served only to worry him more. When he heard Naomi banging on an iron triangle that served for a dinner bell, he gave up and rode back to the house.

Naomi was not at all fearful about riding into town to be questioned by Ernest Robertson and the others, but she was concerned about leaving the ranch with no one there. She would have liked to have left Sammy there to watch over things, but James Levitt had been specific in saying that Sammy was a witness, too. There was no question about Cullen's part, which he had taken on himself. He was to protect them on the trip into town, but to ease Naomi's concerns, he agreed to escort them in and then return to the ranch right away. The thinking was that the danger to them was on their way to the meeting, and not on their way back home. "It's just not a good time to leave the ranch with nobody here," Naomi explained. "We've been seeing a lot of coyotes lately. Sammy killed one the other day nosing around the pigpen, and that old sow just had those pigs."

"If you don't watch 'em," Sammy said, referring to the coyotes, "a bunch of 'em could bring the cow down."

Cullen understood their concern. "I'm bound to see you safely to that meetin'," he said, "but I'll ride back here as fast as I can, so the coyotes and anything else, won't have much time to do any harm." The ranch was less than five miles from town, and he thought it a pretty safe gamble. "They don't need me at their meetin', anyway. I've already said my peace, they know where I stand." That was the final decision.

The party of three arrived at The Texas House with a half hour to spare and with no trouble during the trip. "I sure didn't read this one right," Cullen told Naomi. "And I'm glad I didn't. I'll head on back just as soon as I tell the mayor what I'm doin'."

"I sure will feel a whole lot better if I know you're watching the place," Naomi said. "I'm sorry we have to take up your time to look after us."

"No trouble a-tall," Cullen assured her, then went to tell the mayor he was going to be absent from the discussion.

Robertson was not at all happy about it but understood why Cullen felt he should help the lady. "I guess Fred would appreciate it in his absence. I suppose there's no real reason for you to be here. We already know what you said and did, and you say Mrs. Thomas is willing to tell us what went on at her house."

"'Preciate it, Mayor," Cullen said, then added, "I'm not a member of the community, anyway. Some of your council might say it ain't none of my business." Having said that, he knew that it was very much his business. He was convinced that Prophet had been the leader of the expired Viper Gang and had his sights on holding New Hope hostage when he rebuilt his gang of outlaws. It was his hope that the council would now see the man for what he was and fire him from the sheriff's office. With no one left but his one deputy, the town could stand up to Prophet and rid themselves of Robertson's bad mistake.

With a nod of encouragement to Naomi and Sammy, Cullen walked out of the saloon and almost collided with the sheriff, who was just coming to the meeting. Having not seen Cullen or Naomi in town until that moment, he was taken aback. The confident smile he had worn was replaced by a look of shocked disbelief, as if looking at a dead man. A glance through the doorway revealed a very much alive Naomi Thomas, her son standing beside her. He could not speak for a moment as his brain was trying to right itself. Slim was dead, or had failed him and had not had the courage to return to tell him, instead letting him walk into this trap. Cullen stepped aside and said, "Come right on in, Sheriff, the council's waitin' for you."

Still too shocked to speak, Prophet answered with only an angry glare, as he turned to watch Cullen climb on his horse and wheel away from the hitching rail. Thinking now about turning around and returning to the jail, he heard Mayor Robertson at his elbow. "Come on inside, Sheriff, we're ready to get started."

Still, Prophet hesitated, then his confidence returned, and he was determined to face the council members down. This was still his town for the taking, and there was no man among the tradesmen and shopkeepers who would dare stand up to him. "All right, Mayor," he said, "let's go in and hear what pitiful bit of nonsense your council has to say." He pushed by Robertson and strode up to the first row of chairs that had been placed in front of the bar and sat down in the end chair. Then he turned to glare at Naomi and Sammy, who were sitting in two chairs at the other end of the front row. Members of the council were seated in some chairs placed at one end of the bar, and Robertson took his place on a stool behind the bar.

When he was seated, he called the meeting to order and announced the first order of business. "On the requests by the sheriff to replace his second deputy and increase the sheriff's and his deputies' salaries, the council has voted on it and the decision is to deny both requests." It took a minute for that to sink in with the sheriff. The council had decided they no longer wanted the services of John Prophet as their sheriff. And they had hoped, when he was denied both requests, he would simply resign, pack up his things, and leave town.

Prophet was not so inclined. Speaking forcefully through clenched teeth, he rejected the council's decision. "I'll have what I want, or I'll burn this damn town down," he threatened. His statement was met with only a startled gasp or two in an otherwise totally silent saloon. "You don't believe me? You just try me." He swept the small gathering with his defiant glare.

Forced to use a courage he did not possess, the mayor banged the counter with his hammer and declared, "I'm afraid the council has decided to terminate your contract with the town, effective as of twelve noon today."

On his feet now, Prophet sneered when he said, "I suppose you're thinkin' about givin' my job to that yellow back-shooter, Cullen McCabe."

"No, sir, we are not," Robertson replied. "Mr. McCabe has not applied for the job."

"Yeah?" Prophet barked. "Well, he will. He's a low-down murderin' devil! And he's gonna have to go through me to get this job."

"You're the lyin' one," Sammy Thomas declared. "You sent those two men out to our house to kill us. They said you did!" He turned to the mayor and said, "I can tell you everything that happened."

"Why, you lyin' little snot," Prophet snarled. Unable to control his rage, he drew his pistol and shot the boy. Sammy dropped to the floor as his mother screamed and went to his side. The room was turned into a tornado as everybody dived for cover, turning over tables and knocking over chairs. Hiram Polson drew his six-gun but was shot in the chest before he could raise it to fire. Completely out of control of his temper now, Prophet looked right and left for the next brave soul who dared to challenge him. His gaze paused on Johnny Bledsoe, whose contempt for him was well known by Prophet. Bledsoe was not armed, but Prophet sent a bullet his way that knocked Johnny off his feet. When Jack Myers ran for the door, Prophet stopped him with a shot that caught Jack in the side. Prophet turned around, looking for the mayor then, but Robertson had dropped to the floor and crawled under the counter. With only two rounds left in the six-shooter, Prophet started backing slowly toward the door. "Who's next?" he taunted as he continued backing until reaching the door. Once he was outside, he walked rapidly toward the jail, leaving the saloon in chaos behind him.

His initial thought was to barricade himself in the sheriff's office and shoot down anybody who dared approach him. As he walked up the street, reloading his .44, however, a smidgen of his common sense surfaced in his brain, telling him he could hold out against an attack for only so long. His only option was to run. That notion was seemingly confirmed when he reached the jail to find the door still padlocked and no sign of Slim. It served to make him realize his departure was urgent, so he went inside and grabbed what he needed, then turned and walked down the street to the stable.

The scene back at The Texas House was still one of utter chaos, as those who escaped injury tried to administer to the victims of Prophet's six-gun. Naomi Thomas sat on the floor, holding Sammy in her arms while Darlene attempted to stop the bleeding from the gunshot wound in the boy's shoulder. Darlene's friend Nancy and Rena, the cook, were working feverishly to save Johnny Bledsoe, who was fighting desperately to hang on. Prophet's bullet had struck Bledsoe in his chest but did not appear to have damaged any major organs. That was not the case for Hiram Polson, who was stone dead. Ernest Robertson and Raymond Monroe were working together to bandage Jack Myers, where the bullet had passed through his side, leaving an entry and an exit wound. Dr. Paul Worley, having just arrived, after being summoned by Deke Campbell, was quickly moving from patient to patient. In the aftermath of the shooting, no one gave any thought toward going after Prophet until the victims had all been tended to. It was then that someone finally asked the question, "What are we gonna do about Sheriff Prophet?"

There was no immediate response, as no one appeared anxious to confront the obviously deranged sheriff. Finally, Burt Whitley made the statement no one wanted to hear. "We're gonna have to strap on our guns and go after him. There ain't nobody to protect us but ourselves."

All were thinking the same thought, but it was

Monroe who expressed it. "Where is that fellow, McCabe, when we need him?"

"That's my fault," Naomi confessed. "He woulda been here if I hadn't asked him to watch after the ranch while we were in here for this meeting." It entered her mind, but she refrained from adding that it was because she was worried about a litter of pigs.

"Well, there ain't nothin' we can do about that now," Burt said. "And as crazy as Prophet went, he might not be through with his killin'. I wish to hell I'da strapped on my gun."

"Maybe he's just gonna hole up in the jail," Deke commented. He was standing by the window, looking diagonally up the street toward the jail. Had he been at the window a couple of minutes after Prophet's exit, he might have seen him on his way to the stable.

"Right now, I'm more concerned about us protecting ourselves than going after that madman," Robertson declared. "All we've got is poor Hiram's pistol. Nobody else is armed, are they?" If Prophet was watching the street, it would be dangerous for anyone to leave the saloon to go after a gun.

"I've got a scattergun under the bar," Deke sang out. No one else answered.

"If someone can go out the back door and run to the store, I've got a shotgun there," Jack Myers volunteered, straining against the pain when he talked. "You have to be careful, though. Mildred surely heard the shots and she might shoot you when you go in the back door."

"Well, I'm gonna see if I can get back to the stable without him seein' me," Burt decided. "The rest of you stay here and watch the front door, in case he decides to come back. You've got a pistol and a shotgun.

Use 'em if he walks in the door." He went out the back door while the others crowded behind the bar for protection, with Deke acting as lookout at the front window.

Burt paused for only a moment to make sure Prophet wasn't behind the building before he hurried down to come up behind his stable. It was on his mind also that Prophet might be in the stable, if he decided to leave town, and he was anxious to avoid that. Back of his barn, he paused at the corner of the corral and watched the stable for any signs of anyone. When there were none, he moved up next to the back door, which was only halfway open, and stopped to listen. There was nothing that would make him think there was anyone there, so he peeked around the door. There was no one, so he went inside and hurried to the tack room, where he found his pistol and rifle. He took them both. Armed now, he took another look outside the tack room door before walking out between the stalls. Prophet was not there. He went then to the back stalls and discovered Prophet's gray gelding was missing. Two of the other horses were gone as well. *He's gonna run!* At least, things pointed that way, and that was good news to Burt. But had he left town yet? To try to answer that question, he ran to the front door of the stable and looked up the street toward the sheriff's office. The horses were not there, so he felt confident in walking up to the jail to be sure.

With his gun belt strapped around his waist and his rifle held ready to fire, he walked directly toward the sheriff's office. When he got there, he noticed the padlock hanging unlocked on the door. Certain that Prophet had fled, but still fearful enough to be cautious, he pushed the door open with the muzzle of his rifle. The office was empty. He walked in, seeing ample evidence of Prophet's hasty departure. The gun rack on the wall was empty of weapons and the drawer where ammunition was usually kept was pulled open and empty. Burt had seen all he needed to see.

"Damn!" Deke swore in surprise, still standing by the window. "He's comin' outta the sheriff's office!"

"Prophet?" Monroe responded.

"No, Burt," Deke answered. "He's walkin' up the middle of the street. Prophet musta lit out." He walked over to the door and opened it, while everybody came out from behind the bar, anxious to hear Burt's report.

When it was certain that Prophet was no longer in town, the business of recovery from the young town's worst confrontation with outlaw trouble began. Doc Worley insisted that Johnny Bledsoe had to be transported to his office for surgery to try to remove the bullet lodged in his chest. Myers's and young Sammy Thomas's wounds were pronounced non-life-threatening, so Naomi started immediately for home, with Sammy wearing a sling for his wounded shoulder, but able to ride. After offering his deepest regrets for having put her and her son through such a traumatic experience, Mayor Robertson stood on the front steps of the saloon, watching Naomi and Sammy ride off toward the south river road. Coming to stand beside him, Raymond Monroe asked the question the mayor was hesitant to think about. "What the hell are we gonna do now, Ernest?"

"I don't know," the mayor answered him. "But I promise you this, I'll not hire another sheriff without getting the council's approval first."

* * *

It was afternoon when Cullen came from the barn and saw Naomi and Sammy coming up the path that led from the river road. Relieved to see them at first, he became concerned when he realized that Sammy had his arm in a sling. He walked up to the house to meet them, so he could take their horses to the barn. "What happened?" he asked when they were still several yards away.

"We needed you," Sammy answered before his mother could speak.

"It was a total catastrophe," Naomi said then. And she went on to tell of the disastrous town meeting that turned into a shooting spree by a madman. "He is absolutely insane," she declared. "You told us he was a dangerous man, but I never dreamed he could just start shooting people right and left." She paused to shake her head slowly. "Poor Hiram Polson, it was unlucky that he was wearing a gun. If he hadn't been, he might not be dead now. Dr. Worley said Johnny Bledsoe was in critical condition, but he's got a chance of making it." She shook her head again. "I'll tell you this, though, he didn't look too good when they carried him out."

Her news was doubly distressing to Cullen. There was no doubt in his mind as to what his duty was now. His job was to track Prophet down, if at all possible, and the sooner he got on his trail, the better. And it was a trail that was rapidly getting cold, since he was already too far behind. A conflicting thought presented itself to worry him, and that was Naomi's and Sammy's welfare. Was it safe to leave them alone? Not only tonight, but for the nights that followed. After hearing their accounting of John Prophet's mental breakdown, he could not be sure what the madman might do for revenge. It might be two months before Fred returned from that cattle drive. He would suggest that they go into town and stay in the hotel until Fred came home, but he knew Naomi would refuse to leave their home for that long. They couldn't, anyway, with livestock to take care of.

Almost as if she knew what was troubling him, she said, "You need to get on your horse and get into town right now. I don't know why, but I know you feel some reason to go after John Prophet. I guess just because he's evil. I know you're thinking you can't leave Sammy and me here alone, but you're wrong. We're used to just the two of us when Fred has to be away. What do you think we did before you came along? This time, I promise you, we'll be more vigilant. And now, our cattle are on the way to market, and there's nobody left from that gang of outlaws we worried about to rustle our cattle. So please, go do whatever your conscience drives you to do. Sammy and I can take care of ourselves."

"Don't worry, Cullen," Sammy assured him, "I can take care of Ma and me."

"I know you can," Cullen said. "You take care of that shoulder." He turned back to Naomi and said, "I'm sorry, Naomi, but I have to go after that man. He's responsible for killin' a lot of people, and not just today."

"I understand," she said. "You take care of yourself. Be careful if you catch up with him. He's pure evil." He nodded to reassure her and turned to go to the barn to saddle Jake. "And Cullen," she said, "thank you."

* * *

He rode into a town that was still recoiling from the unexpected shock that killed one of their people, left another clinging to life, and two others wounded. When he dismounted in front of the saloon, Burt Whitley and Deke Campbell came out the door to escort him in, both talking at the same time to tell him what happened. "You sure he's gone?" Cullen asked. Burt assured him that Prophet had taken his horse and two packhorses and had left town. "Don't suppose anybody saw which way he was headin'."

"Nobody said they did," Campbell answered. "Nobody wanted to stick their nose outta here to try to see what he was doing." He looked as if he should explain. "We weren't all carrying guns," he said.

Cullen listened with interest to their report on the incident. It was pretty much the same as the one he had gotten from Naomi and Sammy. One thing that puzzled him, though, there was no mention of Slim Bradshaw. He seemed to have disappeared. "What about that deputy of his?" Cullen asked. Burt and Deke looked at each other, obviously never having thought about the deputy.

"He was going somewhere," Burt remembered then. "He came to the stable and got his horse and one of the other horses last night right after dark—said he was goin' somewhere early this mornin' before I opened up."

Cullen couldn't see how that tied in with what Prophet did today and he wondered if he had Slim to worry about, too. With no place to start, it was damn near impossible to pick up Prophet's trail. He didn't even know if he went north or south. He looked out the window at the fading light of day. Soon it would be dark. That didn't help a hell of a lot. The only shot he figured he had was definitely a long one and might prove an even bigger waste of time. But it was all he had. At least it was a place to start. Burt said Prophet took two packhorses, but he didn't have any supplies to pack on them. But what if he knew he had some supplies at that hideout? The odds were that he did, because that's where the two men he killed at the Thomas ranch had been hiding out. If he was right, it would make sense for Prophet to go there first. Thinking about the deputy again, he wondered if Prophet had planned all along to shoot up the council meeting and was going to meet Slim at the hideout. It didn't make sense. He was inclined to agree with Naomi's opinion, that the sheriff went loco and just started shooting at random. It all boiled down to the very real possibility that Cullen would never find hide nor hair of either man. And the only place he had to start looking was at their camp, so that's what he would do. At least he knew where that cabin was.

He wasn't sure if in the darkness he could find the point where the little stream emptied into the river. It was so well hidden that he would not have found it in broad daylight, had he not seen Deputy Slim Bradshaw drive his horse through a large bank of laurel bushes hanging out over the water. He knew he couldn't afford to waste any time, however, so he decided to ride up to that stretch of the river as soon as he could ready his packhorse. "I'll need to get my packhorse outta the stable," he informed Burt, and Burt said the stable wasn't locked up yet, and went with him to help.

"Ain't none of my business," Burt said as he watched Cullen securing his packsaddle on the sorrel gelding, "but are you thinkin' about goin' after Prophet?"

"Don't seem like much possibility of catchin' up with him, does it?" Cullen asked in answer to his question.

"No, it don't," Burt said, "since nobody saw which way he went when he left here."

"Reckon I won't know for sure unless I try to cut his trail," Cullen said as he untied the sorrel's reins and led it out to the front, where he had left Jake.

"Whaddaya gonna do if you do catch up with him?"

"I don't know, shoot him, I expect," Cullen answered as he stepped up into the saddle.

"What if it turns out he ain't really runnin' and he doubles back to show up again in New Hope?"

"Then, you shoot him," Cullen answered, wheeled his horse, and rode up the street to the general merchandise store.

When he walked in the store, he was met at the door by Mildred Myers. "I'm awful sorry to hear about your husband gettin' shot," he said. "I hope he's gettin' along all right."

"I'm gettin' along just fine, considerin' I've got a hole clear through me." Cullen was surprised, because he hadn't noticed Jack propped up in an armchair behind the end of the counter, his shotgun lying across his lap. "It's gonna take more'n that to put me in the bed."

"Thanks for askin'," Mildred said. "Can I help you with something?"

"Yes, ma'am. I'm gonna need some things. I'm gonna be takin' a little trip and I don't know how long it'll be. So, I'll take enough coffee and bacon to last me a while, maybe some jerky, if you've got some." While she was wrapping up the bacon, Mayor Robertson walked in.

"McCabe," Robertson said, "glad I found you. I

heard you were back in town and I wanted to talk to you." He paused only a moment to nod in Mildred's direction, then seeing Jack propped up in the chair, he commented to him, "What are you doing sitting in here? You oughta be in bed, so those wounds can heal."

"I'm protectin' my business," Jack answered boldly, "in case that maniac comes back." He held his shotgun up for Robertson to see. Then he thought to add, "And my wife."

"Good for you," Robertson replied, then to Cullen, he said, "That's what I wanted to talk to you about."

"About him and his shotgun?" Cullen asked.

"No, about you taking the job as sheriff. I know you said you're just passin' through, but you've done a great deal of good for this town since you've been here." He glanced at the supplies Mildred was collecting to put on the counter. "I don't blame you for deciding to go ahead now and leave town, but we're without the protection of the law, and folks like Jack and Mildred deserve to have decent protection for their business and their home." He glanced at Jack again before saying, "Of course, I'll have to have the council's approval before I can make it official."

"I appreciate the fact that you'd offer it to me," Cullen said, "but I'm not a candidate for the sheriff's job. I don't plan to be in New Hope much longer. I'll be leavin' as soon as I get a few more things done, then I'm gone. I'm only sorry I wasn't here to help you this mornin' and I surely hope you find a solid man for the sheriff's job pretty quick. I may be wrong, but I don't think you'll see any more of John Prophet, or Slim Bradshaw. I believe Prophet and his gang were responsible for the complaints of cattle rustlin' you've had, so you shouldn't have as much trouble with that as you had before." He paused, then said, "But thanks for the offer."

Robertson didn't make any response immediately, instead he seemed to be studying Cullen intensely. When he did speak, it was with an air of one who had discovered something. "Let me ask you a question, if you don't mind," he said. "It looks like you're getting ready to take a trip. Where are you heading?"

"Don't know for sure," Cullen answered.

"You know," Robertson continued, seeming more intense, "a while back, I sent the governor several letters about the trouble we were having here with rustlers, as well as rowdy troublemakers here in town. Then you showed up. Another gunslinger, I thought, but right away, most of the trouble Johnny Bledsoe was having in the saloon started disappearing, then we quit hearing complaints about rustling. And now that I think about it, you were somehow involved with all of it. Do you suppose that might be just a coincidence?"

Damn, Cullen thought, *he nailed it, right between the eyes.* To Robertson, he said, "Hadn't thought about it. Never believed much in coincidences, anyway." As a rule, he never liked to tell anyone that he was a special agent for the governor. He figured it would only complicate his actions if people thought to debate whether he should have done this, or he should have done that. He also was pretty sure the governor preferred not to have it known that he employed a gunslinger to take care of problems he thought the different law agencies were slow in handling.

"I'm thinking you're not interested in the sheriff's job because you've already got a job," Robertson said.

"Well, you're right about one thing, I do have something I've got to do, so I'd best pay Mrs. Myers for my possibles and pack 'em on that sorrel outside." He turned back toward the counter then and waited for Mildred to total his purchases. He paid her and picked up an armload of packages and took them outside with Robertson silently watching him, a smug expression of satisfaction on his face. He turned and gave Jack a wink, then he picked up the rest of the packages and followed Cullen outside, leaving Jack puzzling over the wink.

The mayor stood by Cullen as he tied down his packs, handing him those he carried when Cullen was ready for them. "Much obliged," Cullen said when all was ready. He stepped up into the saddle and turned Jake toward the north end of the street.

"Good hunting," Robertson wished him.

"Thanks," Cullen replied.

CHAPTER 17

By the time he passed by the hotel and struck the road that led north along the Brazos, he was pleased to see a full moon beginning its climb into the starry sky above him. *Good,* he thought, *that'll make it easier to find that one spot where that little stream empties into the river.* This would be only his second time to find the hideout, but he was sure he remembered it well enough to find the particular section of the river. He was certain he could find the wide ravine where he had left Jake and climbed to the top to spot Slim on his way to the hideout. So, with that as his intention, he held Jake to a comfortable lope for a good part of the approximately ten miles to the ravine. When he reached it, he again guided the horses into the wide mouth of it and dismounted. He would leave them there while he went forward on foot, scouting as best he could in the moonlight for tracks that might tell him of recent visitors to the cabin perched on a high ridge above the river. Unfortunately, the heavy growth of trees along the banks of the river shut out the moonlight, making it impossible to find any trace of tracks. He looked along the banks of the river for the thick stand of laurel bushes that hid the tiny stream. He could not be sure if this was the right place, and he hated to think that maybe he was not at the place he remembered at all. There was no way he could be sure until he had light enough to see. And then, his foot kicked something on the dark path. He stopped immediately and knelt down to discover droppings from a horse. He picked one up and examined it. It was fresh, only hours old. A horse, or horses, had been there today! Still kneeling, he looked up and down the river, trying to identify the bank of bushes that hid the trail up to the ridge. It was no use. Without tracks to follow, he could never find the hidden entrance. In the darkness of the trees, there appeared to be no break in the dark wall along the river. He was forced to admit that he would have to wait for morning light. Then maybe the tracks could tell him something. Resigned to it, he went down to the edge of the river and washed his hands.

Returning to the ravine, he took Jake's saddle off him and relieved the sorrel of its load of packs, then took the horses to the river to drink. He had eaten nothing since breakfast, so he made a small fire in the protection of the ravine and ate some of the jerky he had bought with some coffee. He made his bed a little farther up the ravine, cautioning himself to sleep lightly, knowing that Jake would alert him of any visitors during the night. Just in case, he slept with his Winchester close by his side, counting on a single visitor, if there was one, but allowing for the possibility of two. He was still not sure if Slim was now with Prophet or not.

* * *

He was awakened by a single ray of sunshine beaming through a hole in the trees on the other side of the river. Up at once, he took a quick look around him, then at his horses. All was peaceful, so he loaded the sorrel and saddled Jake. He planned to go back on foot to the place he had found droppings the night before. But he wanted his horses to be ready if he needed to ride in a hurry. He had no thoughts of breakfast, not even coffee, so he made his way quickly along the path until he came to a little clearing where he found the droppings. As the light along the banks gradually became stronger, he could now see hoofprints, relatively fresh, and enough to indicate three horses. Burt had said Prophet took three horses. He had guessed right, and he followed the tracks along the bank to a spot where they entered the river. He looked across to see the thick laurel bushes and knew the path up the stream was beyond them. Looking at the tracks at the water's edge, he saw that they were all heading toward the other side. There were no tracks coming back. He was still up there. Having climbed halfway up the rocky stream once before, he knew he could not lead two horses up that climb without alerting anyone up there. He would have to go on foot. Thinking there was no reason to wait then, he waded into the water and started across.

At first, he missed the opening between the bushes, but discovered it after moving a few yards upstream. Pushing through the laurels, he found the path before him, which was actually a tiny stream that trickled over a rocky path to the river. With his rifle ready to fire, he started the climb. Passing the point where he had rolled over the side to escape being discovered the first time he approached the hideout, he got his first glimpse of the cabin that served as the camp for the notorious Viper Gang, now reduced to two men.

Crouching low close to the bushes that nearly enclosed the stream, he studied the rough dwelling for signs of life. There was no one stirring as more and more of the sun's rays found passage into the dark ravine. A few minutes more revealed the rails of a corral directly behind the cabin, but he could detect no movement. Then he realized there were no horses, as the sun revealed more of the corral. Still, he waited there, watching and listening. There was a stone chimney, but no smoke, and the only sound he heard was that of the stream as it washed over the rocky channel. *Already gone*, he finally decided, and rose to his full height, still holding his rifle ready to fire at the first sign of an ambush. He walked up to the door and kicked it open, set to pull the trigger, only to find an empty cabin. He saw what appeared to be a lantern in the darkness of the inside of the cabin. It was sitting on the only piece of furniture in the rough structure. He found a box of matches beside it, so he lit the lantern and looked around him at the evidence of a man in a hurry to escape. There were bedrolls scattered on the floor, some with muddy boot prints on them, indicating someone had walked right over them. In a corner by the fireplace was the remains of what had evidently been a pile of food stores. It was obvious to him that Prophet had taken whatever he could use and didn't bother to worry about the rest. It also told him that Prophet wasn't planning on coming back to this hideout.

The job now was to find out which way he went. At the bottom of the stream, where it emptied into the river, there were only tracks going into the stream, and none coming out. So, there had to be a way out the back. With that thought, he went around to the corral to see if he could pick up a trail. He found that it was not difficult to find Prophet's exit. The corral rails had been removed from the back section and he had not bothered to replace them after he left. Fresh tracks, from what Cullen could easily determine to be those of three horses, led out of the corral toward what at first appeared to be the face of a twenty-foot cliff. Unless Prophet's horses had wings, there was no way they could go up the near-vertical face to the hill above it. So, he searched the rocky surface outside the back of the corral but found it hard to find any discernable tracks. He soon came to the conclusion that Prophet must have returned to the stream and followed it on up the hill. That being the only possibility, he figured he might as well go back and get his horses because his only hope of picking up Prophet's trail was at the top of this steep hill.

He stopped briefly at the foot of the hill to let the horses drink before riding across to the mouth of the stream. Once through the bushes that guarded the entrance, he dismounted, thinking it wiser for him and his horses to walk up the steep, rocky climb. He continued the climb on past the cabin, following the stream until it ended abruptly, going underground. He looked up to see still more hill to climb, but at least he was assured that he was right about his guess that Prophet had to have followed the stream up. Near the stream's underground opening there were definite signs left by Prophet's horses where they had climbed out of the stream. In addition, the branches of some bushes close by the stream were broken, showing the direction Prophet had taken.

He followed the obvious trail for about a dozen yards before he came to a clearing near the top of the hill. The hoofprints led straight across the clearing to a small winding path that led down to disappear into the trees. From where he now stood, high up the hill, he could see the prairie beyond the chain of low mountains. It seemed endless, and he had no clue as to where Prophet might be heading. His only hope was that he had been careless enough to leave him a trail. He stepped up into the saddle and started down the path.

He followed the path all the way to the bottom of the hill and continued for what he estimated to be about seven or eight miles across an almost treeless stretch of prairie. It seemed endless until he sighted a line of trees and bushes that indicated a creek in the distance. When he reached the creek, the tracks told him that Prophet had followed the path into the water. Since he didn't know when he might strike water again, Cullen paused to let his horses drink before pushing across the shallow creek. When he crossed over, he found Prophet's tracks on the opposite bank, but the path they had followed ended at the creek. Only about fifty yards beyond, however, he came to a wagon road, running east and west. The question to be determined was, which way did he go, east or west? That depended, of course, on whether or not he took the road, but after carefully scouting the road, Cullen identified Prophet's fresh tracks heading east on the road. And there were no tracks that would show he crossed over it to continue traveling in a more northerly direction.

Even realizing that his odds of finding Prophet were not good, Cullen was determined to push on, hoping he might just get lucky. Prophet was obviously a mad dog and mad dogs had to be put down. So he followed the road until it struck a river, then crossed it and continued east. From the direction he had come, he knew the river had to be the Brazos. He had been led back to the river, but north of where he had started this morning. Knowing that, it suddenly struck him that the road he was now following had to lead to Fort Griffin. "Well, hell," he swore, "if I'd known that's where he was headin', I coulda saved myself a helluva lot of trouble." It made him wonder why Prophet had chosen to take such a roundabout route, if he was heading to Fort Griffin. "Maybe just to throw anybody off that was trackin' him," he told Jake. Anxious now to get to Fort Griffin as quickly as possible, he nevertheless decided it was time for some coffee and breakfast, only because his horses needed rest. He couldn't be sure, but he figured he was as much as a full day behind Prophet, since he couldn't be sure if Prophet stayed the night at the camp or not.

"Well, I'll be damned, what are you doin' here?" Lon Schneider asked, surprised to see him in his saloon. It had been over two years since John Prophet had shot Long Bob Tolbert down in his saloon for cheating in a card game. Prophet had skipped town before a detail of soldiers from the fort on the bluff above town came down to look for him. Schneider never expected to see Prophet back in Fort Griffin.

"I thought it was time to visit my old friends," Prophet answered, "to see how you're all doin' since the army's been tryin' to run all the outlaws outta town."

"What are you doin' back up here?" Schneider

repeated. "I heard you were operatin' in the cattle business, heard you had some of my old customers ridin' with you south of here somewhere. You still in the cattle business?"

"No, I'm takin' a little vacation from that line of work right now. You ain't seen Slim Bradshaw lately, have you?" Prophet was still thinking that he would dearly love to catch up with Slim, and he thought he might have run this way.

"Slim? No, I ain't seem him since he left to go with you. He ain't with you no more, huh?"

"That's right," Prophet replied. "He left me in a bad fix and I just thought he mighta come this way."

"Is that a fact?" Schneider replied. "I thought ol' Slim was a pretty steady hand."

"He was for a while," Prophet said, "but when the chips were down, he lit out to keep from tanglin' with some gunslinger I ain't ever heard of before. You ever heard of a fellow named Cullen McCabe?" Schneider shook his head. "No, me, neither," Prophet went on. "At least not till he started pickin' off my men."

The longer they talked, the more Schneider began to form a picture of the real reason Prophet was in Fort Griffin. He poured a drink for Prophet and asked, "Have you been operatin' in New Hope?"

"I was the sheriff there till that Cullen McCabe started killin' my deputies, one after another. He got the town council turned against me and was tryin' to get 'em to lynch me." He paused to toss his drink back. "Well, I had to give 'em a little lesson on what happens when you mess with me. I thought it'd be a good idea to let 'em cool off for a spell, then I'm gonna go back to settle up a few scores."

"You need a place to stay?" Schneider asked. "A couple of my rooms upstairs are empty."

"How 'bout that place you used to have on the other side of the river?" Prophet asked, referring to a log cabin Schneider had built to house outlaws passing through town who didn't want to take a chance on getting trapped in town.

"You got somebody on your trail?" Schneider immediately asked, thinking that was the only reason Prophet didn't want to take a room upstairs.

"Not that I know of," Prophet answered. "I just don't want to have to put my horses in the stable—have 'em ready if I need 'em in a hurry." He punctuated with a casual shrug. "Anybody stayin' in that cabin right now?"

"No, nobody but Jess, he's always there," Schneider replied, referring to Jess Sweeney, a little old bald man who was more or less a caretaker. He was there to ensure no one would think the cabin was abandoned and move in. In return, he got a house to live in. "You're welcome to move in there. My regular rate ain't gone up any since you were here two years ago, a dollar a day, unless you're thinkin' about stayin' a long time. Then we can work out a cheaper rate."

"Dollar a day's all right," Prophet said. "I ain't plannin' on stayin' around that long."

"Good enough," Schneider said. "How 'bout you pay me for a couple of days in advance, just in case you do need your horses in a hurry?" He smiled knowingly.

"I told you I don't know of anybody chasin' me," Prophet replied. "But I'll pay you, you ol' skinflint. I ain't lookin' for handouts. I ain't decided yet what I'm gonna do, but I will in a day or two." He pulled some money out of his pocket and paid him.

"Much obliged," Schneider said. "Have another drink. This one's on the house. Glad to see you back in town again."

Prophet stayed only long enough to finish his drink, since he wanted to get across the river and get himself settled in at the cabin. When he started toward the door, Schneider told him to tell Jess, "The kettle's on the stove." That would signal the old man that Prophet was a paying customer. "Here," he said, and handed Prophet a bottle of whiskey. "Give that to the old man." After he was gone, the woman living with Schneider walked out of the kitchen.

"Well, ain't that somethin'?" Marge announced. "The devil himself come back to town. I can't say I'm tickled to see him. Least he ain't with some of that crowd that was with him last time he was here."

"He's back, all right," Schneider said. "But I think he's on the run. He says he ain't, but he was ready to go across the river quick enough. I'd rather that than have him stayin' here again. Always playin' the big shot." He gave Marge a grin. "He said he was the sheriff over in New Hope." They both laughed at that. "I hope them folks down there have got better sense than that."

Prophet rode up out of the river and followed a path that led along the bank until coming to another path that led to a log cabin with a barn and corral behind it. Walking his horse up the path, he was startled when the door of the cabin suddenly flew open and he was met with a wiry little man holding a shotgun. "Somethin' I can do for you?" Jess blurted. "This ain't no empty cabin."

"Put that damn shotgun down!" Prophet roared back. "I'll drill you so full of holes, you won't hold water."

"You might, but this buckshot is gonna make a real mess outta you," Jess came back defiantly. "What business you got here?"

"Put the scattergun down, you damn fool, I paid Schneider to stay here," Prophet demanded. "And you'd best do it quick. I ain't got a lotta patience."

"Maybe you paid Schneider, and maybe you didn't. I don't let just any saddle tramp in Texas stay in my cabin." He raised the shotgun and aimed it at Prophet's head. "Now, you just turn your ass around and go back where you rode up from." He paused, then added, "Unless you know somethin' about the stove."

Prophet remembered then. "The damn kettle's on the stove," he recited, feeling his irritation doubling. "Is that what you want, you damn fool?"

"Well, unload your horses, then, and come on in the house. I've got some coffee on the stove, but if you want somethin' to eat, you'd best bring it in. I ain't feedin' nobody. Did Schneider send me a bottle?"

"No," Prophet lied. "But I brought one and you're welcome to share it." He brought it in with his saddlebags and set it in the middle of the table.

"Thank you, kindly," Jess said. "Why don't we take a drink of it right now, start us off on the right foot." He got a glass from a cupboard and, taking the bottle from Prophet, he filled it along with one that was already sitting on the table.

"Sure, why not?" Prophet said. "Here's to not gettin' in each other's way," and he tossed it back.

"Here's to not havin' to wait this long for a drink

again," Jess said, tossed it down with a grimace, then smacked his lips. "Damn, that's terrible stuff. Wish I had a barrel of it."

Prophet went back outside to unload his horses, making several trips back and forth while Jess remained at the table, working on the bottle of whiskey. Then he led the horses to the barn to look for hay, since there was very little grass around and none in the corral, the only occupant of which was a mule. There was hay in the barn, enough to take care of his horses for the short time he expected to be there. His first introduction to Jess Sweeney was not a positive one. He was not sure how long he could tolerate the feisty little man before he decided to put a hole between his eyes.

While he put hay out for his horses, his thoughts led him to consider his present situation. On the run again, after having built his gang up to a force of twelve hardened men, including himself, and several trips to ship stolen cattle east from Fort Worth on the Texas and Pacific Railroad. On top of that, came an opportunity to take control of a whole town from the sheriff's office. "Damn!" he swore when he thought back on the crumbling of his ambitious plans. He hadn't even been aware of what was happening to his empire, as one by one, he started losing men. When he realized it was all because of one man, it was too late to stop it. He should have shot McCabe after Slade and Luther failed, should have shot him down right in the street with no warning. He could have fabricated a reason for the killing that would have placated Ernest Robertson and the council at the time. *Hell,* he thought, *they would have called me a hero for getting rid of another gunslinger.* He could kick himself now for not doing it. *And now, I'm on the run,* he reminded himself once again. *I shouldn't have let them rile me up,* he admonished himself, thinking of those moments in the saloon when he lost control of his temper. He thought again of going back to settle with McCabe, but it would be at great risk because the whole town was against him now. It was bitter gall to swallow, thinking that McCabe had won out. At the time, there had been no choice for him but to escape before some upset citizen took a shot at him from a window or doorway.

Suddenly aware of pain in his hands, he looked down to realize he had been squeezing the handle of the pitchfork so hard that his hands were bright red. Calmer now, he returned his thoughts to a plan he had been considering on his ride to Fort Griffin, and the reason he was on his way back to Fort Worth. He had not parted on good terms with his two brothers after a fight over who was running the business of buying stolen cattle. Maybe after two years had passed, he could patch up the rift between him and the two of them by offering an opportunity to take over a town desperate for a sheriff. He knew there was no possibility that the people of New Hope could forgive him his shooting rampage at the council meeting. So he wouldn't tell his brothers about that problem. But he would have an opportunity to confront McCabe with the backing of a hard bunch of riders who worked for the Prophet Brothers Cattle Company.

By the time he had taken care of his horses, it was getting around to the time to think about supper. When he returned to the cabin, he found Jess still at the table, his head down on his folded arms, apparently asleep. Prophet looked at the nearly empty whiskey bottle. It was not difficult to guess why Jess had suddenly gone to sleep. Prophet hoped he would stay that way, but Jess had somehow heard him when he closed the cabin door. "Whadda hell?" Jess slurred drunkenly.

"Go back to sleep, you damn drunk," Prophet answered him.

Jess tried to focus his bleary eyes on Prophet but couldn't seem to succeed. "Whaz your name, anyway? We gonna cook some supper?"

"You can cook whatever you want," Prophet said. "I ain't gonna be here to eat. I'm goin' into town." He was in no mood to put up with the old man. He walked back out of the cabin while Jess was still trying to get up from the bench by the table. *That damn Schneider,* Prophet thought, *he ought to pay me a dollar a night to put up with that old coot.*

He still retained distinct memories of Lon Schneider's woman, Marge, and the slop she tried to pass off as cooking. So, he saddled his horse again and went across the river to the little town below Fort Griffin. Originally called "The Bottom" before it took on the name of the fort, the town used to have a hotel with a decent dining room. He hoped it was still there. It was, and he was able to enjoy a supper of steak and potatoes. The meal and the coffee were good enough to partially alleviate the foul mood he had been in since leaving Schneider's Saloon earlier. So, he decided to return to Schneider's for a couple of drinks before going back to the cabin.

"Did you give Jess that bottle?" Schneider asked when he saw Prophet come in the door.

"Yeah, I gave it to him," Prophet answered, "and

I believe he woulda crawled inside it, if he coulda squeezed through the neck."

"Yes, sir, ol' Jess loves his whiskey," Schneider chuckled. "You wantin' something to eat? Marge fixed up something, some kind of stew, I think. We can fix you right up."

"Nope, I just came back from the hotel, had a fine supper in the dinin' room," Prophet replied.

"Oh, you've been over town eatin' with the fancy folks, huh? You coulda et here for about half the price I bet you paid for that supper at the dinin' room."

"I expect I could have," Prophet replied. "But the last time I ate Marge's stew, I got a case of cramps in my belly, and like to never made it to the outhouse in time."

Schneider looked truly offended. "Oh, is that right? I don't know what coulda caused that. Musta been something in the well water." All too aware of Prophet's tendency to wreak havoc on those who cross him, he was surprised that he hadn't shot Marge at the time.

Overhearing the conversation from the kitchen, Marge made a face. *I wish you had ordered my stew tonight,* she said to herself. *I woulda peed in it for you.*

"You can pour me a drink of liquor, though," Prophet said. "I reckon I can risk that." He stayed long enough to have a couple more drinks before he decided to go back across the river.

There was no sign of life from the cabin when he rode up from the river and went straight to the barn. He hoped that meant the old man was completely passed out. He was in no mood to bother with him. After he unsaddled his horse and put it in an empty stall, he walked back to the front door of the cabin and walked into the dark interior. The fire had gone out in the fireplace and there was no lantern lit, which was fine with him. It meant Jess was not awake to irritate him. That thought was shattered in the next moment when he heard the drunken challenge behind him. "Who the hell are you?"

Prophet turned to find Jess silhouetted by the faint light coming through the doorway, his shotgun wavering slightly as he aimed it at him. "Who the hell do you think?" Prophet replied. "I'm gettin' tired of you aimin' that shotgun at me, you crazy old drunk. Put it down."

"Not till you tell me who you are," Jess insisted.

Not in the mood to tolerate any irritation at this point, Prophet pulled his Colt and put a .44 slug into the old man's belly. Jess cried out in pain and collapsed in the doorway. "I'm the man who got rid of an old pain in the ass," Prophet answered his question, then walked over to the suffering little man and placed a second round in his head. "Now, maybe I'll be able to get some sleep tonight." He grabbed the back of Jess's collar and dragged his corpse out of the doorway, so he could close the door, then paused to look at the body again. "Oh, I forgot, the kettle's on the stove," he said, and chuckled in appreciation for his joke.

After a peaceful night's sleep, Prophet woke up with determination to persuade his brothers to back him in his quest to destroy Cullen McCabe. When he walked outside to answer nature's morning call, he barely glanced at the body lying just outside the door. *I'll be gone by the time you start to stink,* he thought. He had no intention of stopping by Schneider's again, even though he considered asking for a refund of a dollar for the second night he paid for in advance. As for the demise of his custodian, Schneider would no doubt find out before very long. So just as soon as he got saddled up, he struck out for Fort Worth and the Prophet Brothers Cattle Company.

CHAPTER 18

It was well into the afternoon when Cullen rode into the town of Fort Griffin. One of the first places of business he came to was a saloon called Schneider's. He figured that might have been a tempting sign for Prophet, so he decided to see if he had stopped in. Lon Schneider looked up from the bar when Cullen walked in. A big man, Schneider thought, one he had never seen in his place before. Cullen stood in the doorway, looking the room over before proceeding to the bar. "What can I do you for?" Schneider asked, cheerfully.

"I think I could use a drink of whiskey to cut the dust in my throat," Cullen answered.

"I know I ain't seen you in here before," Schneider said as he poured Cullen's whiskey. "I'da remembered you. You just passin' through town, or you lookin' for a place to stay?"

"Just passin' through, I reckon," Cullen replied. "Depends."

"Oh? On what?"

"I'm tryin' to catch up with a fellow," Cullen said.

"Maybe he mighta stopped in here to get a drink." He was about to continue, but Schneider interrupted.

"Is his name John Prophet by any chance?" Schneider asked, feeling fairly certain that it was. He saw by the look of surprise on Cullen's face that his guess was accurate. "I'm guessin' your name might be McCabe."

"You're right on both counts," Cullen could only confess, seeing there was no use in trying to play a part. "So, I reckon he stopped in here?" He asked the question, not really expecting much cooperation from the saloon owner, because he guessed a good percentage of the man's customers were outlaws.

"Yesterday," Schneider said without hesitation. He was sizing Cullen up quickly, figuring him to be a lawman and not the gunslinger Prophet described, who was competing with him for control of New Hope. Had he been the man Prophet said he was, he would probably not be tracking him. Most likely, he would have been satisfied to have run Prophet out of town. The man standing on the other side of the bar from him now had the look of a hunter. "He stayed for the night in a cabin I own on the other side of the river," Schneider continued. "He's gone now, left this mornin' after he shot a little old man that took care of the cabin for me. So, I reckon he rode on outta town. If I had to guess, I'd bet he was headin' to Fort Worth."

Surprised that Schneider was so forthright in his information, Cullen could readily attribute it to the fact that Prophet had murdered the caretaker of his cabin. The little old man Schneider referred to must have meant something to him. "Well, sir, I'm much obliged for the information. I reckon I'll head out toward Fort Worth, soon as I rest my horses and get something to eat." Thinking he should give the man

a little more business, since he had been so generous
with information, he asked, "Can I get something to
eat here?"

"Ordinarily, you could," Schneider answered apologetically. "But my cook ain't here today. She's buryin'
her pappy."

Cullen nodded, having put two and two together.
"I'm sorry to hear that," he said, although he had not
been enthusiastic about eating there. "I thank you for
your help." He turned to leave but was stopped by a
question from Schneider.

"Are you a lawman? Ranger, maybe?" he asked.

"Nope," Cullen replied, "I just wanna make sure a
man gets what's comin' to him."

"If you're goin' to Fort Worth, it might help you to
know John Prophet is the middle brother of three.
The other two own the Prophet Brothers Cattle Company. You mighta already known that."

"No, I didn't," Cullen said. "I'm obliged again."
That last scrap of information provided another surprise and caused him to wonder about the business
Prophet's brothers could be running. He never figured Prophet to be more than another outlaw and
killer. Maybe it shouldn't be so surprising that he had
held ambitions to control a town like New Hope.

"I hope you find him," Schneider muttered under
his breath when Cullen went out the door.

As he rode on into the little town, Cullen searched
for a good place to water and rest his horses. When he
came to an establishment close by the river with a sign
that proclaimed it to be KATE'S KITCHEN, he decided
it might serve his purposes. He could water Jake and
the sorrel in the river while he got something to eat.
Expecting to find an enterprising woman who earned

a living off her cooking skills, he found instead a restaurant owned by a man named Ronald Kate. He turned out to be a good cook, however, and the price was right.

Since it was about a hundred miles from there to Fort Worth, Cullen thought it best to send a wire to the governor's office to let them know he was heading there. So when he left Kate's Kitchen, he rode up the hill to the fort and the telegraph office. He figured the governor might be pleased to know that the town of New Hope was no longer threatened by the Viper Gang.

After sending his telegram to Michael O'Brien in the governor's office, he left right away, instead of waiting for any reply. He was afraid O'Brien might order him to forget about chasing after Prophet, and he was determined to bring Prophet to his deserved fate, whether it be prison or death. Riding back down the hill then, he started out for Fort Worth. He had been told by Henry, the telegraph operator, that the main road to Fort Worth was the one that left town between the hotel and the barbershop and headed east. That was the trail that he now rode, and he figured to see the outer buildings of Fort Worth in two and a half days, or less. Once he reached Fort Worth, he was not assured of finding John Prophet. As far as the Prophet Brothers, he had no idea if it was a legitimately run business, or one of the many buyers that dealt in stolen cattle. John could possibly be the black sheep in the family, as suggested by the fact that he was not involved in the business. On the other hand, he was very much involved in cattle rustling with the cows being sold to the Fort Worth shippers. It was a lot to think about and he decided to worry about catching up with a wanted killer. He figured anything more complicated than that was not in his department.

After leaving Fort Griffin about fifteen miles behind him, he decided to make camp for the night when he came to a sizable creek that offered trees and grass, a perfect spot for a camp. When he walked Jake through the wide grassy clearing, he saw he was not the first to find the spot ideal. There were several signs of old campfires around the edge of the clearing. He might have ridden farther before stopping, but he had not given his horses much of a rest at Fort Griffin. Only after they were unloaded and turned loose to water, would he gather wood for a fire. He wasn't really hungry. The beef stew he took on at Kate's seemed to still be holding up, but he always needed coffee, so he soon had his little pot on the fire. It was only after his second cup that he became aware that he had company.

Jake told him at first, causing him to become alert. He poured a little more coffee from the pot and casually backed up against the trunk of a tree and pulled his rifle up beside him. There was no further sound for a little while, then he heard a slight rustling of leaves in the bushes between him and the creek. That told him that whoever was approaching his camp was coming along the creek, and that was why Jake warned him. They must be on foot and Jake could see them, instead of having been signaled by another horse. Cullen readied himself for whoever saw fit to sneak up on him. It could only be someone with evil intent.

Very slowly, he reached down and cocked the hammer on his Colt .44, knowing it would make less noise than cranking a cartridge into the chamber of his Winchester 73. He was not yet ready to let his visitors know he was aware of their presence. The rustling of leaves became more distinct and he listened, ready to fire, until the disturbance stopped in a bank of berry bushes no more than ten yards away. He waited, wondering if they might be waiting for some more of their party to circle around the other side of the clearing. Finally, after a period minutes long, he became impatient. "All right!" he commanded as he cranked a cartridge into the rifle, "come outta there before I cut that bush to pieces!"

There was no response to his command for a long moment, and then there was more movement in the bushes, followed by the appearance of a young girl, her hands up in surrender. Maybe ten or eleven years old was his guess, her clothes torn and tattered, she walked bravely toward him. "Please don't shoot, mister," she begged.

He lowered his rifle, perplexed. Having prepared for a situation he was confident he could handle, he was not sure what to do about this. "Who else is in the bushes?" he finally asked, thinking maybe a parent. "Are you by yourself?"

"No, sir," she answered. "My little brother's in there, but he's afraid to come out."

"Tell him to come on out. Nobody's gonna hurt him." After a long minute, a little boy of perhaps five or six peeked out from the bushes and his sister motioned for him to come out. Finally, he came out and went quickly to stand beside the girl. "What are you two doin', runnin' around this creek? Where are your folks?"

"I think they're dead," the girl answered, her eyes tearing up when she spoke.

"Dead?" Cullen responded. "Why do you think that? Did something happen to them?" Teary-eyed now, she nodded then dropped her chin down on her chest. "Tell me what happened," Cullen pressed.

"Some badmen sneaked up on us when we stopped to camp," she said. Then with his coaxing, she was able to tell him what had happened to her parents. When she finished, he had a picture of the incident in his mind. They had stopped to camp somewhere down the creek, when they were attacked by two men. Her father tried to protect them, but one of the men shot him. Her mother tried to hide, but the men followed them, and her mother told her and her brother to run. So they ran, and kept running until they came upon Cullen's camp. "They got my mother," she said in conclusion.

"How far did you run before you got here?" Cullen asked.

"I don't know," she answered. "A long way, I think."

"How long ago was it?" He figured he would have heard the gunshots if it had happened anytime within the last half hour. Looking at the children's torn clothes, he assumed they had been running for quite some time. On the other hand, they may have found a place to hide and stayed there for a while. "Have you been runnin' the whole time, or did you find you a place to hide?"

"We hid near the creek bank for a long time, but we heard them coming close to us. So, that's when we decided we'd better run again."

So, he thought, their camp might not be that far away from here. "All right," he said, "I'm gonna go back the way you came and see if I can find out what happened to your mother. You and your brother stay right here till I come back. Can you do that?" They both nodded earnestly. "Good," Cullen continued. "What's your name?"

"Carrie," she answered. "My brother's name is David, but we call him Skeeter."

"All right, Carrie, you and Skeeter stay here by the fire. I'll be back as quick as I can." He left them there and started down the creek at a trot, scanning the creek bank ahead of him for signs of any movement. Although cautious as he moved quickly along, he didn't expect the men who attacked the children's parents to spend much time looking for their kids. It wouldn't have been too difficult to catch up with the two, for he passed several places where he saw their footprints in the soft sand near the edge of the water.

He had covered what he figured to be about 150 yards when he saw the smoke of a campfire drifting up through the trees ahead. More cautious now, he checked his rifle to make sure it was still cocked and continued to work his way toward the smoke. A few yards farther and he could hear voices, so he made his way even more carefully, moving from tree to tree until reaching a point where he could look through the bushes and see the camp. It was in a small clearing, much like the one he was camped in, and he assumed it was a popular spot because it had what looked to be a worn path linking it to the Fort Worth road. The campfire was close by the bank of the creek and this was where he saw the two men Carrie had described. They were sitting by the fire and eating something. Back in the clearing, there was a wagon and horses grazing. He felt his blood getting hot in his veins when he saw the woman tied to the rear wagon wheel. Alive or dead, he was not sure, for her head was slumped forward on her breast. It appeared that he had arrived too late to help her. And her brutal murderers were now taking their ease by the fire. Looking closely around the camp again, he then spotted a form lying in the grass near the edge of the clearing. It was about the size of a body, so Cullen felt sure it was the woman's husband. It required no imagination to know what happened here and the thought of it kindled Cullen's anger into a fury he had not known since his own wife and children were slain. With no thought beyond eliminating an evil presence from the face of the earth, he raised the Winchester and laid the front sight on the man whose back was to him. A steady squeeze of the trigger brought the man suddenly upright before falling face forward across the fire as the sound of the avenging rifle echoed through the trees. Stunned, the second man stumbled to his feet in time to feel the solid impact of the .44 slug against his chest. He staggered backward two steps before collapsing.

Cullen remained where he was for a minute or so, waiting for the rage inside him to calm down to the point where he could finish the grim task awaiting him. He must bury the children's parents. First, however, he had to be sure his victims were dead. Cranking another cartridge into the chamber, he walked out of the trees and went to the fire. There was no need to worry about the body lying across the fire, so he checked the second target. He found him to be breathing, but not very steadily. As he stood over him, the man's eyes fluttered open and he managed to rasp, "Finish it, you weasel."

"My pleasure," Cullen replied, and shot him again. He turned back to the first victim, whose body was smothering the flames of the small fire. With one thrust of his boot, he kicked the body hard enough to roll it off the fire, thinking he didn't want to smell it when it started to cook. With burying to do, he went first to the woman tied to the wagon wheel. He reached under her chin and pulled her head up, trying to be as tender as he could. Her head came up with no resistance, telling him rigor mortis had not set in as yet. Her face was cut and bloody, and her clothes torn almost off. While he looked at her, imagining the horror she must have suffered, he was suddenly startled when her eyelids fluttered and she opened them. "You're alive!" he blurted in disbelief. Unaware that he had come to save her, she dropped her head again, awaiting the horror she thought was returning.

Eager to help her now, he gently raised her chin again. "I'm gonna help you," he said. "You're safe now. They ain't gonna hurt you anymore. You understand?" She did not respond, her eyes still closed. Then he thought of the children. "Carrie and Skeeter are back at my camp waitin' for you." Her eyes opened then, searching his face for truth. "I'm fixin' to untie you from this wagon wheel, all right?" She did not respond, but her eyes were now open wide, as she studied his face, still afraid he was untying her with evil things in mind.

She realized that the face she studied was not one she had seen before, not that of either of the men who had attacked them, and she spoke finally. "My children?"

"They're safe and sound," he answered, and repeated, "They're back at my camp."

Gradually, she began to come back to the present.

"David?" she asked then. "My husband, they shot him. Is he . . . ?" She started but could not finish.

"I don't know, ma'am, I ain't checked on him yet. I'll go see about him as soon as I'm sure you're all right." When she was free of the wagon wheel, he laid her down on a quilt he found in the back of the wagon. "You rest up here and I'll go see about your husband."

He was pretty sure her husband was dead, but he had assumed the same about her and had been wrong. There was no question about her husband when he stood over the body, however, for he had been shot four times in the chest and stomach. Cullen knelt down beside him and turned him over, in case there was another miracle working. There was not, so he went back to give the bad news to his wife, news he felt sure she anticipated. She broke down, sobbing violently. Cullen felt helpless to do anything to relieve her pain. "I'm gonna bury your husband," he said. "I'm awful sorry for yours and your children's sakes, but there's nothin' I can do besides dig him a decent grave." He hesitated, then asked, "Do you wanna see him before I bury him?"

"No," she sobbed, "I don't want to remember him all shot full of holes."

Seeing what looked to be a woman's robe hanging near a shovel on the side of the wagon, he handed it to her and said, "It's gonna take me a little while to dig a decent grave for your husband. Maybe it would be best if I took you to be with your children and I'll come back to dig the grave." She anxiously nodded her agreement as she slipped into the robe. He went into the clearing where the horses were grazing and caught the two that were saddled, knowing they belonged to the killers. He helped the woman to her feet, then lifted her up into the saddle of one of them. He stepped up into the saddle of the other one, then holding the reins of the horse she rode, he led her out to the road, where it was a ride of only a hundred yards or more to the clearing and his camp.

He found the two children sitting by the fire as he had instructed. They both jumped up and ran to meet them when they saw their mother on the horse behind him. The woman didn't wait for Cullen to help her down but jumped out of the saddle in her haste to embrace her children, falling to her knees in the process. They reached her before she had a chance to get up, so they embraced while she was on her knees. He gave them a little time to reunite, then told her that he was going back to take care of their camp. "You and your kids might need to have some supper. Do you feel good enough to fix them something to eat? If you do, I'll show you what I've got in my packs and maybe you can find something there. If you don't, I'll try to rustle up something when I get back."

"I think you've done plenty already," she said, making an effort to control her emotions, for the sake of her children. "I don't know what I can ever do to thank you for your kindness. I don't even know your name."

"It's Cullen McCabe," he said, "and I'm just sorry I didn't get to you sooner."

"God bless you, Cullen McCabe," she said. "You should know that the man you're going to bury is David Compton, and he was an honorable man, like yourself. My name is Sarah and you already know

Carrie and Skeeter." She quickly brushed a tear that threatened then. "I'm sure I can find something to cook in these packs." She looked in one of the packages. "Here's some bacon, we can start with that, but I've got some flour and basics in the wagon."

"Good enough," he said. "I'll go see if I can't move your wagon back here before dark." He pulled the saddle off the horse she had ridden and turned it loose with his horses, then he rode back to the wagon.

The first thing he did was grab the shovel and find a spot where the ground didn't look too hard, then he started digging. While he labored, he thought about the situation he now found himself in. Up until this moment, he had not thought about John Prophet since this encounter with the Compton family. He thought he could feel Prophet's trail growing colder by the second, but he had no choice other than to take care of Sarah and her two kids. It would be a bitter dose to permit Prophet to escape to bring more trouble down on unsuspecting folks. But he was going to have to get Sarah somewhere safe.

When he figured he had gone deep enough to keep the body out of harm's way, he went back and picked it up, laid it across his shoulder, and carried it to the hole he had dug. Out of respect for the woman's husband, he tried not to drop the body roughly in the hole. "All right, David Compton," he said, "sorry for you and your family you had to end like this. I'll get 'em somewhere safe for you." Through with the burial, he caught the two horses and hitched them up to the wagon. He relieved the two men he had killed of their weapons and ammunition, then dragged them over into the trees to wait for the buzzards to find them. He found a small sum of money in their pockets and he put that inside the wagon for Sarah to find later. When he was sure he wasn't leaving any blankets or anything that looked as if they belonged in the wagon, he killed the fire. Then with the one saddled horse tied to the back of the wagon, he climbed up into the seat, and drove the wagon to his campsite.

He found Sarah and the kids waiting for him with fresh coffee and bacon. He took care of the wagon and the horses before he sat down across the fire from her. "I reckon we're gonna have to figure out what we're gonna do now," he said.

She handed him a cup of coffee in the one cup she had found in his packs and watched him take a sip of it. "Is it strong enough for you?"

"Just right," he said, and got right to the issue. "Where were you and your husband goin'?"

"A little town west of Fort Griffin, called New Hope," she said. "It's a new town and my father has a business there. You probably never heard of it."

"I've heard of it," Cullen said. "I know it pretty well. What kinda business has your father got?"

"He owns a stable," Sarah said.

"Burt Whitley?" Cullen asked, surprised.

"Yes, that's my dad," she answered, equally surprised. "You know him?"

"I sure do, but I never knew he had a daughter." It was one hell of a coincidence, he thought, since he knew Burt better than anyone else in New Hope. "Matter of fact, I didn't even know if he was married or not."

"That's not surprising," Sarah said. "Mom passed away three years ago. They were living in Fort Griffin then. The doctor said she caught some kind of fever, got pneumonia, and died. David and I have been talking about moving out there with him for a long time." She paused then to bite her lip and wait for an emotion to pass. "I'm just so sorry we picked this month to do it." Cullen could not help thinking what he was bound to do now, and in his mind, he was already estimating how many days it would take to get to New Hope with a wagon, then how many days to ride back to Fort Worth. She seemed to sense what he was turning over in his mind, so she said, "I can drive a wagon. I can't ask you to turn around from wherever you were heading to take us to New Hope. Where were you going, anyway?"

"Well, I was headin' to Fort Worth," he replied. "But after what's happened to you and your family, I can't let you start out to New Hope by yourself. You've got a little way to go yet, about thirty miles or so. In that wagon, it'll take you about a day and a half. I wouldn't feel right about it if I didn't make sure you got there all right, especially since you're Burt's daughter. And that ain't gonna take that much time outta my plans. I'll get back here pretty quick on Jake."

She smiled and shook her head at him. "The Lord works in mysterious ways, I guess. He took David's life today, but he sent you to take us to New Hope."

He shrugged. "I don't know if the Lord would want you to think I was on his payroll or not," he said.

CHAPTER 19

Cullen was sure he heard Sarah crying softly once during the night that otherwise passed peacefully. He was up with the sun, revived the campfire, and had his small coffeepot working away by the time she climbed down from the wagon. "Good morning," she offered when she walked over to the fire to join him. Holding up a cup she brought with her, she said, "That coffee smells good and I really need it this morning."

"Yes, ma'am, I reckon you do," he replied, impressed by the way she was holding up after having seen her husband murdered the day before. "I wasn't sure what you'd wanna do about breakfast, eat here before we start out for New Hope, or wait till we have to rest the horses."

"Whatever you think is best," she said. Then they batted the question back and forth, each of them determined to do what the other preferred, until they settled on leaving now and eating when the horses were tired. "I'll drive my wagon," she insisted. "I've done it all along, spelling David when he got tired." That was all right with Cullen, since he always preferred a saddle to a wagon seat. "I have one request, if you don't mind," she said. "I would like to spend a moment at David's grave before we start out."

"Yes, ma'am," Cullen replied, thinking he had done well in digging an adequate grave that should protect David from predators. At the time, he had suspected that she might want to say good-bye to her husband.

While Sarah got her children up and ready to travel, Cullen hitched her horses up to the wagon, saddled Jake and the two extra horses, and loaded his packhorse. When all was ready, he led her in the wagon back to the original camp. Then he waited while she walked with Skeeter and Carrie to the spot he pointed out and she said her final farewell to her husband. After a short visit, they returned to him and the wagon. Sarah climbed up onto the seat, and with a pop of the reins, turned her wagon around and headed back down the road to Fort Griffin.

On the first day of travel, they covered roughly twenty of the thirty-some-odd miles Cullen figured the distance to New Hope to be. Sarah proved to be capable of handling the team of horses, and the children walked a good part of the way but persuaded their mother to let them ride the two horses tied to the rear of the wagon. Cullen put both kids up in the saddle, since both horses showed no sign of bad temper. Had it not been under such mournful circumstances, it might have been a joyful experience for them. When they camped at the end of that first day, Sarah made some pan biscuits to go with the beans she had soaking since that morning. She substituted some sugar-cured ham for the bacon Cullen had provided before. It was a more substantial supper than the one he had offered them the night before. They ate breakfast before starting the next morning, thinking they would arrive in New Hope to rest the horses there.

They rode past the hotel a little past noon with Cullen leading the wagon down the middle of the street, heading for the stable at the opposite end of town. Along the way, folks stopped to stare when they recognized the imposing figure of Cullen McCabe passing by. Raymond Monroe looked out the window when the wagon wheeled by the hotel dining room. "Well, I'll be damned," he said. "I thought we'd seen the last of him." When Lottie asked who, he answered, "Cullen McCabe. I'm gonna go tell Ernest. He thought McCabe took off after John Prophet, but I swear, he's come back with a woman and a couple of young 'uns."

His remark caused Lottie to walk to the window to see for herself. "You reckon that's his family? He's never said anything about a wife and kids."

By the time the wagon reached the stable, it had attracted several interested spectators, who crowded around it to gawk at the lady driving and the two kids riding the horses behind it. Well known by all the citizens of New Hope by now, Cullen was greeted with a few *howdys* and asked where he got the woman. Cullen refrained from answering. He dismounted and walked back to the wagon to help Sarah down. As she stepped down on the street, she turned to see Burt coming out of the stable to see what the fuss was about. When he saw her, he stopped, not sure. "Papa," Sarah pronounced softly.

"Sarah?" Burt responded, still not certain he could believe his eyes. When she smiled, he exclaimed,

"Sarah," and ran to greet her. "I never thought you'd make it down here. Where's David?" Before she could answer, he turned to the small gathering of spectators and announced, "This here's my daughter, Sarah!" They all welcomed her cheerfully. "And I reckon them two little desperadoes are my grandchildren." He hurried over to lift them down from the horses and give them both a hug. He turned back to Sarah and asked again, "Where's David?"

"David's dead, Papa." Her softly spoken answer brought a hush to the people gathered around her. She went on to tell him of the tragic encounter with the two killers that resulted in the death of her husband. Burt studied her closely as she related the attack, only then realizing the darkened spots on the side of her face were bruises. When she saw the anguish in his eyes, she said, "The children and I are all right now, thanks to Mr. McCabe."

Confused, Burt asked, "Well, how did . . . Where did you . . ."

"He just came out of nowhere," she said. "We wouldn't be here today, if he hadn't, because those men were going to kill all of us."

Burt turned to look at Cullen, who was busy shifting two of the packs on the sorrel, already getting ready to leave. "Yeah," Burt said to Sarah, "that's kinda what happened here in New Hope. We had more trouble than we could handle and one day he showed up." Then seeing that Cullen looked to be about ready to leave, Burt walked quickly to catch him. "McCabe, what's your hurry? I ain't even had a chance to thank you for bringin' my daughter and my grandkids to me."

"I'm just sorry I didn't get to 'em before they killed

your son-in-law. But now I expect I'd better start on back while there's half a day of daylight left. Those two horses the kids were sittin' on belong to Sarah and you now, I reckon. And there's a little bit of money I found on those two killers. I stuck it in the wagon, thought maybe Sarah could use it."

"Prophet?" Burt asked. He didn't have to say more.

"I was on my way when I came upon your daughter. That's why I've gotta get goin'." He climbed up into the saddle. "Take care of yourself and your family," he said, and started back up the street.

Ernest Robertson was standing on the boardwalk in front of the hotel when Cullen rode past. He signaled with his hand and called out, "Change your mind? Job's still open."

"Reckon not," Cullen called back. He planned to make Fort Griffin that night and Fort Worth two and a half days after that. The chance of catching up with John Prophet seemed twice as unlikely as it had the first time he went this way. If he never settled with Prophet, however, he would be eternally thankful that he had been able to save Carrie and Skeeter. *Sarah, too*, he thought.

"Hold on for just a minute," Robertson called out again, and strode briskly toward him.

Cullen reined Jake back. "I 'preciate the offer, Mayor, but I can't take that job here in New Hope."

"I know that," Robertson said, "and I'm not trying to talk you into it. I just want to ask you for one more favor for the people of New Hope." He hesitated. "Well, it's a big favor for me, I guess. I'm sure you think I made a huge mistake when I believed John Prophet was the right man for the sheriff's job. Well, there ain't anybody in town who knows I messed up more than me. As mayor, I know I let my people down. If you hadn't come along, there ain't no telling how much trouble we'd be in."

Cullen couldn't agree more, but he wondered if the mayor was ever going to get around to telling him what the favor was he wanted from him. "Everybody makes mistakes, I reckon. What is it you want from me?"

"Take the sheriff's job," Robertson said, then before Cullen could refuse, he added, "temporarily. Not for good, just for a week or two till things settle down a little and folks aren't scared anymore." When Cullen grimaced in response, Robertson asked, "Can you do that? I guarantee you, the people would be eternally grateful."

"Damn, Mr. Mayor," Cullen started.

"Ernest," Robertson corrected, and smiled warmly.

"Right, Ernest, I'm bound to go after that mistake you said you made. He's got to pay for the trouble he's caused and the people he's hurt. And I'm already way too far behind him."

"Do you know where he's going?" Robertson asked.

"Well, I ain't positive. If I did know, it'd make my job a whole lot easier."

"I'm sure it would," Robertson continued. "But you've got a trail to follow, right?" When Cullen said that he didn't have even a cold trail out of Fort Griffin, the mayor said, "So you don't know for sure where he might be going, you don't even know which way he went after he left Fort Griffin. So, the best you can do is just try to guess where to look for him, right? He could be anywhere in Texas, or maybe Oklahoma."

"It don't sound too good when you put it that way," Cullen admitted. He couldn't really argue with

Robertson's point. He wasn't telling him anything he hadn't already thought, since Schneider was only guessing about Prophet heading to Fort Worth.

"It would do a lot of good for the people of New Hope if they knew you were taking care of the town, even if it was just until we hire a new sheriff," Robertson said. Cullen hesitated, wondering what it was going to take to make the mayor understand he was leaving. He was about to try one more time when they were joined by Dr. Worley, on his way back from visiting Jack Myers.

"Glad to see you're back in town, McCabe," Doc Worley greeted him. "Maybe Mildred Myers will rest a little easier, if she knows you're here."

"I was just trying to persuade McCabe to stay around for a week or two," Robertson said. "Make a lot of folks feel safer."

Doc looked at Cullen and frowned. "You fixin' to leave again?" He paused. "Right now?" He made it sound like it was unthinkable.

"That's right," Cullen replied. "There's something I've gotta do."

Doc turned to Robertson immediately and said, "That means we're without anybody in the sheriff's office again. Ernest, have you talked to anybody about that job?"

"No, who in the world would I talk to?" Robertson insisted. "I had Hiram Polson in mind for the job before I hired Prophet. And damned if Prophet didn't kill poor Hiram."

Doc returned his gaze to Cullen. "That might not have happened if you had been in town."

"All right," Cullen finally conceded. "If it's the only way to get you two to shut up about it, I'll stay here for a few more days, a week maybe, but I'll be movin' on after that."

"The people of New Hope greatly appreciate your help, Cullen," Robertson crowed.

"I doubt if many of 'em think about it one way or the other," Cullen said, "but you'd best start lookin' for a sheriff right now. I'll stow my gear in the sheriff's office."

"You can have your old room in the hotel back," Robertson quickly offered, all smiles at this point.

"Thanks just the same," Cullen replied, "but I'll bunk in the jail." His desire to hunt Prophet down and settle with him was as strong as before. But when he was honest with himself, he could not deny the facts as Robertson had summed them up. He had no idea where to start looking for Prophet. And if Prophet was intent upon disappearing, it wouldn't be that hard to do, in Texas or in Indian Territory. He decided that the hunt for Prophet would be a long one, so a week's delay in starting wouldn't have that much influence on the outcome.

He turned Jake around and headed back toward the stable, where Burt was still outside, getting acquainted with his grandchildren. When he saw Cullen returning, he paused and when he was close enough to hear, asked, "What did you forget?"

"I reckon I forgot how persuasive the mayor is," Cullen replied. "I'll be leavin' my horses with you again."

"Hot damn!" Burt exclaimed. "You took the sheriff's job!" He looked at his daughter and grinned, thinking it wouldn't have happened were it not for Cullen bringing her to New Hope.

"Just for a week," Cullen said, and stepped down from the saddle. He looked at Sarah, standing by her wagon and she gave him a smile. "Your pappy gonna make you stand out here in front of the stable all day?"

"I was just fixin' to pull her wagon around to the house, so we could unload it," Burt answered for her. "First thing I'm gonna do is show her where the kitchen is."

Sarah laughed. "I'm pretty sure the first thing I'll have to do is clean the kitchen."

At almost the same time Cullen was caving in to Mayor Robertson's plea for help, a man several days away walked into a small frame building near the Fort Worth stockyards. "Can I help you with something?" Weldon Jones, administrative clerk for Prophet Brothers Cattle Company, asked. He eyed the tall, dark stranger with interest, thinking he might have seen him before, but was unable to remember where.

"Yeah, you can help me," the stranger replied gruffly. "I need to see Dewey or Graham Prophet. Are they back there?" He nodded toward a closed door that led to the offices.

"Who may I say wants to see them?" Weldon asked.

Impatient to see his brothers, Prophet was in no mood to be delayed. "You can tell 'em Santa Claus for all I care. Are they in there?" When Weldon hesitated, Prophet said, "Never mind, I'll see for myself." He turned and started toward the door.

Weldon jumped up from his desk. "Wait!" he exclaimed. "You can't just go barging in there!" He hurried to catch up with Prophet.

Prophet turned to face him, his six-gun in hand. "The hell I can't," he roared, his nerves already stretched as tense as piano wires. Weldon, terrified, backed away at once. Hearing the office door open behind him, Prophet turned to face his older brother,

Dewey, standing in the doorway, having heard the commotion outside.

"What the hell are you doin' here, John?" Dewey demanded, his tone obviously less than cordial. "I told you not to show your face around here again."

Prophet slowly formed a cynical smile upon his face. "Howdy to you, too, big brother. I thought it was high time I paid a little visit to my only kin. You know, keep the family close. I even brought a little business proposition for you and Graham to discuss." He tilted his head to the side in an effort to see past him. "Where is brother Graham?"

"I'm sorry, Mr. Prophet, I told him you were busy," Weldon started to apologize.

"Never mind, Weldon," Dewey Prophet said. "Nobody's ever been able to talk any sense into him. It's a wonder he didn't shoot you as soon as he walked in the door. He doesn't know how to behave in a civilized world." Turning his attention back to his unwelcome guest, he answered his question. "Graham's down at the stock pens, doing what honest men do. You wouldn't know much about that."

"That's fine talk, comin' outta you," John Prophet replied. "You and Graham are just as bigga crooks as I am. It's just that you don't get your hands dirty, like the rest of us."

"Whadda you want, John? State your business, then get the hell outta here."

"That's a fine attitude, when your brother comes to let you in on a proposition to set us up bigger than this wormy little business you got here. I'm talkin' about ownin' a whole damn town, and all I need is to borrow half a dozen of those men you've got stealin' cattle to help me get rid of a couple of people."

Dewey shook his head impatiently. Once again, he

was hearing the same harebrained ideas he had heard from him before, which was the primary reason the brothers had split up. John was too dangerous. The only solution he knew for any problem was to stick a gun to somebody's head and pull the trigger. "You want our men to go with you to get rid of a couple of people. Tell me, John, what about using your men? I heard that you had put together a gang of outlaws and you were rustlin' cattle. You drove those cattle to some other buyer, I might add. Why don't you use those men to do this job? They all get wise to you and leave?" He paused then, and the two brothers glared at each other in mutual contempt. After a silent moment, thick with anger, Dewey spoke again. "Get the hell outta here, John, and don't ever come in here again."

Burning with the fury raging inside him, John Prophet could feel himself quivering. "You always did think you and Graham were so smart, Mr. High and Mighty. Well, you ain't so damn high and mighty in my book."

"Get outta here, John," Dewey said, turned, and walked back to his office.

John couldn't help comparing him to McCabe and the smug confidence he conveyed. Overcome by the same rage that had taken control of him at the council meeting, Prophet pulled his pistol again and shot his brother in the back as he went through the door. He turned then to Weldon Jones, who, stunned by the horror he had just witnessed, tried to back away. In his fright, he stumbled over his desk chair and landed on the floor. Totally caught up in his insane desire for vengeance, Prophet stood over him and shot him in the head. He then went to the office door, stepping over his brother's body, to see if his younger brother was there. He was not, so he returned to the front office. But before he did, he went through his brother's pockets, then searched his desk drawers, hoping to find money. There was not a great deal in either one, and this served to make him even madder. Feeling he was the victim of his brother's failure to help his blood kin, he pulled all of the papers he could find out of the desks and cabinets. When he had a sizable pile, he struck a match and set it on fire. It took only a few minutes to catch, so he pulled a couple of chairs over and put them on the fire. Satisfied, he decided he'd best leave before smoke began to escape the structure and attract attention.

He pulled his horse to a stop a mile or so away and looked back to see a plume of smoke rising from the stockyards. Even more satisfied, he nudged the gray gelding and started back toward Fort Griffin. With his failure to get help from his brother, he was left without a plan. It only seemed to intensify his desire for vengeance on Cullen McCabe and the town council of New Hope. He had to have time to think and decide what he would do now. It galled him to think his plan to rule New Hope was not possible without some help, but he swore to himself that he would not be denied vengeance against the people who had destroyed his plan. Cullen McCabe, Ernest Robertson, and last, but not least, Slim Bradshaw, were all marked for death in his mind. And right now, there was nothing of higher priority. He started riding again with New Hope his destination. That's where McCabe and Robertson were and after they were taken care of, he felt he was bound to run into Slim somewhere in one of the old outlaw hangouts they used to frequent.

CHAPTER 20

Within minutes after the sun disappeared behind the hills to the west, darkness cloaked the heavily wooded stretch of the Brazos River north of New Hope. Pausing only a moment to be sure, John Prophet guided the gray gelding into the water and waited while the horse drank. After a few minutes, he gave the horse a kick with his heels and started across toward a bank of dark bushes on the other side. When the horse balked upon reaching the bushes, Prophet gave it a harder kick, causing the horse to push through the bushes covering the mouth of the hidden stream. Concerned for the safety of his horses, and his own neck, he dismounted and led them up the treacherous climb to the cabin built into the side of the slope. He paused near the shelf where the cabin sat to make sure no one had moved in while he was gone. Seeing no sign of anyone, he proceeded on up and took his horses to the corral.

Inside the cabin, he looked around at the disarray of blankets, clothing, and discarded cartridge cartons that he had left in his haste to escape pursuit of a posse. He was caught up in a paralyzing fury at that time, after shooting up the saloon at the so-called hearing. Had he not been so furious, he would have reasoned that the helpless citizens of New Hope didn't have the guts to mount a posse and come after him. He was calmer now, he told himself, and no one knew about this hideout. Less than ten miles to New Hope, it provided an ideal base to operate from. He suddenly realized he had not eaten all day. This was not unusual. When his brain was occupied with thoughts of vengeance, there was seldom room for any other thoughts beyond total revenge. And when that score was settled, and the person who had angered him had been slain by his hand, then he had appetite for a banquet. As for now, he got one strip of jerky from his packs and was satisfied. He decided to rest the gray for a while before he rode him into town. His plan was to move in close under cover of darkness and set up somewhere with his rifle, then wait for targets to become available. He knew it would not give him the complete satisfaction he would have if he faced McCabe man-to-man, as he did when he shot Long Bob Tolbert down in Fort Griffin. But he also knew that there was too much chance one of the citizens of the town might throw a shot in his back. So tonight, the citizens would get the opportunity to see how safe they are without him as their sheriff.

When he had waited as long as he had patience for, he led the gray back down the rocky stream, then rode on to New Hope. Holding close to the river, he rode behind the hotel and the general store next to it. When he was even with the back of the saloon, he dismounted and tied his horse on the bank, then made his way through the oak trees and laurel bushes close enough to see activity on the street. Confident he could hit anyone at that distance with his rifle, he moved until he had an angle that allowed him to see the front door of the saloon, as well as the boardwalk in front of the jail across the street. *As good a place as any,* he thought, cranked a cartridge into the chamber, and waited for a target.

He laid the front sight of his rifle on an obvious drunk that staggered out of the saloon and stood for a few moments, as if trying to remember which way he wanted to go. He was an easy target, but no one Prophet could recognize at that distance. So he held his fire, not wanting to waste it on someone of no importance. He waited a few minutes longer before a target arrived. Another man came out of the saloon and stopped to talk to the drunk. Prophet recognized the gangly figure of the manager of the hotel dining room, Raymond Monroe. Monroe was a worthy target. He had spoken out in criticism of Prophet's request for extra pay. So, Prophet's thin lips curled into a satisfied smile as he shifted his front sight from the drunk to rest on Monroe's back. A steady squeeze of the trigger saw Monroe's knees buckle and he dropped to the ground as the sound of the shot rang out. Prophet's grin widened into a satisfied smile, only to freeze moments later when the door of the sheriff's office opened and an imposing figure he recognized immediately came out to investigate. *Cullen McCabe!* The image of the hated man froze the blood in his veins. *He had not left town, and he was obviously the sheriff now. All his suspicions were becoming fact.* Without hesitation, he cocked the rifle again and fired at McCabe, but he missed, so as quickly as he could crank another cartridge in, he shot again.

Cullen had been standing in the door of the sheriff's

office wondering if he was going to have to help the drunk wavering in front of the saloon. Before he decided, he saw Monroe come out of the saloon and stop to talk to the drunk. Moments later, he was startled when the shot rang out and Monroe slumped to the ground. Not sure where the shot had come from, Cullen responded at once, running to help him, and barely missed being hit by a shot that passed within inches of his head. Only by chance, was he lucky enough to see the muzzle blast seconds before he grabbed Monroe by the shoulders and dragged him out of the street, as the second shot kicked dirt up in the street several feet away. He dragged Monroe far enough past the corner of the saloon to get him out of the line of fire. At the same time, he yelled to the drunk to follow him. The closeness of the two shots had a definite sobering effect upon the young ranch hand and he did not have to be told again. Help arrived within minutes when several customers in the saloon came to the door to see what the shooting was about. Cullen and one of the customers carried Monroe inside and left him in Doc Worley's hands. Doc reluctantly left the poker game to tend to Monroe, who had been somewhat fortunate that Prophet's shot had struck him behind his left shoulder.

Having seen the muzzle flash, Cullen knew the shot was fired from somewhere close to the river. He made a quick estimate of the location of the shooter, based on where he would have to have been to get a clear shot between the front corner of the saloon and the front door of the sheriff's office. He needed his rifle, and it was in the sheriff's office. Since the front door of the office was obviously within the shooter's range of sight, he ran out the back door of the saloon, circled around the barbershop, and approached the office from the rear. Luckily, he had the key to the back door in his pocket. If that luck held up, he might possibly get around the back of the buildings and get in behind Prophet. And there was no doubt in his mind that it was Prophet.

Watching the section of the street he could see at his angle, Prophet cursed silently to have missed the opportunity to do away with McCabe. With his rifle still sighted on the spot where Monroe went down, he prayed for Cullen to show himself again. But there was no sign of him and no one else in the street. When it seemed obvious that no one was going to risk exposing themselves to another shot from that angle, he figured it best to move in search of an angle that might give him another target. He backed away from the low mound he had used as a firing platform, but stopped, startled, when a handful of dirt suddenly popped up in the air. It was followed immediately by the sharp crack of a Winchester rifle. He didn't wait. Following his natural instincts, he ran to his horse, back on the riverbank, thinking he could hear the sound of McCabe's feet pounding the ground behind him.

Not sure where Prophet was running to, only that it was somewhere on the riverbank, Cullen ran to the spot he had fired at. He had only been able to guess where Prophet had been shooting from, so he threw a wild shot at a low hummock about thirty yards from the river. He had no idea if that was where Prophet had been. He had only shot at the mound in hopes of drawing another muzzle blast, but there was no return shot. Looking back toward the street, however, he saw that he had a view of part of the front of the saloon, as

well as a full view of the sheriff's office. Then, to verify
his calculations, a tiny glint of light caught his eye,
and he reached down to find a spent shell from a
.44 cartridge. *He was here*, he thought, and immediately looked back toward the river. In the darkness, he
could see the outline of the foliage along the river.
His eye stopped on a group of trees with open spaces
on each side. *The closest place to tie a horse*, he immediately thought. He didn't hesitate but started trotting
toward the trees at once, his rifle ready to fire.

He approached the trees, ready to fall on the
ground if he saw the first sign of an ambush, but when
he reached them, there was no one there. Still not
certain he was right, he was about to search farther
up the river, when he was stopped by a familiar odor.
He looked down just in time to avoid stepping in the
sign Prophet's horse had been considerate to leave
for him. Still fresh, there was no doubt this was where
the horse had been tied. Prophet had chosen to run,
rather than force a confrontation. Cullen's initial
guess was the hideout. Evidently, Prophet had decided
to come back to take his vengeance on the people of
New Hope. And he had decided to take it one by one
as a sniper, possibly to keep the whole town on edge.
At this point, that theory was no more than Cullen's
guess, however. In case Prophet had simply moved to
a new position to shoot from, since this one had been
discovered, Cullen decided to follow his tracks if he
could. In the dark, that would not be easy, but bending
close to the ground, he could make out the horse's
hoofprints in the open spaces where there was no
grass. He found enough prints to give him a general
direction, and they led to the riverbank, and from

there, north along the bank. Cullen had to speculate Prophet was heading back to the hideout. As he stood there, considering that possibility, the moon began its slow rise over the plains. It helped confirm his opinion on Prophet's flight. *Well, I hadn't planned to take a ride tonight, but I don't reckon I've got anything better to do,* he thought. Before he did, however, he thought he'd best tell the people there was no longer any threat of a sniper—for tonight, at least.

When he returned to the saloon, he found Monroe sitting at a table, his wound patched up and bandaged. "Did you catch him?" he called out as soon as he saw Cullen.

"No, but I think he cut out," Cullen answered. "I found where his horse had been tied, and I couldn't find any trace of him."

"I reckon I'm lucky he ain't a better shot," Monroe said. "But I wonder why he picked me out. Who would wanna shoot me?"

"I expect about half the people in this town," Burt Whitley remarked, just coming in the door. His remark brought a wave of chuckles from the customers. He walked over to Cullen and asked, "You reckon it's that damn Prophet back to devil us?"

"That's my guess," Cullen answered. "I'm glad you came in. I'm gonna need my horse."

"I figured that, too, so I saddled him up for you. I wasn't sure the shootin' was over, so I left him at the stable."

"I 'preciate it, Burt," Cullen said, and started for the door.

"You be careful," Burt said.

Cullen didn't bother to go back to the riverbank to

try to follow a trail from there. When he picked up his horse, he set out for the outlaw camp, convinced that the sniper was Prophet. There was very little chance he could overtake him before he reached the hideout, but he could get there soon after. And that might be surprise enough to catch him unprepared for company. While he rode, he couldn't help thinking how things had worked out. If he hadn't let Ernest Robertson talk him into acting as the temporary sheriff, he would be in Fort Griffin, or Fort Worth, or headed for Indian Territory, looking for Prophet. He was dead set on finishing this business with Prophet before he killed more innocent folks in New Hope. The moon, although only a three-quarter one, was rising high in the sky now, lighting the wagon road that followed the Brazos. It might help a little on the treacherous climb up the little stream leading to Prophet's hideout.

John Prophet was talking to himself as he led his horse up the rocky stream bed, interrupting frequently with a swearword whenever he slipped or lost his footing on a loose rock. He had kept up a continuous rant all the way back from New Hope, triggered by the sighting of Cullen McCabe having obviously taken over the position of sheriff. The man was like a plague come to torment him alone, a plague that would not die. He was almost sick with frustration knowing he had the chance to end this curse that the devil had placed upon him, but had missed the shot. Every man he had sent to kill McCabe had failed. Now, he had failed, too. Was it this that caused him to run tonight? All the way back to the camp, he had told himself that he had not run because of a fear of this man. He feared no man. No man was faster with a six-gun than he. No, he told himself, he retreated from New Hope because he needed to plan his attack on McCabe, so as not to be shot in the back by someone hiding in ambush. So, it was best to return to the camp until he was ready to strike again. And he had struck the first blow against the town that rejected him and cast him out. That was certain. *Raymond Monroe was a member of the town council that voted to fire me, and he knows now what it means to act against John Prophet*, he thought. *There will be more before I'm through.*

Once he reached the cabin, he felt he was safe, thinking no one knew of the existence of this hideout. Everyone but him was dead, except the coward Slim Bradshaw, and he was most likely in Kansas by now. The thought of Slim triggered another thirst for vengeance. "When I'm through with McCabe," he announced to the empty cabin, "I might look Slim up." It pleased him when he imagined a picture of Slim trembling with fear upon seeing him. Hungry, now that he had convinced himself that he had struck a blow against New Hope, he got some more jerky out of his packs and picked up the coffeepot on the table. When he went outside the cabin, he paused when he realized he had not unsaddled his horse. He decided the gray could wait until he built a fire and put the pot on to boil. So he walked over to the edge of the stream where the rocks had formed a little pool and dipped the pot down into the water.

When the pot was filled, he started to return to the cabin when he thought he heard the unmistakable sound of a horse coming up the stream. In a panic, he dropped the coffeepot, drew his six-gun, and emptied it, shooting straight down the stream into the darkness. When the pistol was empty, he drew his rifle from the saddle sling and proceeded to empty the full magazine on it as well. In a panic now to think McCabe had found his hideout, he hurriedly reloaded his weapons, not knowing if he had hit him or not. There was no return fire. Maybe one of his bullets had struck home, but he wasn't going to go down to see.

Below him, Cullen was lying facedown, taking cover behind the biggest rock he could find in the brief seconds left to him when he first heard the cocking of the pistol some fifty feet above him. Immediately following the sound of that hammer cocking, he found himself in a hailstorm of flying lead and the only thing he could do was to hug the bed of that tiny, rocky stream. Luckily, he had left his horse at the mouth of the stream, otherwise Jake would be dead, for there was no way he could have avoided catching one of the many bullets raining down the stream. He was sure Prophet had fired every round in his handgun and the rifle, too. He thought about scrambling up the stream before Prophet could reload, but as soon as he started to get up from his cover, his foot dislodged a sizable rock which tumbled down the stream, taking more rocks with it. The ensuing disturbance caused more noise, which brought a second barrage of bullets down upon him from Prophet's half-loaded rifle. When it ended, Cullen fired three quick rounds in response. They were prompted by his frustration, for he couldn't see what he was shooting at. It occurred to him that this could go on all night, or until one of them ran out of ammunition. Reluctant as he was to retreat, he knew it made no sense to continue the standoff, hoping for a lucky shot. He was going to have to find another way to get to that cabin, and the only other way he knew about was to circle around to come up the other side of the hill. He was pretty sure he could find the back door to the hideout in the light of day, but he was not so confident that he could find it in the dark of night.

Above him, Prophet was frantically reloading again, still panicking to realize that McCabe had found the hideout. Suddenly, he felt treed, like a small animal up a tree, with no place left to escape to. And Cullen McCabe waiting below him was the hunter. With both handgun and rifle loaded again, Prophet tried to think what best to do. It occurred to him that maybe McCabe was not alone. He had made enemies of other men in town. They might be riding with McCabe to come after him. It struck him then that he was trapped up here, and the most important thing for him right now was to get out of this trap as quickly as possible. McCabe had found the way up the stream to the cabin, and he might find the back door as well. *I'm not going to wait to find out*, he declared to himself. His horse was still saddled, his packs were inside the door of the cabin. But what if McCabe came up the stream while he was loading the pack-horses? He quickly decided not to risk it, holstered his handgun, and ran to his horse. With no other thought except to leave this trap as soon as he possibly could, he stepped up into the saddle and guided the gray into the stream. When he reached the point where the stream went underground, he came out of it, as he had done once before, and headed down the mountain. Relieved of the worry that he might have been met by some of the men with McCabe, he thought about the fact that he had left horses and supplies behind. But he had money and ammunition. He would find what he needed at Gus Welker's trading post, and that was only fifty miles away.

CHAPTER 21

Having decided it was useless to try to approach the cabin from below, Cullen withdrew from the stream and went back to his horse. It was going to be difficult to find that back door into the hideout, but he figured it to be his only option with the situation he faced. So, with the little bit of help from the three-quarter moon, he started on a circle around the back of the slope that served as a base to a larger hill. He had to push through a thick belt of trees, hoping to come across the small path that led down from the clearing that he remembered. When he was about to decide he had somehow miscalculated the distance to the path, it suddenly appeared as a thin winding ribbon coming down from the slope above. Once he struck the path, he knew where he was in relation to the hideout, and he followed the path up to the small clearing he remembered. From there, he continued up, listening for the sound of the stream gushing out of a hole in the ground. When he found it, he left his horse there, thinking it best to proceed on foot, lest Jake make too much noise in the rocky stream.

When he had descended to a point where he could

see the back of the cabin and the corral behind it, he
picked a spot beside a tree where he could watch
the cabin until deciding how best to approach it.
In the darkness, he could not see Prophet waiting
near the stream, where he expected to find him. It
seemed unlikely that he was in the cabin, since he was
so fiercely guarding the trail up the stream before. He
looked at the corral again. There were two horses
there, so he had to think that Prophet was there as
well. "Damn," he softly swore when it occurred to him.
There was no gray horse in the corral. Prophet rode a
gray gelding. Unless he was pulling some kind of trick,
Prophet had run again, leaving his horses behind. If
that was the case, he couldn't have that much of a
start on him, but it would be more of a start in the
dark when Cullen had a slim chance of tracking him.
First, he decided, *I'd better make sure he's really gone and
not sitting in ambush down there in that cabin.*

   He got up from his position beside a tree and made
his way down the stream to the corral. From there,
he became more cautious, even though he knew
there was no place for Prophet to have hidden his
horse. *Unless he took it in the cabin,* he couldn't help
thinking. There was no trace of light in the cabin, so
with his rifle held at the ready, Cullen walked up to
the door, kicked it open, and jumped to the side
just in case. As he had already concluded, Prophet
was gone. He looked at the packs on the floor, just
inside the door, and realized that Prophet was
clearly in a panic to run. Cullen had a decision to
make at this point. His impulse was to get on Jake
and go after Prophet, but he was the temporary sheriff
of New Hope, and he had no idea how long he might
be gone, leaving the town without a sheriff again. As

peaceful as the town had been for the past couple of days, he felt the only known threat was from John Prophet. So, if he stopped Prophet, he might be protecting not only New Hope, but other towns as well. *At any rate,* he decided, *I ain't likely to be this close on his trail again, so I'm gonna catch him.* With that decided, he got ready to leave.

He wasn't sure how long this chase was going to be, so he decided to look through the supplies Prophet left behind. He soon found enough basic supplies to keep him going for a while, so as quickly as he could, he loaded them on one of the horses left in the corral. Then he took the rails out of the corral to let the other horse go free and led his new packhorse up the stream where Jake waited. He figured he could assume that Prophet had followed the path down from the hills and onto the prairie beyond. So, he continued on, gambling on Prophet taking the path to the creek where it stopped. He remembered the distance to be around eight or nine miles, and at that point, he would have to determine which way he went after crossing the creek and striking the road beyond it.

When he reached the end of the path at the creek, he dismounted to try to confirm his hunch so far. At the edge of the creek the wide stretch of white sand was soft enough to permit him to see the recent hoofprints that led into the water. Knowing he was still on Prophet's trail, he continued on to the road, which he had determined the last time he tracked Prophet to be the wagon road to Fort Griffin. The question to be answered at this point was, did he go east or west? He had to assume he went east to Fort Griffin, so he turned Jake that way, but before starting out on the road, he decided to check one other option. So he stepped down from the saddle and walked across the road. To his surprise, he saw hoofprints beyond the road, indicating someone went straight across. To be sure, he struck a match and held it close to the tracks. He was sure they were fresh. He figured there was no decision to make, so he stood up and took a long look in the direction the tracks appeared to be heading. *Straight north,* he decided. *I hope to hell I'm right.*

Taking a sighting on a distant hill, he held to that direction for what he estimated to be about ten miles when he came to a small creek. He decided he'd best stop and rest the horses, else he might soon be on foot. While he waited, he opened Prophet's packs and pulled out a coffeepot and some coffee. While the coffee was boiling, he took a look around the creek bank for any sign of tracks. He didn't find any, nor did he expect to. He just had to have faith that he was still riding in the general direction that Prophet was. Maybe Prophet was heading for someplace in particular, a town maybe. This far along, Cullen had to trust a great deal to just plain luck. After the horses were rested, he started out again, holding to the same line as before, and within a distance of two or three miles from the creek, he struck another wagon road. It came in from the west and turned almost straight north at that point. It looked to be heading in the direction he was riding. He took it as a sign that his hunch was right and decided to stay with the road from that point on.

Close to the time when he felt he should rest his horses again, he spotted a long line of trees, indicating a river ahead, or possibly a large creek. When he approached it, he decided it was a river, probably a fork of the Brazos, and it came at a perfect time to water his horses. He rode upstream of the road, crossing to a spot under a large tree, and made his camp, wondering where and what Prophet was doing at that time. He wondered also if he had gained any on him, if he had stopped to water and rest his horse. It was tempting to push Jake on a little farther, but he knew if he did, it might cost him later on. Thinking of Prophet prompted him to decide it time to cook some of the side meat he had found in his packs.

Gus Welker turned around from the shelves behind the counter when he heard the little bell on the front door ring. He seemed startled for a moment before he said, "I'll be go to hell, John Prophet. What are you doin' out in this part of the country?"

"Well, I ain't travelin' for my health," Prophet answered. "I need a drink and I need somethin' to eat."

"I reckon we can fix you up with both of 'em," Gus said. He continued to shift his eyes nervously toward the door that led to the saloon portion of his building. "You look like you been rode hard this early in the mornin'. You lookin' for somebody? You ain't got a posse on your tail, have you?"

"What the hell's wrong with you, Gus?" Prophet responded. He was wrung out, both mentally and physically, and he had no patience for Gus's inane questions. "If you think I look like I was rode hard, you oughta take a look at my horse outside. I had to leave a place in a hurry, but I ain't got no posse behind me. So, you ain't got nothin' to worry about but sellin' me some likker and somethin' to eat. You still got that half-breed woman cookin'? What was her name?"

"Mae," Gus replied, "still is. You wait here a minute. I'll go see if she can cook you up some breakfast." He started toward the door to the saloon. Seeing no reason to wait there in the store, Prophet promptly followed. Sensing it, Gus sang out, "Mae! John Prophet is here and he's lookin' for somethin' to eat!" There was an immediate sound of a chair being pushed quickly back from a table.

"What the . . ." Prophet started, unable to believe his eyes. A cynical smile broke across his face. "Well, I'll be . . . If it ain't my old partner, Slim Bradshaw, my trusty old partner. You musta got lost when I sent you to take care of a little job for me." His hand dropped to rest on the handle of his .44.

"Now, hold on, Boss," Slim pleaded, trying desperately to come up with some explanation. "It weren't just McCabe out there at that ranch. They had brought in some help from town or somewhere, guardin' him and the woman." Making it up as he continued, he said, "I stayed out there all night, tryin' to get a chance, but come mornin' I had to give it up."

"Is that a fact?" Prophet smirked. "Well, why didn't you come back and tell me, instead of takin' off and comin' here?"

Unable to create any reasonable reason why he didn't, Slim gave up and told the truth. "I knew you'd be mad as hell, so I figured the best thing for me to do was to take off."

"And leave me to find out that mornin' when that bitch and McCabe both come walkin' into that saloon," Prophet said, the smirk still in place. Feeling himself again, with Slim cringing before him, he watched the worried man literally trembling. Gone for the time being were the feelings of panic he felt when McCabe came after him at the hideout. "You feel lucky?" he said with his hand hovering over his sidearm.

"I don't reckon I got no luck," Slim answered, knowing he was moments away from his death. He had seen Prophet draw down on a man, more than once, and he knew he didn't stand a chance. But he stood there, determined to take the fate he had coming with his head up high. He was genuinely sorry for the life path he had chosen, but he had no one to blame but himself.

Prophet continued to smirk at him for a long moment before suddenly declaring, "I think I'll give you a chance to show me you ain't the yellow-bellied coward I thought you was. I just decided to leave that sorry little town, and I ain't sure that Cullen McCabe ain't tryin' to come after me. If he does, I'm callin' him out. Now, I don't know how fast he is, and right now, I ain't takin' any chances. I just want him dead." Prophet still planned to settle with Slim for running out on him, but he could be useful for the time being. And when Slim still looked confused about what exactly he expected of him, Prophet spelled it out for him. "When I challenge the blowhard to stand and face me, I don't plan to take any chances. When I say, *Whenever you're ready*, that's your signal. Shoot to kill. Understand? Whenever you're ready," he repeated.

"Yeah, I reckon I understand that," Slim said.

"Good. Now let's have a drink," Prophet said, then turned to Gus, who had been watching the pathetic drama as it played out. "Tell Mae I need some breakfast."

"Right," Gus responded, and turned to Mae, who

had been standing in the kitchen door watching the confrontation between the two outlaws.

Before Gus could relay Prophet's request, she said, "Yeah, I heard." She did an about-face to return to the kitchen, disappointed not to have seen a gunfight.

After leaving his camp on the Brazos, Cullen was in the saddle for no more than seven or eight miles when he saw that he was approaching yet another river. Based on the scant knowledge he had of this part of the territory, he guessed it to possibly be the Wichita River. When he got closer, he realized the river forked at that point, and he discovered a building of some sort between the forks. His initial thought was a store of some kind, possibly a trading post, and as he got closer, his guess was confirmed. There was a path to the store leading down from the road, so he turned to follow it, but pulled Jake to a sudden stop when he saw the gray horse tied at the hitching rail in front. There was no doubt, even at that distance, that it was Prophet's horse. The gray gelding looked drawn and weary, telling Cullen why he had not been able to overtake him before now. He sat there for only a second longer before pressing Jake again and riding down the path toward the store, some thirty yards away. He thought it best not to remain a sitting target, in case Prophet might be watching from the store. Halfway down the path, he veered off and rode Jake up to the side of the trading post.

Stepping down quickly, he drew his rifle from the saddle sling and dropped the reins to the ground. Then he edged up to the corner of the building to make sure there was no one on the porch before he walked inside. He lifted the latch and pushed the door slightly ajar, enough to see a portion of the room. Alert to the possibility that he might be walking into a reception awaiting his entrance, he pushed the door farther open. Still there was no one, so in one quick move, he pushed the door wide open and held his rifle ready to shoot anyone behind the door. There was no one in the store. He looked at once toward the door that led to the saloon, where he could hear voices.

Gus Welker, standing near the bar, was the first to notice the imposing figure stepping through the doorway from his store. "Howdy, stranger," he greeted him. "Somethin' I can help you with?"

"You can stand right there on this side of the bar," Cullen answered. At the sound of his voice, both Prophet and Slim turned at once. "Didn't expect to find the sheriff and his deputy here," Cullen said, his rifle leveled at the two seated at the table. "Best keep your hands on the table where I can see 'em," he warned when Prophet started to slide his right hand toward the edge of the table.

Initially speechless from the shock of seeing the man he hoped never to meet again, Prophet gradually regained a modicum of courage, since McCabe didn't come in with guns blazing. "There's three of us to your one," he pointed out. "Ain't too gooda odds, is it?"

"Two-to-one," Gus immediately declared. "I got no part in this, one side or the other." He threw his hands up to show Cullen he was unarmed.

His declaration of surrender brought a glaring rebuke in Prophet's eyes, but he was sure McCabe could not kill both Slim and him. "One of us is bound to get you, McCabe. You oughta know that."

"That may be so," Cullen said. "I reckon we'll see, but one thing you can count on is you'll get my first shot."

"If you had any guts, we'd settle this between the two of us, I'd tell Slim to stay out of it, and it'd just be the two of us, man-to-man. Whaddaya say, McCabe? Have you got the guts to stand up to me in a show-down?"

"Now, why the hell would I wanna do that?" Cullen replied. "I've got you covered right now. One little squeeze on this trigger and you're a dead man." He glanced at Slim, standing now and looking tense and uneasy. "So, I reckon it would be between me and Slim then to see who was fastest."

"I'm a man of my word," Prophet claimed. "I'll tell Slim to step aside. This has been a long time comin' between me and you. We need to settle it man-to-man, if you're man enough to face me in a fair fight. I'm thinkin' you ain't fast enough to take me on. What if I let you use that rifle you seem so partial to? The only rule is, you have to rest the muzzle on the floor before we draw. Gus, there, can call the action, when he says *draw*, we draw. Best man wins. How 'bout it, big man? Are you man enough to face me when we've both got a fair chance?" Feeling more and more confident now that Cullen seemed to be hesitating, Prophet took a step sideways to stand away from the table. He nodded toward Slim. "Back up, Slim, this is between me and Mr. McCabe. You stay out of it, no matter who comes out on top. You understand?"

Slim nodded and replied, "I understand." He backed away from the table.

"All right, McCabe," Prophet said. "It's just me and you now. You walked in here with your rifle, looking for somebody to shoot. I'm waitin' to see what you're made of."

Cullen had to admit to himself that Prophet was right in his assessment of the situation. He had been too anxious to catch up with him. He should have scouted the situation first, but he had not given any thought lately toward Prophet's joining up again with Slim Bradshaw. So, he foolishly walked right into it. What puzzled him, however, was the fact that he was still standing. He would have expected Prophet to shoot him down as soon as he walked in the door. That was more his style, than this challenge to face him in a duel. Also, he was not foolish enough to think Slim would stay out of it. So, it had come down to taking the chance to get both of them before one of them got him. He had no way of knowing just how fast Prophet was, but Prophet was confident enough to think he could draw his .44 and fire before his opponent could lift a rifle and pull the trigger. Cullen was confident that he couldn't, so it seemed like a foolish move on Prophet's part, unless he knew Slim was going to shoot him before he had a chance to raise his rifle. Whatever happened, he decided, he was determined to kill Prophet. Slim was just a simple puppet, dangling on Prophet's strings. It was important to keep Prophet from destroying any more lives of innocent people. "All right," Cullen said. "I'll play your game." He walked over in the center of the room to face Prophet. As Prophet grinned, Cullen lowered his rifle until the muzzle rested on the floor.

Prophet said nothing for a moment while he openly smirked at Cullen. Then he said, "Whenever you're ready," reaching for his pistol even before the words were out of his mouth. The sound of the .44 shattered the silence of a few moments before. Prophet jerked his head back, his pistol halfway out of his holster, and fell face forward on the floor, a bullet hole in his back. Stunned, Cullen nevertheless raised his rifle in time to cover Slim, who stood as if in a trance, his .44 still in hand. After what seemed a long minute, he dropped his pistol on the floor in surrender.

As astonished as Gus and Mae, who had come from the kitchen to watch, Cullen stood speechless for a long moment, his rifle still covering Slim, who seemed to have expected a fatal shot to come from the Winchester. After another moment, Cullen let the rifle sink slowly again, walked over to Prophet's body to make sure he was dead, then he picked up Slim's pistol from the floor. He looked Slim in the eye, waiting for some explanation. Finally, Slim spoke. "I done a lot of rotten things in my life, but that man was more evil than the devil himself. I didn't wanna be no part of helpin' him kill another good man." He raised his face to look at Cullen. "So, I reckon you got me to do whatever you was gonna do to Prophet. I ain't gonna fight you. I reckon I deserve whatever's comin' to me." With that, he had said his piece and was ready to accept his punishment.

Still finding it hard to believe what had just happened, Cullen didn't say anything for a long minute. Finally, he handed Slim's pistol back to him. "My advice to you is to get on your horse and ride way the hell away from this part of the country." He glanced over at Gus and Mae, both with eyes wide and mouths agape. "Folks are gonna talk about this, but the story is gonna be about you bein' the man who shot John

Prophet in the back. It'd be a good idea to change your name, too."

Slim wasn't sure he was hearing correctly. "You gonna let me go?"

"Yeah, I reckon so," Cullen said, and promptly turned his back and walked out the door.

It was suppertime when Cullen rode into the north end of town and pulled his horses into the stable. Burt wasn't there, so he figured he was at his house, eating supper with his daughter and grandchildren. After he put his horses away for the night, Cullen walked down the street toward the hotel. He was tired, and he was hungry, so he gave the jail and sheriff's office only a casual glance as he walked past. Everything looked just as he had left it and the padlock was still on the door, so he figured the town had been as peaceful as he had expected it to be. He walked up to the outside entrance to the hotel dining room and went inside. "Well, lookee here," Lottie Bridges sang out when he came in the door. "He ain't run off and left us after all, and this time he didn't bring a wife and young 'uns back with him."

Hearing Lottie's boisterous greeting, Monroe came from the kitchen to see who she was talking about. Seeing Cullen, he commented as well, "Heyo, Cullen, everybody was wondering what happened to you. I figured you've been sayin' you were leavin' ever since the day you rode in, so you just finally did it. That's what I told Ernest Robertson. He's been worried about what's gonna happen if we ain't got a sheriff."

"I didn't expect to see you up walkin' around,"

Cullen commented upon seeing him up so soon after having been shot."

"I was just lucky, I reckon," Monroe replied. "Doc's got me all bandaged up under my coat. Right now, I just can't move my shoulder much."

"If you folks still sell supper in here, I'd sure like to buy some," Cullen replied.

Lottie was quick to fetch a cup of coffee for him. "I already told Bea to get a plate ready," she said, and stood waiting for him to explain his absence of more than two days.

"Well, damn it, McCabe," Monroe finally blurted, "are you gonna tell us what happened?"

"I ain't gonna bring him his supper till he does," Lottie threatened.

Having been told by someone on the street that the sheriff was back in town, Ernest Robertson came into the dining room at that point. "We'd all like to know if you caught up with Prophet," he declared.

"Well," Cullen said, "you don't have to worry about John Prophet causin' you any more trouble."

"Good," Monroe said at once. "You killed the crazy S.O.B."

"Well, no," Cullen replied. "That's a kinda funny thing." An immediate look of disappointment appeared on all three faces, replaced a moment later by one of surprise when Cullen explained. "He's dead, all right, but I didn't shoot him. His deputy did."

"Slim Bradshaw?" Monroe blurted.

"Slim Bradshaw," Cullen confirmed. He went on to explain the circumstances of John Prophet's execution. When Robertson asked about Slim's fate, Cullen said, "You don't have to worry about him anymore. He's halfway up through Indian Territory by now, headed toward Kansas. He shot Prophet to keep him from shootin' me. Now, can I have my supper?"

When Bea brought Cullen's supper plate in from the kitchen, Robertson sat down at the table to talk. Cullen prepared himself for another recruiting speech but was pleasantly surprised instead. "When you disappeared for a couple of days, I have to admit I was a little worried. I had talked to Dave White about the job of sheriff. He used to be the foreman on John Snyder's cattle ranch, but he got tired of being away from his young family so many months of the year on cattle drives. He had a little experience as a deputy sheriff when he was a lot younger, so I talked to the council and we decided we'd offer him the job if you definitely didn't want it."

"Well, that's good news," Cullen said at once. "I hope he turns out to be a good sheriff. New Hope surely deserves one." His supper suddenly tasted all the better.

After supper, he made it a point to go by Burt's house to tell him what had happened with Prophet and to let him know he planned to sleep in the stable with his horses that night. He was pleased to see that Sarah and the children had made themselves at home. It was obvious that Burt was happy to have them with him, even under such sad circumstances. Cullen wished them all a good night and retired to the stable.

When Burt opened the stable the next morning, he came with instructions from Sarah that Cullen was expected for breakfast. But Cullen and his horses were gone. Knowing it was too early for the dining room to open, Burt thought he would catch him in the sheriff's office. He found the lock missing from the door, so he went inside. The office was empty, and he noticed the padlock and keys lying on the desk. While he was standing there, he heard someone come up on the porch. He turned to see Ernest Robertson come in the door. "Looking for McCabe?" Robertson asked. When Burt said that he was, Robertson said, "I think he's gone. I don't expect he'll be back this time."

"What makes you say that?" Burt asked.

"I don't know. I just have a feeling, I reckon. When he rode into town that first day, things were getting worse and worse in New Hope. He was just a drifter. Nobody knew where he came from, or where he was going. And right from the first, he said he wouldn't be here long, but none of the trouble he came face-to-face with was enough to send him on his way. It would have been enough to send most men along quick enough. Then it seemed like New Hope's problems became his to solve. McCabe single-handedly cleaned out the Viper Gang, and when John Prophet went down, New Hope's problems went away." He paused to emphasize, "And so did McCabe." He waited a moment, but when Burt made no comment, he asked, "What do you know about McCabe? He ever tell you about a family or anything like that? You got closer to him than anybody else in town. Did he ever talk about where he came from, or where he was going?"

"No, for a fact, McCabe wasn't much for makin' conversation," Burt answered. "That might be the only thing I know about him for sure." He chuckled then and continued. "I can tell you what my granddaughter, Carrie, says. She says McCabe rode that big bay horse right down to the bushes she was hidin' in, right after she prayed as hard as she could for the good Lord to send an angel down to save her and her brother. She said she thought her mama was already dead, but McCabe went back to their wagon and brought her back with him."

Robertson grunted, amused by the child's imagination. He shook his head then and allowed, "That ain't a whole lot different from what happened in New Hope, is it?"

"Ain't for me to question," Burt said. He couldn't help thinking about the rare odds that also brought McCabe to appear at the site of David's murder, in time to save Sarah and the children. "Ain't for me to question," he repeated softly.

Keep reading for a special early excerpt!

SAVE IT FOR SUNDAY
A Taylor Callahan, Circuit Rider Western

by William W. Johnstone and J.A. Johnstone

**From Confederate marauder to rebel gunfighter
to repentant preacher man, circuit rider
Taylor Callahan's road to perdition has been a
hellish ride. Sinners beware.**

After riding with Missouri bushwhackers,
Taylor Callahan vowed to never take another
life. He's making good on it in Peaceful Valley.
By day, swamping a saloon. By night, preaching
the Good Book. But this little settlement is
about to become anything but peaceable.
When the marshal takes a bullet in a
sheepman-cattleman skirmish he pins a badge
on Taylor, leaving the circuit rider open to
whole new world of hell . . .

A railroad engineer building a line from
Laramie to Denver is cutting across Arapaho
land, starting a war on Peace Treaty Peak. If
that's not enough to set the county on fire,
Taylor's trigger-happy past comes calling.
The revenge-seeking Harris boys are hot on his
tail. With the marshal down, Peaceful Valley is
ripe for the taking—and blasting Taylor to
kingdom come is part of the deal. If keeping
the peace means breaking Taylor's vow, so be
it. He's looking forward to strapping on his
Colt .45 again. That's the gospel truth.

Look for SAVE IT FOR SUNDAY,
on sale in April 2023

CHAPTER 1

Wyoming Territory, 1876

And it came to pass . . .

It was a stagecoach, moving as thought the hounds of hell were trying to jump into the rear boot. This wasn't a Concord, but one of those Abbott & Downing mud wagons—though the trail wasn't even damp. Boxy-looking, not as big as a Concord, bouncing like it was out of control, with the driver serenading the six mules pulling the coach with every cuss word in his vocabulary. The leather curtains were rolled up. No guard to be seen—perhaps he had jumped off or quit. The horse and rider didn't get a good look at any passengers inside.

Because it *passed* Taylor Callahan, riding that slow-footed white gelding he named Job, like horse and man were standing still like those wind-blown boulders sprinkled across the rolling plains.

Nary a salutation from driver, who spit out a stream of tobacco juice that shot past Callahan's beard stubble like a minié ball.

And it came to pass . . .

Taylor Callahan ran that through his mind again, nodded, and pulled down the kerchief as the dust kicked up by the mud wagon settled onto the grass and rocks on the southeastern side of the trail. Yes, he could use that. It would work fine. *It* being the stagecoach. *Pass* being the verb and . . .

The jangling of traces and more ribald language caused Callahan to turn around.

Could that be?

This time, Callahan eased Job farther off the trail, turned the gelding around to see another approaching mud wagon, also with a foul-mouthed driver and no guard. Time brings wisdom to most critters, one of Callahan's pappies had always said, so this time Taylor Callahan had time and wisdom to pull up his bandanna to cover his mouth and nose.

Once again, the driver paid no attention and made no gesture, friendly or otherwise, to the tall man in black on a white horse whom it passed. But Callahan got a good look inside this coach. He saw a handsome woman, in a fine green dress, hair in a bun, holding what might have been a Bible in her hand. And the woman might have smiled at Callahan, or perhaps Job. She even offered a friendly, fleeting, wave as this coach rolled past.

Once again, Callahan let the dust settle before he lowered the bandanna and nudged Job back onto the road. He looked behind him a good long while before he felt satisfied that no more speeding mud wagons were stampeding north. He forgot about any puns or wit he would display at his next preaching, just let the gelding carry him leisurely north.

Though he did keep looking over his shoulder while plodding across a country that looked like waves on the ocean. He wanted to make sure no other coaches came up behind him. The last thing he wanted was to be greeted by the Major General in the Heavens at St. Peter's Gate and be told that he had been killed after being run over by an Abbott & Downing Company mud wagon.

By then the sun had started to sink behind the mountains far off to the west. Coming out of Denver, Colorado Territory, Callahan thought most of the Rocky Mountains would be like that Front Range just west of Denver. Mountains reaching to the skies, often their tops disappearing behind clouds. But here, in what Callahan figured had to be Wyoming Territory by now, the mountains appeared to be a good ride southwest or northwest.

Oh, these weren't those flat plains Callahan had seen in Kansas, or just last year way down in southern Texas. The way the wind blew the tall grass, Callahan almost thought he was in an ocean. Which reminded him:

I still ain't let my eyes feast on an ocean.

That had been his plan when he was drifting south in Texas. See the great seas, where that whale swallowed Jonah, though some blowhard Texan had told him that he wouldn't see an ocean, just the Gulf of Mexico, or maybe even nothing more than the Corpus Christi Bay.

He had hardly seen anything wet except one of the most vicious flash floods he had witnessed. And coming from a childhood in western Missouri, Taylor Callahan had seen many a flood. The Mighty Missouri was no little crick when she flooded, and one of the first funerals the Reverend Taylor Callahan had ever preached was for a 10-year-old boy who got caught when the Sni-A-Bar got to raging.

Which reminded Taylor Callahan that the four Harris boys, if they had not been lynched or shot down like the dogs they were—*May the Major General in the Heavens forgive me for thinking in such an unforgiving kind of way*—could be after him yet.

He reined in Job, and looked down the trail. The dust from the two stages had long settled. No travelers could be seen as far as Taylor Callahan could see, and he could see a right far piece in this country.

There were hills all around him, popping up here and there, rocks strewn about, and a body could even find a tree, usually along the creek beds, even though Callahan had not seen much in the way of water in those creek beds.

Strange country. Pretty, but different. It looked as though that old Major General in the Heavens had been trying to see what He or She ought to make this Wyoming Territory look like. Maybe the General decided that those mountains off to the west just was too much like Colorado, and the Major General had already perfected the Great Plains when Kansas got created. How about some of these red rocks and boulders and dust to blow? That ain't half bad, but, well . . .

Callahan understood. He had seen parts of that when he had left Texas and ridden up through New Mexico Territory following, mostly, the Pecos River.

The hills weren't consistent, either. Some of them were just rolling like the waves, but here and there he found buttes, mostly barren, some with boulders that appeared to have been dropped out of the sky.

Meteorites? All those shooting stars Callahan had seen, sometimes making wishes on, though rarely, if ever, seeing one of those wishes come true. Those things had to land somewhere. But these rocks like the two Job was riding between right now did not look like

the moon did when she was close and shining bright,
or that little piece of hard rock he had paid a three-
cent nickel to see at that dog-and-pony show in
Trinidad, Colorado, a few months back. The professor
swore that it was a part of a meteorite that had come
past Mars and the moon and landed in Utah back in
'69. But that professor might not have been the most
honest person, since his assistant was peddling bottles
of Doctor Jasper's Patented Soothing Syrup Guaran-
teed to Cure Infant Colic, Consumption, Whooping
Cough, Female Complaints, Malaise, and Warts.

Just before darkness fell, Callahan found a muddy
bit of water where a little creek made a bend around
another boulder, and he stopped here, loosening
the cinch but leaving the saddle on the gelding, and
letting Job graze and drink. He pulled another bandanna out of the saddle bag and used it to strain water
into a coffeepot, just enough for two cups of coffee.

He built a fire, stretched his legs, pushed back his
hat as the water began to boil, and tried to think how
far he had come since Denver.

The carpenter Callahan had been working for said
it was about a hundred miles to Cheyenne, but keeping track of miles traveled came hard for this circuit-
riding preacher. How long had he stayed at Fort
Collins? The carpenter hated to let Callahan go, and
since they were building a church, Callahan had kept
delaying his departure, even though the church already had hired a minister who was coming in from
North Platte, Nebraska, if he didn't get scalped by
Sioux and Cheyenne, and the congregation was de-
cidedly Episcopal, and Callahan had known many a
fine Episcopalian, and even had enjoyed a pilsner

with one of that cloth—before the War Between the States, anyway.

He had moved on to Poudre City, preached a few days at the livery, and then went through Virginia Dale, preached in a saloon, before lighting out again.

Callahan knew he was in Wyoming by now. The beer jerker at Virginia Dale said the territory wasn't more than a hop and a skip away, and while Job had never been inclined to hop or skip, they had gotten a good start not long after breakfast.

"Just follow the trail," the beer jerker said, "and make good time. Indians be on the prod."

"Most of that's way up Montana way," the faro dealer corrected.

"They's enough injuns between Montana and New Mexico to give us fits."

Taylor Callahan drank the coffee, massaged his thighs and buttocks, emptied bladder and bowels, washed his hands in the muddy stream, and waited till the moon rose.

"Best to travel at night," the beer jerker had told him. "Injuns won't attack at night."

"Who told you that?" the faro dealer barked.

"An old-timer at Fort Lupton."

"That ol' coot? His brain left him before the Pikes Peak crowd showed up in Colorado."

"I read that in the *Denver Twice-Weekly Reporter*, too."

"You can't read."

They were still going at it when Callahan pulled on his hat and left the saloon for the stable.

The moon was full.

"Plantin' moon," the beer jerker had said.

"Raidin' moon, you moron," the faro dealer had said.

Callahan figured it would be light enough to follow the road, even if the road was really nothing more than the tracks of wagons—like those fool mud wagons—had made by flattening the grass.

Callahan was used to traveling at night. Back in Missouri, he traveled a lot without even a moon to guide his way. But that's what a lot of Missouri bushwhackers needed to do during the late War Between the States. Carbine Logan's boys made a habit of not being seen. That was a long time ago though, and back when Taylor Callahan was younger and impetuous, and a tad bitter and angry.

He was a changed man now.

He was also broke.

The money he had made working for the carpenter in Fort Collins did not amount to much, and while the livery in Poudre City had paid him in coffee and hard tack, the coins collected in the black hat Callahan passed barely covered the feed bill he had been charged for Job's appetite. He had done a wee bit better in Virginia Dale till that old codger with a wooden leg came in with a story about an ailing wife and all four kids with the croup and not enough money to hire the barber across the way who sometimes doctored folks up.

"Here's what I can give you, old-timer," Callahan said, and dumped his change into the man's calloused hands. "As long as you promise me you ain't buying Doctor Jasper's Patented Soothing Syrup."

"Cures warts," the faro dealer said.

"No, it don't," the beer jerker argued. "But it works wonders on the grippe."

Callahan wanted to get to Cheyenne so he could maybe get enough tithes to spend at least one night in a hotel with hot bath water and decent linens. Maybe even a shave since he had traded in his straight razor for a bit of ground coffee in Poudre City.

The faro dealer at Virginia Dale had told him not to go to Cheyenne, but make way to Laramie. It was closer and had a lot of sinners.

The beer jerker had said, no, the real action was to be had farther west, at Fort Steele on the North Platte because nobody sinned worse than soldiers that far from the civilized world.

That's why Callahan picked Cheyenne.

He kicked out the fire, doused the smoke with the remnants of his coffee, and got to work on Job, tying the coffeepot to the bedroll, tightening the cinch, saying a short prayer, and eating the last bit of beef jerky he had been saving. He waited for the moon to rise just a bit higher, and then he opened the saddle-bags. He pulled out the .45-caliber long-barreled Colt revolver, and checked the loads. He thought about sticking it inside the deep pocket of his black Prince Albert, but decided against that.

Indians might have a different color skin than Taylor Callahan, and likely practiced a different religion, but if the faro dealer was right, then Callahan would rely on his faith, and the Major General in the Heavens, to protect him, His will, or Her will, be done.

He returned the Colt to its place, fastened the buckle, moved around Job, keeping his hand on the gelding hide so not to get kicked, and reached the other saddle bag. He opened it, touched the Bible, said a brief prayer, and found two corn dodgers.

He thought about eating one, but figured the salt would just make him thirsty. Instead, he brought them to Job, and let the horse eat the stale balls of bread.

Callahan led the horse back to the trail, which

would be easy to follow on a cloudless night. He tightened the cinch again, and eased into the saddle.

Job snorted.

"You'll get a fine stall and a good rubdown in Cheyenne," Callahan told him.

That was a bit of a prayer, he realized. But maybe the Major General in the Heavens was listening and feeling charitable.

He laughed when Job bucked twice, an informal protest, but Callahan was a better horseman than many people—at least those who had never known him as one of Carbine Logan's Irregulars—didn't realize.

"You done?" he said, then kicked the gelding into a slow walk.

"That's what I figured." Callahan shook his head and clucked his tongue. "Two jumps and you're played out. Come on, boy, just follow the trail."

Callahan had done some figuring, and the way he figured, those stagecoaches that had almost run him and his horse over that afternoon would not be traveling at night. So he could maybe be out of their way by the time dawn broke if, by chance, they started making a return trip to whatever burgh they had come from.

He could hear his late ma telling him, with some amazement, "You got some brains beneath that hard skull of yourn that I never knowed you had, boy. How come you don't always act like you know somethin'?"

An hour later, he realized he had erred.

And as the stagecoach barreled toward him, he could hear his late ma's voice:

"Boy, you ain't got the sense the Lord give a corncob."

CHAPTER 2

Riding horseback at night had its risks. Taylor Callahan understood that. The odds—and the preacher remembered a thing or two about such things from his wilder years when he saw nothing sinful about wagering on anything—likely favored a stagecoach over a man on horse. Even with a shining moon. A stagecoach, after all, had headlamps. A stagecoach would not likely be started by a rattlesnake or a pronghorn. And most stagecoach drivers did not whip six mules into running at a hard gallop over not much of a road up and down a steep hill.

Thank the Major General in the Heavens, because Callahan—and Job—heard the rattling of the coach, the cannonade of hoofbeats, the snapping of a whip, and the reprehensible language of the driver. That gave the circuit rider time to turn the white gelding off what Wyoming called a road.

What neither horse nor rider expected was for the lead and trailing mules to leap into view on the crest of the hill. The stagecoach went airborne. The mules, and driver—again, no one rode as a guard—spotted Job, beaming brighter that he actually was because of

the big moon—and while mules might not be
spooked while galloping from a rattlesnake or an
antelope, seeing a ghostly figure in black atop a bright
white steed led to a totally different reaction.

The mules turned left, away from Job and Callahan
on the right. The driver shouted out something that
was lost in the chaos that followed.

Taylor Callahan knew he would never know exactly
what happened till that glorious day—many years
from now, he prayed—when he stood at the Pearly
Gates and heard the story from the Major General in
the Heavens. The mules and driver were not the only
ones spooked. Job started bucking.

The top of the stirrups caught Callahan's boots
when the gelding kicked out his back legs, right
before the seat of the saddle caught the Missourian's
crotch when the horse's legs touched ground. Those
moves repeated themselves for four or five or fifty
more jumps. Well, Callahan would concede later, it
probably did not get as high as fifty, but that didn't
mean he couldn't use it in a sermon at a camp meeting now and then. In any event, once his right foot
lost its hold in the stirrup, and Job's twisting, turning,
bending head jerked one rein from Callahan's grip,
he knew he was not long for this ride. He kicked his
left foot free, let go of the other rein, and propelled
himself off his mount on Job's next high kick.

He landed on his left foot, bounced up, twisted
around, and fell on his back. His legs landed next
while the air rushed out of his lungs, and he felt a
sharp pain in the back of his head. Since he had no
idea where Job might be bouncing around, Callahan
did not wait to wiggle his fingers and toes or turn his
head one way or the other. The last thing he wanted

was for eight hundred pounds of glue bait to stomp the life out of him.

Rolling over sage and rocks and cheap grass, he realized that he had not broken his back or neck. Once he stopped, he shoved his hands flat on the ground, and pushed himself upright.

There he stood, breathing in dust. As his lungs worked extra hard, he wet his lips with his tongue, and turned to find Job. The horse had bucked itself out pretty quickly. That came as no shock to Taylor Callahan. But the gelding remained out of sorts, ears flat against its head, staring off to the southwest, and pawing the earth.

"Easy," Callahan said, surprised that his jaw was not broken, but he never got to finish saying "boy."

Behind him came a deafening crash, followed by hideous screams of man and beast.

The next words that escaped from Callahan's mouth would not please the Major General in the Heavens, but the battered preacher could remember to ask for exception and forgiveness later. At that moment he turned around. Dust rose like fog glowing white and tan and ominous in that bath of moonlight. Callahan started up the incline toward the path that pretended to be a road. Then he stopped, turned around, and found his hat.

He took one more glance at Job before, satisfied that the gelding wasn't going anywhere unless someone dangled a carrot, Callahan pounded some shape back into his Boss of the Plains, and rid it of dead grass and some of the dirt, and reached the trail. More dust rose in separate locations. The thickest cloud was down southwest, maybe forty or fifty yards. That would be what was left of the stagecoach and driver. The other dust came from the mules, all six of them, still in their traces and making good time for Virginia Dale, Poudre City, Fort Collins, Denver, Hades, wherever those animals felt like stopping.

He stopped, bit back another unkind word, and turned around. Job stared at him as he approached, but seemed to have calmed down a mite, and Callahan hummed softly. The saddle was leaning far to the right, and Callahan saw that the canteen was missing from the horn. He walked to the horse anyway, maybe just to let the animal know that he was well thought of, which might not be entirely true. Once he reached the horse, he rubbed the white neck, and gently pulled the saddle back into place. He looked around for the canteen, but didn't see it, and didn't want to spend the rest of the night looking for it. Most likely, he would find it or trip over it this evening or tomorrow morning. But right now, someone else needed his attention.

"Easy, boy. Just eat some Wyoming grass and get some rest. I'll be back directly."

Callahan turned, shook his head, sighed, then thought about swearing a bit more, but did not go through with that.

Instead, he returned to the trail and moved in the direction of the crumpled heap that once was a mud wagon. He heard the moaning, but ignored that for the time being, and leaped up onto the kindling that passed for a stagecoach, and peered through the opening. Nope. No one was inside. That was a good thing. He held that thought for a moment when clarity, slow to come after this crazy night, returned, and he understood that, like the moaning driver, passenger or passengers could have been thrown clear of the mud wagon.

Callahan backed up and studied the rolling waves of grass, hills, bounders, and one antelope that had come out to see what was going on. No humans that the circuit rider could see, which didn't mean there weren't any, but the driver, loosely defined, started moaning louder. So Callahan walked toward the groans.

The man lay on his back, boots crossed at the ankles as though he were being laid out for the undertaker, arms stretched out over his bearded head. His nose was leaking blood, which stained his white mustache, and his lips were busted, but the man still breathed, and his breath reeked of bad whiskey.

The eyelids moved, the gray eyes focused, and the driver spit out blood and saliva and asked timidly, "Are you God?"

"No." Callahan knelt.

The man gasped. "The . . . devil?"

"Not the devil you should be seeing." Callahan ran his right hand over the man's ribs, noticing that the man's eyes were wild with fear, but he didn't seem to feel any agony where Callahan applied pressure.

"I could use some whiskey," the driver said.

"You ain't the only one, brother." He looked at the man's hands.

"Wiggle the fingers on your left hand," Callahan ordered.

He waited. And frowned.

"Are you wiggling?"

"Yeah."

Callahan sighed, and turned to look at the man's battered face and broken neck. Something else grabbed his attention, and he fought back that urge to curse again.

"Your *left* hand."

The man looked confused, till the fingers on the left hand began to move. Then he just looked stupid.

"Turn your feet, left to right, or right to left, it don't really matter."

That he did without any stupidity.

Callahan let out a sigh. The Major General in the Heavens did look after idiots. He stared down at the driver. "Where all do you hurt?" he asked, knowing the answer.

"All over!"

"Can you stand?"

"I could use some whiskey."

"Do you think you could stand?"

"I said I could use—"

"I heard you the first time, but your breath tells me you've had enough whiskey. Now, can you sit up at least?"

The man whimpered. But he did bring his arms to his side, and used his forearms to push himself up. Callahan reached around and grabbed the shoulders and eased him till he was sitting in the dirt.

The driver saw what was left of the Abbott & Downing wagon and cursed. "What happened to my mules?" he cried out. "Tell me that ain't dead."

"They were lighting a shuck south last I saw," Callahan answered.

"You shouldn't have startled my team so," the man complained. "It's your fault. You'll have to answer to the Poudre City Stagecoach Line."

"Mister," Callahan said. "I wasn't the one drunker than a bluebelly on payday, whipping a team like a maniac uphill and downhill on a road seldom traveled like there's no tomorrow."

"There ain't gonna be no tomorrow if I don't get to Poudre City before the Peaceful Valley stagecoach does."

That statement brought back memories from the afternoon. The second mud wagon. The one with the female passenger who had smiled—or at least Taylor Callahan had fancied a smile—that was being whipped just as wildly. He looked toward the road and up the hill.

He also listened, but just heard the driver's groans, moans, and then, a stinking, rippling, long whiskey fart.

Callahan glanced at the moon and asked the Major General in the Heavens what he had done to deserve such punishment, but stopped quickly, whispered an apology, and looked down at the battered old driver.

"My name's Callahan," he said. "Taylor Callahan. Circuit-riding preacher bound for Cheyenne."

"Preacher?"

"That's what I said."

"In Wyoming?"

"If this indeed happens to be Wyoming."

The man blinked and stared, which he followed with a stare and a blink. Then he remembered his manners.

"My name's Absalom," the driver said.

Callahan laughed so hard his ribs almost broke. Tears filled his eyes. Drunk as that driver was, as beaten up as he had to be after that wreck, the man had a wicked wit underneath that raw, rank exterior.

"What's so dad-blasted funny?" the driver wailed.

"Absalom!" Callahan shook his head.

"That's my name."

Callahan laughed again, shook his head, and said, "Your name can't be Absalom."

"The devil it can't!" the man barked with genuine sincerity and, if Callahan were not mistaken, a good deal of anger. "Why can't it be?"

Perhaps this drunken fool was a thespian to match the talents of Edwin Booth. The preacher might have felt sorry for the old cad, till he heard Job walking toward him and saw the ruins of the mud wagon and remembered trying to ride out a bucking show by the usually lazy gelding. "Because you ain't hanging between two boughs of a big old oak tree, 'between the heaven and the earth,' though your mules sure had the right idea."

"Huh?"

"Second Samuel, Chapter Eighteen. But don't ask me the verse. Not till morning, maybe afternoon, when I ain't so flustered."

"I don't feel so good, Preacher," the man said, and sank back to the ground.

Kneeling quickly, Callahan placed the back of his hand on the man's forehead. The eyes fluttered, but did not open.

"Where do you hurt?" Callahan asked.

"Everything's just spinnin'," the man whispered. "Spinnin' like a top. Feel sicker than a dog."

Which could be the whiskey, or a bad combination of whiskey and wreck.

"Don't let me die, Preacher." The man's voice barely carried to Callahan's ears.

"You just rest, Absalom," Callahan said. He lifted his eyes to the moon one more time and began praying for a bit of help, a smidgen of courage, and a whole lot of explaining exactly what all he needed to do.

Like many a Western man, Taylor Callahan had experience in patching himself and other people up. Doctors were mighty scarce on the frontier, and where Callahan and poor drunken Absalom found themselves as being beyond frontier. They had to be right smack-dab in that clichéd but omnipresent Middle of Nowhere.

For a circuit-riding preacher who had been traveling across the Western states and territories since before the War Between the States had ended, Taylor Callahan was no stranger to injuries and illness. During the unpleasantness between North and South, and, more specifically, Missouri and Kansas, Callahan had been doctor and surgeon as much as parson and priest. He had amputated fingers, toes, feet, arms, and legs. Some of his patients even survived. He had dug out bullets with knives, spoons, and pliers. He had bandaged bloody wounds, and he had cauterized them. He had held down screaming men while others did the dirty work.

He had also had to tend to the sick. Measles and mumps. Cholera and bowel complaints. Bad water, bad food, bad whiskey. The grippe, broken arms, broken legs, shot-off ears, rope burns, knife cuts, saber wounds, fevers, chills. He had even had to help the wife of one of Carbine Logan's Irregulars birth a baby girl, six pounds and twelve ounces according to the kitchen scales, while six of the boys fought off a Yankee patrol in a cabin deep in the Sni-a-Bar.

But Absalom wasn't pregnant. He wasn't shot or cut. He had no fever or chills. And he wasn't bleeding anywhere except from his lips and nose. Internal in-

juries? Callahan knew of such things, but he had
never had to treat anything.

Concussion. That was Callahan's uneducated guess.
He knew of concussions. But no one had ever told
him how to treat one.

No one was going to right here, either. He would
have to throw this man over the back of Job and get
him to . . . and that was the problem.

Go back to Virginia Dale. Which had no doctor,
but did have a bartender who sometimes cut hair and
had pulled out a few bullets from human beings.

Keep going north to . . . Cheyenne? Wherever and
how far away it was.

Or he could sit here with one canteen—if he could
find his—and wait till someone passed by. Or until
poor Absalom went to hear orders from the Major
General in the Heavens.

The man snored softly.

And he could just be passed out from sheer
drunkenness.

Still Callahan knew he had to do something.

He moved to what once had been an Abbott &
Downing vehicle of commercial transportation. He
picked up the broken spoke of a wheel, about
eighteen inches long, and used it to prod around
the driver's box. He heard something roll, and he
reached against the side and found . . .

A jug of whiskey. Somehow, the thing had not
busted or gotten flung into the scorched grass. He
shook the clay jug. Still some left. He hadn't tasted
liquor in some time, and it took a lot of conviction not
to pull the cork now. Setting the jug on the ground,
he stepped into the driver's box and pulled himself
up to stare across the port side of the coach. Or

was that starboard? Not being a sailor, but being a Missouri lad from the hills, he never could remember those little things.

Nothing caught his eye.

"What would you expect?" he asked himself. "A water keg?"

Then he leaped onto the ground and hurried to the back of the mud wagon. The boot. Yes. The boot might hold something. Canteen. Doctor's kit. Luggage. Water.

Nothing.

And that perplexed Callahan. Why would a stagecoach be making this run without any passenger? Was this Abbott & Downing wreck delivering mail? And what was this deal with the Peaceful Valley Stagecoach Company? That must have been the wagon that had carried the woman in its coach this afternoon.

He wet his lips and walked back to pick up his spoke-stick and whiskey jug.

"Job," he said, and turned to the gelding. "Looks like we got us a . . ."

He did not finish the statement.

Job was telling him what he had to do. And do right quick.